ACCLAIM FOR

Michelle Huneven's

Round Rock

"Classy, absorbing . . . thoroughly old-fashioned in its likable characters and its fine writing."
—*The New Yorker*

"Like a fat, comfortable chair, [a book] you can forget yourself in. . . . [Huneven] lays bare the human heart's deepest fears and yearnings." —*Chicago Tribune*

"Characters that fit like a pair of jeans and an old T-shirt—this is a book you can live in. It is wise, witty, and charming—and, ultimately, deeply moving. Brilliant."
—T. Coraghessan Boyle

"Warm and absorbing." —*San Francisco Chronicle*

"I've not read so knowing and pleasant a book in years . . . superb!" —Barry Hannah

"A wonderfully rewarding good read." —Alice Adams

"Huneven is an audacious novelist. . . . [She] approaches the inhabitants of Round Rock with the same curiosity through which Brian Moore or Graham Greene or Muriel Spark might explore characters in their novels."
—*Los Angeles Times*

Michelle Huneven

Round Rock

Michelle Huneven is the author of *Round Rock* and *James-land*. She was born in Altadena, California, studied at Grinnell College and the Iowa Writers' Workshop, and makes her living as a freelance writer and restaurant critic. She has received a GE Younger Writers Award in Fiction and a James Beard Award. She now lives (again) in Altadena.

Round Rock

a novel by

Michelle Huneven

Vintage Contemporaries
Vintage Books
A Division of Random House, Inc.
New York

FIRST VINTAGE CONTEMPORARIES EDITION, SEPTEMBER 1998

The Library of Congress has cataloged the Knopf edition as follows:

Huneven, Michelle, [date]
Round Rock: a novel/Michelle Huneven. —1st ed.
p.   cm.
ISBN 0-679-45437-3
I. Title.
PS355.U4662R68   1997
813_54—dc21   97-5831
CIP

Vintage ISBN: 0-679-77616-8

Book design by Dorothy S. Baker
Author photograph © James Fee

Random House Web address: www.randomhouse.com

Printed in the United States of America
10 9 8 7 6 5 4

For their expertise and support, the author would like to thank
James Beetem, Bernard Cooper, Gary Fisketjon, Amy Gerstler, Maxine Groffsky,
Arthur Huneven, Tom Knechtel, Bia Lowe, Jeffrey Luther, Arty Nelson, Holly
Pilling, Nicole Reilley, Lily Tuck, Ellen Way, and the MacDowell Colony.

Round Rock

Prologue

Prologue

AMONG the inhabitants of the Santa Bernita Valley, it is commonly believed that nothing there ever goes according to plan.

The valley was settled by two families back in the late 1850s. Henri Morrot arrived from southern France with his wife and infant son to plant vineyards. Discouraged by the adobe soil, he spent thirty years growing lima beans and sweet potatoes before filling the valley floor with citrus.

Tom and William Fitzgerald, two adventurous, often drunken brothers from Chicago, received a land grant for the northern foothills and grazed sheep in a haphazard fashion while Morrot grew rich during the citrus boom in the nineties. Now, a century later, eighty percent of the groves are in the Fitzgerald name, and the only two Morrots left in the valley live in the government-subsidized Buena Vista Rest Home in Buchanan, a small city in the valley's western mouth.

In the narrower, less-developed eastern end, particularly in and around the town of Rito, fate is said to be especially capricious.

In 1947, the Army Corps of Engineers paved the road and erected a pretty little bridge over the river just outside of town. That very winter, the Rito flooded, washed out the bridge, and changed course, using half a mile of new roadway as its streambed.

In 1958, Victor Ibañez purchased a small corner storefront in downtown Rito and opened an auto parts store and machine shop. When his wife, Aida, saw the men standing around waiting for their pistons to be knurled and drums to be turned, she decided to market homemade tamales from an electric Dutch oven. Soon, the men were asking for pop, beer, cigarettes. By 1963, squeezed out by a NAPA franchise, Victor's business became a grocery store with a full meat case and deli.

When Ralph Mills bought the old Frank Morrot residence catty-corner to the Ibañez Grocería, he planned to turn it into a nice, low-budget motel for the fishermen who came to Lake Rito, six miles away. Guests who checked in never checked out, and Ralph found himself the reluctant landlord to an assortment of cranky old pensioners. Death alone generated vacancies.

William Fitzgerald IV had acquired over 400 acres of Morrot groves by the 1960s. He sent his son, John, to study agronomy at Cal Poly, San Jose. His daughter, Billie, went to Stanford, where, he hoped, she'd use her commendable intellect to attract a suitable husband. John now practices entertainment law in West Hollywood. Billie came home from Stanford in her junior year five months pregnant. No husband. She presently manages some 500 acres of avocados, oranges, grapefruit, lemons, tangelos, mandarins, and pomelos.

Yolanda Marina Torres, the novice Sister Katy at the Purísima Sacred Heart Academy near Lompoc, was accompanying a group of other teacher-nuns to a seminar on audiovisual aids in Los Angeles. They stopped at a fruit stand on the Santa Bernita Highway and a man named Luis Salazar asked Yolanda if he could see her hair. She never made it to the seminar. She's now the mom in their mom-and-pop bar and grill, Happy Yolanda's, in downtown Rito.

Libby and Stockton Daw, a young couple from New Orleans, bought a ten-acre parcel four miles from town for an extravagant sum of money. They bulldozed a site for an enormous, postmodern home that Stockton, an award-winning architect, was designing. Within a year, Stockton was living with a TV actress in Burbank and Libby was alone on the property, inhabiting an older-model Manatee house trailer and working two jobs to make ends meet.

The most popular explanation for the valley's haywire history and unpredictable future is geological. The valley is slung between two ridges in the Santa Bernita Mountains, which, contrary to almost every other American range, run east and west. The Santa Bernitas are young mountains, surging in place, their stratigraphy diagonal, their profiles jagged and fanciful, as if cut with a jigsaw in the hands of a child. Erosion and vegetation haven't worn them down or softened the evidence of continual upheaval. Gravity itself has never fully asserted its steadying centripetal power. Pivoting outward from the San Andreas Fault, the region still twitches with frequent, tiny earthquakes. And there's a grade by Harry Zeno's junkyard where cars, if left in neutral at a complete standstill, will roll uphill at speeds up to twenty MPH. Nearby irrigation ditches also run uphill. So it stands to reason that humans, being ninety percent water, should also fall prey to certain reversals and unpredictabilities.

Red Ray attributed the relative success of his drunk farm to the valley's peculiar seismology. Drunks, Red had long since learned, were the world's most assiduous planners. They planned their next drinks, to drink only socially, to stop drinking entirely. They planned to make their first million, to improve their marriages, to live new, perfect lives. Out in the world at large, such plans had predictable outcomes. But here, in the Santa Bernita Valley, where nobody could predict anything with accuracy, even drunks had a fighting chance to surprise themselves.

Although long-term valley inhabitants have learned to tailor their expectations, everybody still makes plans, the more elaborate, the better, if only to take greater delight in the permutations to come. It's a great place to live, they say, if you like surprises: it's just like life, only different.

ONE

LEWIS FLETCHER was waiting to be discharged from the Ventura County Social Model Detoxification Facility. Nobody could explain this name to him. "Social" as opposed to what? Asocial? Antisocial? *Un*social? Yesterday, they—or at least this guy Bobby—told him he'd be able to walk right out come nine o'clock this morning. Walk right out to freedom. Sky. Sidewalk underfoot. Well-aimed sun. Coffee shops. Then, Bobby said, some stuff about him came in over the computer, and now it was known he'd had too many alcohol-related offenses to be released on his own recognizance.

Lewis had trouble accepting this development. Six years had passed since he'd had that drunk-and-disorderly, which wasn't at all what it sounded like, and three years since the DUI, or almost three, and that was a fluke too. The day he got the DUI, he'd been at the beach with friends and hadn't had a thing to drink until a minute before they left. They'd been rolling up blankets, gathering trash, when a girl handed him a screwdriver. He drank it down like orange juice, only she must have put a lot of vodka in it that he didn't taste, because when he was tested, he had a really high blood-alcohol count. Point two.

The drunk-and-disorderly was even more ridiculous. He and one of his mother's boyfriends had been drinking a little beer and got into an argument in the driveway. They were yelling away, with Lewis's mother coming out every few minutes to beg them to stop. He didn't have any idea what was so important that they had to stand there and yell for the whole neighborhood to hear, but he did recall that there was some pleasure in it, a big, freeing fuck-everybody feeling, and neither one of them was willing to give it up. His mom called the cops, and they took both of them to the station. They were joking around in the patrol car on the way down, and probably wouldn't even have been booked if Elkhart—that was the boyfriend's stupid name—hadn't called the cops a couple of pin-dicks to their faces.

Of all the times Lewis had really tied one on, been truly angry at someone or on the verge of doing something profoundly disorderly, it was absurd that these two incidents were the ones that came over the computer to complicate his discharge from detox. Bobby said he had a few choices: his wife or a relative could come and sign him out, or he had to check himself into some kind of treatment program for alcoholism.

Lewis didn't have a wife, so he called his mother, who lived sixty miles away, in Sunland. She was on her way to work, she told him, and couldn't come. She couldn't come after work, either, or tomor-row, which was Saturday. She couldn't come get him at all, in fact. "This time, you have to count on somebody else, because I'm letting you down and making a point of it," she said. "This is a big step for me and I want you to respect it." Okay then, Lewis said, goodbye, and stood there trying to think why she was so mad at him. He had this guilty, sick-at-heart feeling and kept going through his memories until he found one that matched. Sure enough, he remembered the hundred dollars he borrowed from her three months ago for what was supposed to be three days. Funny thing was, he'd had the money the whole time. He could've paid her back. He never got around to finding an envelope, addressing it, buying a stamp.

He sat back down on the plaid couch in the waiting room swamped with shame that he was such a constant disappointment to his mother. Instead of a son, she had a black hole for an offspring, and in their every encounter, he saw, he had never failed to cause her anguish.

Bobby came over and said if Lewis didn't have any other relatives, or if he didn't have a hospital program or halfway house in mind, he could always take a bed upstairs for a month. Lewis had no relatives and didn't know of any programs, but he would kill himself before spending a whole month in detox. Still, to get Bobby off his back, he agreed to go upstairs and have a look.

The detox center, along with other county agencies, was housed in an old junior high school. As he pulled himself upstairs, Lewis saw initials cut into the wooden banister. Some were enclosed in lopsided hearts. Lewis wondered if anybody who ever went together in junior high school actually got married and stayed married all their lives. He thought about a girl he went steady with in junior high, a black girl named June with a French last name he couldn't recall. She was very dark, though her hair was naturally straight. She was the first black girl he'd ever kissed. That he had a black girlfriend was a big deal to everybody. White girls had black boyfriends, but not the other way around. This girl had fine, sharp teeth and liked to bite down on his tongue and lips. A few times, she drew blood. At first, he was surprised and excited by her biting, but soon his mouth was so sore that he lost any desire to kiss her. They broke up, and although they went on to the same high school together, they eventually stopped acknowledging each other. Within two years, they were strangers again. Lewis had run into an old friend who went to their tenth reunion and reported that June what's-her-name, the biter, had won the award for having the most children: six.

In the first old classroom at the top of the stairs, Lewis found half a dozen beds, each with a dresser/nightstand unit in an area made separate, if not exactly private, by chin-high white Formica partitions. The room looked like a secretary pool, only with beds instead of desks. Three guys had gathered in the first tiny bedroom space, two Latinos and a little guy who was white except for arms and shoulders covered with green tattoos. Lewis recognized them from the AA meeting last night. They took this AA stuff seriously and needed to, because to hear them tell it, their lives were all messed up with crack cocaine, heroin, prison, insane women, you name it.

The next classroom didn't have any partitions, just five beds in a row, like an old-fashioned hospital ward. None of these beds was taken. Every surface in the room itself, including the bottom half of the windows, had been painted the same dull pale green. Hand-lettered cardboard plaques were stuck on the walls, each with a saying: EASY DOES IT. LET GO, LET GOD. ONE DAY AT A TIME.

Lewis lay down on one of the beds and lit a cigarette. Somebody had written JESUS CARES on the pillow in blue ballpoint pen. He tried to make this meaningful, something that someone had written just for him to find—a divine message, humbly drawn—but he didn't have the energy for such creative thinking. He didn't believe in Jesus, except as a man and maybe a spiritual genius, a Buddha for literal white people. Once he had a dream about Jesus and Jesus was nicer than anybody Lewis had ever met, and his hair was long and glossy like in ads for cheap shampoo. Jesus also had long fingernails, fetishistically long. Frankly, even though he seemed so nice, Jesus had creeped Lewis out.

Lewis smoked his cigarette and listened to his heart thump. He could see the shadow of a tree through the painted glass. Traffic surged outside. The central furnace rumbled. There was a sweet chemical scent of floor wax he recalled from every school he'd known.

No matter how hard he tried, Lewis couldn't remember how he ended up here, in Ventura County Social Model Detox. Bobby told him that a woman in Oxnard named Clarice Martin had called an ambulance because he was having convulsions in her front yard. "Flopping like a fish in her dichondra," Bobby put it. Lewis had never heard of Clarice Martin and didn't have any idea how he got to Oxnard.

The last thing he did remember was being in Westwood at a small party in married-student housing. He didn't recall whose party it was or what he was doing there, but he was in a knotty-pine kitchen talking to a short, plump girl. Her face was rapt and bright with hope and coming at him like a bucket of fresh milk.

To hold her at bay, Lewis ranted about Rilke, erected a wall of words. Or no, come to think of it, maybe he was lecturing on Goethe. Of course it was Goethe, whom he'd never read. The only thing he knew about Goethe was from an old Time/Life book that said he was the most intelligent man who had ever lived. Someone had estimated Goethe's IQ and it was higher than everybody else's, even Einstein's. Higher by some thirty-odd points than Lewis's, at any rate. Not that anybody was really sure. Goethe, after all, had never taken an IQ test. His IQ and the IQs of other long-dead geniuses had been based on their capacity for abstraction. Goethe's abstractions were the most abstract of all, which is why Lewis had avoided reading him: why read someone just to make yourself feel stupid?

If he'd been boring Miss Bright-Eyed Milkmaid, she didn't show it. She touched his arm. Her face spewed light. Her eyes urged him on. Had he pounced? He had a vague sense of pulling her to him, scrubbing his beard against her incandescent cheeks, stuffing his tongue into her tiny mouth. Yet he couldn't say for sure if he was remembering this or just imagining it.

He finished his cigarette, then stood up so fast his eyesight exploded into sparks of wormy light. He put one hand on the bedstead and waited for the air to clear.

Back downstairs, Lewis shook his head at Bobby. "Can't do it," he said. He resumed his seat on the ugly plaid couch. He kept thinking there were bugs on him, that a line of ants was crawling up his neck and into his hair, but he couldn't catch a one. After a while, Bobby came over and said that there was a man who might take Lewis in his halfway house. He was lucky, Bobby said, because normally there was a waiting list for this drunk farm, as he called it, but he'd just found out there were a couple of empty beds. How did that sound to Lewis—a month in the country on a sliding scale?

ABOUT the time Lewis was staggering down the old schoolhouse stairs, Red Ray was trying to coax Frank Jamieson into the cab of his '46 Ford pickup. Frank was more interested in the sky, which was full of fast-moving horsetail clouds. Frank, it occurred to Red, was looking more and more like Walt Whitman every day: surging gray beard, disheveled, hoary, vaguely vagrant. Unlike Whitman, Frank always had a cigarette in his mouth. Also, Frank never spoke; he hadn't said a word to anybody in eleven and a half years.

"C'mon, you old sacka corn." Red had his arm around Frank's shoulders and was attempting to steer him over to the truck's open door. "Upsa-daisy, into the cab."

Frank was too big to move when he didn't feel like it. Even though Red probably matched him pound for pound—they both weighed in at over 230—Frank had a lower center of gravity and a way of turning his weight into concrete.

"Come *on*, Franky," said Red.

Frank raised his right hand, index finger extended, and touched the unlit tip of his cigarette.

"I'll light the damn thing," Red said, "if you get in the truck."

He next tried sitting in the truck as an example to Frank. Closing the driver's-side door, Red grasped the steering wheel resolutely. "Bus is leaving," he called, turning the key and gunning the engine. He was parked behind the Blue House, the old Victorian mansion that served as Round Rock's dormitory. Behind the mansion were orange groves, Washington navels. Plump, ripe, the oranges spun amid dark leaves like spheres of light.

Red lit a Pall Mall for himself, then extended the lighter toward Frank. Frank pointed to the tip of his cigarette.

"Jesus Christ on a crutch," said Red.

Red used to take Frank with him everywhere—on his morning rounds, to AA meetings, on supply runs, to the Old Bastards Club—but since the farm lost its secretary a few months ago, Red couldn't take the time. Under the best circumstances, Frank was never what anyone would call Johnny-on-the-spot. Before any outing, he had to be taken to the bathroom, combed, supplied with cigarettes and Life Savers and various other prized items without which he became quite agitated. Red felt bad about neglecting him, but only up to a point, because now, whenever he did try to include him in activities, Frank pulled *this* kind of stunt, turned into this *inert* life form.

It wasn't as if Frank didn't want to get out and about: he'd run away from the farm twice in the last month. The first time, a neighbor spotted him sitting on a rock wall about a mile down the road; the last time, Burt McLemoore, the deputy sheriff, found him six miles away, under the Rito River bridge, where he was watching women from the nearby fieldworkers' camp do their laundry on the big white rocks.

Red rolled down his window and blew smoke outside. Though he'd never tell anyone, Frank's escapes hurt his feelings. To take to heart anything a big, mute, brain-damaged man did sounded crazy. Still, Red had kept him out of institutions for all these years, so if Red was a little busy for a change, it seemed that Frank could endure some inattention. Frank didn't have to answer to the board of directors. He didn't have to do paperwork or run into town or apply for grants or listen to the endless river of anger and self-pity that flowed from the mouths of the newly sober. Frank didn't have to write schedules or mop up after suicide attempts or make sure the citrus groves were picked and cultivated and sprayed and irrigated. If anyone deserved to run away, Red thought he himself should have that privilege.

Red smoked and thought about where he'd run. He'd probably go to the mountains, hole up in a cave or some old hunter's shack slumping into the ground. He'd avoid people, become a hermit, even a rumor, like Big Foot. Hikers would tell how when they were lost, he materialized and led them back to their trails. They would show off the splint he made for their broken bones, recount how he fed them elderberry juice and watercress salad and smoked squirrel meat. (Red had eaten squirrel, and it wasn't bad—a little gamy, maybe, but the smoking would help.) The only thing he'd ask for in return would be books—best-sellers, guidebooks, hand-scrawled journals, whatever written matter the hikers carried. He'd accumulate a library, and in the winter he'd read.

In the army, Red had once spent a winter reading books up in Alaska. On one training maneuver, he and another officer built an ice cave, a six-by-eight-foot room dug deep into the snow. They lived there for ten weeks. The ceiling was a tarp, the entrance an L-shaped dogleg dug off to one side. They carved out little sleeping shelves and niches for their food and gear. On their first day, after the warmth from their bodies made the walls sweat, they rolled back the tarp and the walls froze as shiny and hard and refractive as glass. A single candle then threw enough light to read by. Since either Red or his partner was always on watch, privacy was absolute—at least in the beginning. These maneuvers were all part of a staged war, and after a while the enemy developed the bad habit of showing up and asking for a slug of Red's vodka. But before the enemy became a nuisance, there was that warm, brilliant cave of pure silence, and Red missed this more than any other part of his life—certainly more than his childhood, his marriage, or even the heady first years of the farm.

The truck creaked and bounced a little as Frank climbed inside. "Hey, Franky," Red said. "Attaboy." He lit Frank's cigarette, plus a new one for himself, then reached over and closed Frank's door. Just as Red put the truck into gear, Ernie Tola came out of the Blue House waving his arm. Ernie was Round Rock's full-time cook. In his fifties, he looked and often acted like a well-coiffed, temperamental woman with a goatee.

"You might as well bring Frank right back in here," Ernie called out. "Detox just phoned and they got a live one for you."

Red turned to Frank. "Damn it all, Franky, did you hear that?" Then he yelled out the window, "Anybody we know?"

If it was a repeat customer, Red thought, he could leave Frank in the truck, because they—the drunk and Frank—would already be acquainted. But a brand-new fellow might not appreciate such a dramatic example of what drinking can do to you if it doesn't kill you first.

"Naw, just some young drunk who likes his coke," Ernie hollered. "But Bobby thinks you'll take to him."

"Yeah, right." That Red didn't much like cokeheads was no secret. In his opinion, the average alcoholic was above average in intelligence—intelligent about everything, that is, except his drinking. The drug addict, Red found, too often fell into one of two categories: the grandiose, ego-bound hotshot, or somebody so down and out it was hard to locate even a germ of self that could help him begin to recover. On principle, as long as they also identified themselves as alcoholics, Red didn't turn away drug users at Round Rock. Personally, given his own experience, he'd take a garden variety alkie any day.

TWELVE years earlier, Red Ray had bought the old Sally Morrot ranch near Rito as an extravagant, hysterical ploy to distract himself from drinking and thus save his marriage.

The ranch had been part of Henri Morrot's original holdings. A month before he died in 1915, Morrot parceled out his land, in what he believed to be an equitable manner, to his seven children. Famous for their contentious natures even as infants, six of the heirs felt gravely wronged. Old sibling rivalries intensified in the public arena of the courtroom. Feud fueled feud, hostilities became generational, and litigation replaced ranching as the Morrot family business. The courts impounded acre after acre for costs, and the Fitzgeralds bought up the land at auction for a fraction of its worth. After three generations, the Morrot empire had shrunk like a vast landlocked lake until only a few groves remained in the family name.

Sally Morrot, Henri's youngest child, had taken her allotted, lady-sized inheritance of 250 acres without dispute and repulsed all suitors, claim jumpers, and obsequious volunteer heirs for the next sixty-five years. On the west end of her property, she built for "her Mexicans" nine unplumbed, unheated, yet sturdy wooden bungalows, a packing house, outbuildings, and a company store. Her workers lived there year round, raised children, planted perennials, considered the place home. Half a mile away, on a knoll surrounded by two acres of rolling lawn, Sally Morrot constructed a three-storey mansion as spindly and delicate as a wicker throne. A prototype of already outdated Victorian whimsy, the house sported narrow bay windows, gables, balconies for every bedroom, finials, crest work, scrolls, and a wide portico that wrapped around three exposures. Six chimneys and two turrets were pink limestone block. The architect took lace from his wife's undergarments, reproduced it in wood, and mounted it along the eaves and ridges of the roof.

Aloof and iron-willed, Sally Morrot managed her groves like a feudal lord. She made money through both world wars and the Great Depression. When avocados became a viable commodity, she planted 30 acres of the Haas and Bacon varieties. She put over 130 acres in citrus. She gave generously to charities and sent her disenfranchised nieces and nephews through college. She allowed the University of California to use her ranch as a field station and, in exchange, was the first in the valley to implement technological innovations in the citrus industry. She credited her vitality and advanced age to a series of pagan rituals and herb teas provided by her chauffeur, Rafael Flores, who was a *curandero*—a healer—among his people.

Sally Morrot was savvy and indomitable and an institution, but old age eventually wore her out. On her ninety-second birthday, deaf and half-blind, she packed a single suitcase, put her bug-eyed papillon lapdog in a picnic hamper, and took a taxi to her favorite nephew's house in Oxnard, never to return. Even as she lived on, her relatives plundered the nineteen furnished rooms, sold off the valuables, and abandoned the rest, including dirty dishes on the drain board and the dog's bowl on the floor. When Sally Morrot died at the age of ninety-five, her nephew hired a corporation to oversee the groves, and the first corporate decision was to evict the nine families from the village.

Organized by a young firebrand in their midst named David Ibañez, the so-called Mexicans—most were third- and fourth-generation Californians—took their case to court in the spirited style of the Morrots themselves. Unlike their luckless Anglo role models, the workers won, in a manner of speaking: though not allowed to stay in their village, they did receive abundant compensation for the inconvenience and trauma of relocating. Many went off and purchased their own land and homes. This settlement put the first big dent in Sally Morrot's estate. Court battles over the will made further inroads. The corporate overseers continued this downward trend, and in less than five years, the ranch went on the market to pay off accumulated taxes, debts, and court costs.

An associate in Red Ray's San Francisco law firm eventually handled some of the more difficult probate proceedings and tipped off Red to what he described as "the steal of the century."

The ranch didn't look like a steal. The trees had been neglected and whole groves had withered. The mansion had been thoroughly ransacked. An attempt had been made to hammer plywood over the downstairs windows, but vandals had pried it off and entered at will. When Red first walked through, it looked like a stage for cult depravities, gang wars, snuff films. Mattresses and sofas were disemboweled. Half-burned clothes and draperies clogged every fireplace. Obscenities were spray-painted on the walls and shotgun patterns pocked the wainscoting and recessed ceilings.

Such heinous disfigurement of aging beauty caused a great hope to awaken and lumber through Red's thoughts. His marriage of twelve years was faltering—in fact, his wife was conducting a house hunt of her own—and he saw in Sally Morrot's defiled kingdom the groundwork of his own salvation.

Yvette Ray was an urban planner. She sat on the San Francisco planning board and lobbied for historical preservation at any and all costs. A slim, muscular woman with prematurely white hair and a crisp, patrician manner, she had been a promising ballet dancer until family pressure and a foot injury sent her back to college. Thereafter, her histrionics were staged in zoning battles and a few instances of civil disobedience. She'd grown up in the architectural wonderland of Pacific Heights, and as an adult, she fought to restore it to a glory that neither she nor possibly the district itself had ever known. Red had seen her weep with rage at the sight of a bulldozer near the Presidio. Yvette was articulate, militant, and convincing, and her cause was fallen elegance. She was, in short, a rich girl who loved a shambles. Providing, that is, that she could set to and clean it up.

Red Ray made the down payment on the old Sally Morrot ranch with the fat contingency he'd received from helping a quadriplegic become a multimillionaire quadriplegic. He didn't breathe a word of his plans to Yvette, just lured her to a spa in Ojai for the weekend and, on Sunday, took her for a drive through the nearby countryside. He drove up the Victorian's palm-lined driveway and, parking by the sweeping front steps, handed Yvette a key at the exact moment that her mouth started working in silent outrage at yet another crime against architecture. The oxidized, slightly bent brass skeleton key had no function, of course, as there was no glass in any of the windows and any child or dog could've pushed open all the downstairs doors. The key, obviously, was purely symbolic, and it inspired Red to an even greater act of symbolism. He reached in front of a shocked

Yvette, opened the glove compartment, pulled out a bottle of Dewars, and emptied it out on the ground. Joe, their three-year-old son, was asleep in the backseat; Red woke him to extract a pint of Johnnie Walker Black from the accordion file he'd been using as a pillow. Red poured out this scotch as well. Then, he took the keys from the ignition, went to open the Mercedes's trunk, and did likewise with another bottle of Dewars and a liter of clear mirabelle brandy.

Yvette was impressed—stunned, really—by the house, though skeptical about what had already become something of a ritual disposal of booze. She agreed to make the move, take on the restoration, but refused to quit her job, taking a year's leave of absence instead. She also made Red put their Filbert Street townhouse in her name. "I just need a place to run," she said, "if you ever start drinking again."

Red had no official program, no medically supervised detoxification. He simply hoped that in the shuffle of moving his addiction would get lost, like a misrouted box of books or a disoriented house cat.

Yvette decided to serve as her own contractor and hired a crew of carpenters. She subcontracted the plumbing and electrical work. In a gleeful fever, she tore up rotten floorboards, sanded and polished mahogany baseboards and cocobolo mantels. She hired five craftsmen to replace the stained-glass work alone, and drove clear to San Diego to talk to a ceramicist who could copy the destroyed Italian kitchen tile.

Red rented a storefront in the sleepy hamlet of Rito and opened a law office. No more boilermakers for his lunch. He bought homemade tamales and tart pineapple *paletas* at the Ibañez Grocería and washed them down at his desk with Diet Pepsi and selections from a tattered copy of *Shakespeare: The Complete Works*, a book he'd always wanted to read. He'd exchanged big-time for simple—simple personal injuries, simple divorces, simple tax work and wills, and just enough of each to keep him busy five or six hours a day. He came in at nine or ten and left his office at three. Sober as God. Yvette met him in the front hall of the house and, after a few weeks, even stopped sniffing at his breath before giving him a quick kiss. That kiss was never quite what he wanted, not as long or as deep as he felt befitted a dried-out man coming home to a ransacked castle: just the taste of a kiss, a vague and disheartening promise. When he lunged for more, she'd slip from his path, fasten onto his elbow, and guide him through the morning's progress to whatever project she'd singled out as his.

Sweating copiously in the summer heat, closed in by membranous plastic drop cloths, inhaling paint and varnish and lacquer fumes, he puttied and slapped on latex with furious energy. Renovation! Restoration! Preservation! He worked without pause, through what was rightfully the cocktail hour, and prayed to the forces of parallel development that somehow his home and soul and family would come back into shape. When Yvette finally called him to dinner those nights, he was crazed with hunger: ten thousand little mouths sagged open in his veins. She cooked out on the porch using an hibachi and Coleman camp stove, and it seemed to Red that the steaks and canned baked beans and sliced tomatoes could taste so good only to a starving man.

At one time, when they were first married, Yvette used to say Red was the only man she'd ever met to make intelligent use of alcohol. "It brings out the poet in him." Hah! That was before she saw him pass out and crack his head open on the glass coffee table. Before he slugged her on the ear. Before he ruined the new linen wallpaper in the Filbert Street dining room with an attack of projectile vomiting. Before he began disappearing for three or five days at a stretch. Really, Red was grateful for his twentieth or thirtieth second chance, and he forgave Yvette even if her crispness had turned brittle, if her generosity was now grudging. He forgave her for being unforgiving. Just wait: he'd make it up to her, turn it all back around.

During the twilights, they took walks in the groves, an ostensible family. Joe raced circles around them, threw fruit, dug into anthills. Red concentrated only on the flex of distance between Yvette and himself. He took her hand and worried over her reciprocal grip. He did battle with an unceasing urge to drag her to him. Even outside, with miles of room, she could make him feel as if he were crowding her. He felt huge as a haystack, a plow horse, a dump truck—stupidly huge. When she sprang from his side to join Joe, he stood bereft until she returned.

They slept in the spacious parlor of the house on a foam pad with sheets. When he reached for her, she collapsed against his chest obediently, a well-oiled folding chair. This was not the grab and gasp of first love, or even the friendly exchange of familiar intimacy; it was, he feared, good sportsmanship. Afterward, when she curled away from him, he would still be wildly awake, restraining himself from reaching out for her again. He hovered over her instead, paw poised, a bear baffled by a tortoise. He monitored the fluttering of her eyelids, the depth of her breath, and calculated how far she fled from him in her dreams.

Sleep eluded him. With the not drinking, his body was on tilt. He could feel his blood and juices trickling and eddying and sloshing in confusion. He lay wide-eyed and electric for hours on end. He followed the progress of a vigilant moon from frame to frame in the bay window. The house surrounded him, a many-chambered hope.

In the morning, her capable hands tugged him from sleep, pinched him awake. She'd be dressed, her hair hidden under a scarf, sleeves rolled up, breath steamy from coffee. Time for Home Improvement! Fix It! Do It Yourself! And in the middle of this mad race toward perfection, Red Ray decided to go on a diet: one thousand calories a day.

When he told Yvette, she grabbed a handful of his abdominal sag. "I won't object," she said.

In the first week, he lost eight pounds. "I set them free," he told Yvette, "like Prospero released Ariel and all the sprites on the island." The second week, he lost four more pounds. He grew twitchy. His mouth stung from a steady diet of pineapple *paletas*. The iambs in *Coriolanus* thumped in his head, spilled over into unworkable legalese in his briefs. *The client wishes only for some justice. A settlement of forty grand will do* . . . The rumblings in his stomach gave him visions of a Dantean Hell.

When he closed his eyes or gazed at a blank piece of paper, the word "diet" floated there, a photographic afterimage; a diminutive of "die," it occurred to him. In the fourth week of this self-imposed starvation, self-pity staged a coup and took over as the governing factor in Red Ray's life.

"I'm only drinking until I drop twenty more pounds," he informed Yvette. She had already turned her back on him and was striding deep into the house. He stumbled after her, bumping off the hallway walls. From various rooms, workmen stared out at them. He caught up, gripping her shoulders. "Listen," he said. "It's very self-regulatory. I can't possibly get drunk. If I can only ingest a thousand calories a day, that's at most ten shots of scotch or six and a half cans of beer. Or four beers and three shots of bourbon. And that's assuming I *eat* nothing at all!"

THE TOWN of Rito, population 750, had grown up around a large packing house. Most of the inhabitants were descendants of original Morrot serfs who, in one of "Don" Henri's fits of benevolence, were allowed to buy small plots of land. Homes in Rito were modest and varied; a small wood frame house sitting next to a pink cinderblock cube, which neighbored a river-stone cottage whose yard stretched into a weedy vacant lot. Beyond the lot were two shacks sided in asphalt shingle and a fifties stucco tract home replete with fancifully scalloped plywood trim. Then another lot, a whitewashed wood bungalow, and so on, until the orange groves took over. The vacant lots served as a kind of village green where townspeople staked goats and ponies, and chickens roamed freely. If the community ever felt any pressure to cultivate the well-barbered suburban look found farther south in the bright new developments of Simi Valley and Newhall, nobody in Rito responded. Still, there was plenty of front-yard one-upmanship: birdbaths abounded, as did plaster animals of every species and whirligigs made of bleach bottles. There was even a half-ton pair of concrete tennis shoes, and in front of one home, ornamental bombs were planted nose-up and painted Caterpillar yellow and John Deere green. Cacti and the more prickly and primordial succulents proliferated, making the lush yards lusher and the austere, swept-dirt ones more forbidding. The favorite planters were old rowboats and red Cudahy lard buckets. Prized by every household, however, were round rocks from the Rito River. Some specimens were as small as walnuts, others as large as wrecking balls. They were placed atop fieldstone pillars or in gradated rows along flower beds. Boulder-sized matched pairs flanked the entrances of driveways. They were perfectly, naturally, remarkably round! The one coveted variation had a kind of hourglass shape and, depending on its size and who was describing it, looked like a bulbous bowling pin, a model of the moon pulling out of the earth, or a seamless two-tiered snowman. But the most popular rock by far was purely round. The very presence of these granite miracles in a yard was said to ease headaches, lessen female troubles, attenuate baldness, and nip melancholia in the bud.

Rito's busmess district featured the only sidewalks in town as well as a U.S. Post Office, Victor Ibañez's grocería, the Mills Hotel, a laundromat called Casa de Wash 'n' Dry, St. Catherine's Thrift Store, and two bars: the Rito Lito and Happy Yolanda's. Allegiances to these last two establishments cleaved the town neatly in two. Even teetotalers, bedridden grandmothers, and young children could express an immediate, ironclad preference for one bar or the other.

The newly remodeled Rito Lito, which was actually two blocks south of Main Street and across from the packing plant, attracted packers, commuters, trysting suburbanites, and underage beer swillers. An illuminated marquee announced live music and a daily happy hour. The cocktail waitresses, snub-nosed blondes imported from Newhall and Buchanan, served free peanuts and popcorn to generate thirst and profit. Happy Yolanda's was right downtown, up from the Rito River bridge. On warm spring nights, with the door open, the sound of the river filled the pauses between Spanish ballads on the jukebox. Yolie's regulars were the geriatric contingent from the Mills Hotel, neighboring merchants, the occasional adventurous student from the art institute down the road, and all of Happy Yolanda's family, who made up about a third of Rito's population. The back door of the card room was the front door to Yolanda and Luis Salazar's living quarters, and due to the steady flow in and out, it was impossible to tell bar customers from houseguests and family. No gimmicks at Happy Yolanda's.

Red had gravitated naturally to Happy Yolanda's. In addition to Luis's heavy pouring hand, Red also appreciated his respectfully laconic posture. Although versed in local history and trivia, Luis refused to gossip. Nor did he count rounds or cast disapproval on any man's drinking method. He would, whenever appropriate, drive a staggering customer home, and he could be provoked, on behalf of his regulars, to collar an intemperate and throw him into the street. He deferred all confessions and sob stories to Victor Ibañez at the grocería or to Yolanda herself, now a corpulent, middle-aged beauty who sat at the end of the bar with the serene air of a happy queen. Luis and Yolanda both took to Red and tended fastidiously to his dietary needs. If the grill was off when Red came in for a late lunch, Yolanda prepared him a tuna sandwich, no mayonnaise, or skimmed off the orange droplets of fat from the cooling *albóndiga* soup and heated a panful in her own private kitchen. Luis frequently interspersed a free drink among those Red paid for.

As his diet progressed, Red bought drinks for a burgeoning pride of new friends. He arrived home later and later. In fact, the workmen came from his house and he stood them rounds and heard from their mouths how the restoration of his home was progressing. *She hadn't left.* He was drinking and the windows were still being glazed, tiles grouted, floors sanded. Daily, huge appliances arrived. A new septic tank went in, the driveway was asphalted, the columnar palms trimmed. Well, he *was* drinking at a reasonable pace. He had yet to black out or get sick or even insult anybody. This time, it seemed, he could handle it.

On a Thursday in the dead heat of September, Red had eaten the soup-and-sandwich special minus the sandwich, finished beer number three, and was on his way back to his office to meet a client and court recorder and take a deposition. Yvette's work crew met him at the door. Red turned back toward the bar, beckoning them to follow. "Come on in," he said. "I've got a few minutes. I'll buy you all a drink."

They shuffled among themselves like shy boys at a dance.

"Luis!" called Red. "Fix these fellows what they want and put it on my tab."

The plumber stepped forward. A sallow young man of about thirty, he came close and spoke to Red in a low voice. "She let us off, said the work that was going to get done was done. I tried to tell her, just let me finish this one U-joint and I could at least turn the water back on. She said no, we should pack up our tools and go home." He pulled his blue Dodger cap low on his forehead. "We did what she said, put our tools in our trucks, but you know, she owes all of us money—me quite a lot, as a matter of fact, since I'm under contract. So we stood there, thinking she'd come out with the checks. We waited and waited; then she and the boy came out all loaded down with suitcases. Look . . ." He stopped, removed his cap, and looked deeply into it, as if to read his next line or find a way to keep from speaking further, then gave up and put the cap back on. "I hate to be the one to tell you this."

"It's all right," Red said. "Don't worry. Go on."

"Well, I think she was real surprised to see us all there on the porch. I had to step up and ask her for our money. I was real polite about it, I just said, 'If the job's really done, I guess we need to be paid.' She looked at us for the longest time, with that suitcase in one hand, your boy's hand in the other, then told the kid to go inside and she followed him. We stood there for ten minutes, sure she was writing our checks. But a couple of guys swore they saw her peeking out to see if we'd gone. Finally she came out, only this time she had that old shotgun you've been using on the ground squirrels."

"Come on," said Red.

"I'm not kidding," said the plumber. "I know it's just a four-ten single shot, but it doesn't seem all that harmless when it's stuck right up in your face. She was crying, crazy, saying stuff like, 'I know where you guys go every night. You go down to that bar with the dopey name and get my husband to buy you drinks all night.' Said we'd already been paid. She'd seen your monthly tabs, and we'd drunk up all our pay."

"She knows drinks don't cost that much," said Red. "She's just upset."

"Oh, I know she's upset," said the plumber. "And we didn't want to make her more upset. She could be in enough trouble as it is— brandishing a weapon and all. Some of the guys want to press charges."

"Now, hold on," said Red. "Everyone's going to get his money." Red told the men to wait while he went across the street to fetch his checkbook. He hurried back, sat down at the bar, and ordered a shot of Early Times with a beer wash. After another shot, he started writing checks, although his lawyering self feared she'd already cleaned out the accounts. That was always his first advice to female dissolution clients: clean out the bank accounts, rent a U-Haul, and take everything that's not nailed down. Get yourself into a bargaining position. . . .

The men came up one by one, naming their prices and taking their checks, then leaving their drinks and drifting out until only the plumber remained. He folded his check, stuck it in his shirt pocket. "You okay?" he asked.

"I'm okay," Red said.

The plumber left and Red drank some more. He remembered the court recorder and the client, then forgot them again. When the three o'clock whistle blew at the packing plant, he got up and walked outside. Yvette was parked across the street in the Mercedes. Joe was in the front seat next to her. Between Red and his family, two large retrievers slept in the middle of Main Street. Red gazed helplessly at his wife, her face framed and dark within the car. Did she want to speak to him? Did she want him to speak to her? On both scores, he thought not. She just liked these moments of high drama that harked back to her dancing days. Grand finales. Bowing. Bowing out. This was her final pose for him to view. He hitched up his pants, looked up the street and then down. The stoplight hanging in the intersection was green and swaying in the hot breeze. Red heard the diesel sputter of the Mercedes's engine. The two dogs rose reluctantly and made for the sidewalk. The car slid away from the curb. As it turned the corner, Red saw his son's hand out of the window: tiny, white, clutching at the air.

AFTER his wife and son drove out of his life, Red Ray got drunk. Besotted, swacked, stinking drunk, and then some. He drank until he passed out, woke up, and started drinking again. He drank for a week, until he came upon a twilight calm in which he could walk, talk, even think, all without pain. From this dark, incorporeal state, he called Frank Jamieson, his oldest friend.

Married and divorced three times, Frank was an expert on the extinction of matrimony. Red hadn't seen him for over two years, relying instead on the occasional drunken phone conversation. Yvette had banished Frank after his last visit, when he took Red to pick up crabs for dinner and didn't bring him home for three days. Red didn't even know where they'd gone. East, possibly the Mother Lode country, maybe even Tahoe. Red swore that they'd only been gone a day although Yvette and the calendar said otherwise. But that was good old Frank, skilled since childhood in the short tonic excursion.

Frank's father died when he was seven. His mother shut herself away with a well-stocked liquor cabinet and tried to take Frank with her for company. She invented a chronic asthma for her son and kept him out of school for weeks at a time. Frank learned to escape. He memorized bus schedules. By age ten, he knew how to hop a freight train. He discovered transient camps in storm drains and abandoned houses, turning up at school filthy and hungry from these hobo lairs. Red was his sidekick. Frank had the plan, Red had the money and the clothes and the food. Even then, Frank eluded the authorities while Red got grounded or yelled at, once even suspended from school for truancy. In their teens, the two boys discovered an arroyo with several rustic cabins that mud slides had rendered inaccessible by car. For six months, they spent afternoons, and in Frank's case nights, in different houses, entering through screens that parted at the touch of a pocket knife. They sprawled on strangers' sofas, ate canned goods, read old magazines and shopping lists, and drank bottles of wine and

Rock 'n Rye smuggled from Mrs. Jamieson's stores. In those havens of rustic luxury, Red developed a taste for how he'd like to live and drink.

This pattern of brief escape never left Frank. At seventeen, he joined the Air Force, and stayed on for twenty-four years. How many times had he shown up on Red's doorstep, AWOL and drunk? Yet he always gauged the tolerance of his superiors with perfect accuracy; he never saw the inside of the stockade or received more than a stern reprimand. His wives and sidekicks and the wives of his sidekicks suffered more. Whenever Frank came to town, Yvette's love died in chunks: Frank was the proverbial bad influence, a test to the Rays' marriage, a test Red invariably failed.

The Air Force trained Frank to be an aircraft engineer. Upon retiring at forty-one, he was deluged with offers from civilian corporations. He went through four companies in one year, claiming that civilian work lacked the military's standard of perfection. The headhunters soon stopped calling. Frank shed a third wife and moved back to his mother's house. He quit shaving for the first time in his life and spent his days watching game shows and soaps and playing gin with his mother.

The day Red called, mother and son were drinking Safeway-brand vodka, eating jalapeño cheese on Bacos, and betting a penny a point. The score was 7,243 to 5,689 in Mrs. Jamieson's favor. Frank told Red, "I can be there in, say, four hours."

Three hours later, he walked into Red's office. Six foot four, spindly and graceful, Frank carried himself with a polite slouch. Red did something of a drunken double-take. This was not the shaved-neck military lifer Red remembered. Frank's black hair was shoulder-length, slicked back, his beard long and woolly and streaked symmetrically with white. He looked cultish, backwoods, ministerial. Red thought of Tolstoy's fevered Russian saints. Then Frank smiled his old slow smile; it unwound like a revelation, a sly and knowing nudge to the heart. "Here I am," he said.

"I love you for it, too," said Red.

Frank slid into the life of a Rito idler. While Red kept up the semblance of a law practice, Frank had coffee at Yolanda's and afterwards lounged in the sun in the park by the river. Red met him for long lunches. When Red returned to his office, Frank joined the old men on the shady porch of the Mills Hotel. They met again at

Yolanda's for drinks and dinner. Yolanda worried over them, insisted they eat, gave them milk cartons of *albóndiga* soup to take home. They spent nights at Red's house, camped out in two rooms on the first floor. Red connected the water, but everything else remained as it had been when Yvette walked out: Cement had dried on hods. Paintbrushes sat in coffee cans of turpentine. Plastic wheezed in windows. The two men tracked plaster dust and sawdust, formed paths around stacks of lumber and the mammoth crated appliances. They were squatters at the construction site, vagrants at the scene of an abandoned dream. The days bled by.

Red received divorce papers just before Christmas and drove to San Francisco to work out a settlement with Yvette. Problems in property distribution arose only in the Rays' mutual indifference. "All I really want is out," said Yvette. "She can have everything," said Red.

He was appalled when he found himself the sole, uncontested owner of the Sally Morrot ranch. "I bought it for you," he told her.

"I don't want it," Yvette said. "Besides, you'll need a place to die."

Red returned to Rito an ex-husband and partial father. He found Frank at Happy Yolanda's with a pretty sixteen-year-old Mexican girl on his lap. "Here's Red back from the divorce wars," Frank said. "Red, this is Isabel, Luis's niece from Sonora." She had braids as thick and long as arms, equine eyes, and strong white teeth. She lit Frank's cigarette with a lighter shaped like a Saturday-night special, and ignored Red.

Everybody he loved, Red realized, was being taken away from him. "Frank," he said. "Come outside for a minute. I have to talk to you." Out in the blue dusk, he beckoned Frank into his pickup. "Come on, let's take a drive."

They drove for a month or more. They lived out of Red's truck and checkbook. They showered at campgrounds, bought clothes as they needed them. They meandered down the coast through the bars of Oxnard, Malibu, Oceanside. They sat in the sand, passed a bottle, and watched the sun go down over the ocean. "Look at that," said Red. "A path of gold right to me."

"No," said Frank. "To me."

They drank draft beer in pool halls, Rob Roys in hotel lounges, told bartenders and fellow customers, "We're on a drinking tour of the Southland. . . ." Skirting the border, they turned east: Calexico, Mexicali, Yuma, Arizona. Between hangovers and sunsets, Motel 6s and cramped nights in the car, they kept driving. As Frank drove, he sang:

> My daddy loved his bottle
> Lord, it drove him to his grave
> My mama loved her bottle too
> And it done her just the same
> Now there's no one left to love me
> And that old whiskey fills my days . . .

In a town whose name Red never knew, Frank swung too wide at an intersection, jumped the curb, and hit the side of a brick building. Red flew from the cab, then skidded to a stop in an alley. It was dawn in a grimy industrial zone. The sky was wintry overhead. Red saw the links of his watchband mashed into his wrist. He heard footsteps, saw dark forms standing over him, clouds of steam billowing from mouths. Shoes were tugged from his feet, his clothes were patted and probed, the watch extricated from flesh. A man's voice said, "That other one's a goner." And silence. Red rolled over on his stomach. One leg would not work. Blood ran into his eyes, a hot red curtain. He dragged himself along the pavement, inching his way around the back of the truck until he saw Frank hanging halfway out of the cab, his left ear snagged on the handle of the sprung door.

RED RAY rose from that curb a sober man. He spent three weeks in the VA hospital in San Diego, then six months in an alcohol recovery house in Los Angeles. He underwent two operations to repair the splintered bones in his left leg. Except when he was bedridden, he attended AA meetings three times a day. He wrote letters to his accountant and creditors and straightened out his finances. He ate three squares, gained back some of the forty pounds lost on his three-month liquid diet. He lifted weights, read mystery novels, and talked endlessly with his fellow drunks.

In September, he signed himself out and drove north in a rented car. In the Tehachapis, he heard on the radio that a band of anticommunist and anti-Japanese Koreans had met in a plaza in downtown

Seoul, chopped off their little fingers, packaged the digits, and mailed them to the Japanese premier. The premier, however, was in Mexico donning sombreros for reporters. And the Pope was in the Southwest donning feathered headdresses for other reporters. Red snapped off the radio. Finally sober and the world stays drunk.

The pale blond hills were dry and shiny with dead grass. He was on his way to Rito to check on his property before putting it on the market. He planned to return to San Francisco, join up with his old law firm, be a weekend father to his son. The sky was a soft talc blue. He drove west on the tiny two-lane blacktop that meandered like a dry river through the Santa Bernita Valley. Rounding a bend, he was suddenly, unexpectedly charmed by the vista of orderly orange groves, blue foothills, and distant purplish peaks. He'd been steeling himself to come here, to return to the scene of his consummate alcoholic crimes, where he had systematically relinquished and destroyed everything that was precious to him. He'd feared a relapse of fiery thirst, helpless remorse, clouds of pure pain. Instead, he was enchanted. A man could live peaceably in this valley. He could work outside in the air and the trees and soak up strength like sunlight.

Red spent weeks cleaning up after the last siege of vandalism in the mansion. He drove to Rito for meals at Happy Yolanda's, but he drank only 7-Up or tomato juice. Nights, he drove to Buchanan or Ventura for AA meetings. He asked Doc Perrin, a gruff old-timer with eighteen years of sobriety, to be his sponsor. Red called Perrin every day, sometimes twice. "I'm thinking of letting rooms to drunks," Red told him. "Turning the place into a kind of halfway house."

Perrin laughed and wheezed into the phone until Red worried for his health. "There's an idea," Perrin gasped.

"You think it's a bad idea?"

"Not if it keeps you sober. Better get yourself a good strong board of directors just in case. . . ."

Red moved into one of the bungalows in the workers' village on the far side of the estate. He made his intentions known at AA meetings, and by mid-October a volunteer work crew was showing up daily. By the middle of November, the job was done. The mansion was not the restored gingerbread castle of Yvette's blueprints; historical societies would strike it from their records. The repairs were basic, sound, institutional in flavor, heavy on stainless steel and pre-waxed linoleum.

A neighbor filed three appeals to halt the zoning changes, but the court threw them out. So Red hired a full-time cook, a local recovering alcoholic named Ernie Tola. He sent word to all the jails and hospitals, detox centers and halfway houses in a fifty-mile radius that Round Rock Farm for Recovering Alcoholics would open its doors on December first. Over the Thanksgiving weekend, Red drove down to San Diego to pick up the first and only permanent resident that Round Rock would ever have: a speechless, witless, barely ambulatory Frank Jamieson.

LEWIS itched. Having run out of cigarettes, he was smoking butts pinched from ashtrays, first his own Camel straights, then anything that didn't look mentholated. The muscles in his legs and shoulders and back were sore to the touch. He didn't have conscious memories of seizures, only the physical sense that his body had been wrung out like a washrag. Bobby said the seizures were DTs, delirium tremens. Lewis doubted that. More likely, he had smoked some questionable pot at that party, or done a line of something that was supposed to be cocaine. Drugs in academia were always suspect. Undergrad kids drove over to Ramparts, bought whatever was shoved through their car windows, and cut it with baby laxative, veterinary antibiotic, photographic chemicals.

Which is not to say Lewis didn't drink. He drank almost every day. But he didn't, like, *drink* drink, or go crazy to get the top off a bottle or anything. He knew some legendary drinkers, and he, clearly, wasn't one of them. He once drank with a famous writer from Montana who'd ordered round after round, and although Lewis drank hard to keep up, a long avenue of amber-tinted bourbon-and-waters soon stretched out in front of him. Nobody ever called that famous writer an alcoholic, so how could he, Lewis, be one?

Around noon, Bobby wandered up and asked if he wanted a sandwich or a piece of fruit. Lewis preferred not to take food from this small, balding bureaucrat. "That's okay," he said, only you might've thought he'd said, "Sit down and tell me your whole life story, Bobby." It was an AA thing, Lewis surmised: in the two, three days he'd been in detox, several people had launched into long, earnest secular testimonials.

Bobby had a short beard and thick tortoiseshell glasses. As he talked, he patted Lewis's forearm. "I wish you'd eat something." Pat. He just wanted Lewis to know how glad he was to have met him. Lewis reminded him so much of himself when he first got sober. It was important to remember what that used to be like. Bobby had run a sheetrock business that was so successful, he had everything: the car, the house, the gorgeous wife, the kids, the boat, even a plane. Another pat. Did Lewis ever fly a plane? Well, Bobby had discovered how fast you can get drunk in a plane; he'd take his Cessna up to ten, twelve thousand feet and chug a half-pint. After his wife left—because of the drinking, of course—and after he stopped going in to work, all he did was fly and drink. "I figure my last drink was a pint of bourbon at twelve thousand feet." This last glugging episode made him so drunk and lost—here Bobby gripped Lewis's arm—he landed on the first runway he spotted, which happened to be a military airstrip out in the Mojave. He opened the door to a dozen MPs with their guns trained right on him. An amplified voice told him to lie facedown on the tarmac—not that he had any choice, drunk as he was. He detoxed in the stockade for twenty-four hours before receiving any medical attention. He was lucky he didn't choke to death on his tongue or fracture his skull during the seizures. "That was fifteen years ago." A concluding pat, then a pause. "I never did get my plane back."

Lewis didn't know or care why any of this reminded Bobby of him. He let the guy talk and pat away to his heart's content because it seemed to brighten him up, give him a charge. Helping other alcoholics, Bobby said, was the best life he ever could've imagined for himself. This made Lewis sad—that anybody could be so pleased with a crummy administrative job in such a depressing place. Okay, Lewis thought, fine: I can listen. Why not let some poor guy cheer himself up?

Bobby went off in a great mood and came back with Lewis's knapsack. The knapsack held Lewis's notebooks, a few pens, matches, and a falling-apart paperback edition of the poems of Gerard Manley Hopkins. Bobby also handed him an envelope containing the contents of Lewis's pockets when he'd been signed in: matches, keys to the apartment he no longer rented, keys to the car he junked three months ago, a three-inch length of plastic straw. Bobby plucked the straw out of the envelope. "Let's toss this," he said. There was also under two dollars in change. No mention of the $250 Lewis had at last count.

When Bobby went back to his desk, Lewis tried to read a poem. He'd been working on a paper about Hopkins's concept of "inscape" for a Ph.D. seminar in nineteenth-century British literary culture. *I am gall, I am heartburn. God's most deep decree / Bitter would have me taste: my taste was me. . . .* He was too tired to unravel such syntax. He dozed, woke up to the ancient detox doctor jiggling his shoulder.

"Achy? Shaky? Lacka appetite?" the doctor asked, then grabbed Lewis's chin and pulled his lower eyelids down with his thumbs. Lewis looked back into rheumy blue eyes in a face of a thousand wrinkles. "Looking good," the doctor said. "Not so yellow today. Still, we're gonna keep an eye on that liver, friend."

Given the doctor's advanced age and broad body vibrato, Lewis assumed he was a retiree who'd volunteered his antiquated expertise to this shabby institution. The old gent wavered so much that it was like looking at someone through water. Keeping an iron grip on Lewis's cheeks, he said, "Hear you're going out to Red's place."

"I 'on't 'ink so," Lewis said.

The doctor released Lewis's face and scribbled on a clipboard. "You want Antabuse?"

"I just want a cigarette."

"Can't help you there." He scribbled some more. "You'll like Red's. You won't want to go home after your thirty days are up."

Lewis didn't particularly relish going home, period, considering he'd been living in his philosophy professor's garage, sleeping on a foam pad between the washer and dryer and the BMW. Every morning he'd wait until Sam and his wife went to work, then go into the house and shower, read the paper, and drink whatever coffee was left cooling in the pot. The first month, Amanda—the wife—left him a fresh half-pot and something to eat. "There's bread in the toaster for you," she'd call as she climbed into the BMW. "Pancakes in the oven . . . muffins on the table . . ." Soon, however, there were no baked goods, and she got into her car ignoring the fact that Lewis was a couple feet from her right-front wheel well. He didn't know what bent her cross. They used to talk, be close. She'd admired his work, especially a paper he'd published in *New History Journal*. Without warning, she'd stopped being friendly. Lewis took the hint and steered clear. The last night Lewis was there, Sam had called him into the kitchen for a drink. "We haven't seen you," he said. "Are you okay? Staying warm enough out there in the garage?"

In fact, the cement slab was like a block of ice, but before Lewis could answer, Amanda said, "If you get too cold, you can always take a spin in the dryer," and laughed heartlessly.

Oh, sitting there in detox thinking about how Amanda stopped liking him, and how his mother wouldn't come and get him, it seemed to Lewis as if everyone who was ever nice to him had pushed him away in the cruelest way possible.

The old doctor's pencil scratched. His breath whistled, broke into high-pitched chords. "Whaddaya weigh? One forty?" Frowning, gave Lewis an appraising look. "Month of Ernie's cooking oughta put some meat on those bones."

IN THE canned-vegetable aisle at Smart and Final, Red heard someone call his name. Julie Swaggart, his ex-secretary, pushed toward him, her dolly loaded with cases of Murphy's Oil Soap, popcorn, and Tampax. With her rippling hair, shapeless batik dress, and fringed shawl, she looked the same as always, only happier.

Julie once had been a well-known R&B singer, and back then her drugs of choice had been marijuana, red wine, and barbiturates. These substances had so shaped her behavioral style that even after many years clean and sober, her manner was still leisurely, as drowsy and vague as if she'd just pulled herself up off a massage table. "Hey, you," she said in her just-woke-up voice, giving Red a hug. Her shawl folded around him like patchouli-scented wings. "How's life at the ranch?" she asked.

"Going all to hell."

She laughed, but they both knew he wasn't lying. Despite her apparent languor, Julie had run a tight ship. In her reign, paperwork was completed. Quarterly taxes duly filed. Unpaid accounts relentlessly pursued. She'd been gone four months and he hadn't replaced her. He was missing luncheons and speaking engagements because nobody had updated his calendar. He missed the deadline for a major government grant that the farm had really counted on. For the first time in years, there were vacant beds at the Blue House; he'd misplaced the waiting list.

After five years at Round Rock, Julie had decided to open a recovery house of her own, the White Cottage for Women, over by Somis. When she'd told Red, he was stunned. "I wish you w-well," he stuttered. "But you have to be crazy to open a drunk farm. If I'd known what I was in for, I never would've started Round Rock. But I wasn't even a year sober. I *was* crazy. I hope you know it can consume your entire life. . . ."

Today, she looked so satisfied, so radiant, that he knew his advice had been wrongheaded. Then again, for the first four or five years at Round Rock he couldn't wait to wake up in the morning, and working with drunks had seemed, finally and irrevocably, his life's calling.

"How are your women doing?" he asked.

"Working with women is a whole different ball game," she said. "They're so much more willing to look at themselves, examine their behavior. The egos aren't so well defended." There was no remorse in her voice, nor the faintest constriction of regret. "I'm having the time of my life."

"Lucky you."

She searched his face. "You still haven't found anyone."

"Still looking," he said, though he hadn't even interviewed any applicants for Julie's job. Some kind of mental block, he supposed. A protest at her leaving. Maybe he'd run the whole farm into the ground. That'd show her.

She was on the verge of saying something, Red could tell, but restrained herself. They smiled at each other—he wistfully, she with a little shake of her head—and pushed off down the aisle in opposite directions.

Red stopped next at the auto parts store, the hardware store, the produce stand. In the detox parking lot, he sat in the truck, window cracked, and smoked. The day was cold and clear. He could see down the hill to the ocean and, across the dark blue water, the craggy shadows of the Channel Islands. On one of those islands, a woman had lived alone for a dozen years. A Chumash Indian woman. She'd lived by foraging, snaring fish and game, weathering storms in shallow caves. She'd done fine, too, until rescued. Taken to the mainland, given clothes, a bed, human company, and medical treatment, she died within the year.

APPROACHING the detox reception desk, Red was intercepted by Doc Perrin. "C'mon, Husky," Perrin said. "We got test results."

In Julie's absence, Red had also fallen so far behind on staff medical insurance that the policy had been canceled. To be reinstated, the company told Red, *he* needed a physical examination. He'd called on Perrin, his sponsor and friend, expecting him to fill out the insurance forms over a cup of detox's pisswater coffee. Instead, the old sawbones merrily administered an electrocardiogram, a treadmill test, hammered on Red's knees, listened to his lungs, pinched, prodded, and stuck a finger up his ass.

In Perrin's office, they sat down across from each other, the desk between them. "You gotta lose forty pounds, friend," Perrin said with more gusto than Red felt was called for. "And cut out caffeine and stop smoking. And that's for starters. You get that licked, we'll work on cholesterol and sugar. First thing, though, you gotta lower that stress level."

"Right," said Red.

"Might think about cutting down your work load."

"Right."

"Got a new secretary yet?"

"Thinking about it."

Perrin cackled. "Face it, Blue Eyes. You're nothing but a dried-out old drunk still hellbent on self-destruction."

This was hardly news to Red. When his head hit the pillow and he was alone with the sibilance in his lungs and the furious working of his heart, he vowed to quit the coffee, the sugar, the two-to-three packs a day. In the morning, he'd have half a pot of mud and a dozen Pall Malls and be midway through his rounds before he was awake enough to recall these promises. When he did try to go an hour or two without nicotine, the intensity of his craving astonished him. Who would guess that a fifty-two-year-old body could harbor such focused, shameless appetites!

"This kid you're picking up?" Perrin shifted his attention to another open file. "Skinny as a POW. Some liver damage, but I'm not sure the message has gotten through. You might like him, though. Smart."

AN ETERNITY had passed on the hideous waiting room couch, an eternity plagued by crawly bugs, vague, ominous dreams, and Bobby, who insisted on waking Lewis every few minutes: Glass of water? A final Dilantin? This time, Bobby introduced a large, fair man. "Here's Red Ray," Bobby said, and to Red, "I'll leave you to it."

The guy had a gut that swelled out over the waistband of his jeans. From Lewis's vantage point on the sofa, he had a double chin and a protruding, snouty face. His eyebrows, half red, half white, were long and bristly, like a badger's. His fairness seemed a painful, delicate condition.

"So," he said. "You want to come to Round Rock."

Ahh. A friendly sort, with a distinctly visible nimbus of goodwill, a light-flecked shading surrounding his face. Lewis managed to sit up straight. Then again, there was a light-flecked shading around everything—thanks, no doubt, to the many meds he'd been given in detox. "What I want," Lewis said, "is to get outta here. Why can't I just leave?"

"With your record, you walk out of here, get drunk, and hurt someone, detox is liable. So somebody else needs to take responsibility for you."

"Yeah, but I can't ask anyone to drive a hundred miles up here on a stupid bureaucratic technicality."

"Why not?"

"No," Lewis said darkly. "I just couldn't."

"I'm sure Bobby told you there are beds upstairs."

"I couldn't stay here."

"If you don't come with me, you know, they'll send you over to the state hospital."

This was the first mention Lewis had heard of a state hospital. "And where would that be?"

"Camarillo," said Red Ray. "The alcoholism ward. It's not so bad. Can get pretty hairy, but some guys actually like it."

Lewis knew about Camarillo. Who didn't? The big nuthouse. One time he'd been driving with a girl through the Santa Monica Mountains, trying to find a route back over to the coast, and they ran across the place. Tucked up against green rolling hills, the hospital formed a whole little town unto itself. There was no checkpoint, no guard, and they drove right onto the grounds. All the buildings were white with red tiled roofs. The streets were wide and freshly oiled and lined with healthy, thick-trunked palm trees. Expanses of green, closely cropped lawns shimmered in the sun. The girl he was with said she wanted to make love. It would be funny, she said, to have sex at the nuthouse. They drove around looking for a likely spot. The flower beds were all low to the ground, and there were no shrubs. No walls, no nooks.

That was the thing about a nuthouse, Lewis guessed: no privacy. Curiously, nobody came out and asked why they were driving around in slow-motion circles. In fact, the only person they saw was a huge-headed man tottering down a red-painted sidewalk. Lewis suggested they do it in the car. The girl said that wouldn't work for her, so they drove on down the coast.

Lewis was shocked to hear they'd ship him to Camarillo. He was angry, too, that neither Bobby nor the breathing-impaired doctor had mentioned this possibility. On the other hand, it would be ironic if he did wind up inside. He could call that girl and say, "You'll never guess where I am. Here's a hint: *no place to do it*."

Red, meanwhile, was standing with his hands splayed on his hips, fingers drumming at high idle.

"Sorry," Lewis said. "Just thinking about this girl I used to know. . . ."

Red regarded him without interest. Not in the mood for reminiscence, Lewis guessed. "And, uh, your place—what goes on there?"

"You'd work. Go to AA meetings. Get back on your feet. There's counseling. Three squares a day. Softball on Sunday."

Lewis knew about AA, and not only from the meetings at detox. He'd had to go to six meetings after he got that DUI. He'd heard a few good stories about people shooting dope with famous musicians, stuff like that. Once, a leader had called on him to speak—or rather, to "share." Would he like to share? No, he wouldn't, but he didn't want to hurt the guy's feelings, either. He told that meeting he was impressed by the rigor with which they were trying to solve their problems. He had no doubt that their efforts would pay off. When he finished talking, the man next to him thumped Lewis on the shoulder. "Keep coming back," he'd said.

"I'm not crazy about AA," said Lewis.

Red shrugged. "We do have one requirement, and knowing it might save us both some time. The only requirement is a desire to stop drinking."

Lewis had heard that phrase before, in the AA rules. His first impulse was to say, Yeah, yeah, yeah, let's just forget it then, but his present options were beginning to compute. Upstairs. Nuthouse. Remote drunk farm. He felt compelled to cry out against the mounting absurdity. "I'm just not so convinced I *need* any of this. It feels like a big mistake, as if I've been caught up in the system, like I've found myself in a tomato soup factory, only I'm not a tomato. I'm not a tomato, I tell all the machines, but they say, Well, you're on the conveyor belt, you're in the boiling vat—as far as we know you *are* a tomato."

Red chuckled. "Oh, hell," he said. "You can get out of here *like that*. Call a friend, anybody—that girl you were thinking about. Have her pose as your sister and sign you out. They won't check. They just want a signature."

Lewis focused on a few square inches of the brown plaid couch and thought about who to call. Sam, his philosophy professor, would probably come, but in a year or two, Lewis would be asking him for recommendations. *He was a brilliant student, but I did have to bail him out of the drunk tank.* As for the girl who'd been to Camarillo, she might not be so pleased to hear from him. He wished he knew the name of that girl at the party, the one with the bucket-of-milk face. And there was Sergei, a Russian physicist whose papers he edited, but with all the vodka Sergei swilled, Bobby would probably take one whiff and lock *him* in the rubber room.

Lewis couldn't think of anyone else, anybody he wouldn't be too ashamed to ask. Fear set in at a low hum. Dark winged things flickered in the corners of his eyes. Or maybe he was just glimpsing Red's fingers drumming with impatience. Down the hall, someone was cheerfully whistling "The Battle Hymn of the Republic."

Lewis reached for his knapsack and stood up. "Let's blow this pop stand."

Lewis's abrupt lurch upwards startled Red Ray, and it practically made Lewis pass out. His blood still wasn't moving at normal speed, and the room burst into bright squiggles.

"Easy now," Red said, grabbing Lewis's shoulders. They swayed, and briefly it seemed that they might go down together. Red recovered first, then righted Lewis. "I take it," Red said, "you want to come with me."

EWIS slept all the way to Round Rock and through much of his first week there, or as much of it as he could. He was awakened for meals and also for AA meetings, where he stayed conscious long enough to say, during check-in, "Lewis, alcoholic." In detox he'd learned it was easier to go with the flow than explain to a room of the newly converted that he personally was not a member of their tribe.

He shared a room with Carl, the snoring virtuoso. Carl was a high-school biology teacher; he had a wife and three towheaded little girls whose pictures occupied the nightstand between his and Lewis's single beds. A binge drinker, Carl kept getting arrested with underage hookers he picked up at a bar in Oxnard called the Joy Room. After arrest number three, Carl's wife had thrown him out of the house and he had come here, to Round Rock, presumably to wreck Lewis's run on sleep. Lewis, awakened in the early morning hours, swore the curtains rose and fell—indeed, that the entire room shuddered—with each of Carl's snores. There was nothing to do but get dressed and wander around.

He didn't know, really, where he was. He hadn't seen a map. He knew he was north of L.A., north of the San Fernando Valley, and perhaps not far from the ocean. Sometimes, as he roamed the house at night, he watched fog billow up against the windows, a series of ghostly shoulders. By day he noted citrus groves, clear skies, a thick yellow afternoon light.

The mansion itself seemed a comic travesty—a ravaged, once-lavish confection, a villa turned loony bin. It was called the Blue House, but the name barely hinted at its peculiar exterior color, an insistent, almost process blue, the color of robins' eggs, swimming pools, or glacial fissures. Inside, rooms with twenty-foot ceilings were cluttered with sprung sofas, ugly coffee tables, and folding chairs;

parquet floors were strewn with fake Persians and rag rugs. AA meetings took place in the ballroom, whose pillars were carved into ornate hanks of twisted rope, the slate floor hand cut in a wild sunflower pattern clearly inspired by van Gogh's work at Arles. Meals were eaten in the formal, wood-paneled dining room at six chrome dinettes, the kind Lewis spilled milk on as a child, with surfaces that looked like cubed Jell-O. Rackety older white refrigerators were shoved up against the dark wood wainscoting and stocked with milk and juices and packaged pastries you could heat up anytime in battered toaster ovens. Experienced residents said this was Round Rock's biggest selling point over other recovery houses: always enough to eat.

Lewis located two pay phones in closets off the living room and the lobby. Once, he shut himself in and, depositing the last of his change, called his philosophy professor. Amanda answered, and Lewis hung up without speaking.

He bummed cigarettes until Carl told him he could get small loans from the house manager—it would all show up on his bill. The notion of a bill caused a twinkle of alarm and then was blissfully forgotten, a twenty-dollar loan immediately sought and granted.

On his second Friday night, after dinner, Lewis squeezed into a Buick with five other men and rode through rural darkness to a town called Buchanan, where a large AA meeting was held in the domed auditorium of a former Masonic Temple, now a Teamsters union hall. There were women present, the first Lewis had seen in days. He sat next to one, a plump and fortyish knitter, who kindly gave him an unpleasantly sour lemon drop. He stayed awake for some of the speaker's story, so as not to appear rude; but the lulling tick of her needles wore him down and sleep, in a heavy green wave, reclaimed him.

On one early-morning ramble, Lewis slipped into the parlor, where the TV played all night to a host of chronic insomniacs. "If it isn't Rip Van Winkle," said Chuck, a small old guy with a white butch cut. A plumber, Chuck had retired to tend bar in a two-bit beer joint in Castaic and promptly drank himself into bankruptcy. Even sleeping through most AA meetings, Lewis had absorbed more biographical data about his companions than he cared to know. He knew, also, that this was Chuck's second visit to Round Rock; after his first discharge, he'd made it as far as the bar in Rito called Happy Yolanda's before his first scotch rocks.

"Remember how Harlow slept when he came here? Laid his head on a hamburger steak one night like it was a boudoir pillow." This was John, the house manager, a blue-eyed Irishman whose nose and cheeks bore a permanent, bright webbing of red capillaries. John, sober for five years, had no discernible sense of humor, bullied the men, was rumored never to sleep, and otherwise, so far as Lewis could see, provided clear inducement for a person to keep drinking.

A late-night talk show was turned down so low that Lewis had to stop breathing to hear a gospel-pop singer describe her work with Haitian orphans. Then Gene, a tall and doughy ex–football player holding a pot of fresh coffee and mugs, blocked his view.

"Jesus," Lewis said after his first sip. "No wonder you guys stay up all night, drinking this tar."

"This ain't strong," said Chuck. "Drink a cup over at Red's. He has that burnt-tasting stuff in little cups."

"Espresso?"

"Shit, I don't know." Chuck had a forearm tattoo of a woman sunk ass-first in a martini glass with a banner that said MAN'S RUIN.

"Who's been over to Red's?" asked Gene.

"He had me over there fixing a drain," said Chuck.

"He never once asked me over," said Gene.

"He doesn't ask anybody over," said John. "He lives there for a little privacy. I catch one of you over there buggin' him, you're out the same as for drinking or drugging."

"I wish he still lived over here with us," said Gene.

"Red never lived in this house," said Chuck.

"That's right," said John.

"Did so," said Gene. "I heard he was here till he was going to get married. Then he fixed up his place. Only the girl dumped him."

"Pure caca," said John.

"That's not what I heard," said Lee. With long blond hair and rock-star good looks, he was, at nineteen, the youngest guy at the farm. "I heard Red lived here till Ernie chased him out with a shotgun."

The men in the parlor burst out laughing, even Lewis.

"I'm just telling you what I heard," said Lee.

"It's those voices in your head again," said John.

"I don't have voices in my head," said Lee.

"You're crazier than a rat in an oil drum," said John. "You all are. A bunch of moody, sad-sack girls. Red this, Red that."

Lewis slipped from the room. Except for John, he didn't much mind the men. Or even being here at Round Rock. The almost heady lack of responsibility is how he'd always imagined life in a pricey private mental ward. Things could be a lot worse; he'd already heard stories of treatment programs where residents were made to pick up fields of dog shit, march in formation, and stay in group therapy sessions until everyone was blubbering. Here, nobody said boo as he slumbered through the days. Still, moving on through the dark, shabby rooms, he finally had to park himself on a dusty sofa, light a cigarette, and puzzle out how he, Lewis Fletcher, had come to be in a facility for recovery from alcoholism when, so far as he could tell, he wasn't alcoholic.

Young Lee had confided at dinner that his last high was an ounce of hash, an eightball of coke, six Quaaludes and a dash of crystal, all hastily washed down with Cuervo shooters as police crossed a dance floor to arrest him for punching a bouncer. "Pooped my pants in the squad car," he concluded cheerfully. At another meal, the men at Lewis's table discussed what they drank when the booze ran out. Vanilla extract. Mouthwash. Aftershave. Everybody agreed aftershave was the worst—because of the burps it gave you. Lewis had never owned such a stash as Lee's, nor had he sampled any one of the potions listed by his tablemates. At worst, he'd been playing a little fast and loose with alcohol in the last term.

He'd taken the last two quarters off to save money and finish a raft of incompletes. Six incompletes. Six incompletes out of nine courses. Without classes to attend, he began to feel peripheral, like the hangers-on lurking around every graduate program. The papers haunted him. "Flaubert and Racism in Late-Nineteenth-Century France," "Swedenborg, Blake, and Valuation of the Imagination," "Inscape and Individuation: Concepts of Self in Hopkins and Jung" . . . Where to start? Always, it seemed, with a little lubrication, a quick stop at the Think Tank, where he invariably ran into a colleague or a professor, someone, at any rate, who bought him one more drink, and one more after that. Many Round Rock residents blamed their drinking on raging fathers, pillhead mothers, overcontrolling wives and girlfriends. Lewis blamed his on literary culture.

LAWRENCE, a sweet homosexual speed freak who manned the clothes room, took Lewis under his wing, at least sartorially. "You have to class up. Beatniks are so passé," Lawrence said, and slipped him freshly laundered, donated clothing, all of it cleaner, newer, and more fashionable than anything Lewis had left in his professor's garage.

Chipper in his new clothes and increasingly well-rested—he had a sense of swimming through viscous green liquid toward a dim light—Lewis began to seek out intelligent conversation. Carl liked to talk about waterskiing. Lee punctuated the briefest exchanges with fast, furious jamming on the air guitar. Lawrence spoke knowledgeably of designer labels and suit cuts. The only person who displayed anything resembling a literate sensibility was the head honcho himself. Red Ray was the only speaker at AA meetings who didn't put Lewis out cold: he was funny and modest, and once he'd even quoted from a Blake poem: "I give you the end of a golden string. . . ." Also, when Red laughed, it was quiet, inward, almost like a sob. Lewis found this endearing, especially in such a large man.

The trouble was, everybody else wanted a piece of Red Ray, too. Whenever he came into the dining room, there was an obvious, communal hush. Hands reached for Red's hand. Men interrupted their own conversations to greet him. This reminded Lewis of the time he and a girlfriend went to see a man who trained animals for Hollywood. The man had trained a bear for beer ads and a stag for insurance ads and now ran a riding stable. When the three of them walked out to the barn, the farm dogs leapt joyously in front of the trainer, dropping sticks and toys at his feet. In the corral, horses edged toward him, pushing and nudging and surreptitiously nipping at one another to get closer, to be the one spoken to and petted. That's what it was like when Red Ray came into the Blue House—the same animal magnetism. As Red passed his table, Lewis didn't reach out a hand, but inside he craned and yearned with the rest of them, one more beast nuzzling up.

ON HIS second Sunday, visitors' day, Lewis felt strong enough—and social enough—to play softball. A diamond had been chalked into the base of the mansion's gently sloping lawn. The game served primarily as a diversion for residents who, like Lewis, had no visitors, although a few visitors also played, and any number of Round Rock alumni arrived to flesh out the teams. Lewis was instructed to choose a side: Shitheads or Doodads. He chose the former—Red Ray was their pitcher—and thus made what he learned was a lifelong commitment. As the day warmed up, his teammates peeled off their sweatshirts, revealing T-shirts that read, ONCE A SHITHEAD ALWAYS A SHITHEAD. Lewis played both the morning and the afternoon game, back to back, a total of twenty-two innings. The next morning, his ninth at Round Rock, he could barely walk and couldn't move his neck at all. Lewis was, in fact, in worse pain than when he was fresh out of detox, and John informed him that R & R was over and it was time to go to work.

W HEN Round Rock first opened, Red started out thinking—his first mistake, he always said—that if he put the drunks to work in the groves, the farm would support itself. This didn't play out precisely as planned: the groves were in such a state of neglect, the handful of newly recovering alkies so shaky, and Red's farming knowledge so halting that the first project—removing deadwood from a two-acre grove—took three months.

One day, on his way to the farm-equipment dealership in Buchanan, Red stopped in at Victor Ibañez's grocería for cigarettes. The small, cavelike grocería was crammed with shelves of canned goods and fishing equipment, and racks of gloves, Chap Stick, sunglasses, and car deodorizers. Faded piñatas and dust-furred coils of chiles hung from the ceiling. Two highway patrolmen sat on stools near the register, and on the counter itself sat Billie Fitzgerald, who lived with her father and son in an historic adobe on the banks of the Rito River. It was Billie who had instigated the court orders to prevent Red from opening his drunk farm.

To give Billie room to leave or move, Red hung back by the bulletin board near the door, pretending to read ads for pygmy goats and lawn mower/outboard motor repair.

"Hey, Red Ray," Victor Ibañez called out. "What d'ya need?"

"Smokes," Red said and reached for the flying pack of Pall Malls. "Thanks." He still had to step forward to pay.

Billie slid off the counter, moving to one side. She was quite tall and fit. Muddy clothes only underscored her imperious, pedigreed good looks. Her neurasthenically pale skin was scrupulously covered even in this dry summer heat.

"What brings you to town so early?" Victor said.

"On my way to pick up an auger," Red answered quietly.

"What do you need an auger for?" said Billie.

"I ordered a couple hundred trees to fill out a few groves and I need to dig the holes."

"I thought you were raising souls out there, not fruit."

"Hopefully, the souls will raise the fruit."

Billie stared at Red and pulled absently at her springy black hair. She harvested a few long, curly strands in her fingers, then dropped them on the old wood floor. "If I remember right," she said, "Sally had a couple augers in the warehouse."

"They went at the auction."

Billie painstakingly dropped more hair onto the floor.

"I'm gonna make you sweep before you leave," Victor said.

She ignored him. "Okay, Red." She sighed as if accepting an endless, onerous task. "I'll bring you an auger."

She came that very afternoon, and after a twenty-minute walk down the roadway, she told Red he had to lease the groves if he wanted to save his shirt. "You don't seriously think," she said, "you can run a drunk farm *and* a major citrus ranch?"

"That's the whole idea. The men work the farm."

"C'mon, Red. You're too nonprofit to be a farmer. You can't make money and help people at the same time. And even if you could, farming's not the way to do it. Now, you can lease 'em to me or you can lease 'em to Sunkist."

He leased them to her; she, in turn, hired her work crews off the farm. Given her reputation for machismo and slave driving, any resident who worked for Billie soon called her, among other things, the Amazon Next Door.

LEWIS didn't want to work for *any* Amazon, especially one he pictured as a steely older woman wearing jodhpurs and carrying a quirt. Neither did cultivating the organic vegetable garden appeal to him, nor joining the grounds crew. That left the garage.

In his twenties, at a loss at what to do with a B.A. in European history, Lewis had worked in a friend's garage in Monrovia. Karmachanics hadn't lasted long; instead of recycling the proceeds, the owner spent them on cocaine, which he ingested or sold to his employees at cost. When the business went under, right about the same time Lewis's marriage ended, he found a job in an auto parts store in Pasadena.

To be a good parts man—and Lewis had been an excellent one for five long years—you have to be a demon for details and compulsively, even supernaturally, tidy; otherwise chaos boils up so fast that you might as well shut down the store as try to find a Volvo alternator. While Lewis wasn't particularly neat about his own person or living space, he was used to a workplace where everything had—and was in—its designated place. The Round Rock garage, then, was a version of hell.

On the far end of the farm, near the workers' village, the garage was an old-fashioned setup with two wide bays that originally served the tractors, trucks, spray rigs, and forklifts of Sally Morrot's ranch. Instead of hydraulic lifts, each bay had a narrow trough where a man stood to work beneath a vehicle. "It's like a grave," Lewis complained to Gene, the only other mechanic. "You know how monks used to sleep in coffins? Well, we get to work all day in graves."

They were to perform simple, tax-deductible tune-ups and oil changes for the few patient locals who brought in their cars. Since both Lewis and Gene had less than thirty days of sobriety, neither could leave the farm for parts; they had to phone in their orders, then ask someone else to pick them up. Gene liked handling this procedure, having quickly figured out that by asking the *wrong* people, he could delay a single parts delivery for days, during which time he could watch TV in the parlor with impunity.

While Lewis waited three days for an oil filter, he gradated socket sets and crescent wrenches, labeled drawers, and matched various tools to outlines painted on pegboards. Gene, putting in a brief, guilty appearance, said that Lewis was exhibiting the classic symptoms of an adult child of an alcoholic—overresponsibility, workaholism, obsession with control. Lewis wondered to what condition, then, did one attribute avoidance, laziness, and chronic messiness?

After that first, interminable oil change, Lewis resolved to track down his own parts. His next project, the reconditioning of a recently donated, ice-cream-white '65 Ford Fairlane, might require any number of parts orders. He wrote a preliminary list—*points, plugs, spark plug wires, belts*—and went in search of Red Ray.

A FEW hundred yards west of the garage, two shady cul-de-sacs branched off from the roadway, with nine small bungalows scattered between them. The former fieldworkers' village looked like tourist courts Lewis had seen in Pasadena, although not as quaint or well preserved. Red's house and the office, both painted a rustic redwood brown with ivory trim, had been landscaped with lawns and roses and house-swallowing bougainvillea. The other seven cottages were boarded up and sitting in hard dirt like studies in decrepitude: crumbling chimneys, listing porches, silvery clapboard shedding a few last flakes of paint.

Lewis's knock and tentative "Hello-o" drew no response, but the office door was unlocked, and he let himself inside.

Another mess. Psychology and recovery books were shoved this way and that into shelves. Wastebaskets overflowed with styrofoam cups, the holey edges of computer paper. The desk was a thicket of stacked files, newspapers, and fast-food wrappers. A large calendar mounted on an easel displayed November, and this was the first week in February. Lewis cleared a space to sit on the plump green sofa, then plucked a brochure from the stack on the coffee table. A brief description of how Round Rock worked was followed by three lengthy testimonials by former residents. Lewis skimmed these, finding the usual earnest litanies of personal loss and physical decline followed by triumphal recovery. The back page featured a few shorter endorsements:

> Until I came to Round Rock Farm, I thought nobody cared. How wrong I was! *George L.*

> In my six months at Round Rock Farm, I found the freedom to become the person God intended me to be—myself! *Bob K.*

He flung the brochure aside—how corny can you get?—snuggled into the cushions, and sleep, his dearest ally, carried him off. The next thing he knew, Red Ray was standing over him, hands full of mail. "Jesus, Mary, and Joseph! How the hell'd you get in here?"

Lewis struggled into a sitting position. "The door was open. . . ."

"Scared the wits out of me."

"Sorry. I need some car parts picked up."

Red tossed the mail on the desk. "Just came back from town." He sat down, still breathing hard. "It'll have to be tomorrow. Okay?"

Lewis nodded. Red slipped on a pair of half-frame reading glasses, pushed papers off his blotter, and began sorting through the mail. "Everything else okay?" he asked absently. "We treating you well enough?"

"Yeah. . . ."

"Good." Red gave him a quick, over-the-glasses glance.

Here he was, finally alone with Red Ray—and tongue-tied as a starstruck teenager. He recalled his mission, however: to let Red know that he, Lewis, wasn't one more run-of-the-mill juicehead. He wracked his brain. "I was wondering," he said finally. "Is there a typewriter or computer I could use?"

Red stacked letters in piles as if playing solitaire. "And what would you need a computer for?"

"I'm a Ph.D. candidate in cultural history and I have to give a paper at a conference in March."

Red swiveled in his desk chair until he faced the calendar. Absently, he lifted the month of November, then the month of December. Behind December: empty space. They both gazed into it. The phone began to buzz. Red made no move to answer it.

Lewis said, "If you let me use this computer, I'd be happy to answer the phone for you, take messages."

Red turned to Lewis. His eyes were kind. "How much time do you have now, Lewis?"

Lewis knew what Red meant: how long had he been sober? "Fifteen days."

"Terrific! And you're here for how long?"

"Thirty," said Lewis.

Red's forehead pleated. "Lewis, you have the rest of your life for cultural history. Why not take the next two weeks to get grounded in sobriety? Read the Big Book. Talk to other alcoholics."

"I'd clean this place up for you."

"You would, would you?" Red smiled, rueful, and tapped the corner of an envelope on the blotter. "Tell me, Lewis. Who's your sponsor?"

Lewis picked at the piping on the sofa arm.

"You have a sponsor?"

"No."

Red aimed the envelope at Lewis. "It's a good idea to have a sponsor."

"Yeah. But . . ." The whole concept of sponsorship gave Lewis the jitters. One of the more excruciating things about life in the Blue House was hearing grown men say, My sponsor says I should do this; My sponsor says I shouldn't do that—as if no one could blow his own nose without special dispensation.

"Tell you what," said Red. "You get yourself a sponsor, and if he thinks it's a good idea for you to work on your paper, we'll talk. Okay?"

Lewis couldn't say how unokay this was. He clutched the sofa arm, trying to think. Red returned to the mail and, after a few minutes, shot Lewis another sharp look.

Against his own will, Lewis was embarrassing himself, behaving like a fool, like a clingy girl who wouldn't take no for an answer— like that girl from Texas in his Shakespeare class. He'd slept with her once and she'd glommed on like industrial-strength adhesive. Dogged him everywhere. He would be at a bar and suddenly, on the next stool, there was Tex primly sipping a beer and radiating pain. He'd ignore her as long as he could, then break down and talk to her. Eventually, he'd grown curious: just how long *would* she sit there without acknowledgment? Hours. Several times, in fact, she outlasted him.

Lewis, so strangely paralyzed, prayed he wouldn't sit here for hours, a pathetic, groveling supplicant.

Red spoke abruptly. "You say you like to write?"

"I don't know how much I *like* it," Lewis said. "But yeah, I do a lot of writing."

"Tell you what. You write something for me, you can have a couple hours on the computer. But I don't want you over here all the time hiding out with the damn thing."

"I was thinking you need some help with your correspondence."

"No," said Red. "I'd like your drinking history."

"My *what*?"

Red wanted a narrative about how Lewis's family drank, how Lewis drank, and whatever trouble alcohol or drugs had caused him—arrests, humiliations, jobs and friendships jeopardized or lost, all of it. "I don't want the *Encyclopaedia Britannica*," Red said. "But try to be thorough."

Lewis assumed Red needed text for another brochure and was certain he'd only disappoint him. Next to the stories told at the Blue House AA meetings—including Red's own impressive saga, which had achieved the status of legend—Lewis's drinking career had the dramatic content of skimmed milk. A guy named Oscar had come out of a blackout with his arms torn up and bleeding only to find his beloved cat drowned in the bathtub. Chuck had woken up married to a woman he didn't recognize. Lawrence had been stabbed in a kidney while shooting dope in a West Hollywood alley. Lewis could count maybe half a dozen blackouts, total, and he'd always woken up at home and in bed, safe and sound and—regrettably—alone. "I don't know if I can provide what you're looking for," he told Red.

"I'm not looking for any one thing," Red said. "Just tell the truth. Can you do that?"

The truth, thought Lewis, was just what would make 'em snore.

AFTER Lewis left, Red Ray locked the door and slit open a letter from his ex-wife. A note, really; half a sheet of heavy, ivory stationery, the message typed and brief. Evidently, Joe wanted to go out for track. The meets were on Saturdays, which meant he couldn't come down to Red's for three months, four if the team made the state finals: "You could come up here and see him run." She signed off "Best wishes" and typed her name, initialing it with a large, loopy "Y" in bleeding blue ink.

Old fears arose, tireless as waves. Was this another ploy to disenfranchise him? Or was Joe trying to avoid him? Was Yvette exacting punishment for yet another perceived failure in parenting?

Not that Red was a terrific father even by his own standards. He ached for Joe, yearned to spend more time with him, yet often felt awkward, shy, almost afraid around the boy. At fifteen, Joe was going through such rapid physical and emotional changes, Red worried he'd embarrass or appall his son, miscalculating him from one visit to the next. And then there was the steady bass beat of dread that Red would unconsciously emulate his own intemperate, well-meaning father, who, through no effort or guile, had managed to harm everyone in his path.

Red shared with his father the same name, John Robert Ray, which neither ever used. John Senior went by "Jack." He was a tall, lean man who had both the gift of gab and "the failing." He would gauge the needs of others with uncanny accuracy and then promise to fulfill them—which, of course, he never did. In a few short years of marriage, he gambled away the farmhouse in Azusa and a modest sum of money his wife had inherited from her father. Red distantly remembered a series of shabby motel rooms made huge, almost infinite with waiting, always waiting for his father to return from the bars.

His parents separated when Red was five, and his mother took a teaching job in Glendale. Red was left behind, to be shuttled among his aunts and grandmother. He saw his father with increasing infrequency. At one point, Jack was enlisted to move Red from his aunt Maude's house in Redlands to his grandma Iris's house in Pomona.

"We'll make a day of it," Jack told Red over the phone. "Get you moved, then pay a visit to the water gardens. Sound good to you, son?"

Red, seven years old, had no idea what water gardens were; he envisioned a landscape where running water was piped and channeled to flow in the shapes of trees and flowers, a park whose foliage was transparent, boisterous, ever in motion. And yes, that sounded very good to him.

Red waited for his dad in the front yard with two suitcases and Smoky, an adolescent barn cat he'd acquired from the ranch next door. From the way Jack Ray slammed on the brakes and spun his tires in the gravel drive, Red sensed that his father was in a terrible hurry and that he, Red, was to blame. Jack Ray had a craggy face and sandy hair. Aunt Maude called him "a tall drink of water" to Red and "a long list of troubles" to everyone else. Jack grabbed Red's suitcases and loaded them into the trunk of his '42 DeSoto coupe. "Put the cat down and get in, son," he said.

Red would not put Smoky down. Smoky was his cat. He rolled Smoky up inside his sweater, ran to the edge of the property, and refused to get into the car until Aunt Maude appeared on the porch and told Jack that it was okay, Iris was expecting Red to bring the cat.

Jack reached an arm impatiently toward Red. "Give him here. I'll put him in the car."

Reluctantly, Red handed Smoky to his father. Jack tossed the cat into the trunk and slammed it shut.

At dazzling speed, they drove west on Foothill Boulevard, Route 66, through stretches of scrub desert alternating with vineyards and orchards. The front seat was black leather, warm and slippery. Red clung to the armrest and saw mostly sky over the dashboard. They'd gone only a few miles when Smoky started to yowl, a desperate, guttural noise of impossible length and resonance. Red's father said nothing. The yowling persisted, in waves, each louder and more protracted than the last. Red glanced around and saw that, somehow, Smoky had crawled up between the roof and the sand-colored headliner, and was slowly coming their way. Red could make out four convex points—Smoky's paws—as he advanced, step by step. Occasionally, a translucent claw broke through the headliner's weave. With a series of ripping sounds, the liner pulled free from where it was glued to the roof. Soon Smoky's yowling was directly overhead, chordal, extended, bloodcurdling. Between Jack and Red, the headliner sagged with the cat's weight and shape. Jack gazed straight ahead, driving faster and faster toward smeary clouds and washed-out blue sky.

When they arrived at Grandma Iris's house, Jack drove up on the lawn. He leapt out, went to the trunk, and threw Red's suitcases onto the grass.

"Get out of the car," he said to Red and took out his pocket knife, pried open the blade. Red scrambled away and watched as Jack plunged the knife into the headliner, cut a long gash, reached in, pulled Smoky out by the leg and hurled him, a black fright wig, out into the yard. The cat sprang to his toes, unhurt, and dashed into nearby orange groves. Without another word, Jack climbed in his car and drove off, his face curtained by the flap of torn headliner.

Red never saw his father alone after that. Subsequent meetings were stiff, virtually silent half-hours in the presence of a grandmother or aunt. When his mother married Giles Southerly and brought Red to live with them, it was easier for everyone if Jack stayed away.

Eight years ago, a private investigator sobered up at Round Rock and Red let the man work off his bill in trade. Red asked him to locate his father, an assignment both assumed would result in the address of a cemetery. Within a week, however, Jack was found traversing the country in a mid-size motor home with a Choctaw woman named Winnie. Red sent a telegram to a Kansas KOA campground, and ten days later Jack and Winnie rolled into Round Rock. Almost forty years had passed since Red had seen his father. Jack was now a fragile stick of a man, face wattled in loose skin, head crowned by a wavering white flame of hair. Jack and Winnie parked the motor home next to Red's bungalow and drank gin around the clock until

Red had to ask them to leave. Two years later, Red was summoned to Monrovia to identify his father's body and collect his possessions: one green woolen overcoat, one pair of black steel-shank boots, sixteen dollars and change.

Since his father's death, Red had had a recurring dream. There was no story or sequence of events, merely landscapes of water: hills and mountains of water, and, of course, gardens, with sparkling clear dahlias, surging hedgerows, weeping willows.

Red smoked and reread Yvette's note until he knew for certain no rebuke or threat simmered between the words. He laughed a little at the strength of his own inexhaustible fears. The boy just wanted to run track, for Christ's sake, to be on a team with other boys. Red could go up there to see him. Cheer him from the sidelines. There was still hope, after all: it was just possible that he and Joe would not end up lost to each other, two heartbroken strangers.

L EWIS showed up in Red's office the following afternoon.

"Yes?" Red looked up from the computer.

"I finished that writing."

Red looked confused, so Lewis held up a sheaf of pale-green
paper covered with blotchy ballpoint scrawl. "My drinking history,"
he said.

Red's face cleared. "That was fast! What'd you do? Stay up all
night?"

Lewis shrugged—three a.m. was all—and started to hand the
pages to Red.

Red crossed his arms. "Read it to me."

"Oh, that's okay. You can read it."

"I'd rather hear it, if you don't mind."

"Really? Right now?"

"Is there something else you need to do?"

"No. But you . . ." Lewis couldn't imagine that Red didn't have
other, more pressing items on his agenda.

"I'm here. I'm ready. I'm listening."

Lewis sat in the green armchair closest to the desk. "All of it?" he
asked.

"All of it."

Lewis straightened the pages and began to read.

FAMILY DRINKING PATTERNS

The one grandmother I knew, my mother's mother,
went to a bar every afternoon. The bar, on Loden
Street, was called Lloyds of Loden, which made my
parents laugh and laugh—I didn't understand why for
years. When this same grandmother took us trick or

treating, she wore a big heavy serape and a wide brimmed hat and carried a heavy coffee mug. At each door, she held out the mug and boomed, "Me want fire-water!"

"Is this the sort of thing you had in mind?" Lewis asked. "Precisely. But slow down, please. And speak up."

My parents had cocktails every night, and when I was very young, they threw cocktail parties. The specialty glassware came out of its closet. The parents of my nursery school classmates arrived, the men in starched white dress shirts unbuttoned at the neck, the women in floral prints and spaghetti straps. My father was loud and jolly in a way he never was with us. My mother bared her shoulders, drank martinis, and kissed her way through the room, leaving a wake of smeary red lipstick.

In the morning, my older brother Woody and I drank all the unfinished drinks.

Red was smiling.
"What?" Lewis said.
"I'd say you wrote the hell out of it."

My father drank bourbon. Gin, my mother's drink, disagreed with him, although he never did refuse a mar-tini. A short time before he moved out—I must have been nine or ten—I woke up in the middle of the night and went into the kitchen for a glass of water and he was drinking straight from a bottle in big long chugs, like he was dying of thirst. He'd take the bottle away from his lips and pant until he caught his breath, then drink more.

Years later, his second wife told me he had to stop drinking—doctor's orders. She said he had drunk so much that not only his liver but his eyes and his bone marrow were damaged.

"That's it for 'Family Drinking Patterns,' " Lewis said.

Red leaned forward. "What about your brother? Does he drink?"

"Woody?" Lewis squinted at the fireplace. "Maybe. He's in the merchant marines, I hardly ever see him. He's more into pot, always has some gourmet bud or opiated hash."

"Okay," said Red. "Go on."

"Let's see. 'My first drink'?

> Sips from my parents' glasses. Wine. Beer. Liqueur. And those party leftovers Woody and I drank—I still remember how they made me feel rubbery, hot, bursting with energy.
>
> I smoked pot for the first time when I was twelve. A neighbor kid stole a joint from the stash hidden in his stepfather's shoulder holster. Woody and I also filched pills—white crosses, Dexedrine, Seconal—from my mom.
>
> I went to my first kegger at fifteen. I remember rolling on the grass, laughing like crazy, then throwing up in someone's car. My friends dropped me off down the street from my house. I slept for two days.
>
> I had my first bourbon at sixteen. We were on a rooftop smoking pot when an older guy showed up with a quart of Bourbon Deluxe. Even at the time it seemed one of those signifiers of adulthood, like a first cigarette, a first pair of dark glasses. In the mercury vapor streetlight, I looked at the clear, shiny brown and thought, Here it is, here it is.
>
> Drinking was never the focus in high school. Only jocks and parents drank seriously. We took drugs to have visions, push through the cracks. Pot was weaker then, more fun. It arrived from Mexico in sugary bricks the size of shoeboxes; you could smoke a whole joint and all you'd do is laugh and eat everything in the fridge.
>
> I got busted once, with friends, for smoking a joint in somebody's front yard. When my mom's boyfriend came down to get me, the cops arrested him for all the

unpaid parking tickets I'd accumulated on a car registered in his name.

"I laugh about it now." Lewis glanced up. "But when he got me alone, he broke two of my ribs."

I dropped acid and mescaline in college until I had a bad trip on some so-called psilocybin. Psilocybin's supposed to be so benign, but on this stuff, dark, glittering chasms opened up between blades of grass, along rooftops, around people's faces. The civilized world seemed the flimsiest construct, frantically devised to shore up against the pure terror of existence. It was hours before I came down and years before I went a whole day without seeing dark chasms in the edges of my eyesight.

No more psychedelics after that. I couldn't even smoke pot without rekindling terror. Booze was okay. Booze was all I did, until I discovered cocaine.

My ex-wife Clare and I discovered cocaine together, but once we got married, she decided coke was too expensive. I was working at a garage and the owner sold us blow at his cost; still, by the end of the week, when I went to get paid, I often owed him a hundred dollars.

After the divorce, I took a job at a parts store and went out with the guys after work. Prodigious drinkers, they ordered round after round. A few times, I woke up the next morning without knowing how I got home.

I quit the store when I was twenty-nine. I didn't want to be thirty years old and working in parts. I stopped drinking. I started running seven to ten miles a day, applied to grad school. When I started drinking again, sometimes one beer made me drunk. Another time, I could drink half a quart of bourbon and not feel a thing. I got a DUI after just one drink. (Maybe I shouldn't have sung the alphabet.) I was fined nine hundred dollars and sent to six AA meetings.

So, in the last two years I only drank on weekends

or at social functions. Recently, because I took time off from school, I was drinking more often. No more than four, five drinks a night, though. I only got drunk once or twice a week, usually when I did editing for an expat Russian physicist—he'd always give me ice tea glasses of frozen vodka.

I don't remember my last drink. I remember being at the Russian's house and, less clearly, at a party in married student housing. Then I woke up in my underwear in the detox rubber room.

"That's it." Lewis folded his writing, set it on the desk, and looked at Red.

Red was sunk in thought. His index fingers pushed his lips upward toward his nose. "What I want to know, Lewis . . ." he said, and focused slowly, "is *how*, after writing all *that*, you can have any doubt whatsoever that you're an alcoholic?"

"You're kidding, right?" Lewis *was* flattered that Red thought his paltry story measured up. Still, the diagnosis, delivered so unequivocally, felt like a punch in the chest. He'd drunk heavily at times, sure. But he never drowned any cats or committed vehicular manslaughter or had to glug alcohol in the middle of the night. He never even *thought* about alcohol all that much, and wasn't alcoholism an *obsession*? "What makes you so sure?" he said.

"What normal drinker could write a document like that?"

Lewis drew his knees up to his chin and wrapped his arms around his legs. Any guy he knew, any guy he went to school with, could produce a similar narrative, if asked. The misunderstanding, Lewis thought, was generated by the structure of Red's assignment: the form alone pre-empted the content. "I can see that it sounds like I had a big long thing with alcohol," Lewis said. "But if I'd written an essay concentrating only on all the times I've *laughed* you'd think I was a total laughing fool. Yet I'm *not* a big laugher."

"And so?"

Lewis rested his forehead on his knees, breathing his own scent: tobacco, motor oil, almond-scented solvent, a whiff of goaty sweat.

"Sit with it for a few days," Red said. "See how you feel."

"Well, here." Lewis tried to hand Red the written pages. "Don't you want it?"

"Hang on to it for the time being. Might be useful later."

Lewis was baffled: if the drinking history was so well written, and smacked so conclusively of bona-fide alcoholism, why didn't Red snatch it up for one of his brochures?

AT 5:30 A.M., Libby Pollack Daw curled over her journal and listed everything she missed about Stockton, her ex-husband. The flood of divorce-inspired fury had finally subsided, and in its wake lay a most alarming nostalgia for: *(1) That formal thank you kiss before he sat down to meals. (2) All his highbrow charm. (3) Good, smooth lips. (4) Well-shaved jaw. (5) The great pleasure of making him laugh in bed.*

Libby regarded this list, then wrote: *Am I turning into a Tennie?* Tennie had been a next-door neighbor on Carondelet Street in New Orleans. When Libby first met her, Tennie was a bright, normal, divorced hospital technician, dating a Cajun shrimper, and moderately unhappy like everybody else. Tennie had two kids her ex-husband was good about seeing and supporting. Then Tennie was born again in some Pentecostal sect and decided that her ex was her one true husband under God, and that no man, including any judge or even the former husband himself, could put it asunder. They'd been apart three or four years by then, and the ex had married someone else, but Tennie began to cook dinner for him every night, setting his place at the head of the table. She'd call him up across town: dinner's ready, honey. Before long, there was a restraining order and threats of a custody battle.

Tennie relayed these developments matter-of-factly. When Libby, benumbed secondhand by the humiliation, asked what his new wife thought of all this, Tennie replied, "I'm his one true wife and the mother of his children." Libby didn't challenge or contradict her, partly because Tennie seemed nuts and partly because, well, what if she was on to something? What if Tennie eventually wore him down and he capitulated, sat himself down before his steaming plate of limas and rice?

"Come home, husband—it's dinner time" . . . imagine trying that out on Stockton! Libby could see his lips curl back like razor-cut paper. Still, she now could admire the mad plunge of Tennie's approach, the disregard of civility and civil law in lieu of a higher administration. "Your bed is made, dear, your clothes laundered and laid out." In thrall to such devotion, Libby thought, one simply bows to the yoke of contempt, welcomes it, suffers it gladly in Jesus' name. . . .

She wrote: *I'd rather stick my head in the oven.*

She pushed her hair back from her face and began writing in earnest. She'd been keeping a journal long enough to know that self-indulgent speculation, however gratifying in the moment, wasn't half as fascinating or useful in a month's time as brief, factual notes that could evoke otherwise forgotten days. *Dinner last night with Billie and the Bills. Rack of lamb cut into little chops, tiny yellow potatoes. Wine so good it made me want to cry. They ridicule environmentalists. Their ranching is an unrepentant rain of herbicides, miticides, pesticides, fungicides, etc. Am surprised, as ever, they want me around. They don't, can't, have any sense of who I am, but have decided, for reasons not apparent, that they like me. . . .*

Libby closed her journal and dressed for work. She packed jeans for practice later with the Cactus Pharaohs, a not-bad band who, in addition to all the sappy covers required at every wedding, played a mix of Western swing and barnyard jazz. Grabbing fiddle and purse, she left the trailer.

Libby's car was a 1960 baby-blue Ford Falcon. Reaching for the driver's-side door, she paused. Every little hair on her body rose up, as if an army of tiny bugs blanketing her skin all raised their antennae at the same time. Her crazy first thought was, I've been cut in two at the stomach. Then time slowed down, way down, and she actually observed her mind filter the information before her: the huge, bearded man sleeping in the backseat of her car.

Libby stepped back carefully, soundlessly, and dashed to the trailer in two or three bounds. She locked herself in and, fingers noodly, called the sheriff. The phone rang and rang—she could have been stabbed fifty times at least—before the woman dispatcher picked up.

"There's a guy sleeping in my car," Libby said, "and I have to go to work."

The woman took her name and address, then asked for a description.

"He's big and has a gray beard and . . . I don't know. He looks like he lives in a pumpkin patch."

"Keep your door locked," the dispatcher said. "I'll send Burt over."

Libby was about to call Billie Fitzgerald, but remembered Billie and her father, Old Bill, drove her son, Little Bill, to prep school in Ojai every morning.

Libby sat at the kitchen table, where she could see the car. Nothing moved. She took a knife out of the drawer: a well-weighted twelve-inch chef's knife. She considered sharpening it, since you were supposed to do so before each use.

She blamed Stockton for abandoning her out here like a litter of kittens. He would say, You should've locked your car doors. But wasn't no locked doors one of the pleasures and payoffs of living in the country? Libby never locked her trailer, either. Thank heavens her visitor liked car seats.

She jumped when the phone rang, Victor Ibañez calling from the grocería. "Heard you got Frank over there," he said.

"Victor! God!" Libby said. "Who's Frank?"

"Big old guy with a bushy gray beard. Probably wearing slippers. Looks like he lives in a pumpkin patch."

Would small-town telegraphy ever cease to astonish and appall her?

Victor laughed through his nose, like a snuffling dog. "A pumpkin patch! That's *perfect*!"

"Victor," Libby said. "This is not funny."

"Frank won't hurt you, honey," Victor said. "Just light his cigarette, you'll make a friend for life."

"I'm not going anywhere near him! Is Burt there? You tell Burt to get over here."

"Just a moment." Without covering the phone, Victor said, "It's your wife, Burt. Are you here?" Into the receiver, Victor said, "Burt says he's not here."

"Come on, Victor. Please," Libby said. "I'm seriously freaked out. If you don't let me talk to Burt, I'm going to call the marshal."

"She's gonna call the marshal, Burt," said Victor.

"Damn it, Victor."

"Now, now," Victor said. "Burt's already on his way. I just wanted to call ahead to say Frank's harmless. But lately he's been taking these little walks away from home."

"I don't think going around and terrifying single women who live alone in the country's exactly *harmless*."

Libby heard gravel crunching outside as Burt McLemoore pulled into her driveway.

LEWIS woke up early in the morning from a dream in which the earth had tilted off its axis and everything was sliding away from everything else. Chairs flew from tables, pillows popped from sofas, highways lifted off the ground like kinked ribbons. In the next bed, Carl snored pianissimo, almost a purr.

Lewis decided to go running. He pulled on pants and loped downstairs. Movement was good. He pushed through the front door, jogged down the driveway, one footfall between each palm tree. It was cold out, gray and dewy, and Lewis's wool sweater produced a faint wet-dog stink that intensified as he warmed up. His hands grew pink. Was it possible that his jerky start-and-stop pattern of drinking constituted a real disease, the same one his father had? His father seemed another species: a red-faced television exec, a five-martini luncher fixated on racehorses, already on his third family and second open-heart surgery.

Lewis hit flat ground and picked up speed. Light seeped slowly into the sky. As if hand-tinted, oranges and lemons acquired the faintest pastel hues. Near the garage, he heard the familiar glass-packed rumble of Red's truck and looked around for a place to hide in case he was doing something wrong by being out at this hour. It *felt* like he was. Then again, he usually *did* feel like he was doing something wrong.

Red rolled down his window. "Beautiful morning, eh?"

"Just taking a run," said Lewis.

"You and Frank both," said Red. "I gotta go fetch him. Want to come along?"

"Sure." Lewis clambered into the truck. He'd been only vaguely aware of Frank's existence. Frank spent his days in a lawn chair in the kitchen, where Ernie Tola could keep an eye on him and light his cigarettes. A couple times Lewis had seen Frank sitting on the front porch, and once Lewis went into a downstairs john and found Frank, pissing away with surprising accuracy: the big mute seemed too dim to have mastered even that basic art.

"Any more thoughts about the writing you did?" Red asked.

"No." Lewis accepted a Pall Mall and light. "Although I don't see how you can be so sure I'm an alcoholic."

"Oh, I could be wrong," Red said cheerfully. "Although normal drinkers don't drink ice-tea glasses of vodka. Or get DUIs. Have four or five drinks a day and get drunk twice a week. Not to mention the blackouts. Then there's the secondary stuff. Living in a garage. So alienated from family and friends you can't call on anyone for help. Dropping out of school and—"

"Look, alcoholism is *your* paradigm," said Lewis. "I say it's more a basic, chronic misanthropy."

Red smiled. "You'd be surprised what sobriety does for basic, chronic misanthropy."

Lewis glowered at the passing groves. This was the first time he had been off Round Rock's premises during the daylight. A river ran on the left, the water swift and green among willows and naked cottonwoods, the riverbed wide and filled with smooth, pale rocks. Lewis rolled down his window. The air was heavy with dampness and oxygen. "It's nice up here," he said.

Red ducked his chin as if accepting a compliment, then waved to an old man riding a bicycle. "Rafael Flores," said Red. "The local *curandero*—witch doctor. The old gal who used to own my ranch supposedly swore by him. Said he kept her alive for years with a special tea. Whenever we kill a rattlesnake, we save it for him. He makes some kind of powder from the skins."

"No shit?" Lewis twisted in his seat to get a better look at the elderly rider, whose long white hair fanned out behind him like a veil. "Think he does peyote and mushrooms?"

Red chuckled. "That, I wouldn't know," he said, and turned at a mailbox with "DAW" painted on it in red nail polish. The gravel spur climbed steeply through a silvery olive grove and up to a grassy plateau where a house trailer sat between two willows. A squad car was parked behind a Ford Falcon. Frank was leaning against the Falcon's back door and smoking. Red said, "He does look like he lives in a pumpkin patch, don't you think?"

The deputy was standing on the deck, talking to a woman in a flowered skirt and a down vest. The woman rubbed her arms. When Red parked, she put her hands on her hips and glared at the truck.

She was not unattractive—slim legs, shiny brown hair—but the allure of uneducated females had dimmed for Lewis after five years of dating checkout girls at the parts store. This woman looked like the kind you hear screaming at a loser boyfriend through the flimsy walls of a fleabag apartment. And what were trailer houses if not the rural version of fleabag lodgings? This one in particular, an older white model with a broad turquoise stripe, looked like a large, discarded laundry-soap box.

Lewis sat in the truck as Red tried to cajole Frank into leaving. Frank didn't so much as blink. The deputy stood by until another call came in, and he backed down the drive. The woman stood out on the deck for a while, still rubbing her arms, then went back inside her trashy home. Frank took a few steps, only to stop, pull a cigarette from his pocket to his mouth, and point at its unlit tip.

Bored, Lewis got out and walked to the edge of the olive groves. The sun was burning through the mist. A breeze gusted through the trees and tiny fruit hit the ground. He tried to imagine life without another glass of wine or pull of mescal or ice-cold beer on a hot summer day. Who could camp without a whiskey bottle? Or endure a hard day's work without the promise of a good stiff drink? Or face conversation without a little lube? How could he write papers without bourbon to ease him through the hard spots? Who would he even *be* without alcohol's rambunctious energy? He could just see himself in thirty years, a wizened monkey out in suburbia, pushing a lawnmower while sucking sports bottles of headache-sweet ice tea. A fat wife. Casseroles. Golf on TV. A library filled with *National Geographics*.

Something large and brown rustled in the olive trees. Lewis threw a stone and the thing turned into a rabbit and bounded out of range.

Almost 7:45 and I'm still home! The famous Frank is from the drunk farm up the road. Brain damaged, apparently. His mahout arrived, but Frank isn't ready to leave. Some other guy is down by the olive trees, maybe taking a leak. Why is it the men you want to stay leave, and the men you want to leave won't budge?

She could go to work now, obviously, but she wanted to see everybody cleared out first. Actualize the departure, as they say in the mortuary biz. *Who knows?* she wrote. *Maybe I'll sit here all day writing dreck in this journal. My last great remaining pleasure in life, this kinked string of words that has led me through the previously unimaginable—*

Libby paused to answer the phone. Billie, back from Ojai, was calling from Victor's grocería. "Frank's fine," Billie said. "I've known him for years. Since even before he got that way. Never hurt anyone. But hey, when Red shows up, have a good look at him."

The mahout? Libby glanced out her louvered window. The guy was waving a lighter in front of Frank's face. Red Ray. She'd seen him around town. He was fat. "What about him?"

"Just look him over."

Not only fat, Red was old and, to be honest, kind of dopey; he was practically dancing for the big, bearded man. "I don't get it," said Libby.

Billie laughed. "I wish you were here," she said. "Oh, how I wish you were here. Because then you could see Victor's ears burning off his head."

Libby could, in fact, hear Victor Ibañez cackling in the background.

"Do me a favor, Billie," Libby said. "Don't start anything, not at my expense." Libby hated sounding like a prude, but Victor had a mind like a nuclear reactor. The tiniest piece of fodder was all it took for him to conjure an outrageous scenario he then would trumpet as fact. "I have to live in this town."

"Okay, okay," said Billie.

"I'm just trying to keep my head up as—"

"*Now* we've upset her," Billie said to Victor. To Libby, she said, "I'll shut up." Long pause. "There, I've shut up."

Libby didn't answer. Frank had started to move. As he lumbered toward the truck, he looked like a large, upright animal in overalls, a panda or giant sloth.

"I'm only looking after your best interests," said Billie. "I wasn't making fun of you. I wanted you to check out the valley's most eligible bachelor."

"They're leaving now," said Libby.

"Do you have time for breakfast at Yolie's?"

Surely she deserved some compensation for the early-morning adrenaline bath. "Order me *chilaquiles*," she said.

RITO was a tiny town, and brown, the few buildings industrial brick. Red pulled to a stop at the Ibañez Grocería; he wanted cigarettes, and also to call the farm, he said, to tell them that Lewis wasn't AWOL but with him, and safe. Across the street, a man was sweeping the sidewalk in front of Happy Yolanda's. "Our illustrious mayor," said Red. "You mind staying here, keeping an eye on Frank?"

"No," Lewis lied, even as he craved a retail moment. Unless you counted using the cigarette machine at the Blue House, he'd gone over two weeks without a single cash exchange—no doubt his personal record, considering he usually hit several convenience stores and coffee shops a day. Besides, if Frank chose to toddle off, he could do so at will; he had a good eighty pounds on Lewis, not to mention the ineluctability of a mudslide.

Lewis nevertheless sat in the warm cab and watched as the mayor swept dirt into a yellow dustpan and carried it to the trash can on the corner, where he paused. Then, carefully lifting the can, he upended it until a small yellow possum scuttled out, its tail pink as ham. Using his broom, the mayor nudged the creature down Main Street and into the azaleas at St. Catherine's.

Red Ray emerged from the grocería with three to-go cups of coffee and trailed by a tall woman—six, six-one—dressed in muddy work clothes. Cheekbones like a shelf. Dark, flashing eyes. Curly black hair in a thick ponytail. She stuck her head in the truck's open window, her face just inches away from Lewis's. Her skin was smooth and white. "Hey, Frank, you old devil you," she said, ignoring Lewis completely. "Have Red run you by Fat Judy's, then maybe you'll stop scaring all the gals."

Frank clearly didn't distinguish between inanimate and animate objects, even objects as animate as this woman. She couldn't elicit a twitch from him. Pulling back, she gave Lewis an unabashed once-over. "Hey there," she said. She had the kind of wide, beautiful mouth you see in toothpaste ads.

She looked to be about his age, thirty-four, thirty-five. Lewis nodded faintly and looked down, not keen to meet friendly, attractive women while sitting in the drunk-farm truck beside the drunk farm's resident wet brain.

After giving him another moment to speak, the woman made a teasing, sour face and, waving to Red, crossed the street and slipped into Happy Yolanda's.

"Billie Fitzgerald," Red said, climbing into the cab and passing Lewis a cup of coffee.

"No way." This was the so-called Amazon Next Door? "How come nobody ever says what a fox she is?"

"She's a piece of work, all right." Red carefully uncapped a coffee for Frank. "Let's drink these down some before we start moving."

"Major good looks," said Lewis. "Hey, you ever go out with her?"

"Me?" Red chuckled. "I do business with her. That's all I can handle."

"But she's single?"

"Oh, yeah. Lives with her dad and her son. Billie and the Bills."

"And the husband?"

"Never was one, so far as I know."

"So the kid?"

"An indiscretion in college." Red took a long sip of coffee.

"Does she hit the bar first thing every morning?"

Red smiled. "No. Yolanda's also serves breakfast. Great *huevos rancheros*. And Luis makes his own *chorizo*. Big write-up in the *Times* a while back."

"Well, I could go for some *huevos rancheros* about now."

Red appeared to consider this, then cranked the engine with a decisive roar. "Another day," he said. "By the time we got Frank in and out of this truck, it'd be tomorrow."

So it was back to the monastery, the brotherhood, the lousy food. Lewis leaned his head out the window into the moist, green breeze. The air now was almost warm. It would be spring in a few weeks, and today was a sneak preview. Outside of town, orange groves briefly gave way to lush hay fields. A coyote crossed one field at a diagonal, leaving a slash of darker green behind him. A hillside of flat-paddled cactus burst with waxy yellow blossoms. Bees swarmed around the flowers like electrons and hit the truck with little clacks, tiny explosions of honey on the windshield.

Lewis turned to Red. "Fat Judy's?" he said.
"Don't even ask," said Red.

"BILLIE FITZGERALD?" said Lee. "Yeah, I see her every day."
"I think she's stunning," Lewis said.
"A frigid bitch," said Gene, "is what she is."
They were eating tuna casserole in the dining room. The two refrigerators quaked and hummed behind them like small cars idling in place. "You guys don't know class when you see it," said Lewis.
"She's old," said Lee. "And bossy."
"And butch," said Lawrence.
"And she never wears underwear," said Gene.
"That's bad?" asked Lewis. "And how would you know, anyway?"
"Oscar's sister is her housekeeper and she's never seen any women's underwear in that house. Bras, panties, nothing."
"Probably wears boxer shorts," said Lee.
"I can't believe what juveniles I'm sitting with." Lewis shook his head. "What do you guys care about her *underwear*? Sometimes the level of discourse in this place makes me want to weep."
"Jeez, Lewis," Lee said. "You brought it up."

EARLY in the afternoons, once he had his fill of Gene's mechanical fumblings and nonstop Raiders commentary, Lewis scrubbed down, walked to the office, and sat down in front of the computer. He didn't have his notes, or access to a research library, or any real desire to work on his incompletes—he'd mentioned the paper for the conference only to spark Red's interest—but Red had given him another assignment. Lewis was supposed to define a power greater than himself, and come up with his own definition of sanity.

The purpose of this, Red had explained to Lewis's mortification, wasn't to fill up some brochure, but simply to explicate the Twelve Steps of Alcoholics Anonymous, in this case Step 2: "Came to believe that a Power greater than ourselves could restore us to sanity." While Lewis had no yen to be brainwashed in AA dogma, after so many critical essays in graduate school he found it amusing, even gratifying, to write about himself for a change.

> As an atheist, I have had no conception of a god or
> higher power. In my earliest childhood, however, I in-
> explicably thought of God as wrinkly green hills. Then
> my father drew diagrams of atoms and the solar system.
> I saw that the solar system closely resembled an atom;
> clearly then, the solar system was an atom in something
> unimaginably vast. For some reason, I located the sun
> and its orbiting planets in the thigh of a giant clown, a
> clown that looked exactly like a stuffed toy I owned:
> soft red velour body and a maniacally grinning hard
> plastic face.

Sanity he defined as "not letting people or stuff bug me. Having equanimity, concentration, clarity. Minimal self-deceit of mind and body. Good instincts. Feeling comfortable being alive. *Wanting* to be alive."

"ALL RIGHT," Red said when Lewis read him this writing. "Now, using your own definitions, can you believe that a power greater than yourself can *restore* you to sanity?"

"Aha! A trick!" said Lewis. Could the worship of wrinkled green hills encourage flexibility of mind and body? Would the knowledge that he was imbedded in some giant, antic thigh give him equanimity, clarity, and ease in his daily life?

"HOW MUCH time do you have now, Lewis?"

They were in Red's old truck, en route to the Blue House for dinner on a starry, moonless night. There had been rumors of a freak late frost, and men were lighting smudge pots in the groves.

Lewis hesitated. Every time he answered this question, something was denied him. "Twenty-four days."

"Great! And what are your plans after you leave?"

Hang in coffeeshops, read books, get laid. "Go home. Find a job."

"And where's home, again?"

"I'll stay with my philosophy prof in Westwood."

"In the garage?"

Lewis shrugged. The cold slab, he had to admit, had limited appeal.

"Would you consider staying on here? I could offer you a full-time job, with benefits."

Very flattering. A small triumph, even. He, Lewis, had charmed Mr. Detachment, had been singled out, chosen. Nice to know he could still pull it off. Still, the answer was definitely no. Stay in this depressing backwater joint stocked with sad, boring men? No way. "I already told my prof I'm coming back."

"You don't have to decide this very moment," said Red. "Think about it, and let me know."

STAN, THE gentle, gray-eyed Round Rock shrink, conducted Lewis's exit interview on a bright sun porch in the back of the mansion. He read questions off a form and took notes as Lewis talked. "Did you work with a sponsor?"

"Nope. I don't buy the whole sponsor-sponsee deal. It infantilizes grown men."

"I see. And will you continue to attend AA meetings?"

Probably, thought Lewis, but why give Stan any satisfaction? "I don't know. Maybe."

Stan wrote intently. "Do you feel comfortable with your sobriety?"

" 'Comfortable' isn't a word I would use, no. I'm *interested* in sobriety. Does that count?"

"Absolutely. Interest is a very important motivator. Now, what did you like best about Round Rock?"

"The architecture. I mean, when will I have another opportunity to live in a place like this? And I always wanted to live on a citrus ranch. I grew up in the San Fernando Valley and watched the last groves bulldozed for tract housing. Killed me."

"There's something to be said for geographic affinity, all right. And what didn't you like about Round Rock?"

"Don't get me started. No. It's a cool place. But I didn't like being coerced into coming here. And it would've been a lot easier if I could've run to town for parts. And I didn't like having a roommate, not one who snored. And there was too much meat at every meal. Who *is* Ernie Tola, anyway? He's not a very good cook, like sub–short order. And that fakey beard. I told you, don't get me started. And I hated visitors' day—all those strangers milling around looking at you like you're a zoo exhibit."

"Did you have any visitors?"

"No."

"Did you invite anyone to visit you?"

"My mother."

"She didn't come?"

"No, but she sent a note and some money."

"You must've been disappointed."

"Par for the course." The note had said, "It's good you're getting help. Here's some mad money. Love, Mom." A folded ten-dollar bill.

"Was there anything else you disliked?"

"No. But I just thought of something else I liked. I did this writing for Red. Stuff about my drinking and my childhood. My history of this and that. My idea of sanity, higher powers, that kind of stuff."

"*Red* had you write that?"

"It wasn't any big deal."

"Red hasn't sponsored anyone new in years."

"This wasn't sponsoring. He was just trying to show me some things."

"Ahh." Furious jotting. "All right, then." Stan reached into a side drawer, brought out a packet, handed it to Lewis. "Keep in touch," he said. "Let us know where you are and how you're doing."

Lewis hoped that the packet contained money, but found only an AA meeting directory, brochures for several halfway houses, and a list of community health clinics where psychological counseling was offered at little or no cost.

LEWIS did feel guilty, as if he were letting Red down by not taking the job. He decided, as retribution, to give the office a good going-over. File some stuff and toss the junk. Lose those brown roses on the mantel.

He hauled a vintage Hoover out of the storeroom and was merrily bashing into baseboards when Billie Fitzgerald walked through the door. She was dressed, as before, in mud-splattered coveralls, barn coat, rubber boots. Off went the vacuum, in a dramatic decrescendo.

"I knocked but you didn't hear," said Billie. "I'm meeting Red." She plunked down in an overstuffed green chair. She sat like a man, knees splayed open, coat bunched around her shoulders. Her hair was twisted into a loose knot. "Hey"—she pointed a gloved finger at Lewis—"you're guy in the truck, right? Who wouldn't say jack?"

Lewis shot her a surly look.

She laughed. "Red said you're a scholar. You know, I always think about going back to college. Just to catch up on all those books that supposedly shape our lives but nobody ever reads."

"Yeah? Like what?"

Pulling off one glove with her teeth, Billie let it drop from her mouth into her lap. "Well, there's the Bible. You ever read it?"

"Parts," said Lewis.

"Well, this whole wrecked civilization is based on a book most people have only read parts of." Her eyebrows were glossy, superbly arched, like flexible brown feathers.

"The Bible's a good one," said Lewis. "What else?"

Billie unbuttoned her jacket. Beneath the jacket, her coveralls were open far enough to reveal a few inches of a brown plaid shirt. Layer upon layer: Lewis gleaned no sense of her breasts, waist, thighs.

"Red says I'm a total and complete Machiavellian, but I can't even remember what he wrote."

"*The Prince*. And you don't need to read it to be Machiavellian."

"Evidently not." She began worrying her other glove off with her teeth, finger by finger, which somehow seemed either profoundly lazy or obscene. When the glove came free, Billie leaned forward and dropped it into her lap, a mother cat depositing a kitten. "How 'bout Freud? He gave us the unconscious, right? And the Oedipal complex? And polymorphous perversion?"

Was she flirting? Or was he crazy?

"Can you name a single one of Freud's books?" she asked.

"*Totem and Taboo*," he said. "*The Future of an Illusion. The Ego and the Id.*"

"So you *are* a scholar."

"I didn't say I've read them."

Billie grinned and whacked her gloves into her palm. She looked like a little girl who set fires just to watch adults panic.

"Okay," said Lewis. "What else haven't we read?"

"I never read a word of Emerson, but I heard he'd greet his friends by saying something like 'What has come clearer to you since we last met?' That's been my number-one conversational ploy for years now."

"I like it," said Lewis. "Makes you realize conversation was so much more an art in the nineteenth century."

An eyebrow flexed. "Well, then, what has come clearer to you since we last met?"

Lewis thought of several answers, each more personal—and therefore unutterable—than the last. "Oh, my *brain*," he said vaguely. "And what has come clearer to you?"

"That you talk, for one." She laughed, then grew pensive. "I guess it's that my son gets more beautiful every day."

The son. Lewis had forgotten about the son. Some other man's kid. Lewis had had his problems with other men's kids. "Uh, how old is he?" He forced interest into his voice.

"Little Bill? Almost sixteen." Billie's face softened. "He's as tall as I am. Physically, he's a man—his voice has dropped—but it hasn't hit him yet. He still loves and trusts women. He hasn't gone all embarrassed or ironic on me. He's the sweetest human being I know."

"I was sixteen once. And my mother sure didn't like me very much." Lewis forced a stupid little laugh. "She still doesn't."

"But she's your mother," said Billie. "She's crazy for you, I'm sure."

Lewis thought of his mother's scaling hands, her thin, querulous voice, the pull of her incessant melancholy. "No, not really."

Billie glanced behind her, as if wondering how long she'd have to wait here.

"There must be more books we haven't read," said Lewis.

"No doubt." She sounded bored.

There was a thumping on the porch. "I know," Lewis said. "*Faust*. Have you read *Faust*?"

But Billie had turned to greet Red Ray. Pink in the face, he apologized for being late and tossed the mail onto the desk. Billie caught his hand. "You're freezing!" she said. "And what, my friend, has come clearer to you since we last met?"

Red gently and firmly withdrew his hand and stuck it in the pocket of his brown leather jacket. "Only the futility of saving money so long as I do business with you."

Billie turned to Lewis. "He hates it when I tell him he has to spend money. But I'm always right."

"If I spent money every time you said to, I'd be on the street selling pencils."

Lewis, stung that his *Faust* question had been ignored, picked up the mail and started sorting it.

Red said, "The PVC's in my truck."

Billie said, "I've got couplings."

When Lewis glanced up, the door was closing behind them.

"Hey!" Billie swung halfway back inside with a high-voltage smile. "To answer your question—*no*. I never read *Faust*. But I fucked a Goethe scholar once. Does that count?" The door flew shut.

Sure, thought Lewis. Sexual relations are a very important motivator.

When Red returned at dusk, the office was in pristine condition. No unfiled paper, not a speck of dust. A fire blazed in the hearth. Lewis was on the couch reading the Reader's Digest condensed version of *Pride and Prejudice* he'd found in the storeroom.

Red lowered himself into a chair. "Hey," he said. "Looks terrific in here!"

"Thanks, Redsy." Lewis put down his book and gave his scalp a long, vigorous scratch. "Okay, then," he said. "I'll take the stupid job. But only for six months, and then it's back to school."

AFTER five hours of overtime, everything in Libby's office had begun to shiver. Papers in her out basket fluttered. The computer screen vibrated. Down the hall, an AA meeting was producing intermittent bursts of laughter and clapping. It was nine-thirty. She'd missed dinner and band practice, not that she minded missing the practice. Al Keene's girlfriend was in town, anyway. Not that Libby was jealous; if anything, she felt strangely protective of this woman. Libby knew what it was like to learn your man has been sleeping with someone else, though she would spare the girlfriend any grim revelations. Libby had no aspirations to be Al's official other. The girlfriend could have his Kmart western wear, cheap cologne, and trashy pillow talk. The only thing Libby liked about Al Keene was his generic willingness; he fell into bed with an impersonal enthusiasm she found undemanding, rollicking, a balm to her loneliness.

When a column of numbers on her screen began to wriggle and defect, Libby called it a night. She left just as the AA meeting was dispersing. Thirsty, she joined a short line at the drinking fountain. A guy behind her said, "If you'd rather have coffee, there's some in the kitchenette."

She did not feel entitled to the group's refreshment. "Oh, I'm not . . ." Well, how *do* you say, politely, "I'm not an alcoholic"? "I . . . uh . . . work here."

"Not a drunk, huh?" He hooted. "That's okay. You can still have a cup of coffee and a cookie. Come on." He touched her arm. His curly black hair needed a cut, his beard a trim. His name, he said, was Lewis. After a fourteen-hour work day, Libby couldn't resist such overt friendliness. She followed him through the meeting hall, where men were stacking folding chairs, and into a small kitchen area.

"I've seen you before," Lewis said, pouring her a cup of coffee. "Frank slept in your car."

She remembered vaguely that there were two men that morning, now months ago—the mahout and the trespasser—but she never would have pegged Lewis as the latter.

He tapped on her violin case. "Taking lessons?"

"I play."

"In an orchestra?"

"In a band right now." Was she imagining it, or did his face fall? Why was it that things considered so aphrodisiacal in a man—being smart and funny, self-sufficient, playing in a rock 'n' roll band—are such turn-offs in a woman?

"Huh," he said. "And you know Billie Fitzgerald, right?"

"Yeah."

"Billie's cool," he said.

Libby was glad he mentioned Billie, who'd called an hour ago with a migraine and wanted Libby to pick up a prescription. "That reminds me, I gotta go," Libby said. "I gotta get some medicine over there before her head explodes."

He walked her out to the Falcon. He had an old car too, he said, as if this signified some deep psychic affinity. "Let's have coffee again sometime."

"Sure," she said. "Well, maybe not *that* coffee."

His laugh was good, if a little loud. "Drunks'll drink anything. Listerine. Lemon extract. Aftershave. This coffee's nothin'."

"To tell the truth," she said, "I haven't had a decent cup of coffee since I moved up here."

"Oh, I'm lucky," he said. "Guy I work for has his joe sent UPS from Berkeley. Best coffee in the world. I could get you the address of the place. I'll call with it tomorrow, if you give me your number."

"That's okay," she said.

"No, seriously. It's nothing. I'd have to read a label, no big deal."

She would never order coffee from Berkeley, and she wasn't sure she'd go out with this man, either. But somehow, she found herself writing her number on the proffered matchbook. After nine years with Stockton, she'd forgotten that this part, the phone-number exchange, was accomplished so obliquely, as if it was about *coffee*, for crying out loud.

BILLIE was lying on the floor in the library with one ice pack supporting her neck, another covering her eyes. All the lights were out. Banked coals yielded just enough light to prevent Libby from crashing into furniture as she brought Billie a glass of water and two Vicodin. "Met your friend Lewis tonight," she said.

"Do I know any Lewises?" Billie the lifted the ice pack. Blue hollows cupped her eyes. "What does he look like?"

"Tall. Black frizzy hair. Thin. Yogi thin."

"I like the sound of 'yogi thin.' " Billie put the pills in her mouth, gulped down some water, then pressed the ice pack back down over her eyes. "Oh, I know," she said. "Grubby? Kinda sullen?"

"Grubby, yeah. Sullen, no. Good laugh, actually."

"Yeah. That's who it is," said Billie. "Red Ray's secretary. I've talked to him. We've seen him at Happy Yolanda's."

"We have? He's not weird, is he? I gave him my phone number."

"Tries a little too hard. Smart, though." Billie pointed weakly toward the fire. "You mind sticking another piece of wood on that? This ice is freezing. But, you know, that gives me an idea. I *should* take you out to the drunk farm. Two dozen men at any given time, you're bound to find something."

"You mean to *date*?"

"Why not?"

"They're alcoholics, for Christ's sake."

"You think you'd do better at the bars? At least at Round Rock, they've *stopped* drinking. And there's always Red Ray, who's adorable. I know you don't think so, but . . ."

Libby most certainly didn't think so. Ever since she and Stockton had separated, people had been offering to set her up, and it was always with someone they, the setter-uppers, wouldn't be caught dead with: someone too eccentric or old or pathetic. Her mother's best friend took her to meet a man obsessed with grandfather clocks. His living room and dining room were so packed with the clocks and their components, only a narrow path ran from room to room, and there wasn't a single place to sit. Who, except her mother's oblivious friend, would ever think this man wanted another person in his life? And then a friend in Hollywood introduced her to a gorgeous man— a homosexual, it turned out, who was contemplating going straight.

Libby wedged a split oak log into the fire. "If Red's so great, Billie, why don't *you* go for him?"

"What do I need a man for? I've got all the money I could ever want. I've got Little Bill and Dad and you. And besides, Red and I aren't a good match. I don't mind that he's—"

"Old and fat?"

"Built for comfort, let's say. But he's too good for me, too pure. Monkish or something."

"And you think that suits me?"

"You're good, too," said Billie.

"Oh, right." Libby turned to leave. She had to get home, go to sleep, and be back at work, all in eight hours. "That's okay. I'm resigned. This may well be a long dry spell when it comes to men."

DURING the first four months of his sobriety, Lewis had suffered from more or less constant low-level pain. Something was always aching. He moved his head and a clear, electric flash of pain shot down his spine. Other times, the pain seemed to rise out of his blood like a fog. The roots of his hair hurt, or his teeth. Sometimes his entire skin seemed tender to the touch. He gobbled aspirin by the handful and found that lying facedown on the ground worked wonders. Floors were okay, but grass, even asphalt or dirt, was better. When he was flat out against something solid and gritty, inhaling the smell of soil and rocks, the pain seeped out like moisture.

"I know exactly what you're talking about," Red said when Lewis described his symptoms. "When I first got sober, I thought I had the flu all the time. Come to find out, I was angry."

According to Red, the pain was part of Lewis's detoxification: as residual alcohol was leaving his system, the anger he'd avoided by drinking was now surfacing. What would help him through the long, slow process of shedding this anger was an inventory of everything and everybody he felt uncomfortable about—Red suggested he write separate lists of grudges, fears, money problems, sex problems, and secrets. "That'll bring all this unresolved crud to light," Red said. "Often the light alone makes it shrivel up, like pulling weeds and leaving them in the sun."

Before he went to sleep at night, Lewis composed a list in his head. Money, starting with outstanding debts. Better than a sleeping pill.

BEING the new secretary of Round Rock was okay. To make order from someone else's chaos *was* satisfying. He did everything from updating client files on the computer to fetching Frank from his rambles, and was in charge of making follow-up calls to track the progress of former Round Rock residents. Against his better judgment—it seemed like prying—he routinely asked men if they were sober, going to meetings, and weathering crises without drinking.

He went with Red on supply runs, ostensibly to learn the route. Red had sold him the reconditioned Fairlane for two hundred dollars so he could make the runs himself; but after several months, for sociability's sake, they were still doing them together. Lewis was using the Fairlane mainly to commute from Rito, where he had rented a room in the Mills Hotel. Red had tried to talk Lewis into staying on at the farm, even offering to refurbish a bungalow in the village for him. But after ninety-six days and four roommates at the Blue House, Lewis wanted more freedom and more privacy.

Living at the Mills, Lewis found, was not, in fact, all that different from living at Round Rock, though the architecture wasn't nearly so grand and the Mills's winos were still putting away the quarts of Tawny Port. The important thing was, Lewis had his own room—single bed, bureau, wobbly desk, minimal bathroom—and no curfew. And no rules about women, either.

He drank his first cup of coffee each morning at the grocería, leaning against the counter as Victor Ibañez delivered a crash course in small-town life. "That Fairlane you're driving? Used to belong to old Tillie Prouch," said Victor. "She's been legally blind for years, but kept nosing her way downtown every day for mail and groceries. Then the county put in a stop sign up on Church Street. Same day they put it in, Tillie took it out. That crease in your front bumper? The end of one woman's driving career."

Victor was bold, too, with medical advice: "That rash on your arm? Looks like eczema. Old Rafael Flores got rid of mine overnight—a little vinegar and a sweeping's all it took. Want his number?" Lewis, picturing his arm being scraped raw with a steel brush, demurred.

Lewis ordered takeout breakfast burritos from Happy Yolanda's, bought vintage gabardine shirts at St. Catherine's Thrift Store, did laundry at the Casa de Wash 'n' Dry. Where, on a Saturday morning in June, he found a phone number on a matchbook pulled from a pair of jeans. Under the number was an H or an L, followed by a squiggly line. While kids raced wire carts inches from his toes, Lewis sat in a yellow molded-plastic chair and tried to remember whose number it could be. The prefix was local. Probably a newcomer he'd met in a meeting. Dodging crazed children, Lewis left the laundromat and crossed the street to a pay phone. Once the ringing began, he remembered.

I told Al I wouldn't sleep with him anymore, Libby wrote in her journal. *I said it was getting too weird with the girlfriend, the lying, etc. He said he was sorry about the lying, sorry it had to end, and sorriest about all the sex we wouldn't have. I feel nothing but detached. Maybe this is what it's like to be a man. Going in, taking what I want, getting out fast. The Billie Fitzgerald approach: use 'em and lose 'em, she always says. I asked her if she's ever been in love. I hope not, she said. I hope none of those regrettable skirmishes with the opposite sex was love.*

Not even with Little Bill's dad?

Her face gets that plaster of Paris look. That's not a topic for today.

How can she be so intrusive and so secretive at the same time? Maybe that's not such a—

The phone rang.

"Sorry I never got back to you about the coffee," Lewis said. "I lost your number, but I'm doing my laundry and and I found it in a pocket. I don't have the coffee information with me. Maybe you'll talk to me anyway. Laundromats make me so forlorn. Am I taking you away from anything?"

Were all men going to apologize to her this week? Was she insane to be charmed by this outburst?

"Before I forget," she said, "are you Red Ray's secretary?"

"Yeah! How'd you know?"

"When I described you, that's who Billie thought you were."

"And how did you describe me?"

"Thin, black hair, good laugh."

He demonstrated the laugh, then said, among many other things, that he was born and raised in the San Fernando Valley, son of a Hollywood producer—a TV producer, nobody famous. He'd been married once, and divorced, "back in the Neolithic."

"What about you?" Lewis said abruptly. "Ever played your violin in a symphony?" He was a particular fan of Beethoven and Mahler, he said, and she could've guessed. Wagner, too. The tonnage. The origins of gravity.

"So you want to have dinner sometime?" he said.

"Okay." She felt a little worn out just from listening to him.

"Saturday? A week from today?"

She checked the calendar, half-hoping the Cactus Pharaohs had a gig. No dice. "That's fine."

Should he come pick her up? At first she thought, no, no, better to agree on some public place. In Rito, however, that meant bars—not such a good idea, given his AA status. Then she remembered that Lewis had already been to her trailer; if he'd wanted to come and chop off her arms at the elbow, he could have done so months ago.

"That would be good," she said.

Falling asleep that night, it hit her. Unless she counted caving in to Al Keene's ever-present horniness, this was her first real date in nine years.

With a drunk, no less.

EWIS bit into his sandwich, a peculiarly fluorescent-pink ham salad on white, yet another Round Rock variation of shit on a shingle. Friday was Ernie's day off, and the replacement cook reliably presented food that made everyone grateful even for Ernie's meager abilities. "Where do you take someone out to eat around here, anyway?"

"The Basque Garden in Buchanan's pretty good," Lawrence said. "It'll run you, oh, twenty per person."

"I'm looking to spend about half that."

"Jeez, Lew. Who's the lucky girl?"

"A friend," said Lewis.

John, the house manager, lowered himself into the chair next to Lawrence, and Lewis regarded him warily. Since Lewis had joined the staff, John's private mission, apparently, was to cut him down to size whenever possible, preferably in front of residents. John had once come up to a group and said, "Lewis, you may be one of those guys who's just too smart to stay sober." A few days later—similar scene, a few guys talking—John approached him again: "You know, Lewis, I was wrong. You're not so smart, just lucky." Then, a couple nights ago, John handed him what looked like a business card; one side said "KISS" and the other side, "Keep It Simple, Stupid." Was this hostile or what? Yet the other guys seemed to like John. He sponsored eight or nine of them, including Lawrence.

"Is this a friend-friend," asked Lawrence, "or a girlfriend?"

"A friend."

"Better not be a girlfriend," John said.

"Excuse me?" said Lewis.

John unloaded his tray and pushed it to the end of the table. "You better not be getting into a relationship so soon."

"So soon to what?"

"Your first year of sobriety."

"What's that got to do with anything?"

"Hasn't Red told you? No relationships in the first year."

"Why would Red tell me that?" This was the first Lewis had heard of such a thing. He turned to Lawrence. "Is he making this up?"

Lawrence gave Lewis a sad, anxious look. "Don't ask me. I haven't had a date in five years."

"I hate to be the bearer of bad news"—John's eyes twinkled with malice—"but really, it's in your best interest. Face it. What do you have to offer anyone, anyway? What kind of woman goes for someone who's bankrupt—emotionally, spiritually, *and* financially? All I have to do is think about what I dated my first year to—"

Lewis told Lawrence, "I'm going out to dinner with a *friend*."

"Good," John said. "See that it stays that way."

Lewis got up, shoved his plate into the bus tub by the kitchen door, and set out walking back to the office. In early June the heavy morning fogs turned dingy and yellow by mid-afternoon; if he didn't know better, he'd say it was smog. He hadn't made it very far when Red drove up, leaned an elbow out of the truck's window. "Want a ride?"

Lewis scuffed around the back and climbed in.

"Want to talk about it?" Red said.

"No."

Red drove leisurely, humming. A shiny black snake stretched out in the road, straight as a javelin. "King snake," Red said, steering around it. "They eat ground squirrels and rattlesnakes, supposedly, although that's hard to imagine." He resumed humming.

Lewis looked at him. "So what's this about no women in the first year of sobriety?"

"Says who?"

"That paragon of tact and mental health you have managing the Blue House."

"John? He's one to talk. He shacked up with a heroin addict his whole first year."

"So it's not true."

"Nowhere is it written in stone," Red said. "Though it's not such a bad idea to take a break from sex until your sobriety's stabilized. I've seen more guys get drunk over women than anything else. But people do what they're going to do. I say, so long as you're willing to observe your own behavior, do what you need to."

"So I can take someone out to dinner Saturday night without breaking the eleventh goddamn commandment?"

"Is that what this is all about?" Red grinned. "I don't see why not." He gave Lewis a sidelong glance. "Although it never hurts to do a little housecleaning before inviting people over."

"Meaning?"

"Meaning you might want to write that inventory before plunging into something."

"Before one crummy date?"

"Just a suggestion," Red said mildly. "Some light housekeeping today could prevent a big shambles down the line."

"I know, I know. . . ."

"On the other hand, it is possible that you can get a house so clean, you won't want anybody coming in and messing stuff up." Red's voice grew even softer. "Then, I guess, the challenge is to open up, allow a little chaos in. And that can be a . . ." Lewis strained to hear, but Red appeared to be talking to himself.

Red parked in front of the office, then headed across the street to his bungalow. Lewis started up the office steps, shook his head, went banging on Red's door. "How come you haven't even asked who I'm going out with?"

"Well, God, Lewis . . ."

"What if she's a succubus or something?"

Red burst out laughing. "A *what*?"

"Who knows what kind of woman would go out with me?"

Red walked over to the coffee maker, dumped some old grounds into the trash. "Okay, then: who *are* you going out with?"

"That woman in the trailer—where Frank spent the night? Libby."

"Libby Daw? She's a plum."

"A *plum*?"

"She's got such a warm, open face."

So far as Lewis could remember, Libby's face was okay. Round eyes. Tanned skin. A cute kink in her lip when she talked. She wasn't ugly or anything, but not beautiful, either: more like cute, even droll. He would never have singled out her face for comment. Her slimness, maybe. Her playing the violin. Her connection to Billie Fitzgerald.

"Yeah, well, anyway," he said, "I wish I knew someplace good to take her. I wish I could cook, it's so much cheaper, but I don't even have a hot plate at the Mills."

"Cook here," said Red.

"What, so you can chaperone?"

"I'll hit the starch wars." That's what Red called eating at the Blue House. "If I stay for the meeting and the movie, I won't be home till eleven."

"A woman here, after dark, at Round Rock?"

"Why not?"

"Isn't it against regulations?"

"Only at the Blue House. I used to look the other way there too, but guys started pulling them in off twenty-foot picking ladders."

"I wish I'd known that." Lewis slid down in his chair so he could stretch out under the table and nudge Red's shin with his toe. "Why do you think I moved to town? I couldn't hack the celibate life. You might've adjusted, but I never could."

Red swung his leg away. "What makes you think I'm celibate?"

"I don't know—all the lingerie strewn about your house? All the women I see trooping in and out?" Lewis cackled and stood to leave. "I hope to *God* you're whooping it up over here, big guy."

RED POURED himself a fresh cup of coffee and watched through the window as Lewis went back to the office. "Celibate," he muttered. Such a priestly, ecclesiastical word, and not one he embraced. True, he'd gone long stretches without women, but not because of any vow or conscious effort. As a younger man, a drinking man, a bachelor, he'd hit the hay with the first willing victim. Get him divorced, sober him up, add another thirty pounds of padding and behold: a shy, self-conscious, stuttering man.

He was two years sober and three years divorced before he asked a woman out. Cleo Barkin, who ran the alcohol crisis line, seemed the obvious choice. Beige-haired, whiskey-voiced, and widowed, she was older by six or seven years and unflappable. The whole recovery community, including Cleo herself, considered the match inspired and had them married off long before Red even kissed her. So he never did.

Four or five years later, Doc Perrin told him, "I never thought I'd say this to anybody I sponsored, but you gotta get laid, Blue Eyes. Before that armor of yours gets any thicker."

Red took two more years to comply.

Roberta was a state health inspector, a tall brunette with dark eyes and big bones who wore some ancient sadness like a murky perfume. They met for lunch in Ventura, then drove around, two large people curled in her Toyota Corolla, until they came to the Jet Motel outside of Santa Paula. After five or six visits to the Jet, Roberta asked Red to be her date at the state inspectors' Christmas party. He wasn't ready, Red told her. He didn't know when he would be, if ever. Roberta broke it off, changed her mind long enough for another afternoon at the Jet, then broke it off again. Back and forth, Red never knowing whether she'd be furious or welcoming. Eventually he withdrew. For months, she called "to hash things out," until he grew phobic around the telephone. He finally spoke firmly, then harshly, to her.

"I inadvertently engender expectations I can't meet," he complained to Perrin, who in turn accused him of perfectionism, sexual anorexia, priestliness.

Thank God, then, for Christina. Twenty-seven years old, seven years sober, Christina was an M.F.A. student at the institute down the road, a conceptual artist who earned her tuition by dancing at a strip joint in Valencia. They met at an AA meeting in Buchanan. She asked him out for coffee, then asked to come home with him. The first and only woman he'd had in this house, Christina came almost every night, sometimes arriving very late, after her job, sliding into bed next to him, not even waking him up. She never moved in a single thing, and made do with his toothbrush and combs. They drank coffee together before she left for school. A few times, she brought food and made dinner. He gave her a little money, a ten here, a twenty there, whenever she indicated a need. Eighty dollars, once, for art supplies. He was surprised and pleased she turned up for as long as she did, about two months. They would lie in the darkness and discuss her problems at school, her artwork, and her stripping, which she didn't mind because her boss was so fierce with the customers. She had gotten sober young, and was self-contained and direct in a way Red admired. Her body was long-waisted and supple and strong from hours of dancing, and with it she pulled him back from a lost, deep place where he'd long ago abandoned his own desires and sense of possibilities.

When she didn't appear for a week or so, he knew it was over. She did show up once more to tell him she'd met an artist, someone closer to her age, and was going to New York when school was over. She spent the night with Red—one last time, her request. She said that he'd steadied her, calmed her, and thanked him. Now, every so often, there was a postcard from New York, Connecticut, London, all addressed to "My Fine Friend. . . ."

LIBBY had a hard time deciding what to wear. Persona problems, as her old shrink Norma might have said. Which mask to don? She settled on a black T-shirt and a black-and-white polka-dot circle skirt, which turned out to be a little too dramatic.

Lewis showed up ten minutes early in khakis and a green sweater darned, poorly, at the elbows. He roamed around the living room while she applied lipstick and finished drying her hair. She was aware, for the first time, of the preponderance of postdivorce self-help books on her shelves. He asked to borrow a beginner's Spanish language text.

Dinner, he told her, was at Red Ray's house. "I've been cooking all day. Well, not all day—unless you count soaking beans as cooking."

"Oh," she said weakly. She'd been expecting a room full of other people, a waiter, a menu, a ritual to contain them.

"If you'd rather have Basque food or a swordfish steak, just say the word."

But he'd cooked all day. "No, no. That's fine," she said, and hoped it would be.

Red's house was pretty enough, especially his roses, but all the shabby, shut-up houses surrounding it made her uneasy. Anything could go on in there; she stopped herself from imagining specifics. "Red lives here all by himself?"

"Beats living cheek to jowl with twenty drunks," said Lewis.

Once inside the cottage, Libby relaxed amid the oak built-ins and glowing wood floors strewn with good Bokhara and Kurdistani rugs. Books filled the walls, and photographs, including a signed Ansel Adams and a Stieglitz. Red also had an impressive collection of Native American pottery and artifacts. "Nice," she said.

"Red's such a closet aristocrat. Now, listen to this," Lewis said, and, using Red's antiquated stereo system, played Yma Sumac's *Voice of the Xtabay*, an album he'd found at the farm's rummage sale. "Andean birdcalls," he explained, "by a Peruvian princess." Libby didn't tell him Yma Sumac was really Amy Camus, born and raised in Chicago, who later fell into the hands of an imaginative promoter. Some things you didn't do on a first date, like smash illusions.

Lewis had made red beans and rice. A green salad with Thousand Island. Roasted beets. "What's the underlying principle of this meal?" he asked her twice, but she didn't guess until he brought out dessert: a large, domed *pan dulce* encrusted with hot-pink sugar.

"It's all pink?"

"Right! Right! Now we don't have to eat this hunk of leavened lard." Opening the kitchen door, he slung the pastry out into the night, and served her strong, truly delicious decaffeinated espresso. He drank the high-octane stuff himself.

At least she didn't have to worry about what to say. Lewis talked like a radio. No dead air. He kicked off his shoes, perched on his chair like a cat on a fence post, and held forth. He kept to his topics, where he felt safe: music, books, alcoholism, God. Even if he wasn't a real dyed-in-the-wool, black-out-on-your-first-drink alcoholic, Lewis said, he was fascinated by the spiritual aspects of recovery. "Do you have any kind of spiritual practice?" he asked.

She felt, immediately and for the first time ever, spiritually inferior. She'd never gone to church. Her mother was a defiant nonpracticing Jew, she explained; her father, a guilty nonpracticing Catholic. She grew up unaffiliated, just defiant *and* guilty. "I fish," she told Lewis. "Every Sunday morning. At Lake Rito. I commune with the catfish. They bring me messages from the deep."

"Spirituality doesn't mean organized religion," Lewis said. "It's more about intuiting or inventing something you believe in which helps you have a rich and loving life. Do you believe in God?"

"Sort of." Stupid answer. Still, what a relief to be with a man who (a) talked, (b) but not about architecture, and (c) used phrases like "a rich and loving life."

Around eleven, Red Ray drummed lightly on the door and stepped inside. Next to Lewis's dark looks, Red was so pale that he glowed. "Look what I found in the driveway," he said, and held up the pink *pan dulce*. "At first I thought it was a beautiful seashell.

Want some?" He broke off a piece, crossed himself, and held it out in offering. "Eat this in remembrance of me."

They all took a bite, road dust notwithstanding.

I like these men, thought Libby.

Lewis drove her home at midnight. Once in the car, he was hyped up and nervous; then again, he'd had about five hits of espresso. He told her how a Russian theologian had distinguished between being and existing. "Things have *being*," he said, "and the spirit has *existence*. Or maybe it's the other way around."

AT FIVE-THIRTY the next morning, Libby was making an egg salad sandwich to eat out at the lake when the phone rang. "You alone?" Billie asked.

"Yes."

"So why aren't you fishing?"

"I'm going as soon as I can get out the door."

"So, how was it with the scholar?"

"Fun."

"It can't have been too much fun if you're alone."

"No, really, we had a good time."

"What base did you get to?"

"Don't beat around the bush or anything," Libby said.

"Well?"

"I never did know which base is—"

"Just remember the four F's."

"And I really don't want to know," Libby said loudly, "thank you very much. He didn't even kiss me good night, okay?"

"Frenching, feeling—"

Libby held the phone against her thigh for a few seconds. When she lifted it back to her ear, Billie was laughing. "So where'd he take you to dinner?"

"Round Rock."

"What? You ate at the cafeteria?"

"No," Libby said, "at Red's."

"Red's house? And where was Red?"

"He came home later."

"Did he know you were there? I mean, was he expecting you?"

"Of course. What's the big deal? He's very courteous."

" 'Courteous,' " said Billie. "Sometimes you kill me. So our history buff—he didn't even try to kiss you?"

"That's okay."

"Did you want him to?"

"I guess."

"Did he ask you out again?"

"Not yet."

"You think you'll see him again?"

"Well, I lent him a book."

"I gotta give you credit," Billie said. "Dating takes such stamina. Score me a roughneck at the Gusher Inn any day. At least I know what I'm getting—and getting it right away. I couldn't stand the suspense. I get all the delayed gratification I need from raising citrus and a child. So does this mean we'll be staring at the phone for the next three weeks?"

"Jesus, Billie, you're worse than Victor Ibañez."

"Victor! Somebody's gotta call and give him an update!"

"Billie," Libby said. "Billie, I'm warning you. . . ."

What a relief, then, to get to the shores of the deep, cold lake, its gray-blue water napped by the wind. Here, thought Libby, is my private life.

She didn't say so to Billie, but she already knew how this thing with Lewis would end, and part of her was as unmoved as the lake's muddy depths where the catfish lurked. She and Lewis would have an affair. She couldn't say why. Objectively, he wasn't all that attractive. Still, she knew what would happen from the way she couldn't quite talk to him. When he stretched and yawned and rubbed his bare feet together, these movements played directly to her flesh and bones much like music. He'd fall hard. Eventually, there would be the problem of extrication. Libby pitied him already.

LEWIS had the definite sense of getting something out of his system. He'd needed to know that women were out there and that he could make contact, be admitted into their presence and become, however briefly, the object of their attention. He felt a few twinges about his behavior—overexcited, he'd talked too much, as usual—then decided not to think about it anymore. He'd spent all day worrying about what to cook and grocery shopping, soaking beans and picking flowers and washing up after himself, and was in no hurry to do it again. Too time-consuming, too expensive, altogether too harrowing.

BILLIE'S white dual-wheeled Chevy truck roared over the Tehachapis and into the hot, pesticidal bathtub of the San Joaquin Valley. It was dusk, and still in the nineties. The oleander blooming in the center divider exuded a sweet, poisonous perfume. "I'm overdue for this creep," Billie said. "I haven't been outta the valley in two months."

Libby had heard so much about these excursions, Billie's famous "creeps," she had a mental image of every element—the drive over the mountains, the Gusher Inn, the roughnecks. The Gusher Inn she imagined as a cozy, knotty-pine tavern with shelves of arcane oil equipment and maybe a mural featuring a fat geyser of black gold. The roughnecks would be rugged and soiled, a pride of grease-dappled cowboys.

The real Gusher Inn materialized as a cinderblock cube set amid scrubby desert and squat oil derricks. One dirty picture window framed a view of the gravel parking lot.

On entering, Billie spotted a tall, sallow guy with a waxed handlebar mustache. "I'll be right back," she said to Libby, and went outside with him. Libby sipped a beer at the bar, the only woman in the room. A man named Ted bought her another beer. Libby wasn't much of a beer drinker, but the Gusher served only beer or cheap wine-from-a-box. "I'm waiting for my friend," she told him.

"Billie?" Ted said. "You'll have a long wait, then. She took off with Moe."

Libby checked the parking lot. The truck was still there, but no sign of Billie. Libby counted how many cinderblocks high the wall was; counting, the pastime of a prisoner. "Baby," Ted said, "you got the best legs to walk into the Gusher all year."

"Thank you," Libby whispered.

He turned to the bartender. "Pour another beer here. Loosen her up, maybe she'll give us a lesson. A love lesson. These uptight types can be real tigers in bed."

"Easy, Teddy," said the bartender. But he pulled another draft and set it behind the first one Ted had bought. When Billie reappeared, Libby had three full glasses awaiting her attention. Billie nodded to the untouched beer. "I see you're doing all right for yourself."

"I really don't appreciate being left alone like that."

"You will, when you see what I got for us. Come on, let's powder our noses."

In the bathroom, Billie chopped out two lines of cocaine on a pocket mirror. "This'll lift your spirits."

Stockton was fond of it, but Libby had tried cocaine only once; to her, it tasted and felt too much like going to the dentist. "Requisite creep candy," said Billie. "This'll give you the *oomph* you need."

The cocaine did put Libby in a better mood, except that for the rest of the night, she kept thinking something was falling out of her nose. She and Billie and three men piled into a large, boaty American station wagon. Jammed in the backseat between two men, Libby concentrated on not looking as tight-jawed as she felt. Billie, in the front, played with the neck and hair of the driver, a handsome, bulked-up blond guy called Mike. Bottles of sweet, strong liquor were passed, then a joint as they drove to a campground on the Kern River. Libby sat on an ice chest and watched a young woman with long, straight, flaxen hair make a pot of boiled coffee over the smoky campfire. They sat drinking the coffee laced with whiskey, Libby wondering why they'd come out here at all. The woman with the white-blond hair went into a tent and, once inside, called out for Mike. He went into the tent and came out almost immediately. The woman called him over and over, at intervals. Mike and everyone else pretended nothing was happening, but after a while he stood up and said, "I'm outta here."

Back in the station wagon, drugs were passed in brown vials. Libby politely refused. At a new apartment complex on the edge of the oil fields, they took an elevator to a nearly empty apartment on the third floor. In the living room, there was only a wide-screen television and two beanbag chairs; in the kitchen, only chips and hard liquor. Billie disappeared into a room with Mike. Libby sat in a beanbag chair and watched a *Planet of the Apes* movie without any sound. The other two men came in and out. One said, "Hey, Billie, want some of this joint?"

"She's not Billie," said his friend. "Billie's the pretty one." Then, hearing himself, he slapped his face. "It's not that you ain't pretty, hon. It's just, well, Billie's about the prettiest thing."

Libby refused joints, shots of whiskey, and lines of coke, while sending telepathic emergency signals to Billie. Finally, when the apes were silently clobbering each other in the bloody, frenzied climax, Billie burst from the room—hair wild, eyes half-lidded—and threw an arm around Libby's neck. Her breath smelled of alcohol, her words were slurred. "You look miserable, Lib. I knew this wasn't for you. Come on. Let's get you out of here."

Billie snatched some keys from the kitchen counter. In the parking garage, moving by feel, she tried various cars and finally unlocked the door of the station wagon. "Don't worry," said Billie. "We'll leave it where Mike can find it."

Libby insisted on driving. She was so glad to be leaving that driving around oil fields in a stolen vehicle passed for heaven: derricks lit up like Christmas trees, soft cobalt sky, fat stars, the clustered yellow lights of Bakersfield. Billie suggested a turn here and there. Like a vision, the Gusher Inn materialized and beside it, Billie's enormous truck as white and loyal as Trigger.

Libby touched Billie's shoulder. "Sorry to truncate your creep."

"I knew you weren't creep material. I never should've let you come."

"You invited me!"

"I invited you because you were all sad your historian hasn't called."

"I'm not sad about that."

"You're a total misery guts about it."

"You're out of your mind."

"Your heart was broke and I took pity on you."

"I don't even know the guy. I just went out with him once."

"Your heart is in a zillion beensie pieces."

Libby drove home. The dual wheels whistled on the asphalt. Billie slumped against the door, passed out. Libby listened to a talk show on the radio. One of the guests had taken a nationwide poll on happiness. Statistically, the woman said, the two happiest groups in America were married men and women who'd never been married.

"That's me!" Billie sprang up. "What have I been telling you? I'm one of the happiest people in America. Aren't you jealous? Don't you wish you'd never been married?"

My mouth tastes like an electrical short, Libby wrote. *My eyeballs are dry. My nose is packed with crystallized scabs which bleed when picked. I am not fishing—the first Sunday I've missed in a year.*

I'm depressed, thanks, I think, to the cocaine. I've forgotten why I live here in this valley-so-low. I can't find a decent job. Or a decent man. And my closest friend . . . How does Billie do it?

WHEN Libby returned the following week, the lake was socked in with fog. The air was was cool, even cold, but the weatherman said to expect temperatures in the high eighties by noon. She set up two poles, wrote in her journal, and caught one fish, which somehow slipped off her stringer. She dozed in the warming air, a slow bake.

Someone called her name and Lewis pulled out of the fog like creation itself. Her first reaction was, How dare he? Her second, pleased surprise. Or maybe the two thoughts were simultaneous: How dare he cause her pleased surprise?

"This is the second week I've come looking for you." Lewis squatted by her chair. He threw back his head and gulped air. "This *is* a cool thing to do. I normally hate man-made lakes, but there is something to be said for large bodies of water. You're right—it *is* like going to church, only better." He touched the cane pole. "And murdering fish is the sacrament. Hey, want to go to Miserable Yolanda's for breakfast?"

"Can you go there?" she said.

"Why not?"

"Isn't it a bar?"

"What, you think I'm going to drink?"

"No, no . . ." she stammered stupidly. Alcoholism etiquette, she sensed, was a minefield for the uninitiated.

He punched her arm lightly. "I'll be safe with you. You won't let me partake, even if I want to, right?"

His dark eyes danced with what? Derision?

"Sorry," she said to him. "It's none of my business."

"Don't worry about it."

When they got to town, he was too hot and wanted to change out of his sweater. "It'll just take a sec," he said. "You want to see my room?"

She wasn't crazy about ducking into the Mills with a man in clear sight of Victor Ibañez's window, yet she'd always wondered about the fine white clapboard building with wide porches under tall, graceful deodar pines.

The lobby, though dingy, was clean, with scarred, stunted cacti in pots, an atmospheric plein-air painting of red rocks and cypress trees, and rugs so worn that their patterns were mere tracery. Lewis's room, at the top of creaky wooden stairs, was tinier, if possible, than her trailer's spare bedroom. He barely had space for a bed and a bureau. Thumbtacked to the wall was a T-shirt silkscreened with a caricature of Wallace Stevens. A postcard of a blue jar was tacked upside-down above the T-shirt's neck. "It's a joke," Lewis said. "Wallace Stevens wrote a famous poem about a blue jar."

The only poem of Stevens's that Libby had read, which a pianist friend had recommended, was about somebody at the clavier. The vocabulary had cowed her, and she lacked the training, or possibly the patience, to decode the work. Lewis shuffled a stack of library books, suddenly determined to read this blue-jar poem to her.

Libby sat down on the bed since there was no place else to sit, unless she wanted to roost on a big clump of laundry in the room's only chair. Through a small window, she looked out on the bone-white limbs of a eucalyptus tree. Lewis began to read. She didn't understand this poem, either. Lewis's room smelled of old varnish and dust. The tap in the bathroom sink dripped. Her hands were chapped and speckled with fish blood. Her hair snarled from wind. The room was hot. Lewis was reading another poem now, with more dizzying words. "The Idea of Order at Key West." At least she didn't have to think of anything to say. Then, he put the book down on the foot of the bed—she assumed he was going to rummage in the laundry chair for a shirt—but without a word, he placed his hands on her shoulders and then slid them down her arms. He came in close; it was a stare-down, an ophthalmic assault. Her mind sped. He couldn't kiss her when she was all fishy like this, and bundled up in shirts. But he did. He was relentless, even, nudging her down on the bed, kissing her neck and jaw, licking his way back to her lips. In no time he was undressing her, a series of insistent tugs. She didn't mind. In fact she liked this focused, no-nonsense approach. This was what she thought would happen, although maybe not so quickly, and she couldn't have predicted that he would have such authority. She was naked and he was still in that old wool sweater and jeans. He looked her straight in the eye. Scary, but fun. Really fun.

Sprawled across the bed, he pushed his pants down, rolled away from her to put on a condom, and re-establishing eye contact, promptly guided himself inside her. His eyes flickered. It was a little much, a little intense, so she looked over his shoulder to where a wall met the ceiling. Jean buttons snagged on her thigh. The musty sweater was itchy, abrasive, like his beard. She didn't even like beards, thought them slovenly. The whole grungy room was slovenly. She came fast and hard. Like I'm the man, she thought. Premature. He paused until she looked him square in the face. He smiled and, without pulling out of her or looking away, took off his sweater and T-shirt. His chest was hairless, the ribs pronounced. His olive skin was granular, like muscled sand.

"Do you want to talk about this?" he asked, still inside her.

"Not now!"

"We're doin' it," he said. "Shouldn't we talk about it?"

"God, Lewis." She bundled his butt in her hands and, to shut him up, pushed him into her.

"No?" Laughing a little. More in control than she ever dreamed he'd be. "You sure you don't want to talk about this?"

She couldn't talk if she wanted to, and he knew this. That was the point.

Afterward, they lay there like gasping fish. He held her forearm, squeezed it occasionally, kissed her ear. He got up first, and brought her back a mug of lukewarm tap water. They shared a cigarette. When she returned from the bathroom, his pants were on. "Breakfast," he said.

At Happy Yolanda's, they found Billie and the Bills sitting with Red Ray. Little Bill and Red jumped up to drag over another table. "We've been fishing," Lewis said. "It's so cool. Libby goes every Sunday."

Libby blushed and sat up straight. Did she smell like sex? The back of her hair was a bird's nest. Billie winked at her at least seven hundred times. Lewis and Red Ray talked about the softball game later that day. She drifted, chewing *machaca* and eggs, sipping burnt, weak coffee. Lewis grasped her hand under the table and placed it on his erection. She inhaled coffee, coughing until Red handed her a glass of water.

She and Lewis walked outside with everyone else. She hung back, thinking he might want to say something to her. But suddenly he was half a block away—"Bye! So long! Thanks for the fishing!"— and she was still standing next to Billie outside of Happy Yolanda's.

"You're hooked," Billie said.

"I'm not hooked."

"You're hooked, all right. Your eyes have turned to goo."

"I HAVE before me a monster lasagna," said Lewis. "And Red says you should come help us eat it. We have a meeting at eight, so it won't be a long evening. If you got here at six . . ."

Libby went straight from work, pulling off her pantyhose at a stop sign. Dinner with the guys. She liked the idea. When she reached the bungalow, Red was inside and Lewis was out picking lettuce.

"How's our friend Billie?" Red asked.

"Wild and woolly," said Libby. "You hear she's got a court injunction against the county? Doesn't want 'em chopping down those eucalyptus trees. I agree with her."

"Me too, this time." Red's eyes were blue and kind. "She filed three injunctions against me when I started Round Rock." He laughed quietly. "Once she lost, she leased the groves and saved my hide."

"She filed against us when my ex-husband and I brought the trailer onto the property," said Libby. "I think it's her way of saying hello. Some communities have welcome wagons. We have Billie and her court injunctions."

Lewis walked in, his arms full of greens. Libby dried the leaves as Lewis washed them. She was careful, as was he, to reveal no hint of intimacy. "Sorry," she whispered when she brushed his arm.

They ate on the porch, in a cave of bougainvillea. Red had set the table with a white damask cloth, sterling silver, a jar of pink roses. Lewis's lasagna was made not with meat sauce and gloppy cheese but with layers of skinned tomatoes, bitter greens, roasted squash, and noodles brushed with olive oil. Sparrows hopped on the porch railing, begging bread crumbs.

"You ever been to an AA meeting?" Red asked Libby.

"I hear them when I work overtime at the union hall," Libby said. "I always wonder, what's everybody laughing at?"

"Their pathetic, desperate lives," said Lewis. "That's what they're laughing at."

"You should stop by some Friday night," said Red. "It's open to everyone, and the speakers are usually top-notch."

"I'd feel like a voyeur." Libby turned to Lewis, who was lining up bits of bread for the sparrows. "What do you think?"

"Do what you want," he muttered. "I hated my first hundred meetings."

"I wouldn't want to make anyone uncomfortable," Libby said.

There was a long silence. Red stood up and started clearing the plates. "Speaking of meetings . . ."

Lewis walked her out to the Falcon. The sun had set and the gray sky was darkening.

"Who's that?" Libby asked, pointing at a man standing between two bungalows across the way. A tall man with long dark hair.

"I don't see anybody," said Lewis.

Indeed, when Libby looked back, the man had vanished.

"This place is kind of creepy," she said. "All these empty houses." She turned to face Lewis. "Thanks for dinner."

He wrapped his arms around her waist and yanked her flush up against him. Over Lewis's shoulder, Libby saw Red Ray framed in the bright orange light of the kitchen window. "Red can see us," she hissed.

"I don't care. I couldn't stand it in there. All that arm's-length crap. Can we get together later? I want to crawl into your clothes with you. Sorry if I'm being a boor. I can't help it. Can I come over after the meeting? Ten-ish? To your trailer? Jesus, I never thought I'd be begging to come to someone's trailer."

"What's the matter with my trailer?"

"Nothing. I hate trailers. Except your trailer. Your trailer seems like a big candy bar with a nougat inside. You're the nougat."

Nobody had ever called her a nougat before.

THE MAN Libby pointed to was David Ibañez, born and raised in the very bungalow he'd ducked behind to elude her gaze. Thirty-eight years old and living in Tijuana, David was up visiting his uncle and teacher, the *curandero*, Rafael Flores. Taking an after-dinner walk at dusk, David had wound up here, through no conscious intention, trespassing at his childhood home.

As Libby and Lewis embraced, David wandered off behind the bungalows, running his fingers over silvery siding, termite-tunneled sills. The citrus perfume and spicy sourness of decomposing oranges from the surrounding groves was as familiar to him as breath itself. David's father had been Sally Morrot's ranch foreman. His family lived better than most in the village, their house furnished with her discarded mahogany nightstands, linen draperies, couches whose small rents and tears loosed feathers or wiry horsehair.

Otherwise, conditions had been primitive: woodstoves, outhouses, peddlers, milk goats. The village generator went off at nine in the evening; afterward you lit kerosene lamps with fat cotton wicks and blackened globes that gave the air an acrid burnt-petroleum edge. The bungalows were plumbed when David was three—toilets, sinks, and tubs carried into bathrooms hastily constructed from sleeping porches and sections of hallways. A persistent image of black boxes, monolithic and evil, surfaced in David's dreams for decades until, during a hypnotherapy session last year, he identified the ominous cubes as the septic tanks buried in the village of his youth.

David peeked between the houses; the couple by the Falcon were still embracing, so he slipped back into the shadows. He preferred not to be seen. Seventeen years ago, after Sally Morrot died and the villagers were evicted from their homes, David had called in the union and the press. He'd organized the civil action suit that failed to bring them back to these houses, but provided each family with enough money to scatter where they pleased; some stayed in town, some found farm work in the San Joaquin Valley, and others, like David's parents, moved to the city—Boyle Heights in Los Angeles. Such activism hadn't endeared David to the valley's Anglo ranchers, some of whom still bore grudges. On past visits, he had been cited for jaywalking across Main Street, not leashing his dog, and tossing an apple core into the weeds; so he now kept such a low profile that only relatives and old family friends knew when he was in town.

Since leaving the village, David had traveled all over the world, dogged by a persistent homesickness for the valley, this ranch. He wandered back again and again, driven by a need to check on things, see what new twist fate had taken. Like many people who had grown up in the area, he was an ardent student of the curlicued local history, all its false starts and surprises. When the ranch was sold to a wealthy San Francisco lawyer, for example, everyone anticipated subdivisions and commercial development. Then Red Ray turned out to be a profligate drunk and there were rumors of bankruptcy, repossession, a pending sale to Arabs. When Red sobered up and started the drunk farm, David had laughed about it for months; he himself had gotten sober, and this connection made it seem as if the ranch had, in a manner of speaking, stayed in the family after all. Someday, David thought, he might even risk slipping into an AA meeting to sit among fellow alkies in the former ballroom where once Sally Morrot and her companion, Dora, had tried to teach some of the local teenagers, including David, how to waltz.

David heard the Falcon drive off. Peering across the way, he saw Red Ray come out of his bungalow. David had followed his successes—the humanitarian awards and government grants Red received were well publicized in the local papers David's aunt Gloria saved for him. And he'd observed Red out here on many occasions, alone in the village that fifty-odd people once inhabited: reading on his front porch or tending his rosebushes; smoking at his kitchen table or dozing in the living room. This was the first time David had seen any visitors.

Red and the younger man lit cigarettes and started walking east together down the road. Red walked calmly, hands in pockets, at a stately pace. The other guy loped sideways, gesticulating broadly, veering off first to one side, then the other, talking all the while: a man clearly desperate to make his point. They looked like king and frantic petitioner, or hunter and fractious spaniel. Hanging back in the shadows, David watched until the two men rounded the bend out of sight; then he struck off in the opposite direction toward his uncle's house.

BY ELEVEN-TWENTY, when Lewis knocked on her door, Libby had given up on him and dressed for bed in nightgown and kimono. She let him in and saw at first glance that his earlier, pressing enthusiasm had dwindled. He slunk into her kitchen, bad news incarnate.

"You okay?" she asked.

"Sorry it took me so long," he said. "Red and I had to have a little chat. You mind if I smoke?"

"Go ahead," she said, suddenly queasy. "What did you chat about?"

"You don't want to know."

"About me?"

"In the abstract."

"What'd you say?"

"I didn't tell him anything."

What was to tell? "What'd he say, then?"

"He told me to watch my step in all this." Lewis flung an arm to indicate her kitchen, her house, her.

"That makes two of us."

"Maybe I should go," he said. "No sense in dragging both of us down. I'll finish this smoke and leave you the hell alone. Unless you want to make some coffee. I could stand a cup of coffee."

"At this hour? Won't it keep you up?"

"I only wish."

Libby pulled the can of Yuban from the fridge and filled the coffee maker with water.

"This is it, this is who I am," Lewis said. "Up and down, up and down, ever since I got sober." He sat cross-legged on a kitchen chair. "This is me, the dull lump."

Libby laughed softly. " 'Dull lump' is the last term I'd apply to you."

"I just think too much. My mind is an alternate digestive tract. I chew myself up. I make myself sick. I'm a living, breathing wreck. Hey, will you walk on my back?"

Holding on to the back of the chair, Libby took cautious, wobbly steps along his spine. He grabbed her ankle, reached for her hand, and pulled her down among the chair legs. After all that gloom, it was good to be thrashing around on the linoleum and kissing. When he took the condom from his pocket—she loved that he took care of such things—he said, "We might as well hit the bed. If you don't mind. I mean, nothing against your cold, hard, gritty floor."

He insisted on constant eye contact, an intensity she found compelling and connective. Did he know what he was doing?

They smoked afterwards, sharing a cigarette. Libby made herself get up to pee, otherwise it was cystitis for sure. When she returned from the bathroom, he was dressed, drinking coffee. Her heart sank. She'd been expecting him to stay. "You don't have to leave."

"You want to sleep," he said. "I want to pull up trees. Or juggle chainsaws. I'd just keep you awake." He sat on the bed to pull on his socks. She curled around him and it was true, his body hummed. "Maybe I'll have one more cup of coffee." He fetched it himself and drank, sitting on the edge of the bed, stroking her back.

In the morning, Libby wrote: *Running late, but will not abandon this journal just because I'm seeing someone. Don't let me stop flossing either.*

First man in my bed since Stockton. How do I feel? My emotions slide right off that question. I'm still in a sexual blur. Already feel a bladder infection coming on. Guzzling cranberry juice.

Lewis was trouble, she decided, but mostly to himself. She should leave him alone. But her whole body—muscles, skin, eyes, even her hair and teeth—wanted more of him first.

RITO'S Fourth of July parade began with Luis Salazar, the mayor, driving through town in his marrow-red Mercury Cougar. Placards hung on the front doors:

NO SMOG

NO FREEWAYS

NO HUNGER

NO BETTER HOMETOWN

RITO, CALIFORNIA

Behind the mayor came twenty little girls in silver tutus, twirling batons. Some batons were only partially tamed. "This is the sort of thing I see with a really bad migraine," Billie told Libby.

The entire town had shown up to watch: Victor and Aida Ibañez, Happy Yolanda's staff, all the old guys from the Mills, the art institute students who rented a storefront in town. Libby stood between Billie and the Bills. She spotted Red Ray across the street with a group of men. Lewis wasn't among them.

The Rito Lito bar was represented by a flotilla of Harleys; Happy Yolanda's by their mariachi band. On a Sunkist truck, the Methodist youth group formed a tableau of the founding fathers. The Catholic youth group rode on a buckboard alongside several bales of hay, a goat, and a bug-eyed, wobbly Holstein calf bellowing in fear, no doubt terrified by the high-school band marching up behind him playing a curious arrangement of "Stairway to Heaven."

Billie elbowed Libby's ribs, nodding at a red tractor pulling the Round Rock float. Lewis was driving, staring straight ahead like a farmer intent on a perfect furrow. Detached, possibly excruciated. In a black T-shirt, very skinny, his hair drawn back in a ponytail, he looked good to Libby in the daylight. Real. She would've thought he was too cool for such goofiness, and liked him for participating. The float's theme was Snow White and the Seven Dwarfs. Perched on a sofa, the man in the Snow White mask wore a low-cut ivory wedding dress, his chest bristling with lush black hair. He waved as if screwing in an invisible lightbulb. Men in dwarf masks sat along the edge of the flatbed. Not all seven were represented, and there were multiple Happys and Sleepys. Their placards read: ROUND ROCK FARM . . . FREEDOM FROM BONDAGE . . . A NEW FREEDOM AND A NEW HAPPINESS! . . . HAPPY JOYOUS AND FREE. Nothing identified Round Rock as a drunk farm, although one Dopey held a bumper sticker pasted on a piece of cardboard: IF YOU MUST DRINK AND DRIVE, DRINK PEPSI.

Libby's favorite entry was the Vince's Bait-and-Tackle-at-the-Lake float: a yellow El Camino with an enormous papier-mâché largemouth bass lashed to the hood like a dead deer.

THE BILLS dropped Libby off at her trailer in the early afternoon, just in time for her parents' inevitable holiday phone call.

Evelyn and Francis Pollack still lived in Montrose, California, in the same house where Libby had grown up, but they were hardly ever home. For the last six years, they had traveled incessantly, as if her father's retirement had unleashed a profound, compulsive restlessness. They called Libby faithfully, once a month and on holidays. Today, they were in British Columbia at an Elderhostel.

"Are you doing anything fun today?" her mother asked.

Libby had learned to divulge few personal details. Since she'd married Stockton, not much had met with Evelyn's approval, including—paradoxically—the divorce. "Just taking it easy."

"I wish you lived some place where you knew more people."

"I have friends here."

"Yes . . ." Libby could tell her mother was fighting to mince words, swallow her opinions. The struggle was brief. "I would so love to see you around people of your own caliber. And in a job worthy of your talent. I think of all those hours of practicing, all those lessons. . . ."

Libby now heard her father murmuring in the background. Without warning or transition, he took over the receiver. "How's my girl?"

"Fine, Dad."

"Glad to hear it. Need anything from British Columbia? They make mighty good marmalade up here. I'll send you a jar."

"Sure, Dad. Thanks."

After hanging up, Libby dragged herself to her small vegetable garden, pulled listlessly at weeds, ate a few ripe Early Girl tomatoes. It got too hot to stay in the sun, so she took a long cool bath and a short, nervous nap. *Why was she still living in this valley?*

Billie and the Bills picked her up at dusk. They drove to the Rito Town Park and set up lawn chairs between two other families. Billie served fried chicken and potato salad and covertly poured white wine into Dixie cups. Cherry bombs and M-80's exploded around them. A mariachi band played in the parking lot. Sparklers swirled in the falling darkness like tiny, short-lived galaxies.

Libby saw Lewis in the assembled Round Rock contingent in the picnic area reserved for larger groups. She liked the way he moved among them, watchful, keeping an eye on everybody, sure of himself. She heard a gust of his laugh. He crouched next to a long-haired teenager, flung an arm over his shoulder, and talked until the kid cracked up.

Libby had never gone out with a man who did low-paying, service-oriented work. She'd always preferred the grand achiever, the ungainly ego, the high-performance, Stocktonesque characters. Everything she was not. Could selflessness be sexy?

Fireworks rose up over the trees in spidery arcs of light. Ash drifted onto her lap. Dogs howled. From the hills, coyotes answered with a wild, laughing bark that made Libby's skin prickle.

Something touched her arm and she squawked, even as she looked into Lewis's bright eyes.

"Didn't mean to scare you," he said.

"I can't help it. I already feel like I'm in a war zone."

As if to illustrate this statement, a great volley of booms erupted. When the noise died down, Lewis waved to the Fitzgeralds. "Hey, Billie," he said.

"Hey, Lewis. Not read any good books lately?"

"Dozens. And you?"

"The Complete Works of Everybody."

"And what's come clearer?"

"Since we last met?" Billie tipped her head. "Oh, I do keep hearing what a great cook you are."

"I love the small-town life," said Lewis. "You make one pan of lasagna and suddenly you're Paul damn Bocuse."

Libby couldn't help noticing Billie's easy way with Lewis, while she herself was tongue-tied, not to mention abashed by her Dixie cup of wine. When Lewis stepped forward to shake Old Bill's hand, she tucked the cup under her chair.

"I'm here with the Round Rockers." Now, he was talking to her again. "Our big field trip. No casualties so far. Nobody carried off by booze or wild women. Yet." He gave the back of her chair a shake. She did want to heave him up, sling him over her shoulders, and haul him home. Lines of white light reached into the sky. Something—his fingers?—swept her cheek.

The fireworks, intermittent before, were now continuous; this was the grand finale, a preview of the end of the world. In the tiny gap between a high-pitched whine and the ensuing detonation, Lewis leaned down. "Gotta go. Bye." And he was gone. *Boom!*

Billie dragged her chair closer to Libby's. "Happy now?"

"I thought you didn't know him."

"I've only really talked to him once."

Little Bill knelt between his mother and Libby. "Is he your new boyfriend, Libby?"

Libby loved Little Bill. He was soft-spoken, considerate, and, for a teenager, exquisitely gentle. "Oh, I don't know."

"He's cool," said Little Bill.

"You think so?"

"Especially his ponytail."

LEWIS helped Libby haul a futon onto her front deck, where they slept naked under the stars. Their sex was grunty, unabashed, undiscussed. Once, during foreplay, he'd asked her what she wanted from him sexually. "I hate that question," she said. "I just want to be *ground* into the bedsprings."

He constantly expected the other shoe to drop. He wasn't hauling her to the opera, after all, or even to the movies. He wasn't mowing her lawn or completing any bridge foursome. Just dinner at Red's a couple times a week and fishing on Sundays. He was getting away with something; specifically, sex, free and clear. Occasionally he wondered—could it really go unpunished?

Libby intuitively played according to his rules. No accidentally bumping into him around town. No hangup phone calls at work. No surprise visits, ever. He made it clear he was leaving the first week of September, and she'd made no attempt to weave any connective threads into the future.

"It's not serious," Lewis assured Red in one postprandial walk over to the Blue House. "It's just fun."

"You're seeing her three, four times a week? Sounds full-steam-ahead to me."

"Don't worry. I'm not about to move in with her."

"But you've considered it?"

"I could never live in a trailer. Not with Libby, not with the Queen of Sheba."

Red's lips twitched in a smile, instantly suppressed.

"And if you must know, Libby's not really my body type."

"That matters so much to you?"

"I'm not saying anything's wrong with her. She's not accountable for my taste." Lewis honestly did prefer either tiny, slim women or tall, strong, regal women—the dainty or the glorious—and Libby was neither. "She's more like a friend than someone I'd fall in love with."

"Ah, all this self-knowledge," said Red. "Could it be the result of a fearless and searching moral inventory?"

Lewis balled up his fist and delivered a light punch to Red's shoulder. "Nag, nag, nag," he said.

IF PEOPLE wanted to know about Deputy Sheriff Burt McLemoore leaving his wife for the babysitter, they had to go to the grocería. If they wanted to know about town council and school board meetings, weddings and church news, blood drives and how promptly the fire department responded to a man in anaphylactic shock from a bee sting, they turned to the *Rito River News*, a small-town tabloid leavened with local advertisements. Round Rock placed the same ad every week: a photo of an unidentifiable man hunched over a bottle and a glass, with the caption "Sick and Tired of Being Sick and Tired?"

The most entertaining writing was usually found in short pieces from a third-rate wire service, stories selected solely on the basis of how much unsold ad space needed to be filled. WIFE BEHEADS HUSBAND—HEAD FOUND IN BREADBOX. CANNIBALISM IN ECUADOR. WOMAN MARKETS GRANDMOTHER'S SECRET WART CURE.

Libby was paging through the paper as Lewis cooked dinner and Red arranged small, heat-kissed roses in a vase. "Hey, you guys," Libby said, spreading the paper over Red's kitchen table. "Read this."

HUMAN TOUCH PRESERVES

Home Experiment Spurs UC Scientists

Santa Cruz, CA. In a home experiment, local massage therapist Heiko Hakuono may have found proof that human touch is capable of preserving perishable organic matter.

Hakuono, who owns Full Body Care, Inc., has long been convinced of the healing power of human hands. One day, when a friend of hers gave her half a dozen fresh eggs, Hakuono came up with a way to prove it.

Hakuono cracked three of the eggs into a jar and stored the jar in her cupboard. The other three eggs she cracked into an identical second jar which was distin-

guished by a small daub of red nail polish. Hakuono
held the second jar in her hands for two hours every
day. "I held it as I talked on the phone, as I watched TV.
I held it in both hands as if it was something very precious, something alive." In six weeks, the untouched
eggs in the cupboard were, according to Hakuono,
"foaming up and looking very toxic, very scary,"
whereas the eggs she had held for a minimum of two
hours a day were as bright and fresh-looking as the day
they were laid.

Hakuono and her eggs have made a number of
appearances on local television talk shows. Several
leading scientists at U.C. Santa Cruz have vowed to
re-create her experiment under laboratory conditions.
"Some people may be surprised by such results," says
Hakuono. "As a massage therapist, I merely saw new
proof of what I observe daily in my work."

"Doesn't surprise me," Red said. "In AA meetings, you can see
people relax when they hold hands for the prayer or hug each other."

"Ugh," said Lewis. "Hugging and the Lord's Prayer. What I hate
most in AA." He jabbed the article with his finger. "Did this massage
therapist open that jar of eggs? The real proof would be if she scrambled 'em up for breakfast."

"I bet she could've," said Libby. "I'd like to try this experiment."

"Why?" said Lewis.

"What if it's true?" Libby asked. "Wouldn't you like to know?"

"No."

"I have fresh eggs." Red opened the refrigerator. "Dropped off
this morning."

"Are you guys serious?" said Lewis.

Red and Libby rummaged through the cupboards until they
found small, matching jam jars, which they sterilized in the water
Lewis had boiling for pasta. After the jars cooled, they carefully
cracked three eggs into each one. One jar went into the pantry next
to cans of Progresso soup. Throughout dinner, Libby held the other
jar on her lap, cupping it when she could.

Both Red and Libby became positively religious about those eggs.
Lewis would find Red at all hours, at the table or watching television,

clasping the jar as he would a crystal ball. "Hey," he'd say, "how's Operation Stinkbomb?"

Red would hold up the jar, three slumpy yellow orbs in two inches of viscous, slightly cloudy fluid. "Looking pretty darn good, don't you think?"

LAKE Rito on Sunday morning was the color of tarnished silver. The damp morning air was heavily spiced with sage. The sun was up elsewhere, but not in the narrow inlet where Libby and Lewis set up the poles. Libby cut the bait, pork livers that looked like clumps of solid blood. Lewis couldn't watch or he'd gag. Instead, he positioned the chairs, secured poles against them, divided up the Sunday paper.

They each manned two poles, drinking coffee from a green metal Thermos. Fishermen trolled past, their engines a low throb. Libby wrote in her journal. Lewis meditated. A Tibetan Buddhist monk was drying out at Round Rock—a guy from Cincinnati named Simon—and he'd given Lewis meditation techniques, such as counting outbreaths up to ten, over and over, which supposedly could quell the ceaseless inner dithering. Lewis practiced this every morning for twenty minutes. Here at the lake, the sun appeared as a thin red line between his eyelids. The wind funnelled empty space into his lungs. He experienced infinitesimal stretches of mental rest.

Lewis rubbed his eyes, stretched his legs, pulling out of his meditation. Libby kept scratching away in her little cardboard-bound notebook. That killed him. Here he was, the published essayist, just loafing, while she filled page after page in her almost-daily journal.

Lewis touched her arm. "Hey, Lib. Read me something from your journal. I won't be critical." He jiggled her shoulder. "Something about me. I know it's in there."

"Don't be so sure," she said, and thumbed through pages of her symmetrical, clever handwriting. "Here's where you and Red and I talked about who would write the novels of our lives. Remember?"

The conversation at dinner last week. "Sure. Read that."

He hoped to follow along over her shoulder, but she canted the journal so all he could see was the faux-marbleized cover.

"Lewis, barefoot as usual, sits perched on the kitchen stool, picks

at his toes. Picking at one's toenails, he says, is one of the great un-sung pleasures of life."

"I can't believe you wrote that down!" said Lewis. "Jesus!"

"I won't read if you're going to interrupt me every two sentences."

"I'll be quiet." He was so curious now, he would've agreed to almost anything.

"I consider collecting his peeled-off nail bits in case I ever need to send them to Madame Wanda the Wangateuse."

"Wait just a second. Madame what?"

"Madame Wanda," said Libby, "is a Haitian hoodoo doctor I knew in New Orleans."

"You'd send my toenails to a hoodoo doctor?"

"Hopefully I won't have to." She gave him a round-eyed, leveling look. "But I can't read if you're going to keep flipping out."

"I'm not flipping out. I just don't want my toenails going to New Orleans. But go on. Please."

"Red comes in and says he just was at the grocería, and Victor Ibañez told him we were having chicken and red potatoes and choco-late mint ice cream for dinner.

"Can't you buy one damn bag of groceries in this town without it becoming a matter of public record? Lewis says. Don't people around here have anything more important to talk about?

"We can't all be gloriously profound like you, I tell him.

"Me? says Lewis. I'm not so profound.

"Oh no, Red says. You only think you're living a Dostoyevsky novel.

"What's wrong with that? Lewis says. If anybody were to write the novel of my life, I'd want it to be Dostoyevsky.

"I can just see it, says Red. The Genius. A companion volume to The Idiot.

"Hey thanks, Redsy. But more likely it would be The Obsessed, *companion volume to* The Possessed.

"I say, Who would write the novel of Red's life?

"Red says, I could see myself as a bit player in a Dickens novel. One of those good-hearted ninnies running a hopeless institution.

"No, I say, I mean the novel of your life. You can't be a secondary character.

"*Red thinks for a while and says, So how about Henry James? He's suitably stylish and unflinching.*

"*Perfect! Lewis yells. Perfect! It could be* Portrait of a Saint, *companion volume to* Portrait of a Lady.

"*Red's face reddens. Uh, I was thinking maybe,* The Ritonians, *like* The Bostonians.

"*Lewis says, I know who'd write Libby's novel. Jane Austen.*

"*I don't think so, I say. All she could do was get people married. And I've already been married. I need an author who can write beyond the happily-ever-after. Maybe Emily Brontë. Isn't* Wuthering Heights *about how the wrong boyfriend wrecks life for two generations?*

"*Lewis rolls his eyes.*"

"I did not," Lewis said. "I did not roll my eyes."

"Yes you did, and you said 'Priceless,' too, really sarcastically."

"It *was* priceless. I just wish my nineteenth-century-Brit-lit prof could've heard your synopsis." He slipped his hand around Libby's thigh. "Go on. Please. I'll be good."

"*Red says, It could be titled simply* Libby Daw. *Like* Jane Eyre.

"*Wuthering Heights* was a house, I say. So mine could be* The Manatee.

"*You mean the sea cow? says Red. I don't get it.*

"*Manatee's the brand of my trailer.*

"*Lewis says, How 'bout* In the Belly of the Manatee?*"

Lewis burst out laughing. "Sorry, sorry," he sputtered.

"Ha, ha, ha," Libby said, and read on.

"*Who knows? says Red. Maybe Lewis will write the book of all our lives.*

"*What, hollers Lewis, and bore everyone to death?*"

Lewis kicked the mud flats under his heels. "You're already writing the book! I have to start watching what I say around you!"

Libby stuffed her journal into her canvas tote and turned away. He saw then that he couldn't joke with her, not about her writing. "It's good, Libby. Really. You even make me sound funny."

"Right. Like that's my whole purpose in life."

JOE, Red's son, spent every August at Round Rock. During the last week in July, Red drove up to San Francisco to fetch him. Red hadn't been gone six hours when Libby's car pulled up in front of the Round Rock office.

Lewis's heart sank. Did she think, now that Red was out of town for a few days, she could come over any old time? He didn't want this casual dropping-by business to start. He'd say he was too busy to talk. Nip the impulse in the bud. As he waited for her knock, the phone rang. He talked to a woman about her husband's medical insurance for ten minutes. When he got off the phone, Libby still hadn't come to the door.

He found her in Red Ray's living room. "Oh, hi!" She was curled up on the sofa watching the local news and drinking a glass of ice water. She had on a black tank top and snow white shorts. Her skin was the color of roasted peanuts.

"Hi," he said.

"Done with work for the day?" she asked.

"Nope. I'm swamped with stuff."

She held up the jar of eggs, then nestled them back between her legs. "Egg sitting," she said.

"Why not take them over to your house?"

"Red and I agreed that the two jars should be in the same place, the only variable being human touch."

Lewis stood between her and the television. She smiled up at him, a question.

"I got a lot of work to do," he said.

"So you said." She leaned to one side, to look past him at the television.

Back at the office, he kept wondering if he should go over again and act a little nicer. In the meantime, the Falcon disappeared.

Libby showed up the next day, too, going into Red's without so much as a "Hi, how are you?" Red and Libby's little science project was beginning to irritate the hell out of him. What was so damn fascinating about a couple of rotting eggs?

He found her in exactly the same circumstance: sofa, ice water, TV on, eggs nestled in lap. Lewis knelt and slid a hand inside her tank top, over her lace-harnessed breast. She held the eggs up and over to the side. "Put those damn things down," he said, taking the jar from her grasp, "and let *me* demonstrate the benefits of human touch."

YVETTE released Joe to Red with the familiar litany of instructions: Do things with him. He's at that age when he really needs his father.

Joe had grown four inches in the last six months. A trauma, Yvette told Red, and physically quite painful. The boy's skin was so pale and his limbs so skinny that he looked long, cartilaginous, new, as if he'd just uncurled from incubation. His eyes were blue, his hair ash and likely to turn white in his twenties, as his mother's had.

The two of them drove down the coast. Joe talked about baseball until it became obvious that Red didn't know who was on any of the teams. The boy then read a *Rolling Stone* and the Sunday sports section. Spend time with him, Yvette had said. Do some projects together. These instructions sounded more and more like Zen koans.

Once at Round Rock, Joe was independent, intent on amusing himself. He'd brought fat science-fiction and spy novels. Every morning, while Red showered and made breakfast, Joe took a forty-minute run, returning flushed, bright red, every capillary in his sheer skin pumped full of blood. In the evenings, when Red went to his meetings, Joe ran again. Once, Red stepped out on the Blue House's front porch and spotted Joe moving noiselessly down on the roadway, his skin gray in the dusk, his arms and legs pumping, spidery.

Think of some interactive activities: Yvette spoke with such a plea in her voice, Red wondered if Joe had any friends at all in San Francisco. Here in Rito, at least, he had Little Bill Fitzgerald. They hiked together, rode bikes, swam in the river, and, he hoped, amused themselves without resorting to anything illegal. When Red was Joe's age, Frank was his best friend and their favorite activities were breaking-and-entering and drinking, naturally, whatever they got their hands on.

Yvette's imperatives heightened Red's already firm sense of

parental inadequacy. "His mother says I'm supposed to think up interactive activities," he told Lewis.

"Take him fishing," Lewis said.

"I haven't fished for years. I wouldn't remember which end of the line to put in the water."

"Nothing to it," Lewis said. "Take him to the lake, fish from the bank like Libby and I do. It's great. Fresh air. Big body of water. Something always happens."

"I don't know," Red said. "Rods, reels, hooks, tackle boxes, bait—it's overwhelming."

"Talk to Libby. She's got it down to an art. Want me to ask her? We go every Sunday, anyway, so maybe we could all go together. Whaddaya say?"

Somehow, through no effort of his own, Red and son were booked for Sunday's excursion. The night before, he took Joe to the Kmart and bought rods and reels. At five-thirty a.m., Libby and Lewis drove up and loaded an ungodly amount of fishing and picnic supplies into the back of Red's pickup. Joe was thrilled to ride in the back while Red, Libby, and Lewis were crammed into the cab. Libby, in the middle, kept one hand against the dash to brace herself from leaning into Red. He had to touch her thigh every time he shifted gears. Her ponytail switched his face. She smelled of sandalwood soap.

"Maybe we'll have bass for dinner," Libby said. "Makes me hungry just thinking about it. Did anyone have breakfast? I'm starving. Lewis," she said, "could you hand me one of those apples in the bag at your feet?"

Lewis dug around in the canvas sack and found an apple. Libby's enormous, thirsty bites sent juice spraying. "Wanna bite, Red?" She held the half-eaten fruit so close to Red's face that he could smell the cider, see her lipstick staining the crumpled white meat.

"Naw, no thanks, Lib," he muttered, blood suffusing his face.

In all the years he'd lived in Rito, Red hadn't spent much time at the lake. A CCC project from the thirties, a reservoir for Los Angeles, it looked to him bleak and inhospitable, simply a valley in chaparral foothills plugged up and filled with water. An enormous county park with spaces for four hundred RVs was often filled to capacity during the summer, and you had to pay six dollars at the park entrance to visit two small, overcrowded stretches of sandy beach.

Libby, however, directed him down a dirt road outside the park gates. The road, cut like a shelf in the hill, ran alongside a skinny inlet. Red parked behind three other vehicles and a trash can spewing beer cans and soggy garbage.

Toting a rusty cooler, lawn chairs, old quilts, and thickets of fishing poles, they picked their way down a steep bank of sharp fill rock. The water was as opaque and green as a farm pond. The wedge of sky overhead had a lemon-colored tint. Lewis led them along the shore halfway to the main body of the lake, then stopped and planted the ice chest a few feet from the water. The mud-flat bank looked like a floor of warped tiles.

"Best catfish hole in the whole lake," Libby told Red. "But with your high-dollar equipment, you'll want to fish further up there." She pointed to where the finger of water widened into the lake itself. "I guarantee you'll catch at least one crappie." Deadpan, she pronounced the word obscenely.

Red smiled. Out here in the warming day, Libby seemed more physical and energetic, truly spirited. She was one of those people who seemed familiar to Red from the moment he laid eyes on her, as if, contrary to fact, there'd never been a time when she wasn't somewhere in his life. As she unfolded chairs, assembled poles, her face was guileless and happy. Her shin-length pedal pushers made her calves look muscled, her ankles bony, her feet strong and capable of traversing great distances.

In the time that Red had one pole ready to go, Libby had all four of hers snapped together and threaded with line. She called Joe over to her. "You ever been fishing?" she said.

"Once, with a friend. Didn't catch anything."

"Your luck's about to change, knock wood." Libby rapped the side of her head with her fist. "Let's get these lines in the water." She spread out newspaper and opened a Tupperware container of pork livers. She tipped the bowl toward Joe. "Gross, huh?"

"Really gross."

"Catfish go crazy for it." She cut the meat into bloody chunks, baited the line of the first pole, rinsed her hand in the lake, and cast expertly. The liver sailed out and plunked in the water. Libby leaned the pole against the back of one chair. "Watch that for me, Joe, until Lewis gets it secured?"

Lewis clustered rocks around the handles until the poles stood on their own.

Joe frowned. "Don't you hold the poles in your hands?"

"Not these," she said. "You'll hold the spinning poles your Dad bought, but this is catfishing. Nothing labor-intensive about it. Just bait and wait. You need your hands free. I mean, what if you have to scratch an itch?" She baited and cast the next pole. "Hold this now, okay? Couple of weeks ago, I leaned a pole up against the chair and before I knew it, both the pole and the chair were in the lake. Lewis had to go in after them. Got a big old catfish."

Red was wishing by now that he hadn't gotten the spinning rods. They were too fussy and fragile, the three-pound test like spiderwebs in his fingers. He was grateful Libby was distracting Joe, lest the boy witness his ineptitude.

Once their gear was ready, Red and Joe had to walk a good distance away from Libby and Lewis, and then from each other, in order to cast. Too far apart to talk. So much for interaction; fishing, it seemed, was yet another exercise in solitude.

The night before, Joe had spent a long time practice-casting in the Round Rock roadway. He cast until he could send out a lure in a fine, long arc in any direction. He hit specific rocks and trees and other targets. Now he fished with ease, casting, reeling in, casting, reeling in, his face expressing the same focus and intensity as when he read or ran. After a fruitless half an hour, Red worried that the boy was bored, and tried to project confidence that there were fish that *would* bite. And sure enough, Red had a strike and pulled in a pan-sized bluegill. Libby jumped to her feet and ran up whooping. Joe stared long and hard at the fish, as if memorizing what he should aim for. "All right, Dad," he said.

They resumed casting. The morning was warm and still. Water lapped at the shore in tiny waves. From the mechanical daze of repetitive motion, Red heard Joe quietly and pointedly say, "Dad." Joe's pole was curling in a tightening parabola. Libby was over in an instant. "Good!" she cried. "Now keep your pole up. Relax, don't panic. Let him swim. Don't haul him in too fast. Right, good. Pole up! Let him run a bit. Jesus, Joe, what do you have there?"

"I don't know!" Joe was jubilant.

Lewis came over for a closer look. An old man fishing farther down the spit shaded his eyes to see what was going on, then put a rock in his chair and ambled up.

"Big, huh, Dad?" Joe said.

"I'll say," said Red.

The nylon line unzipped the water.

"You're doing great," said Libby.

"You sure are," Red said.

Indeed, Joe grew calmer by the moment. He kept his pole up, maintaining a constant, steady tension, as if he'd been fishing all his life.

"So what do you think?" Libby asked.

"I think I'll bring him on in now," Joe said.

Red realized this was no pretty little panfish long before it broke the surface. He thought maybe sheepshead or sucker, though, and wasn't prepared for the way it kept coming out of the water. At first Red thought it was a snake, but in the next instant, he realized it was an eel—worm, snake, and bottom fish combined. Mud-brown, yellow-eyed, its girth triangular, its skin dented and scarred. The five of them stood there as the eel writhed on the parched mud, two barbs of the brass treble hook imbedded in its jaw. The tiny eyes, spaced so far apart, seemed barely functional or necessary.

"Straight from the Pleistocene," Lewis said.

"Some eat 'em," said the old guy. "I never would."

Joe looked around, his face white and his eyes wide with excitement and fear. "So what do I do?" he asked loudly.

"Oh, we'll throw it back," said Libby. "No big deal."

Red reached to touch his son's shoulder and caught sight of an entire family approaching: father and mother, boy and girl, all wearing brightly colored nylon windbreakers and carrying new-looking picnic gear and tackle boxes. They could have marched straight off the camping pages in the Sears catalog. The father, a fit, handsome man in his early forties, led the way. Over his windbreaker, he wore one of those special fishing vests with dozens of pockets. This man, Red thought, would know how to catch the right fish. This man's son would never catch some freak species of aquatic life.

"Whatcha got over there?" the man called.

When nobody answered, he said something to his wife and kids, then started toward Red's group. He squeezed into their circle between Joe and the old man. "Freshwater eel," he said, glancing at Joe. "You caught this?"

Joe looked from Red to Libby to Lewis and said nothing.

The man unsheathed a knife on his belt and crouched down, the blade as bright and clear as a mirror. He flicked the side of the eel with the tip.

"What the—?" Lewis blurted.

"Used to see these all the time in Asia." He grunted, edging forward, and lowered his foot onto the eel's head. "Ugly suckers." With one strong, fluid pull, he sliced the eel in two. The uneven sections, head and tail, went crazy. Everyone hopped back. The man stood up and wiped the knife on his pantleg. "There you go." He nodded gravely at Red, at Lewis, at the old man. Everyone kept backing away from him and the bloody, flopping eel halves. "Y'all have a good day now."

They watched him rejoin his family. Then Libby reached down and lifted Joe's pole from the dirt, the eel's twitching head hanging from the hook. She took a pair of needle-nosed pliers from her back pocket, grasped the eel's head, and began to pry the hook loose.

Red roused himself. "I can do that," he said.

"Done," said Libby, tossing the head into the lake. "And a free meal for the catfish." Then she picked up the tail end and threw it in. "Dessert, too." She rinsed her hands in the water and flicked the moisture off her fingers at Joe. "Some first fish," she said.

AFTERWARD, Joe sat by himself on the rocks above the shore. Red let him be for half an hour, then climbed up. "You okay?"

"Yeah," Joe said.

"We can leave if you want."

"I just need to think about it."

Red went back to his casting, if only to demonstrate his continued faith in fishing, and caught another bluegill. As the sun gained strength, so did the wind. Lewis was in his chair reading a book. Libby, behind sunglasses, stared straight ahead, as if willing fish to her hook. The old guy down the way packed up his chair and poles and left, raising a hand in silent salute. Red wished Joe would start fishing again, but he just sat there above them, scratching a big rock with a little rock.

Suddenly, Libby leapt to her feet. "Here's dinner," she called, and pulled in a five-pound catfish as big as Red's arm.

Joe came down to inspect it, crouching over the fish with Libby. Red couldn't hear what they were saying, but as soon as Libby got the fish on a stringer, she stood up. "I don't know about you other fisherpersons," she said, "but Joe and I are going to have some brunch."

They sat on quilts and Libby passed out bacon and egg-salad sandwiches. In this fresh air, Red's hunger was shocking. His first sandwich was gone before anyone else's was even unwrapped. Libby handed him another one. He restrained himself from devouring it on the spot by reaching into a bag of *chicharrones*, dipping a dry blistery rind into a carton of fresh salsa.

"Eee-ow, Dad," Joe said. "You're really going to eat that?"

"Why not?" Red said.

"They're delicious." Libby reached for a rind to prove it.

"Fat fried in fat," Lewis said. "Makes my arteries harden just to look at them."

The *chicharrón*, tasting faintly yet pleasantly like sweat, shattered in Red's mouth. The salsa filled his eyes with tears. Libby handed Pepsis all around.

Stretching out, Red absently ate *chicharrones* and watched Lewis hesitate over the sandwich Libby offered. "Come on," she said softly, "I know you like egg-salad sandwiches. That's why I made them. But if you don't want it, I'll just throw it to the catfish."

Red wanted to laugh out loud at Lewis's recalcitrance—such a classic alcoholic need to control. Lewis had no trouble feeding other people, but balked when offered nourishment. Lewis's biggest weakness, Red thought, might be his inability to accept the incredible gifts that life hurled his way on a regular basis.

After building a little stack of food in front of Lewis, Libby turned her attention to Joe. "Don't take that militaristic jerk personally. We've run into some real doozies out here, I swear. Once, Lewis and I decided to go fishing at night and a huge family was encamped right along this inlet. Mom, dad, grandparents, fifty million kids, two mean little mutts barking all the time. They had Coleman lanterns, radios, a portable TV playing the ball game. They must've had about fifteen lines in the water. Lewis and I were forced way out on the spit"—Libby waved toward the lake—"where we'd never catch anything. After an hour or so, we gave up.

"We're walking back to our car, trying to sneak past the dogs, when the grandfather calls us over. Do we want some catfish? he asks, only we don't understand him right away. He has a funny accent, or maybe a speech impediment. 'Got morn we kin et up,' he says. 'Got three freezers full at home.' Lewis—the cook here—says, sure, we'll take some catfish." Libby paused to take a drink of Pepsi.

"We didn't know what we were in for," Lewis said.

"No lie," said Libby. "The old guy takes us to his wife. 'Mammy,' he says, 'give these folks your fish.' So the old gal hauls a stringer out of the water, hand over hand. Meanwhile, the kids gather around us, close. I keep thinking they're touching my clothes, but when I turn to look, they shrink back. The dogs are sniffing our ankles. The whole family is, I don't know, a few bricks short. Big, wide faces. Thin, almost nonexistent lips. Eyes really far apart.

"And the fish! They were the biggest cats I've ever seen. Twelve and fourteen pounds. Bigger than the dogs. The woman pulls one fish off the stringer, hugs it around the middle and gathers it to her chest like she's cuddling a baby. The fish isn't dead, so it's writhing all down her chest, slithering out of her arms, down her legs, probably stinging her like crazy. When it finally hits the ground, one of the boys pins it with a sharp stick until Lewis and I can get it on our stringer. We take the other fish too, don't ask me why. I don't know what we were thinking."

"We were thinking," said Lewis, "about fried catfish with my jalapeño sauce."

"Yeah, but when we got home, we had to skin the damn things before we could go to bed." Libby reached over and touched Red's pant leg. "You ever skinned a catfish?"

"No," Red croaked. He took a swig of Pepsi. Something had lodged in his upper chest, his gorge. It hurt to swallow.

"Normally," Libby said, "you nail their heads to a piece of wood and pull the skin off with pliers."

"Yuck," said Joe.

"It is yucky," said Libby. "But it's the easiest way. Except these fish were so big, I didn't have a nail long enough to go through their heads and stick in the wood."

"You'd need a railroad spike," said Lewis.

"Oh, God, it was five in the morning before we finally got to bed, and then neither one of us could sleep."

Libby stopped talking and looked at Red. "You okay?"

Red found that by sitting perfectly still, he could ignore the sensation in his chest. He gave what he thought would pass for a confident nod, although even that quick tilt of the neck shot needlelike sprays of pain through his chest.

Libby frowned, but went on with her story. "So anyway, we're lying in bed and Lewis starts talking. And it's like he's saying exactly the same things that were running through my mind. 'All I can think about are fish,' he says. 'I feel like I'm swimming in a school of fish. I feel like I *am* a fish. Where did those people come from? Why were their eyes were so far apart?' And then, Lewis sits bolt upright in bed and yells, 'They weren't people, they were *catfish*!' "

Red tried to laugh, but the obstruction in his chest was too big and too painful. It felt, he had to admit, exactly like his heart. In fact, there was no doubt: his heart was swelling, about to burst. He put his palm on his chest and pushed. He was in big trouble. He tried to conjure a way back to the car, to town, to the emergency room, but he'd never make it up those sharp rocks.

He heard Libby talking as if from a great distance. "They probably looked so much like catfish because that's all they ate," she was saying. "But where was their car? How'd they get all that junk down there? I think . . . Are you all right?"

Libby's face loomed in front of him, her eyes enormous with concern.

"I don't know," he croaked. "My chest . . ."

Libby stared at him hard, her eyes darkening, then broke into gasps of laughter. "Look!" She held up the near-empty cellophane bag of pork rinds. "Jesus! You have the *chicharrón* choke! My God, Red, you can't eat these things without washing them down with something!" She tore off the pull tab and handed him another Pepsi. "They get stuck and expand. Oh, you poor baby. I know, it really, really hurts—doesn't it?" She stopped talking to laugh some more. "Drink. But it's going to get worse for a minute before it gets better. They'll really swell now."

Red drank, and the waddage of rinds indeed seemed to balloon beyond his capacity to contain it. Drawing breath was like taking a thick, blunt knife in the chest. When slowly, miraculously, the pain began to ebb, he wanted to weep with relief.

"My God," said Libby, "this expedition's been a disaster from the start. What time is it—almost ten? What say we pack up?"

The pain stopped. Red took a deep breath. His heart was fine. He wouldn't die. He was so relieved he probably would've agreed to anything. "Great," he said. "Let's."

"Hear, hear," said Libby, getting to her feet. "I like a man who says 'let's.' "

Red liked her too. Her thick ponytail and bright laughter. Her knobby ankles, the bold way she handled bait and fish and pieces of fish, not to mention her kindness to Joe. She managed with ease the small acts of attention he found paralyzing.

As Red drove them all home in his truck, the vague ache lingering in his chest became a specific sadness: that age and weight, his own inarguable fate, had disqualified him from Libby's romantic consideration. Though she was undeniably fond of him, when it came to love he was clearly out of the running.

LIBBY AND LEWIS watched meteor showers from her front deck. Single stars sprang out of nowhere, shooting this way and that. "Buddhists," Lewis said, "believe our true nature is really the great sky mind."

"Mmmm." He could, it seemed, deliver a lecture on almost anything.

"And this miserable, fragile biological existence is just a place to work out karma. Eventually, though, if you play your cards right, you can cycle out of existence."

"Who wants to do that?" said Libby.

"It's supposed to be okay. Like that period between falling asleep and dreaming. What the Tibetans call the Great Illumination."

"Why am I not convinced?"

"It takes training. Once you're trained, you'd be aware of that state, and then you'd know what's so great about it. It sounds good to me—an end to endless mental sausage-making."

"I'd rather be reincarnated."

"So would Bodhisattvas. They won't settle for enlightenment until they've helped everybody else get there too. Which is what this life is *supposed* to be about. Helping others." Sighing, Lewis stretched his arms over his head. "Red Ray does a pretty good job of it."

"You think he's a Bodhisattva?"

"Almost. Maybe in his next life, since he's spent so much of this one in service to others."

"But you're that way too," said Libby. "Your job is pure service. I mean, you can't be doing it for the money."

"But Libby!" Lewis nosed into her neck. "I *am* doing it for the money!"

"You're so tender with the men." She strummed his ribs.

"Not really. They bug me."

"I've seen you," she said. "They bug you but you still help them."

"Oh, Libby." Lewis snaked his arms around her, tangled his legs with hers. "I like your version of me. Very generous. And totally full of shit."

Cosmic debris rained down as she slid her leg along his. Skin, hair, muscle, bone. Nothing else felt as real, as astonishing or gratifying as another human being.

It was still mostly dark when Lewis brought coffee outside to her. She raised up on one elbow, took the mug. The coffee smelled rich but was too hot to drink. She could hear a distant train, although she knew of no tracks anywhere in the valley. In the morning chill, she caught a first whiff of autumn.

"Hey," said Lewis. "Did I tell you I'm staying on at Round Rock through the end of the year?"

"You *are*?"

"Yeah. I've got some papers I need to finish, but I can do that here. And if I keep squirreling away the dough, I won't need a loan for the winter quarter."

"Oh, good for you," she said absently. Only later, as she processed insurance claims at the union hall, did she wonder if he maybe was staying on because of her. Uh-oh. It was like having a romance at summer camp and then being told you have to stay through Christmas. What was acceptable in the short run—unheated cabins, primitive plumbing, a lover with countless quirks—became a jail sentence.

He had yet to take her to a movie, to spend the whole day with her or even two nights in a row in her bed. Since Joe had come, she hadn't even been invited to dinner at Red's. Everything was on his terms. If they were going to keep seeing each other, Libby decided, there would have to be some big changes.

Libby had a tough week at the union hall, what with the end of the quarter, and everyone rushing to get accounts balanced. She worked late four nights in a row. Coming home on Thursday, hungry and exhausted, she lowered two slices of bread into the toaster and the lights went out.

This had happened once before, and Stockton had taken care of it. She remembered where the fuse box was and found two scorched fuses but didn't know if she should touch them. She phoned Billie and got her machine. There was no way to call Lewis; he didn't have a phone at the Mills. She lit candles and got ready for bed, prepared to leave home repairs for the morning, then remembered all the catfish in the freezer.

"Red?" she said. "You're not asleep or anything?"

"No. Joe and I are sitting here with the eggs, as a matter of fact."

"Oh, God, I haven't been over to hold 'em for a while."

"That's okay. Joe's taking up the slack. I have to fight him for them. Everything okay?"

She explained her situation.

"I'll be right over," he said.

"Oh, no. Not for a blown fuse," she said. "Can't you just tell me what to do?"

"I can try." He instructed her to throw the breaker and pull the fuses, and stayed on the phone until she returned.

"Okay," she said. "I got 'em."

"We can get your lights back on," he said. "But first you have to promise me one thing."

"Depends."

A chuckle. "Promise you'll buy new fuses first thing tomorrow."

"Oh, that's easy," she said.

He told her to wrap the offending fuses in aluminum foil and again stayed on the line while she went back outside, inserted the silvery cylinders into their clamps, and threw the breaker. The trailer's windows glowed yellow; a nimbus of bugs formed instantly around the porch light. The air conditioner rumbled back to life. Libby ran back to the telephone. "Let there be light," she said.

She pulled the bread out of the toaster and decided to make herself a drink instead. She found a few inches of scotch Billie had brought over last spring, mixed it with Diet 7-Up, and added a wedge of fresh lemon. Why *had* she stayed in this stupid valley?

Headlights lanced the windows and climbed the wall behind her as Lewis's pale Fairlane rolled up behind her Falcon. She went out to the deck to meet him. He bounded up the steps, grabbing her around the waist. They kissed, then he pushed her away with such force that she stumbled backward on the deck. His face was wild, as if she'd bitten his tongue.

"You've been drinking!" His voice was a strangled squawk.

She fought a surge of laughter. "You could taste it? I'm sorry."

He worked his cheeks, rolling the taste around in his mouth. "It's so weird after all this time. Seven months."

She touched his arm. "I didn't know you were coming," she said softly. "You okay?"

He took a deep breath, steadied himself. "What a rush! It all came flying back to me. How much I loved drinking." He took hold of her wrists, held them tightly at her sides. His eyes glistened. "It was like meeting an old friend, but one who betrayed you. Who tried to kill you. It's all so complicated. I really loved alcohol. I did."

"I'm so sorry," said Libby. "If it's any comfort, I don't think I had three sips. But I had a hard day, and I blew a fuse, and I was feeling sorry for—"

"That doesn't matter," Lewis said. "You can drink whatever you want. This is my issue." He let go of her wrists, lowered himself onto the futon. Scratched his head. "Scotch, right? What did you mix it with, club soda?"

"7-Up and lemon."

"Jesus. That's disgusting."

"I wanted something weak, nothing I'd feel."

Lewis, leaning back on his elbows, started to laugh. "You didn't want to feel it?" He patted the mattress, inviting her down. "What's the point of drinking, then? You're such a lightweight, Lib. Straight up or on the rocks!"

"Look, I'm sorry I had alcohol on my breath," she said. "But I'm not going to apologize for what I drink."

"Hey, no big deal. I'm just joking. Please come here."

She stepped back. "Just a minute," she said, and let herself into the trailer.

In the bathroom, she slipped out of her clothes and pulled on a cotton kimono. In the kitchen, she poured the drink down the drain. In the living room she sat down on the sofa.

The candles were still lit from her blackout and she could see her mandolin, a present from Huey Labette, the lead singer of the zydeco band she'd fiddled for in New Orleans. And the antique standing lamp she'd bought for two dollars at a yard sale in Carrolton—although the glass sconce, a large frosted bowl, cost sixty at a lamp store. The Franklin stove Stockton had installed a week before he told her he was leaving.

Lewis tapped on the door and poked his head inside. "What are you doing?" he said. "Is something wrong?"

"Does everyone have to be a heavy-duty alcoholic to be taken seriously by you?" she asked. "Did it ever occur to you that other people have their own emotional lives?"

"What are you saying?"

"How come only your emotions matter?"

"Me? Libby, I don't even know what emotions I have. I wouldn't recognize an emotion if it slapped me in the face."

"Oh, no. I think you're *very* eloquent about them. Kissing me, for example, is like meeting somebody who betrayed you."

He stepped inside, closing the door softly, and knelt down before her. She kept her arms wrapped tightly around herself, so he began rubbing her left foot, pressed the pressure points, and jiggled each little toe before pulling it out with a small, knuckly pop. She stared over his head in the dark.

Lewis set down her left foot and picked up her right. He gave it the once-over, then lifted it to his jaw like a telephone receiver. "Hey, grouchy girl," he spoke into the heel, "let's go to bed."

He made love to her slowly, with uncharacteristic tenderness. Her resistance gave way in stages, like fine strings breaking, their ends snapping in weightless arabesques. He stroked her face and whispered something in her ear—his first blurred endearment? Afterward, she wept soundlessly, tears coursing from the corners of her eyes. Lewis stanched them with his thumbs, smiling down.

I did not expect, Libby wrote, *to be tumbling dangerously toward love. Not at this time. Certainly not with this man. He has a beard, for heaven's sake. And smokes.* And *makes even less money than I do. His feet are usually dirty. My mother will hate him on sight. Stockton will say I'd landed even further down the social ladder than he predicted.*

She wanted to see him right away, the next night, but he clearly had more self-control. She actually expected him on Saturday night—

so they could go fishing on Sunday, as usual—but he neither called nor appeared, and Libby fished alone.

This late in the summer, the water was shrinking, the band of crackled gray mud now wide as a highway. *Don't know what's going on with Lewis,* she wrote in her journal. *I'm not worried. He's been fairly consistent. Still, it feels strange, a little* bleak, *to be here without him.*

She felt better after catching a decent catfish—about a pound, maybe more—and better yet after catching another. She gave both to two young men who were trying to fish with string and gnawed-on chicken bones. The men spoke no English and appeared to be living in the hills. She also gave them one of her bamboo poles, some hooks, and the rest of her pork livers, which, she feared, they probably cooked up with the fish over a campfire for lunch.

RED INVITED her to dinner on Tuesday night, and she was surprised not to see Lewis there. He was invited, Red said, but claimed to have overdue schoolwork. She downplayed her disappointment. She promised to take Joe fishing again, and they set a date for the following Sunday. Then, Joe showed her the eggs.

The cradled eggs did not look good, and in fact they were quite cloudy, almost opaque, whereas the control eggs in the cupboard had only a skin of white foam. "Whatever you do," Libby told Joe, "don't drop them."

"YOU ASLEEP?" Lewis asked.

What did he think? It was past eleven on Thursday night. "Where are you?" she asked.

"At Denny's in Buchanan."

She was too sleepy to make sense of this. "You coming over?"

"I'm real busy this week," he said. "I've got to get these incompletes out of the way. I thought I should check in, though."

"Oh."

"Is something wrong?"

"I didn't know why you weren't calling."

"I'm busy. That's all."

She pushed herself up into a sitting position, wanting to say something she couldn't say while horizontal. If you're going to start with the weird stuff, let's just cut it off cleanly. . . .

He began to talk as if she'd actually spoken. "Libby, I'm no good at meeting expectations. I go right into reverse. I really do have a lot of work right now. I've lost seven months to getting sober. I don't know where I've been. Detoxifying. In a sexual fog. It's been great, too, but now I've got to get out from under this academic wreckage. I miss you, though. Tell me—are you outside?"

"No. In my room."

"Got any clothes on?"

"Lewis . . ."

"Okay. Be that way. But I'll see you soon. Don't worry. We'll get together. If I don't blow town first. Just joking. Don't worry. I'll show up one of these days. That's the thing. I'm sober now. That's what sober people do. Suit up and show up."

She had trouble sleeping for the rest of the night, a stomachache high up under her ribs.

"YOU LOOK like hell," Billie whispered to her. "Get your brains fucked out last night?"

"Shhh . . ." Libby checked to see if either Bill had heard. They were at Happy Yolanda's for breakfast. "No such luck," she whispered.

"Too bad," Billie whispered back, then said in normal tones, "Here's the thing. Dad and I want to give you a no-interest loan."

"That's so sweet of you," Libby said, as noncommittally as she could. She smiled at Old Bill. He nodded gravely and looked away. Old Bill was eighty-eight years old, slight and elegant, with snow-white hair and, as always in the summer, oatmeal-colored linen slacks and a white shirt. Libby was never certain how much Old Bill heard; he was, according to Billie, selectively deaf. Although Billie related stories of verbal cruelty, Libby had never known Old Bill to be anything but flawlessly polite.

When Red Ray and Joe walked in, Billie had them pull up a table. "Help me convince Libby to build a house on her property."

Red sat down next to her. "Sounds like a good idea."

"I don't even know if I want to stay," Libby said. "Besides, I'd have no idea what to build."

"I thought the bastard left you plans," said Billie.

"Too expensive," Libby said. "And awful. All cement and steel, like a jail." She stopped, struck by her own observation: Stockton had designed them a jail!

"What kind of house do you like?" asked Red.

"Tiny, since that's all I could afford."

"Money aside," said Billie. "If you could have any kind of structure, what would it be?"

"What I like they don't build anymore. Something wooden and old-fashioned. A classic orchard house. Like yours, Red."

Everyone burst out laughing.

"A teeny twenty-room mansion," Billie said. "Now we're talking."

"Not the mansion," Libby cried. "Red's house. The bungalow."

"That's easy," Red said. "Take one. I only have nine of them. They sit on stone supports. You could almost move one with a forklift."

"You don't have any plans for them?"

"Every conceivable plan," he said. "A retreat center. A sober resort. Low-income housing. Anything I'd do, Billie would fight me every inch of the way."

"Someone has to preserve this ranch land or this valley would be"—Billie looked directly at Libby—"one . . . big . . . trailer court."

"I do love those little houses," Libby said.

"Think about it," said Red.

"You think about it. And if you're serious, come up with a price."

"Oh, hell. You could pay for the moving. I should probably pay you to take one off my hands."

A small white bungalow sitting snugly against her hill: she wanted it so much, she was afraid to fully imagine it. Yet there was something else, too. A dark spot, an ache. Libby, surrounded by generous friends, suddenly missed Lewis keenly. Where was he? Why wasn't he sitting here next to her, taking her hand under the table and placing it on his admirable erection?

HE'D STOPPED reading. He'd stopped writing. He'd stopped thinking. He'd essentially stopped living his life. From the moment he came to Round Rock, he'd put his personality, work, and future on hold, and now he was in trouble. His advisor had told him he couldn't register for the fall term because he was on academic probation. Over half his courses were still listed as incomplete, and three were already past due. But for the ineptitude of the registrar's staff, he'd be facing three F's. If he wanted extensions, he had to petition right away.

As a last resort, Lewis pleaded getting sober. When he explained how he'd been interned at Round Rock, his advisor softened. "You're very brave," he said. "We want you back. So get your work in."

Inspired, Lewis devised a routine. Every night, after AA meetings at the farm, Lewis drove in to Buchanan, to Denny's, where he sat in booth twelve. Six days a week, this booth was in Phyllis's section. Phyllis was a skinny bottle-blonde with a chronically bloody nose caused, he was certain, by snorting methamphetamines by the spoonful. Not that he had any proof, but this theory explained her low weight, her frequent trips to the restroom, and her edge, although she was nice enough to him. Phyllis didn't care if he kept the booth all night. She sat across from him for brief spells, during which she doled out her life's story in terse sentences, which he, in turn, jotted down and fashioned into a poem. He considered including it in an appendix to his paper "Found Elements in Poetry, Art, and Architecture." He called the poem "Shit, Yeah."

> I married at fifteen.
> Of course I was pregnant.
> Did you really have to ask?
> You'll meet Ralph one of these nights
> I can't find a babysitter.
> He looked like a lizard when he was born.
> Long and lipless.
> You bet I'm divorced.
> He was a college man, too.
> Bad news with a big mouth.
> He had forcible sex with my sister.
> And my mother.
> And me, too, of course.
> If that counts.
> Rape. Right.
> You *are* smart.

He said he'd kill Ralph if I left.
No kidding, I believed him.
His hands had a life of their own,
Snapped off doorknobs.
See this nose?
Feel it.
Feel that?
That's just how it healed.
One night I put ant poison in his food.
Shit yeah, he got sick.
What'd you expect?
He ate ant poison, for chrissakes.

Phyllis read it over several times. "Pretty bitchin' poem," she said.

LEWIS wore pressed khakis. A bright white T-shirt. A black linen sport jacket. Black sneakers. His hair was pulled back in a ponytail. In the porch light, framed by the doorway, his face had a carved, princely look.

"Want to get some dinner?" he asked.

"I already ate."

"I thought we could go to Buchanan. Eat dinner and catch a movie."

"Wish I'd known. I wouldn't have eaten that lousy *torta*."

"We can still catch a movie."

"Come inside," Libby said, "so I can think about it." Three steps into the trailer, she stopped. "Maybe you should go along without me."

He frowned, as if he couldn't quite see her.

"I'm tired. It's almost nine. This doesn't feel good."

"I'm doing the best I can, Libby. I've just been getting work done. I called you, didn't I? Tonight I decided to take a break. I wanted to do something with you. Take you out for a change."

"How 'bout letting me in on these plans, so I know better than to eat dinner by myself?"

"I'm sorry. I don't know what the fuck I'm doing, in case you didn't notice. I'm no good with this dating stuff. When I used to drink, whatever happened, happened. This is all new to me, doing things consciously. I don't have the rule book."

"It doesn't take much imagination," Libby said evenly. "If you want to take someone out, you arrange it ahead of time."

"It wasn't that premeditated! At eight o'clock, I finished at the damn laundromat. I had clean clothes. I put them on. Lawrence just gave me this jacket. I put it on. And that's when I thought, Now I can take Libby out. Now that I look halfway decent. Was I supposed to squire you around town in ratty jeans and a T-shirt?"

"Well, I can't go. Not tonight. I have to get to bed early. I told Joe I'd take him fishing tomorrow at five."

Lewis looked around him. "May I stay?"

"If you want." She went into her bedroom and undressed, then washed her face and brushed her teeth. Out on the deck, she found Lewis lying fully clothed on the futon, smoking. She slipped under the covers, curled away from him on her side. The night was noisy with the high-pitched oscillations of mosquitoes, distant traffic, birds and beasts scuttling in the trees. Lewis switched on the clamp lamp and picked up a book he'd left next to the bed, whose pages had grown fat and wrinkly in his absence. After a while, he turned off the light. He stood, took off his jacket and slacks, and hung them carefully over the railing. He crawled in beside her. "Oh, Libby," he said. "Come over here."

Her eyes were open. She didn't move. He clambered over her, kissing her shoulder, licking her neck. "Come on," she said. "I have to sleep."

He rolled away. She thought for sure he would leave, fell asleep expecting it, and was wakened, hours later, by a shriek.

She thought at first the noise was a large tree falling to the ground, or a coyote's otherworldly wail. Only after she'd seized his arm did Libby realized the sound came from Lewis. He was gasping for breath, covered in sweat.

"Nightmare," he panted. "A curly blond wig was eating me."

She held him, could feel his heart pounding in his chest. "You're okay," she said. "No wigs in sight."

He smashed himself against her, inadvertently pinching one of her breasts. "Ouch," she said.

"I was driving a car that was getting more and more stripped down, until it was more like a go-cart. The steering wheel was a screwdriver stuck in the column. I couldn't steer away from the wig."

Libby tried to free her breast. "Don't leave," he said.

"I'm not going anywhere. You're squashing my breast."

"I hate it when you freeze up," he said.

"Me? *Me?*" Libby was pushing at him as hard as she could.

"You turn into a rock, a frozen rock in a frozen sea."

"You're hurting me!" she hissed, and finally he gave her some room. "And you're the one who froze me out all week."

His arms started tightening again. "I know I'm a jerk. An incredible jerk. God. It wears me out."

"It wears *you* out?" Libby cried. Then, "For God's sake, stop squeezing!"

"Sorry." His body was flush up against hers. "Listen." He spoke into her ear. "I want things to be different. I don't know if I can manage it, but I want it."

"Different how?"

His lips moved for a while before any sound came out. "I didn't expect to feel this way. So attached to you. To like you so much." As if moved by his own declaration, he began nudging her legs apart. "I don't want to lose you," he said. "You're so good for me."

They began making love, though all she could think about was how much sleep she wasn't going to get before she had to pick Joe up. And Lewis was so tireless that she finally had to tell him to go ahead, come without her.

Then he wanted to gab. "Did you ever notice how the Big Dipper is always up there, hogging the sky? Every time I've slept over here, that's all I see," he said. "We should build a deck on the back of your house, maybe we'd see some other constellations. You awake?"

She didn't answer, hoping he'd get the hint.

"I could live here, Libby. I could—if you let me." A moment later, he was snoring.

She was too tired to think clearly. Maybe she didn't understand some vital part of the evening. The word "scimitar" drifted into her mind. With a scimitar, she could slay Lewis. Off with his head. Like in those fairy tales where the princess sends her suitors on impossible errands. Harness the four winds. Suck up the Seven Seas. Eat a stableful of beef, including hide, tails, and hooves. Everyone who fails is slain. With a scimitar. She did want to live with Lewis. Maybe. Or slay him with a scimitar. One, the other, or both. No way she could fall asleep.

But she must've dozed off, because when she next looked at her watch it was 4:12 and Lewis's side of the bed was empty. He was in the kitchen, dressed and pacing before the gurgling coffee maker.

"Would it be okay if I don't go fishing?"

"I wasn't expecting you to," she said. "Only hoping."

"I can't take Red and Joe together, the whole father-son thing. Red's so nervous around the kid."

"I don't think Red's coming," she said.

"Yes he is. He told me yesterday." Lewis poured a cup of coffee.

Libby sat in a chair. She could go to sleep right here. Or maybe she was asleep. She felt a dry peck on her cheek and the door clicked shut.

At the lake, Libby huddled in her flimsy folding chair. The water was very low. Birds pealed in hunger. Red and Joe were a hundred yards away, slip-stitching the air with their fishing lines. A chilly breeze tempered the sun. A bird flew past like a black, disembodied hand waving across the horizon. Bye, bye, bye, bye.

RED CAME into the office and started picking things up—a geode paperweight, a pamphlet, a pencil sharpener in the shape of an orange—and putting them down. Lewis, updating files on the computer, couldn't concentrate. "You okay?" he asked.

"Fine, fine." Red lifted a vase off the mantel, studied its bottom. "So what's cooking with you and Libby these days?"

Lewis groaned. "What, she been boohooing to you?"

"I was hoping we could all have dinner tonight."

"I haven't talked to her for a few days." Lewis squinted at the ceiling, counting how many. "Four or five days," he added. "I'm probably in purgatory. She wears me out, Red."

"Relationships do take a lot of time and energy."

"I hate that word. And besides, it's not *relationships*. It's Libby. She so damn oversensitive."

"*She's* oversensitive?"

"What, you think *I'm* oversensitive?"

"You?" Red pretended to think. "Oh, no, never. Not you."

"Trust me. You should try her out for a few days. You'd see."

"Why doesn't that strike me as such a grisly proposition?"

Lewis snorted. "I wish you would take her off my hands. You'd be doing me a big favor. You take Libby and *I'll* become the monk." When Lewis stood, his leg was asleep, and he staggered around the desk. "You'd come crying to me, man." Lewis yawned. He was at Denny's last night until past three, then up at seven. He wished Red would leave so he could take a nap, but His Corpulence lowered himself into an armchair and slumped in thought. Lewis straightened stacks of paper, banging the edges against the desktop with percussive glee.

Red glanced at his watch. "Joe'll be landing any minute."

"Joe?" said Lewis. "Oh, yeah. Gone, huh?"

"I'm never ready to put him on that plane."

Red's sadness was unnerving. Lewis was supposed to be distressed, and Red the steady one. "Hey, Redsy. You want a cup of coffee?"

"I'm about coffee'd out, thanks."

"You want to, uh, take a walk or something?"

"I thought it'd be good to have dinner with friends, that's all."

"Well, all right, already. Why didn't you say so?" Lewis called Libby at work. "Red Ray requests the honor of your presence at dinner tonight."

"Tell him thanks," Libby said, "but I need more notice."

"Come on, where's your sense of adventure?"

"I can't jump every time you say so, Lewis."

He looked at Red and rolled his eyes. "I'm not asking you to jump—Red is. Just kidding. But seriously, Joe left today and the old man's moping."

"I still need advance notice."

Lewis said, "Okay, okay," and "Goodbye," and slumped in the armchair opposite Red's. "I told you. She's on a kick."

"Oh, well." Red was philosophical.

Now, they were two men with bad posture lost in thought. Lewis had to admit sitting there like that felt good. Guts bulging, mouth-breathing: a form of meditation for sunk white guys. All they were missing were a couple six packs and a wide-screen TV. Red's eyes grew hooded and even his freckles started to fade. They sat without moving for six, nine, twelve minutes, until the phone rang.

"If Red's really sad," Libby said, "is that invitation still open?"

RED AND LIBBY took both jars of eggs, the neglected and the cradled, and examined them endlessly, as if rotten eggs were the *prima materia*. The eggs that had been held were now dark gray, with a rim of white froth. The yolks, when they rolled into view, were still a deep yellow, but their sacs were pocked with gray lesions, knots of stringy membrane. When Lewis shook the jar, there also seemed to be something solid in there, too, like butter forming in a jug of cream. " A whole clot of rot," he said.

"Joe says it's the Alien," Red said.

"A homunculus in vitro," said Lewis. "The child of your applied touch and affection." Lewis picked up the other jar. "Ah, the slower, younger brother." The control eggs still looked like regular eggs, only slightly cloudy, with the smallest fringe of now-pink froth. "I wonder which jar stinks worse."

"We should probably set them lightly in the Dumpster," Red said, "and have done with the whole business."

"Seems a shame to waste two perfectly good Mason jars," Libby said.

"And a much greater shame to bring them this far and never smell the final product," said Lewis. "Let's take them out to the groves and throw rocks at them. Then run like hell."

"What a boy thing to do," said Libby.

Lewis held a jar at eye level. "Mustn't we conclude from this that human touch is harmful and degrading? That prolonged contact leads to putrefaction?"

"You would say that," Libby said.

AFTER dinner, they walked around the boarded-up bungalows so Libby could look them over and pick the one to move onto her land. On closer inspection, the houses were sturdy, simple, ingenious. The architect, said Red, had been a friend of the ranch's former owner, and he'd used structural elements he'd seen in India and Japan: raising their elevation, extending the beams, placing windows for cross-ventilation. The same architect, said Red, eventually designed the first motel in San Luis Obispo. To open a door, Red pulled out nails with a cat's paw. He swept a powerful flashlight over bubbling wallpaper and boarded windows. The air was sour, musty, old.

Lewis started sneezing and had to wait outside. He watched as stars came out in the soft violet sky: a tricky pastime. A tiny sparkle. Then nothing. Nothing. Nothing. He'd look away, glance back, and there it was, a pinhole to another, brighter realm.

Libby came up behind him, snaking her arms around his waist.

He leaned against her, her breasts squashed cozily against his back. "You coming over tonight?" she whispered.

He closed his eyes. "I have to work."

Her body stiffened and her arms withdrew. A chasm of air opened between them. "I need to see you alone," she said.

He closed his eyes. Here it is, he thought.

He'd had a good run with Libby. Three months of happy, have-at-it, laugh-it-up sex. He'd known all along it couldn't last forever. "Okay," he said. "Why don't you meet me later at Happy Yolanda's for a drink?"

"A drink?" she yelped.

"I can drink water or juice," he said. "Milk, Coke, whatever. A Virgin Mary. A virgin martini." He laughed, bumped her arm. "A virgin martini—that would be an olive, right?" Libby wasn't laughing. "Okay, then," he said. "Meet you at ten for an olive."

HAPPY YOLANDA'S door was flung open. Inside the warm darkness, a coppery blur of faces and a sad Spanish love song rasping on the jukebox. Bottles clinked. A drunken laugh rang out. Lewis inhaled the sour breath of his old life: smoke, spilled alcohol, disinfected air.

What if he walked in and ordered a double bourbon, neat? Surely nobody would say, "Hey, aren't you Red's assistant out at the drunk farm? Sure you want to throw away all that hard-earned sobriety?" The bartender would more likely pour the drink, his face blank as lumber.

Libby sat on a stool at the end of the bar, talking to Arvill Hartwood, a big-shot rancher in the valley. Lewis had seen him around town. Though not in Billie's league, Arvill was still rich by anybody's standard. He was famous for having both Morrot and Fitzgerald blood, and for his kindly nature. Even Victor Ibañez, who praised no man, admitted Arvill was sweet, but he called Arvill's wife, Charlotte, "the Barracuda." The Barracuda had walked out on Arvill for the fifth or sixth time two months ago—which was probably why Arvill was slumming in Happy Yolanda's—and Victor had a pool going for the exact date of her return.

Arvill, thought Lewis, was probably just the right man for Libby; maybe fifteen years older, and not bad looking if you don't mind grizzle. Wiry, charming, and rugged in spades. Arvill raised longhorns for a hobby in the pastures around his ranch-style home; if Libby married him, she could admire lunky cattle with silky, speckled hair and handlebar horns from various picture windows.

Lewis sat at the other end of the bar. Libby spotted him, said something to Arvill, and carried her drink over. She'd been home and changed into jeans. Her hair was shiny and floating around her face. Her green, ribbed shirt was tight enough that Lewis could see bra straps and nipples. "Swacked yet?" he said.

"It's club soda, dummy. I know better than to drink around you."

Arvill was watching them. Lewis stood up. "Let's get out of here. That guy creeps me out."

"Arvill?" said Libby. "He's all right."

"He wants to fuck you."

"He does not."

Lewis put his hand on her back and urged her off the bar stool, steering her out onto Main Street. The night was bright, with an almost full moon. You could see the bricks in the buildings, the green bridge arching over the river, the brush-covered hills rising up behind town. He nudged her up Main to the Mills, then through the lobby and up the stairs. In his room, he pushed her down on the unmade bed. "Lewis," she said. "We're going to talk."

He evaded her hands, peeled her shirt up until she lifted her arms, and her breasts, in her lace bra, sprang free. She covered her chest in an ineffective show of modesty. "This isn't talking," she said.

"We'll talk," he said, and unhooked the bra. He pulled her hands away, kissed her breasts, yanked the buttons of her Levi's, which opened in a rapid arpeggio. She kept trying to cover herself, but she was also starting to laugh.

He put two fingers inside her and looked her in the eye, which she never endured with equanimity. She bit her lower lip. "Talk to me now," he said. "What's on your mind?"

"I remember this trick," she said, and arched away from his fingers. With his other hand, he held her pelvis in place. She tossed her head and began moving against him. He climbed on top of her, still using only his hand. She felt juicy, warm, complicated. She couldn't look at him for more than a second. She kept pulling stuff out from under her—a balled-up T-shirt, a pencil. She twisted and squirmed, cried out, pulled a book from under her thigh, and finally came, as if to get away from him.

She was still, eyes closed, breathing hard. Then she reached for his belt buckle. "Take off your clothes," she murmured.

"I'm fine," he said, and moved away from her. He stood, found the cigarettes, lit one. She reached for it; he gave her a puff. She closed her eyes and patted the bed. He sat down beside her. "So," he said. "Let's get this over with. I gotta get to work."

"Work," she whispered. "I need a minute to recover."

"I work at Denny's," he said. "In Buchanan."

She sat up in bed and looked at him carefully. Her hands began reaching for her clothes. "You really don't want to live with me, do you?"

"Not if you push me into a corner."

"I see." She dressed in rapid, hurried movements.

"I need more time to think things out," he said.

"You got it."

Holding the door open for her, he saw that her bra strap was twisted under the ribbing of her tight little shirt, and this made him want to kiss her. He always appreciated Libby at moments of departure. She was such a trouper. Tonight, he was soppily grateful she was leaving without a fight. He disappointed her, he knew. She wanted and deserved more than he could give. Someone like Arvill would do far better, could help her along in life.

Libby turned as he moved forward, his lips aiming for that anger-flushed cheek. Before he got there, she kicked him—hard—on the shin. He could tell she'd meant the kick as a jokey, incomplete gesture, but his momentum had swung him into her oncoming foot. The gently pointed toes of her black pumps connected with his shinbone like a dull axe.

He muffled a shout and she grasped his arm. "I'm sorry! Jesus, I'm so sorry," she whispered. He pulled away from her, away from the pain. Even so, he felt a thrill: for once, *she'd* done the wrong thing. "I'll be okay," he said. "Just go. Get away from me. Please."

She sprang away, into the stairwell, quick and light as a cat. Her swiftness startled him, and he realized how heartless he'd sounded. Hobbling, he pursued her to the first landing. "No hard feelings, Lib," he called after her sotto voce. "I'll call you soon. Take care, now."

AS LIBBY turned up her road, she saw white and yellow lights hovering and swirling in the sky. Is this what UFOs looked like? The lights seemed to come from the area of her trailer. Would she be captured, probed, and then spend the rest of her life trying to convince people that such events actually occurred?

The lights, she soon saw, came from vehicles parked in front of her trailer. Trucks. Large trucks. Fire trucks. And Billie's great white Chevy.

Her first impulse was to drive away, come back, and have it all be different.

Billie's foreman, Rogelio, had been out on patrol when he smelled something. He drove up to investigate and saw smoke seeping from the trailer, called the fire department on his CB, then busted down the door on the off chance Libby was inside. "The fumes could've killed him," one fireman told Libby. "Just be happy you weren't in there asleep." He snapped his gloved fingers. "It happens that fast in these tin cans."

The firemen had thrown what they could onto the deck, covered it with a tarp, then gone back in and sprayed like hell. Now they shined spotlights so she could see to gather up some things.

"Get everything of value out of here," the fireman said. "There'll be looters before morning."

"Looters!"

"They come out of the woodwork." He nodded toward the olive grove, as if that leafy darkness were full of eager eyes.

Billie and Little Bill helped her pile as much as they could into the Chevy. Her musical instruments were safe, and a lot of her furniture seemed fine except for a terrible acrid smell. They worked for an hour or so, loading what they could, locking the rest in the sodden trailer. Back at the Fitzgerald adobe, Billie and Libby drank scotch in the library. "I must be numb," Libby said. "It just doesn't seem so bad. Not as bad as it could have been."

Billie put Libby in what she called the guest suite, two lovely wheat-colored rooms on the second floor. Wheat carpeting and curtains, wheat sofa and bedclothes. There Libby dreamt of trash heaps swarming with looters shaped like giant sow bugs. One turned, and the face in the gray carapace was Lewis's. She woke, kicking at the sheets. What had they even been fighting about?

While Billie was out doing irrigation, Libby dressed and drove back home. In the colorless dawn, the trailer looked bombed. She walked around it slowly. Where the south wall buckled away from the east wall, she could see into a cavern of spongy soot. Side windows had been blown out by the heat. Insulation hung from the ceiling in pendulous stalactites. One willow was scorched, its leaves yellowed and crisped.

At least the trailer had contained most of the fire. One fat flying spark and the hillside would've ignited as if sprinkled with gunpowder. Chaparral actually flourished with fire, since many of its plants and grasses reseeded only after a burn-off. Even this fire, Libby thought, wasn't necessarily a tragedy. The insurance money would pay for moving one of Red's bungalows, and surely a house would appeal more to Lewis.

She unlocked the door and found no signs of looting. The smell, however, was unbearable. It clung to her skin like a pervasive and adhesive evil, a scent of scorched hair and incurable anger that contaminated even her tastebuds; her saliva tasted like tincture of burning tires.

She checked her watch to see if Lewis might be at the office yet. Guess who? she'd say. It's me, the Little Match Girl.

Her phone, however, was dead.

WHEN Red Ray told him about the fire, Lewis was eating a chocolate doughnut for breakfast. He was going through a sugar phase. He woke up in the morning and thought of canned peaches and doughnuts even before coffee and cigarettes. He wasn't getting fat—so far.

"Billie stopped by this morning on her rounds," Red told him.

"She said Libby's bearing up. The fire smoldered in the kitchen walls. It was only beginning to spread when the firemen got there."

"So she didn't lose everything," Lewis said.

"It might've been easier if she had. As it is, she's got a big job on her hands."

"Good thing you're giving her a bungalow," Lewis said. "You want half this coffee?" Before Red could answer, he picked up a styrofoam cup and filled it. Lewis broke the doughnut apart, scattering flakes of frosting over the carpet, and offered half to Red, who patted his paunch and shook his head. When Lewis gestured again, he accepted.

"So go ahead," Red said, "take the day off."

"What for?"

"She'll need all the help she can get. That trailer needs to be emptied."

"I thought," said Lewis, "I'm not supposed to make any serious moves at this stage in my sobriety."

Red's face clouded. "Don't be an asshole. I can't exactly see how helping a friend will land you back in detox."

"You don't know Libby," said Lewis. "I have a hunch somebody's going to try to make her housing problem *my* housing problem."

Red put the last bite of doughnut in his mouth and chewed unhappily, as if the sweetness itself were upsetting. "You know, Lewis," he said, "it is remotely possible that this fire isn't just about you."

"I know, I know." Lewis ducked his head, embarrassed. "Okay, big guy, I'll do the good deed." He struck a muscleman's pose, arms flexed, fist curled to forehead. "I'll clean the Augean stables."

Once in the Fairlane, Lewis could barely lift the key to the ignition. He was genuinely sorry about Libby's trailer. She didn't need any more grief, and he felt guilty enough for bringing up cohabitation the other night; some things seem like a good idea at three a.m., especially in the middle of an anxiety attack. But he wasn't the answer to Libby's problems before the fire, so what use could he be to her now? If Red cared so much, let him rescue the maiden in distress.

At the farm's front entrance, Lewis checked for oncoming traffic and, sure enough, saw a familiar blue Falcon coming from the east. How right can you be? She didn't waste two minutes!

LIBBY was experiencing a heady, if inappropriate, bout of elation. Tragedy struck and missed! The day itself was exhilarating—
last week's tinge of fall now deepened to a cool current, soft gray
clouds blowing across the sky. Anything was possible. She could drive
on, past Round Rock, out of this valley, turn north on the interstate
into the Great Central Valley, land so resolutely agricultural as to still
support general stores, grange halls, and tractor dealerships. She'd
get a job in a small cafe, on the morning shift, and listen to the crop
report on her way to work. She'd wear a fluted polyester uniform, let
her hair go limp. She'd learn to make wisecracks about sorghum
prices and hog bellies.

Or she could take one of Red's bungalows, paint it a woodsy
green with white trim, set it high upon her hill, run bougainvillea on
trellises, build a series of decks like rafts among the flowers and trees.
There would be opera—Verdi or Puccini—in the air. She could see
Lewis there, too: he'd be outside watering, or pruning fruit trees, his
unmistakable brooding self, now sufficiently domesticated. We had
our troubles, she'd say to people. Oh, believe you me. He didn't know
what he wanted. Spooked as a bird . . .

She slowed for the turn into Round Rock's front entrance and saw
the familiar off-white Fairlane at the stop. The curly silhouette wag-
gled this way and that. He looked right at her—his head ticked back
in recognition, *didn't it?*—and then he made a fast, sloppy righthand
turn. The Fairlane skidded on a patch of gravel, slid, and she was sure
it would go off the road. But a wheel caught, and in a big fishtail he
was gone.

She pulled over to the side of the road. "Okay," she said. "Okay."
If she stayed absolutely still, she thought, she might not feel a thing.

RED RAY found her twenty minutes later. The worst was over;
that throat-corroding cry. She'd spat gobs of black-streaked mucus
out the window and dried her eyes on her stinky, soot-smeared sleeve.
Red peered in her window. "What are you doing in there?"

His T-shirt was so white it hurt to look at. "Thinking."

"Coming up with anything?"

"No."

"Sorry to hear about your trailer."

"You already heard?"

"Welcome to Rito," he said.

"And Lewis heard?"

"He left a while ago to give you a hand."

She frowned, thinking this over. "I don't think so. He saw me and took off. We had a fight and he didn't want to see me. That's pretty clear."

Red watched her without speaking.

"I'm okay, now," she said. "I really should get back."

Red reached inside to touch Libby's shoulder. "Let's take my truck," he said.

BILLIE was waiting for them at the trailer, her truck bed stacked with empty 3-Bill brand orange boxes. Libby packed the boxes while Red and Billie loaded them onto their trucks, along with the salvageable furniture.

As she worked, Libby kept thinking she heard a car and hoped to see the Fairlane crest the hill. There was still time for him to relent—or was it "repent"? "Sorry, I choked," he might say. "I flinched, but I'm here now, aren't I?" She tried not to glance down the driveway too often, in keeping with the watched-pot principle. Also, she was embarrassed that, after all his antics, she still wanted Lewis to appear. She couldn't help it. Some part of her—her heart or guts—hadn't gotten the message yet, not quite. She found herself chanting under her breath what was surely a prayer, that Lewis would come, and come soon, before it was too late and this lapse became irreparable.

NEXT STOP: the laundromat. Though reluctant to leave her alone, Billie and Red agreed to take the boxes and furniture to Billie's warehouse while Libby monitored ten loads of stinky wash. "I need time to myself," she'd said. "Please."

Once the clothes were sloshing, Libby walked up to the Mills. Why am I doing this? she wondered. Her trailer had burned, her life was in complete disarray, and all she could think about was Lewis? Clearly this was some kind of post-trauma derangement.

She wanted to find him at home and miraculously equipped with a convincing explanation: his car exploded en route to her, he'd done an L.A. turnaround to fetch her bags of money, he had amnesia, anything. All she wanted was a wild story whose upshot was, We're fine, we're good, our future is bright.

She knocked, then tried his locked door. She stood in the hallway, approximately where she'd kicked him only twelve hours ago. "Oh, God." She was talking out loud now, like a crazy person. "Don't let this be happening. Not to me. Not right now. Not again."

Hearing movement in the room, she became as quiet as air. She would wait him out, stand there motionless, barely breathing until he peeked to see if she'd gone. A knob squeaked and a door swung open—the one next to Lewis's. An old man, his gray hair matted in clumps, staggered into the hall, legs hobbled by the pants around his ankles. His shirttails didn't quite hide his genitals. He gazed at Libby without seeing her, slumped against the wall, and, with great concentration, began urinating on the carpet.

LIBBY transferred ten wet loads into five huge dryers. Red and Billie showed up in time to help her fold. Libby was so happy to see them, she grew weepy. They were such good friends. And such lousy laundry folders. Billie had never folded a thing in her life, and thanks to his military training, Red was so ultraprecise and slow that he probably didn't fold ten items total.

Afterward, they went to Happy Yolanda's for burritos. As soon as they ordered, Billie's beeper went off. "Don't say anything interesting," she told them, and left to use the pay phone.

Red asked Libby about her insurance—she always forgot he was a lawyer. "The only thing that worries me," she said, "is whether I took Stockton's name off the policy."

"Shouldn't be a problem," Red said. "If there's a hitch, I'll handle it for you."

Her eyes filled with tears.

"You okay?" he asked.

"Everybody's being so nice to me."

"Why shouldn't they?" he said. "Anyone who knows you wants to be nice to you."

"Not Lewis."

"Lewis's difficulties in that regard have nothing to do with you."

Libby hated to cry. It hurt, and the back of her throat was already raw, her sinuses already ached. She put her head in her hands.

Red smoothed her hair. "Lewis is a fool," he said. "A *total* fool."

Libby, surprised by the force of Red's words, pulled back to look at him.

"Aw, c'mon," he said. "It's no secret, Libby. Hell. Ever since the day Lewis made a date with you, I've been kicking myself for not getting there first. Not that I deserve the time of day. But I am grateful for the time you give me."

This made her cry even harder, only this time it didn't feel so bad. Less bitter, as if she were a fountain of pure emotion. Red put his hand under her chin and lifted her face. All she could think was how blotchy and swollen she must look. She ducked her forehead against his shoulder. His hand slid over her hair again, a caress so comforting and tender that she sobbed aloud. Red kissed the side of her head and she lunged up, out of her chair, wrapped her arms around his neck, and kissed him on the lips.

He clearly thought it was just a friendly buss, but she insisted, mashing her opened lips against his. Let him be shocked. After a very long moment—long enough to understand she was probably making a total fool of herself—his arms rose up and encircled her, and he actively began to kiss her back.

They stopped, each took a breath, and then *he* kissed *her*: calmly, nicely. How had she never noticed his lips were beautiful, full and pale? She thought, fleetingly, she might actually pass out from all the emotions rampaging inside her, then remembered Huey Labette's zydeco song "Fat Guys Are Great Kissers." This made her smile mid-kiss, which Red felt. They stopped, pulled apart, his eyes amused and electric-blue. She sat back down in her chair. "Yikes," she said.

"Likewise," he said.

"Sorry."

"Don't be," he said.

"Don't look at me. My face is blotchy."

"Not too bad."

"At least I stopped crying," she said, and reached for his hand, which he gave over. They held hands, a moment of insane happiness. Truly insane. "I'm probably certifiable right now."

"I feel pretty good myself," said Red.

Whole geographies were shifting inside her, washed by tidal waves of fear. She retrieved her hand.

"I wish Billie would get back, because I have no idea what to say or do next," she said. "Can we talk a little more about the insurance?"

"Sure." Red smiled at her.

She dug in her purse. "I thought I should take this before anybody else saw it." She held her fist under Red's face. Opening her hand, she revealed the fuse, exploded through its tinfoil casing.

Red closed his eyes. "Libby," he said, "how long did you leave that thing in your box?"

"Just a few days, I think."

"I'd say more like two weeks."

"Don't go bawling me out."

"I'm not bawling anybody out. I'm just amazed. You better give it to me." He went to pluck it from her palm, but she was quicker, and shoved it back in her purse.

"What do you want it for, anyway?" she asked.

"As your legal counsel, I want to be sure it's in the right hands."

Billie returned, sliding her chair out and sitting down. "Rogelio found a company to haul your trailer away. Is Thursday morning okay?"

"Fine," Libby said. "If the insurance inspector gets there by then."

Billie lifted her burrito, paused. "What's going on? Did I miss something?"

Libby lowered her forehead to the tabletop.

"Billie," Red said. "Eat your lunch."

She obediently took a bite, and started talking with a full mouth. "If what I think is happening *is* happening, you have to let me know. I got fifty bucks riding on you two over at the grocería."

"Eat," said Red.

Libby, her face resting on the cool Formica, confronted these questions: Can a person change just like that? Can Red Ray go from being the fat old sidekick to someone's favorite living thing?

N L.A. it was the dregs of summer. Ninety-five degrees, with filthy, red-brown air and yellowing lawns. Never was Lewis so happy to see smog, and traffic, and poor Central American boys selling maps to the stars' homes on Sunset Boulevard. In fact, only the stoplights bugged him. From Round Rock, it was four miles to the nearest stoplight, in downtown Rito; from Rito, another nine miles to the first Buchanan light. In Westwood there were stoplights on every corner, every few hundred yards something telling him what to do.

His philosophy professor's house was barely visible from the street. Set back, shaded by enormous oaks, overgrown with ivy and shrubs, this was what real estate agents called a "hideaway charmer," the perfect choice for an academic embarking on a second marriage with his student bride.

The yard was dusty, the leaves pinched from lack of water; hollyhocks were brown and long on the stalk. Ivy climbed over oak trees, camellia bushes, porch supports, alike. Sam's vintage yellow-and-white Rover was in the driveway, its right fender battered and rusting from when he'd gone after it with a hammer one morning after it refused to start one time too many. Ringing the doorbell, Lewis could hear a television or radio humming loudly within. When nobody answered, he walked around to the side, tapped on the kitchen window. No response. The back door, however, was open.

His professor was asleep on the sofa in the living room, the TV blaring a talk show. A glass sweated on the end table.

"Yo, Sam," Lewis said.

Sam opened his eyes. "Lewis," he growled. "Shit, man." He stood up, stretched for half a second, then walked over to give him a hug. Sam was a hugger. He was okay at it, nothing clingy or sexual. Like you were on his baseball team. Still, Lewis's skin constricted: the guy reeked.

"When did you blow in?"

"Today. It was time to come home."

"Terrific. Great to see you. I hope you're staying here." Sam picked up his sweating glass, drained it. "What do you want to drink?" Starting for the kitchen, he spoke over his shoulder. "Amanda's gone, by the way."

Lewis followed him. "On a trip?"

"Gone." Sam stood at his kitchen counter and gave an unconvincing laugh. He scratched his stomach through his T-shirt. "She fell in love with her boss at the studio. Some asshole hyphenate. That's writer-hyphen-producer." He rubbed his head so his hair stood on end. He looked like a little boy.

"Sorry, man," said Lewis.

Sam shrugged. "At least now you won't have to stay in the garage. You can have her office."

In the kitchen, Sam opened the cupboard where single-malt scotch, rare clear brandies, and private-stock bourbons were lined up like books on a shelf. Lewis stared, not so much with longing as with attention and respect: O *beautiful deadly spirits*.

"What's your pleasure?" said Sam.

"Water's fine."

"That's right," he said. "You've been drying out. There's juice and beer in the fridge." He pointed.

Lewis located a carton of orange juice in a near-empty refrigerator and handed it to Sam.

"I was surprised to hear you're an alcoholic," Sam said. "I mean you *drank*. *I* drink. Hell, we all drink. But I never noticed any problem."

"I had three arrests involving drunkenness."

"Not when you lived here."

"I drank every day," said Lewis.

"Who doesn't?"

"My life was unmanageable. I lived in a garage, for God's sake."

"Only because Queen Bitch wouldn't let you in the house."

"It's more than that," Lewis muttered.

"If you say so." Sam added a short burst of water to his scotch. "I never saw it."

THE NEXT day, after his former boss at the library agreed to give him another chance, Lewis drove over to Sunset to see his friend and fellow Ph.D. candidate Ed Hunkle, who tended bar in the lounge of a large, expensive hotel. Although the adjoining restaurant was busy, the cool, gray bar was empty. Ed threw back his head when Lewis walked in. "Hello, stranger!" he called, and laid a napkin on the bar. "What'll it be? On me."

"Coke," Lewis said.

"*Coke?*"

"I haven't had a drink in almost eight months."

"I'll be darned." Ed squirted Coke from the gun. "So what's new?"

All Lewis could think to say was, "I'm sober"—and hadn't he already said so?

ON SATURDAY night, Lewis drove to Brentwood for an AA meeting that proved to be an intimidating fashion show. The speaker, a studio executive with fourteen years of sobriety, called Alcoholics Anonymous a "womb of love" where people could discover their true human nature as affectionate, compassionate beings. Such talk made Lewis nervous. He remembered that today Lawrence was finally leaving Round Rock, after almost a year's residency. Lewis had missed the standard farewell party with the crummy supermarket cake. He hadn't gathered on the porch with the others to wave napkins and handkerchiefs like so many disconsolate war brides until Lawrence was gone from sight.

"We alcoholics routinely, constantly, save each other's lives," the speaker said. "If that's not love, I don't know what is." Lewis slipped out before the closing prayer.

Sunday morning, Lewis read the paper and waited for Sam to appear. He wanted to take him out to breakfast. At noon, Lewis left the house alone, ate eggs in a coffee shop, then walked past closed shops down Westwood's littered streets. He took himself to a movie, a thriller, and when he came out, the fog had rolled in. A gloomy darkness fell fast.

Back at the house, Sam was watching a news program. During a commercial, he stood up. "Want a beer?"

"No, thanks."

"Can't you drink beer?" he called from the kitchen.

"It's got alcohol, Sam."

Lewis had forgotten how much avid drinkers despise those who refuse their hospitality. Back in his own drinking days, Lewis always took any trace of abstention personally; anything short of whole-hog swilling, in fact, was the equivalent of a moral rebuke.

Sam returned with a fresh drink. "So tell me about you and Amanda," he said.

"What's to tell?"

"She turned on you."

"You could say that."

"You ball her?"

"Sam."

"She turns on everyone she balls."

"I didn't ball her."

"You can tell me. I don't care."

"There's nothing to tell."

"I wouldn't get mad. I already know you balled her."

"Can we change the subject, Sam?"

"I won't throw you out. I'm just trying to get the complete picture of my fucked-in-the-ass marriage."

Delving any further into such a sensitive and personal matter with a drunk person didn't seem wise—or avoidable. Without another word, Lewis went to bed. It was eight-thirty. The small office smelled of burnt dust. He raised the blinds, intending to open the window. Long arms of ivy had snaked in behind the screen and across the glass as if desperate to get inside. The window itself was painted shut. He lay on top of his sleeping bag in his underwear and slid into a sticky sleep, a pit of dreams swarming with police, glass elevators, and an old lady in a blue dress who gave tours of Hell. He woke to the tell-tale clink-glug-splash of Sam making a scotch-and-water; by the digital clock it was 4:04 in the morning. Pulling on pants, rolling his clothes and books into the sleeping bag, Lewis waited until the kitchen was silent and carried everything down to the Fairlane. In a black sky, stars glinted dully like chips of cloudy ice. The weather had shifted and Lewis was chilled. The Fairlane's heater spewed the dry citrus smell of the Santa Bernita Valley. He stopped for gas in Pacoima and pulled on a clean T-shirt. In forty minutes, he was in Rito. He decided against stopping at the Mills and drove directly to Round Rock.

All I want to do is kiss him, Libby wrote. *He's such a good, patient kisser. He came to my bedroom last night under the pretext of seeing the upstairs of Billie's house. (Billie said, I'll just stay downstairs and read a big, fat book,* The Rise and Fall of the Third Reich.) *We started kissing and unbuttoning a few things. He was very sweet, checking with me each step of the way. I was practically dragging him on, then he put a hand on my bare breast and the panic hit like someone was standing over us screaming:* Toying with this poor sad man—What the hell are you doing?

I said, Maybe this is too much too fast.

Red removed his hand. Fastened my bra and buttoned my shirt.

I need to stick to kissing for a while, I said.

I can live with that, he said.

Red's body is so expansive and meaty after Lewis's skin and bones—an armchair versus a wooden folding chair. I know I shouldn't make comparisons, but just Thursday, three days ago, I was in Lewis's bed.

Red said, I'm not in any hurry. Two months, six months, whatever you need.

Six months! I said, One month seems like an eternity, considering how much I already like to kiss you.

Red laughed. I think we both need to get used to this idea.

A month, we decided then, for just kissing. A month minimum. After a month, says Red, we can renegotiate.

RED MADE a late-night call to Doc Perrin. "I've done something I think you should know about," he said.

"You're interrupting Koppel," said Perrin. "This better be good."

Overcome by muteness, Red listened to emphysemic squeaks followed by a lengthy sigh.

"Let me guess," growled Perrin. "You bought yourself a puppy."

RED RAY! Same shell-pink skin, cornflake freckles. Same barrel chest hauling a gut. "Hey, Redsy!" Lewis, crouching in front of a small fire in the office's hearth, looked up and grinned. "How ya doing?"

"Thank God it's you," said Red. "I smelled the smoke. . . ." He put a hand on his heart and nodded to the flames. "Guess I'm a little jumpy after Libby's fire."

As Lewis watched, the friendliness in Red's face receded. "What?" he said.

"You tell me."

"I went to L.A. for a couple days. Now I'm back."

Red waited, hovering.

"I didn't drink if that's what you're so worried about."

"It crossed my mind."

"I even went to an AA meeting. Jesus, you should've seen it. Rock 'n' roll. Fashion-model city. Everybody in black leather. I kept spotting people I thought I knew, only they were famous actors."

Red continued to gaze dispassionately at him.

"What, I can't take a couple days off?"

Patient and merciless, Red loomed over him, and Lewis, suddenly uneasy, stood and walked around the desk. "Okay, I know I fucked up. And I'm sorry. I had to blow Libby off. We were breaking up. I couldn't go running to her like nothing was wrong. That would've only got her hopes up, don't you see?"

"What happens between you and Libby is your business."

"That's not what you said the other day! You practically guilt-tripped me over there! I couldn't handle the disapproval."

"Are you going to leave every time I disapprove of something?"

"I came back, didn't I?" Lewis was plaintive. "You're yelling at me now, and I'm staying put."

"I'm not yelling, Lewis."

Lewis picked up a stick of orangewood and poked at the fire, which collapsed. "Okay, okay. But I learned my lesson. I can't go back there. My philosophy professor drank around the clock. I mean, what can you say when someone thinks two doubles an hour is moderate?"

"When you take off like that," Red said evenly, "you leave everyone in the lurch. It's one thing that there was no coffee at the union hall meeting Friday night. But then, people wanted to know: Where's Lewis? Is he okay? Is he coming back? We were pretty damn worried about you."

"Why do you think I came back? I felt like shit, too. I'll make amends to the meeting and everybody. What more do you want?"

When Red frowned, Lewis prepared for the worst: would Red tell him to move back to the Blue House, start all over again as a lowly resident?

"I want you to take things in order, Lewis," Red said finally. "Amends are made *after* an inventory."

"*Yeah?*"

"I want you to write your inventory, the way I assigned it to you. I'll give you one month." He walked behind the desk to lift a page of the master calendar. "If you don't have it done by Tuesday, October twelfth, I'll have to let you go."

Lewis gave a short cough of laughter, and didn't point out that this was actually five weeks. "I can't believe you're still hounding me about that dumb inventory. You want it that bad, Redsy? You got it."

THE OLD BASTARDS CLUB, a local group of alcoholism and recovery professionals, was formed four years earlier in response to a crisis at Round Rock Farm. Doc Perrin had called the meeting to rally support for Red Ray. Staff members from Social Model Detox, the Alcohol Hot Line, and the AA Central Office gathered at the union hall in Buchanan.

Red had spoken first that night. He was exhausted, he said. The last suicide at the farm had taken the starch out of his sails. This was a great guy, well liked, who'd borrowed Red's shotgun to shoot a rattlesnake in the vegetable garden and then blew his brains out in the groves. Red was fed up and furious. And he couldn't even remember the last time he'd told anybody what was really bothering him; at the Blue House meetings, he shared only strength and hope with the newcomers. He'd been ignoring his own recovery, kept mum about his own problems, and now everything had reached such a pitch.

His outburst broke the ice, and for the rest of the night, all the sober-forever do-gooders talked about *their* troubles: wanting to drink, hating God, their difficulties with forming strong human attachments. Such mutual discovery made everyone unreasonably happy. The meeting didn't break up until after midnight, and only then after everyone had agreed to meet again. They'd done so ever since, as the Old Bastards Club, on the first Monday of every month.

Tonight, Julie Swaggart led the meeting. Her new recovery house was doing well; she'd instituted yoga classes, group meditation, bake sales.

Red braced his forehead against his hand, averting his eyes. He was glad Julie was thriving, and he should ask her about the yoga. But he couldn't stop worrying—about Libby and Lewis, and mostly about his own inappropriate behavior.

When he'd told her Lewis was back, Libby couldn't speak, her face so wan that it frightened him.

"Give me your hand," she'd said. "Say I don't have to give you up."

"You don't have to give me up. Unless you want to."

She held his hand to her face. "Did you tell him about us?"

"The opportunity didn't come up. And even if it had, I wanted to talk to you first. I don't think *we're* sure what's happening here."

"We don't owe him any explanations."

"We should say something eventually," Red said. "I'm not going to force anything, though. It's too fresh."

Now, in the Old Bastards meeting, he faced one irrefutable fact: when you sponsor a man, you don't move in on his girlfriend.

Red's angst did not pass unnoticed. At the break, Doc Perrin seized his arm—"Okay, lover boy. Outside"—and escorted him to the front steps. The fog was thick, the street lamps haloed in purple. "Spill your beans," Perrin said.

"The boyfriend's home."

"And the girlfriend scampered back?"

"No, no, not yet."

"Smart gal. So what's the problem?"

"I'm his sponsor, for God's sake," Red finally got to say it, and to someone who understood that bond. "And I finessed his girl."

"Does she want him back?"

"I don't know. I don't think so."

"Does he want her back?" asked Perrin.

"If so, he hasn't said anything about it."

"You sleeping with her?"

"No."

"You proposed marriage yet?"

"Of course not."

"What the hell have you done that's so goddamn momentous?"

"Kissed."

"*Kissed?*"

"And agreed to something, I suppose."

"Agreed to what, exactly?"

Red winced at the thought of describing what was still unspoken with Libby. "To try . . . I don't know . . . to love each other."

"Ahh. And it's gotta be this kid's ex-girlfriend?"

Miserable, staring at the ground, Red couldn't deny it.

"Congratulations," Perrin said. "I been waiting ten, eleven years for you to become human. Hallelujah! Welcome to life, in all its messy, tangled splendor." The old doctor threw a bony arm across Red's back and planted a sloppy kiss on Red's cheek.

"Feh," said Red. After all these long, lonely years, why was everyone kissing him *now*?

SUMMER mustered a final blast, vanquishing the early autumn chill with a heatwave of almost unendurable dryness and clarity. The air trembled like a dog trying to behave. Heat ignited the aroma of sage in the chaparral, the spicy, slightly rotten citrus dust in the orchards. Throughout the valley, people complained of bad sinuses, itchy eyes, and extended sneezing attacks.

David Ibañez was in town again, staying with his uncle. Both he and Rafael suffered from terrible hay fever and nursed cups of a naturally decongesting tea made from the mahuang plant, brewing more tea for anyone else who needed some. David had brought the mahuang seeds from an herbalist in Shanghai, and Rafael kept a good crop of the low, scrubby bush in his yard at all times. He said it was the best hay fever treatment he knew, and whenever Santa Ana weather kicked in, he was the most popular man in the valley.

David's aunt Gloria was actually fond of this dry weather, since it reminded her of meeting Rafael. She was fifteen and living in L.A., in Lincoln Heights, when she'd fallen in love with an older man. After her sisters saw this man with another woman, her parents forbade her ever to speak to him again. Heartbroken, she couldn't get out of bed, and wept for weeks, until her parents finally sent her to the country, to her aunt's house on the Sally Morrot ranch. Rafael Flores lived in the next bungalow. He was eighteen, and *no muy feo,* said Gloria; but it was summer and there were Santa Anas, as now, and he was sneezing day and night. He sounded, she said, like a drowning man crying for help. And she could hear him snoring all night long. Although everyone was hoping the two of them would fall in love, Gloria said that wouldn't happen until chickens could fly and vests grow sleeves. "But then," she said, "it rained—in the middle of August, if you can believe it!—and Rafael stopped sneezing and he stopped snoring, and when I lay in bed at night, the world seemed far too silent and empty."

LEWIS woke in the mornings with a sore throat, his aching face tender to the touch. Yet he was champing to get to work, continue the long slow crawl back into Red's good graces. In a sense, it was a relief to have relinquished the favored-son status and all its attendant pressures. Red was holding back—no more meals together, no more late-night chats—until the inventory materialized, and who could blame him? Lewis himself knew it was a crap shoot.

First of all, Lewis had trouble with the categories: Fears, Resentments, Money, Sex, and Secrets had too much overlap. Working at Karmachanics, for example, he'd changed spark-plug wires and charged for engine work—did that fall under Secrets or Money? The majority of his Secrets also could be listed under Sex. It was all too confusing! Then, when he sat down to write, all he truly confronted was throbbing sinuses.

THE WINDS started up and blew all night. Old limbs fell from trees, and thousands of ripe grapefruit bounced on the ground, a ponderous, yellow hail. In front of the Blue House, fronds hurtled like kamikaze pilots from the sixty-foot palms. By day, the world was a shambles and preternaturally quiet, the sky a dry, blue ache.

Red finally gave Lewis half a Sudafed. This antihistamine, the first drug Lewis had taken in almost nine months, made him deliciously sleepy. He put his head on the desk and swam in near-sleep for over an hour until the office door burst open with a bang. Billie Fitzgerald entered with her head thrown back, blood streaming down her neck and soaking into her collar. *"Nosebleed!"* she yelled.

Lewis guided her into an armchair. He knew how to treat nosebleeds. Once, when he was in college, he went to pick up his grandmother for a drink at Lloyds of Loden. But when he entered her house, it looked like someone had thrown cups of blood all over her face and kitchen. He made her lie down on the floor and packed ice on her nose; then blood started running from the corners of her mouth. Terrified, he drove her to the emergency room, where a nurse promptly scolded him. "Don't *ever* make someone with a nosebleed lie down. Do this," she said, and pinched his nose so hard, tears squirted from his eyes.

"Forgive me," Lewis said, grabbing Billie's nose. Her eyes snapped open in alarm. She tried to tilt her head back, but he held it in place. "Don't," he said. "Or the blood will run down the back of your throat."

"You bastard," she said, her voice hoarse and full of self-pity.

"Shhh . . ." His hand was dark like a savage's against her face. The sight of blood made him faintly nauseous and dissociated; his lips began to buzz and he sat down on the arm of the chair. Billie's springy black hair was in a sloppy French twist. She glared at him sideways. Yet her upper arm was wedged against his thigh, generating heat. Was she actually leaning into him? "Remember to breathe," he said, trying to discourage an erection. He demonstrated a deep inhalation and they breathed together.

Her beeper went off but he held her in place by the nose. "It can wait," he said. She settled back against his thigh—there was no doubt now, she was snuggling—and he held her there for as long as was credible, four or five minutes, before letting go.

She daubed at her nose with the back of her sleeve, leaned forward. No blood came out. "Huh!" she said. "Hey, thanks." She stood up cautiously. "This fucking wind. Can I use the phone?"

Giddy, Lewis wandered around the office until she hung up.

"I have to run." She came around and grasped his wrist. Her eyes emitted raw wattage. "Wish we had more time to talk," she said. "I'm dying to hear how *you're* faring in this soap opera."

"Soap opera? Oh, you mean with Libby."

"Aren't you a cool cucumber." She gave his arm a rousing shake. "Still, your ego's got to be a little bruised."

"I know I'm an asshole, if that's what you mean."

She worried his arm again. "We'll talk. Definitely. Thanks for the first aid."

His right hand was mottled with her blood. Moist and red in the creases of the palm, it turned brown, grainy as it dried. These cells, he told himself, had strained through her liver, run fast through her heart, engorged the walls of her womb, and wound up here, on him, a form of concentrated, indecipherable knowledge.

EVERY time he set foot out of the Mills, Lewis checked to see if the coast was clear. He stayed out of Happy Yolanda's even if the Falcon was nowhere in sight. What he feared more than a scene was a rapid, if temporary, reconciliation that would land them right back in the sack. Libby was incapable of holding a grudge—Lewis already knew that. Not that he would have minded another turn on that pony ride. He just didn't want to start up again with her if he had any chance at all with the Princess Fitzgerald.

He saw Libby one afternoon from a window in the office storeroom. She and Red were across the road, peering underneath first one bungalow, then another, apparently studying the foundations. The heat had broken and Libby wore a denim jacket, her hair was in a ponytail. She looked exactly like herself, which made Lewis a little sad. He all at once remembered her warm skin, her leveling looks, her generous assessments of his character.

Lewis dug through boxes for mailing labels and, finding them, gave a final look outside. Red was pointing to something up on the ridge that Libby couldn't see, so he nudged her into his line of sight. She nodded, and Lewis could hear a distant scrap of her laughter. Red then dropped his arm around Libby's shoulder and gave her a paternal squeeze. That she clearly required and accepted such gestures of comfort—still, so many weeks later—evoked in Lewis a wave of pure, bone-melting guilt. He grabbed the labels and fled.

Red is giving me a house, Libby wrote, *very similar to his own.* She paused. Exactly what this gift implied, she and Red hadn't discussed. She'd have a house on her property, he'd have one on his; it was, she thought, like evening up the sides before the contest began.

At any rate, she needed a house. She couldn't live forever at Billie's, and she couldn't move in with Red, not yet. To own her own square footage of personal sanctuary couldn't hurt. And no matter what happened with Red—be it true love or a mutual or one-sided waning of interest—she would have a home. And that, she supposed, was the point.

She called a bulldozer man to regrade the site Stockton had surveyed. She called a house mover and applied to the county office for a house-moving permit. The house had to be moved between midnight and five a.m., when it wouldn't impede traffic. Since this trip was only three miles on rural roads, the escort requirement was waived. Then the house mover said he didn't want to lose a night's sleep, so couldn't he do the job on Sunday evening? Back to the permit office, then, for another waiver.

THE FIRST Sunday softball game ended at noon. Doo-dads 21, Shitheads 14. Lewis, once and always a Shithead, left amid the pleas and boos of teammates, who wanted him to stick around for game two. "Some of us," he told them, "have inventories to write."

He locked himself away in his room at the Mills. He crawled into bed and wrote two entries in the Money category before his mind went blank. He didn't want to lose his job. No doubt his past was littered with crimes both grave and inconsequential; they just weren't lining up for inspection. He thought a little nap might help.

He woke up after three in the afternoon, the room hot as a greenhouse. And he was out of cigarettes. Face swollen, hair smashed and linty, he sleepwalked barefoot across the street and smack into a late-afternoon coffee klatch at the grocería: Victor behind the register, Arvill Hartwood and Deputy Burt McLemoore perched on stools, and Billie Fitzgerald on the counter, swinging her muddy rubber boots.

Conversation stopped when Lewis entered. Victor's eyes danced. Billie's fabulous eyebrows inched in place. Lewis stepped between Arvill and Billie. "Camel straights," he said, putting down his money.

Billie nudged his thigh with her boot. "Good pillow perm."

He ignored her. Out on the sidewalk, he opened the pack. Two dogs were asleep in the middle of Main Street, a black Lab and a red dachshund. The afternoon was breezy, and when he tried to light a cigarette, Victor's cheap-ass matches, one after another, wouldn't stay lit.

"You mad at me?" Billie bumped up against him. "Sorry if I insulted your do." She reached to ruffle his hair.

He dodged her hand.

"Cranky, aren't we?"

"Not in the mood for this town." His next match caught and he exhaled smoke. Billie was in dusty gray coveralls, her hair lumpy under a black baseball cap. "Pretty high-fashion yourself," he said.

"On my way to check a couple irrigation pots we mended yesterday up by the lake. Try some water in 'em and see if the fuckers still leak." She pointed to her hulking white truck. "Feel like taking a ride?"

"Got work to do," he said. They started moving anyway. At least he could walk her to her truck.

"So, how's it going?" she asked. Friendly, no edge.

He looked behind him, toward the Mills. The dachshund had left the Labrador retriever and was trotting up toward the stoplight. "No complaints."

At her truck, she knocked on the hood. "Come on, hop in. Won't take an hour."

He shot another look behind him. The dachshund stopped at the intersection, then executed a perfect left turn—left lane to left lane, just like a car. Lewis climbed into the cab as Arvill and Burt came out of the grocería.

"Libby still staying at your house?" he asked.

"You want information about Libby, ask Libby."

"I don't want information about Libby," Lewis muttered. "I was just wondering how this is going to sit with her—you and me in one truck—because she'll hear about it in about five minutes."

"Why should she care?"

"Yeah." They were passing the Mills. "Good point."

Billie drove slowly, although the truck's V-12 engine could've hauled the whole town into another state. "We'll go cross-country," Billie said, "if you don't mind," and a mile out of town she turned between two huge round river rocks into the groves. They bumped along even more slowly, the windows down. Fumbling in a box of tapes, she handed him one—Mozart's Sinfonia Concertante for Violin and Viola—to stick into the tape player. The orchestral introduction blazed from the speakers, magisterial, perfect.

Billie turned down the volume. "You having second thoughts about Libby?"

"Naw. It's just chickenshit how I handled it."

"So you're not jealous?"

"Why should I be?"

Billie grinned, then spoke in singsong, "Oh, I don't know."

"Is she seeing someone?"

"You haven't heard?"

"No. But good for her if she is." That someone else—by his estimation, Arvill—now had sexual access to Libby didn't thrill him. He gave his head a good scratch, then stretched his arm along the back of the truck's bench seat, his fingers inches from Billie's neck.

"Don't you want to know who?" said Billie.

He could see she was dying to tell him. "No. Just so long as she's happy."

Billie gave him a funny look. "Aren't you curious?"

"If I was that curious, I'd probably still be seeing her."

"What went wrong with you guys, anyway?"

"Nothing. Ultimately, I wasn't all that interested."

"You must not have gotten to know her."

"I knew her, all right."

"What did you know about her?"

"All sorts of things."

"Like what?"

"You know. Sexual things."

"Ahh." Billie's lips curved into a smile. She slowed to a crawl over a patch of washboard ruts.

"And other stuff," he said.

"Yeah?"

"She's a talented musician. She has an okay mind."

"Just okay?"

"You writing a book?"

Billie smirked and rolled her eyes. The violin and viola took turns saying the same thing in different clefs. They came out of the groves, crossed a canal on a reverberative wooden bridge, and dove back into dark foliage, cold shade.

"Libby's a good person," said Lewis. "She was born good. It's her temperament. Life's no big struggle for her. She accommodates, adjusts, goes with the flow. But she lacks the kind of empathy you find in someone who's really suffered. I couldn't connect with her on a deeper level. Intellectually, she's obviously bright and capable. But some people have more interesting, complicated minds, and bring more intelligence to everyday living."

Lewis touched Billie's ear so gently, he wasn't certain she felt it. "I need someone who's intellectually nimble," he said. "Who's emotionally and spiritually aware. Someone more . . ." He searched for a word.

" 'Tweaked'?" said Billie.

He laughed. "That'll do."

Billie raised her eyebrows as she navigated a series of deep ruts. "You two never did strike me as the *best* match," she said.

"Why, did you have a better one in mind?"

"For her or for you?"

"Ha! Exactly." Fine black curls clung to the back of Billie's neck. With his thumb, he nudged one, and traced the cording of muscles below her ear. "I like quick, complex, one-of-a-kind minds," he said.

As the violin and viola teased each other through a cadenza, they crossed a road that was either the Round Rock road or a paved spur down to the river. Lewis withdrew his hand, letting it rest on the seat back. They entered another grove on something less than a road and bounced grandly on those thousand-dollar shock absorbers as if on great swells at sea. The second, slower movement of the concerto began. The shade was submersive as water. Dried weeds brushed the underside of the truck's chassis.

"You don't ever get lost back in here?"

Billie didn't reply, and they climbed back into sunlight on a dirt road carved out of the hillside. This road followed the folds of the ridge for maybe a mile, dropping back into trees and rising to hug the hill again. "I still don't have a drip system in these older groves," Billie said. "Until I do, it's one pot after another crapping out."

She stopped a good twenty yards above the orchards. The irrigation pots in question, small, squat cement cylinders extruding four spouts, resembled crude ancient fountains.

"Should I wait here?" Lewis asked, not keen to climb barefoot down the steep embankment.

"I gotta be down there until they fill. Could take fifteen, twenty minutes," she said. "Come on."

He followed gingerly. He'd gone barefoot all summer, his feet were toughened up, but this clay was bristling with small sharp rocks. By the time he reached the first pot, Billie was on her way to the next one, four rows away. He hurried to catch up. Water gushed up from the bottom of the second pot until it closed over itself, swallowed its own roar. The smell of wet concrete dilated his memory, bringing to mind wet sidewalks and playgrounds, the dankness of large, holy places.

He turned to face Billie. The zipper tab on her coveralls glinted like an insect wing. He pulled it down to reveal a man's heavy blue and white plaid shirt. He reached inside and threaded his arms around Billie's waist. She was still as a tree. He remembered to breathe. He put his face against hers. Her arms slid up around his neck and locked.

She started moving against him then, and there was nothing subtle or slow about her desire. Her tongue entered his mouth, a strong, wet muscle. His arms were tangled in her clothes. She slammed herself against him, again and again. He stumbled backward, stepped on something sharp, couldn't regain his footing. They went down rolling. Blue sky flickered by, and the crude terrazzo of rock chips in pink adobe clay. They rolled into the moist shade of a citrus tree, lemon or grapefruit, Lewis couldn't tell. She was on top, sucking his tongue as if drawing water from a rag. He tried to roll her over, wanting to get his bearings, to be on top. She almost allowed it, but as he was rising over her, she shifted her weight—she must have known some kind of Eastern self-defense—and again, she stretched above him, smiling wickedly.

She'd lost her hat. There were foxtails and stickers in her hair. Her cheek was bleeding. He craned upwards to kiss her. She bit his lip. Tasting blood, he squeezed handfuls of cloth and breast and she arched her back for him to unbutton her shirt. Braless, her breasts wobbled out, far, far larger than he ever dreamed, cubic feet of boneless flesh, the nipples small and dark. What to do with such excess? He cupped them ineffectively; pinched the nipples, sucked on one. Her eyes half-lidded, Billie lapped her tongue at him, a trick he'd seen only in porno movies, and he tried to feel the intended erotic force. She continued to move rhythmically, forcefully against him, her breasts swinging and looming. Desperate to please, to enter the spirit of their grappling, he grabbed crotch, breasts, ass. She grazed teeth along his chin. He felt the skin come up in thin curls.

"You've got condoms, right?" she said.

"Huh?" Lewis struggled to pull back, look at her face. "Are you kidding?" He wasn't entirely sure, at that moment, if he had an erection.

As if she heard his thoughts, Billie grabbed his dick and, assessing it, frowned. "No condoms? Is that what you're saying?"

"I don't even have shoes on! Jesus! I went to the store for a pack of cigarettes. I didn't expect this."

"No?" Her hair formed a dark bower around his face. She kissed him sweetly, for which his heart lunged in gratitude. She hovered, panting into his mouth. "Libby said the best thing about you was that you took care of the rubbers."

"*What?*" He scrambled in the dirt in a useless effort to turn her over.

"Don't worry," she whispered, "I got some in the truck."

"Here?" he said idiotically.

"In the glove compartment." She leaned over as if to kiss him, bit his lips, and gave his wilted dick another efficient squeeze. "Better work on that. I'll be right back." She lifted herself off of him, revealing empty blue sky, weak autumnal sun. "You wait here."

Lewis sat up, stunned. His matches had fallen out of his pocket. He gathered them, and Billie's hat, and gazed stupidly at the hat's tree-nursery logo. From the crushed pack, he extricated a cigarette. His hands were shaking. His knuckles were bleeding. Scratches cross-hatched his arms. He was fearful, exhilarated, jangled. This was not what he expected, and yet a certain gratification twanged: Billie Fitzgerald did want to fuck him. Could he go through with it? Her style wasn't at all what he would've guessed. He took a deep breath. Sure, he told himself, I'll fuck her hair straight. He tried to light his cigarette, match after match, as the truck started up back behind him somewhere. Smart, he thought, she's moving it closer. Mozart flew through the air like beautiful laundry. His cigarette lit and nicotine entered his brain like a cloud of cleansing sparks. He turned to watch the truck's approach. From this angle, he saw the grinning chrome grille, the wheel, the mighty armature under the front end. Billie drove up even with him, then past. He turned, looked over his other shoulder. The engine idled. She lowered her tinted window. She had a hat on. This confused him: he had her hat in his lap. She was also wearing sunglasses. He sprang to his feet.

"Hey!" he cried, and started up the embankment. Rocks and dirt slid away underfoot. He paused, used her hat to swat stickers off the bottom of one foot. She revved the engine. He looked up.

"Tell me something," she said. "You *really* think you're so much smarter than Libby?" Without waiting for an answer, she hit the gas, and took off.

HE BECAME a connoisseur of orchard floors: some, mulched with shredded prunings, were a pithy mat; others, pink clay imbedded with sharp granite shards; the best were recently irrigated, the moistened adobe plumped up, softened, astringent and cool on his burning feet.

Although he didn't know where the highway was, he couldn't get too lost. The valley floor slanted south, toward the river. If he kept walking he'd come to a road. He needed another cigarette, but his last two matches went out before he got it lit. Instead, he contemplated a month spent pulling an encyclopedia of burrs, stickers, and splinters from the bottoms of his feet. Eventually, at dusk, he came to the lake road—the oiled asphalt warm and silken underfoot. He stuck out his thumb and wasn't surprised when the few cars sped past. After all, he was filthy, barefoot, and his hair, full of debris, stuck out in every direction. He looked precisely like something risen from the orchard floor.

He started down the road to Round Rock in deepening blue twilight, up and down a series of shallow dips. He heard a truck grinding closer; then the beams of its headlights crisscrossed above his head. Coming over the hill, he saw not only the truck but a whole house moving toward him. Clapboard siding, windows shuttered with plywood. He recognized it, of course: a Round Rock bungalow, his old girlfriend's new home. Standing on the shoulder of the road, he watched this slow, twilight procession, regret filling his mouth with the taste of rusty window screens. As the house passed, he had an urge to hop inside. That way, when the house was set down and Libby walked across the porch to open the front door, he could step right up. "Hello, dear."

BILLIE gave a dinner to celebrate the house-moving. Red arrived late, claiming a crisis at the farm. Oh, well, Libby told herself, I might as well get used to it.

Modeled after chapels in California missions, the Fitzgeralds' dining room was a white hall with dark hewn beams overhead and stenciled geometric patterns on the walls. A chandelier held sixty-five candles, which Billie had lit for the occasion. And dinner was more a feast—sea bass with fennel and roasted vegetables, salad with avocado and grapefruit, a spicy steamed persimmon pudding.

Billie was in high spirits. "Why shouldn't I celebrate when the universe coughs up exactly what I want?"

They had coffee in the library, and after Old Bill retired, Libby asked Red up to her room to look at some insurance papers. There were no papers, of course, so they took off most of their clothes and lay down on her bed. She didn't even think he was fat anymore; she saw only his lived-in, fully mature male body and luminous smooth skin. His legs were remarkably strong. Against his considerable chest, she felt tidy, compact. "Remind me again why we're not having sex?" she said.

"Maybe because we want to do it someplace where Billie Fitzgerald doesn't have her ear to the heating vent."

"Oh, that." She nestled on his chest until her nerves calmed and she could hear clearly the hum of his body and its strong central heartbeat.

He gave her back a few absent pats, cleared his throat, then spoke into her hair. "I didn't want to tell you during dinner, but the reason I was late tonight was Lewis."

Libby carefully lifted herself away from his body, which somehow seemed appropriate.

"Apparently, our friend Billie sweet-talked him up to the hills and then ditched him."

"She *what*?"

"He walked to the farm barefoot. His feet were pretty torn up, so I gave him a ride into town."

Absorbing this information, Libby felt an unexpected protectiveness toward Lewis. Then she giggled. "God. You'd think he'd know better than to mess with *her*."

"Strolled right into the bear's cave," said Red.

"Poor Lewis!"

"He'll live," Red said dryly.

"We shouldn't laugh," Libby said, and bit the pillow to stop.

NO SOONER had Red gone home than Billie tapped on Libby's door, let herself in, and climbed onto the bed. "You guys consummating yet?"

"You'll be the last to know."

She lifted the sheets. "I gotta see if there's a wet spot."

Why in the world had Libby ever mentioned that she and Red were waiting? Some misguided notion that Billie would appreciate— or be instructed by—such restraint? Whatever the inflated moral purpose, Libby was now paying dearly for it. "There's something abnormal about your interest in these things, Billie."

"There's something abnormal about two perfectly healthy adults not fucking. Can't Red get it up?"

"You want to tell me what you did to Lewis?"

Grinning, Billie wiped a cloud of hair back from her face. "Yeah. I took him on a little one-way trip."

"But why?"

"Because he was there." She shook Libby's foot through the covers. "And because he can't fuck with my friends and walk away whistling."

"I can fight my own battles."

"Not to my satisfaction."

"Oh, Billie."

"What did you see in him, anyway? He's got a little dick."

"If you'd seen it, you'd know it wasn't little."

"I didn't have to *see* it. It's little."

"Lewis has a perfectly respectable, above-average penis."

" 'Penis'? Listen to you. All those intellectuals have teeny weiners. I knew a Goethe scholar once whose dick was the size of a baby carrot."

"You weren't really messing around with him, were you?"

"What would you care, even if I was?"

The answer was a tangle Libby couldn't begin to unravel—not at this hour of night, nor with this conversationalist. "How'd you get him up there in the first place?"

"He's easy, Libby. I don't want to ruin any sacred memories you might have, but the guy's kind of a dog, if you know what I mean."

"He always had a thing for you," Libby said bitterly.

"Not anymore he doesn't."

"So you drove him out in the hills and made him get out of the truck?"

"We were checking irrigation pots in the tangelo grove and I went back to the truck for a wrench. The old you-wait-here trick. I actually said that. 'You wait here.' And this beautiful inspiration came to me: Why not just leave? You should've seen the look on his face."

"I have to feel a little sorry for him," Libby said. "He was so out of his league."

"I only wish I'd gotten his clothes off first. Made him walk home au naturel."

That unexpected protectiveness again. "Lewis doesn't mean any harm. Not really."

"You're defending him! After how he treated you? That's sick, if you ask me. You dump Red and go back to him, I'll kill you."

"I'd kill myself first."

Trying to sleep, Libby couldn't stop thinking about Lewis, naked, striding through the woods, elusive as wildlife. She felt the old tug his elusiveness engendered. She recalled how he stared at her during sex so that small leaping sensations started up in her stomach and heart; and the expert, authoritative way he handled her body. Only then what? A cup of coffee, a shared cigarette, and back to their separate worlds until *his* desire—forget hers—built back up.

Insomniac, rehashing these old facts, she realized that *this* was the reason she and Red weren't rushing into sex: so her long-legged and saturnine former lover could roam her thoughts a while longer, until she banished him for good. No matter how deeply or urgently she wanted Red, she wasn't quite done with Mr. Fletcher. What more did she want—a final parting, a solemn handshake? Should the occasion to speak with him arise, she doubted she could even be civil. Nevertheless, part of her waited for him, for *something*, like an orphan girl sitting on a back stoop staring down an empty road.

ON HIS next visit to town, during one of his evening rambles, David Ibañez would notice the missing bungalow and ask his uncle what happened to it. "Up Howe Lane," Rafael said.

David walked there through the orchards. The bungalow had belonged to the Rosales family, Octavio and María and their four boys;

Eduardo, a.k.a. Eddy, had been his great friend. Like David's parents, the Rosaleses had used their settlement money to move to East Los Angeles. David had seen Eddy a few months ago; he was married with two teenaged daughters and worked as a lineman for Water and Power.

David slipped up to the empty house and hoisted himself onto the porch. There was a bright three-quarters moon, and through a low, gauzy blue mist he could see lights down among the trees and a brightly lit oil well on the far hill across the valley. Though the bungalow's windows were still boarded up, he could remember the many times he had sat at the rickety wooden table eating beans and grilled corn on the cob and María's handmade tortillas. Who could have imagined then that the Rosaleses' small, tidy home would come, as if airlifted, to this hillside well above the valley floor, to be inhabited by a divorced, violin-playing white woman?

RED HAD assumed—even hoped—that the inventory would never materialize and Lewis would essentially fire himself. Yet here he came, at the last possible moment, loping across the roadway, a fan of paper in his hands.

"Thanks," Lewis said as he came inside. Red didn't know what Lewis was thanking him for; then again, since the incident with Billie, Lewis had been consistently polite and subdued.

Red nodded at the coffee maker. "Fresh pot of mud."

Lewis helped himself and took a chair at the end of the table. "Ready to hear this?"

"You want to read it to me?"

"Sure. Hell, I wrote it for you."

"Let's have it, then."

"I'll start with Fears," said Lewis.

Red had heard so many inventories that the only thing he still found surprising was the candor of the writers. In addition to the standard fears—death, disease, intimacy—grown men had admitted their mortal dread of crossing bridges or riding escalators; accomplished, intelligent men feared that they were transmitters for space aliens, possessed by devils, or turning into wood, or thin air.

Lewis was afraid he'd start drinking again, that he didn't deserve sobriety, that some invisible signal had gone out, and no woman would ever again desire him and he'd spend the rest of his life alone. He was afraid Red would fire him.

Red forced a smile and said, "Good secretaries are too hard to find." He lit a cigarette; the cool air outside drew the smoke through the cracked window in a sinuous white rope. I should tell him now, he thought.

" 'I resent my father,' " Lewis continued, " 'for his taste test approach to families, UCLA for its endless red tape, my philosophy pro-

fessor for drinking, and'—don't get mad, Redsy—'Red Ray, for holding me at arm's length since I got back from L.A.' "

"If you didn't include me," Red said, "I'd know you were lying."

Money was a list of falsified invoices, petty thefts, uncompleted
drug deals, and Sex a litany of impulsive encounters. He'd slept with
his fourteen-year-old stepsister, cheated on his wife, slept with the
wife of his boss at the parts store, with the wife of his philosophy professor in grad school. Pulling his feet onto his chair, Lewis hugged his
knees and admitted to having sex with men, twice, in high school.

"Am I supposed to be shocked?" Red said. "Sorry, but that's been
in every inventory I've ever heard, including my own. Sex with men—
and usually a particularly charming chicken, too."

"Chickens? *Really*?" Lewis threw his head back and exhaled
loudly. "So you don't think I'm really a homosexual?"

"Do I care? You're sure not *my* type."

Lewis laughed long and loudly. Too loudly.

So far, so good, thought Red. Normally, he might've asked why
Libby and Billie weren't mentioned—an inventory should be current—but for this omission Red was inordinately grateful.

Secrets was mostly recap. Lewis had cheated on a final in college.
And once, when drunk, he'd slugged his mother in the mouth. He
told lies. Stole this and that. And for several months when he was
very young—"I still don't understand this one," Lewis said—he'd
used the backyard as his toilet and *didn't bury it*. When confronted,
he blamed it on his brother, Woody. "I don't know why my parents
believed me," he said. "But they sent Woody to a psychologist. Every
week, *for years*, he went to see Dr. Weiss. Makes me sick to think
about it." And Lewis did look pallid, scared, and tenderly young, as
if in this room he'd become the very boy who dropped his trousers
behind the eugenia bushes.

Never, Red knew, was it the ten thousand dollars embezzled from
a business partner, or the drunken slapping of a new bride, but always
this kind of ancient, shame-soaked, thumb-sucking, bed-wetting
memory around which the personality had knotted, kinked, grown
stunted. "It was probably the biggest favor you ever did for your
brother," he said. "At least he got outside help."

"God. I never thought of that."

When Lewis was finished, Red poured him a fresh cup of coffee and squeezed his shoulder. "Good work," he said. "How do you feel?"

"Pretty fucking weird. I thought I'd die before telling this stuff to anyone. And here I am." Lewis patted his own face. "It's almost embarrassing to see it spelled out so clearly. Always wanting the woman I couldn't have, never the one I was with. Just like my dad." Lewis sipped his coffee. "You know what I've been thinking?"

"Mmm." Red gazed out the window at dry, bleached grasses and dark-leaved groves. The sunlight was fragile.

"I was thinking I'd stay on here indefinitely. Work for you. Commute to school a couple days a week. And maybe patch things up with Libby."

Red nodded carefully, trying not to panic.

"All the time I was with her, I thought I liked Billie. My head was screwed on backwards." Lewis smoothed the pages he'd written. "You were right. I had to do this work. See myself more clearly. Get a grip."

Red gazed at his own thumbnails as if into tiny pink hand mirrors.

"I heard she's seeing somebody, but how long could that have been going on?" Lewis shrugged. "She can't be too far up the tubes, can she?"

Red combed his dim Catholic boyhood for guidance: who was the saint of the worst-case scenario? "Lewis," he said, "there's something I need to tell you."

THE HOUSE sat on jacks while masons built a reinforced cinder-block foundation. Libby climbed onto her new porch, which sat some fifty yards above the trailer's former pad. She could see clear over the olive trees and a sea of darker citrus to the distant blue hills. In the foreground she saw the plume of dust from Red's truck winding up her driveway.

She rushed down to meet him. "Look! It's all here!" Taking his arm, she dragged him around the home site, pointing to pilings as if they were the most fascinating lapidary west of Egypt. She found herself tugging. He soon grew sluggish, then rooted. His skin had a grayish caste, a thin film of sweat. "Are you okay?" she said.

"Did Lewis come by?"

"Lewis? No. Why?"

"He and I had a talk this morning."

"Oh, right, I forgot. You heard his inventory. How'd it go?"

"He did a good job. Took a good look at his shortcomings. And now he'd like to get back together with you."

Libby gave a short, unbelieving bark. "Are you serious?"

"That's what he said."

"Did you tell him about us?"

"I felt I had to."

"Thank God! And?"

"I shouldn't have heard his inventory," Red said. "It was a rotten thing to do. I thought I could get away with it."

Libby reached to clasp his face in her hands. "I would've told him myself, but I never had the chance."

Wincing, Red caught her hands, returned them gently to her sides. "He said he loved you, Libby."

She swung away. "That's just another thing he's cooked up in his head." She shaded her eyes and surveyed the crisped, golden-brown hills behind her house. "Oh, I suppose it is gratifying, a little, to know that I don't thoroughly disgust him. Otherwise . . ." She grasped Red's hand and kissed it.

"He quit, of course," Red said. "I stopped by the Mills just now to drop off a check, but he'd already left. Told the desk clerk he was moving back down south. I thought he might've come by here."

"No. And it wouldn't have made any difference if he had."

"I had to tell you what he said, though." Red closed his eyes. "If not, I'd always wonder."

Libby moved to caress Red's face and again he shied away. "Also, he punched me."

"No!"

Red turned to show her the faint dark smudge emerging on his jaw.

Libby grazed it with her fingertips. "This is only nervous laughter," she said, trying to hold it back.

"It *is* funny." Red smiled ruefully.

Libby grabbed the edges of his jacket, pulled his sternum against her forehead. "It's been a month, Red. More than a month. I want to go to your house and lie down with you, skin to skin, no clothes."

She sensed his resistance assembling—a pause, an alertness in his muscles, an intake of breath . . .

"This isn't just a reaction to Lewis. Although I *am* thankful to him." She looked into Red's face. "Without him, I never would've got to know you. He made it easy. You were the one I talked to. You were the one who courted me. Lewis was just a smoke screen: when he cleared out, there you were. And I already loved you." Libby tugged on Red's jacket. "Now," she said.

They drove in his truck without speaking. A few nervous smiles. Hands clutching. Libby felt empty and light. Once inside his bungalow, Red latched the screen door, then closed and locked the kitchen door. He moved down the counter, unplugged the telephone, untangled cords to the matchstick blind above the sink.

"You locking us in," she said, "or them out?"

"Don't ask me."

The blinds fell in a soft clatter and the room filled with reticulated light.

He faced her, his weight resting against the counter, a swimmer about to push off. They looked at each other. Heavy furniture, it seemed, was being dragged around Libby's chest. He's a man, she thought stupidly. And then the panic arrived, the same she'd felt the first time she kissed him, the first time they lay down on a bed together. The panic came in hot waves, scalding, insistent. You can't love him, she told herself. You don't love him. This is just a silly experiment to see how far you two could go. A laugh on Lewis . . .

Red smiled at her with such kindness, her thoughts stopped in their tracks. "The back door's still open," he said.

She smiled too, then thought: Why, he's a played-out loser who stinks of loneliness, a pathetic old drunk.

Red pulled himself away from the counter and was coming toward her, slowly. But I like this man, she told herself. I want this.

Red put one hand lightly on her hip, twisting her around until he was standing behind her. They started walking and her panic redoubled with such force, she grabbed for the doorframe between the kitchen and the bedroom. *Was* she just toying with him?

Red waited as she steadied herself. The same sorts of doubts had assailed her as she stood in the church narthex waiting to join Stockton at the altar, and had made her withdraw into sarcasm when Lewis behaved tenderly. They were the protests of a frightened, atrophied virgin dwelling in some coal bin of her psyche who spoke up only to rail against the invasion of love.

Red's hands were lightly on her hips, and they were moving again, into the bedroom. There was his bed, the comforter in its brown paisley cover, the pillows at odd angles. And the back door—such an easy leap! She imagined the cold, ridged roundness of the doorknob, the sudden abyss of daylight and vivid blue sky.

She took a long breath and spun instead within Red's fingertips: a neat, perfect ballroom spin. He was smiling and she kissed him, gingerly because of his bruised jaw. As he lifted her onto the bed, she knew this was the most serious, and most adult, and most appropriate thing she had ever done.

TWO

DAVID IBAÑEZ, now forty-one years old and seventeen years sober, worked at the Villa de San Miguel Arcángel, a clinic for the alternative treatment of chronic pain in Tijuana. He'd been at the Villa for four years now, and had moved in with the woman who ran it, Pauline.

The clinic employed a variety of pain specialists: an M.D. from India with a vast knowledge of Tibetan medicine, two yoginis, a hydrotherapist, a hypnotherapist, a *curandero* named Olivero who'd attended chiropractic college in Utah, and David, who practiced his own syncretic mix of tantric medicine, acupuncture, and *curanderismo*.

In early May, when Olivero was at a conference in Dallas, David met with his clients. One old woman came in with severe headaches, and David treated her with acupressure, herbs, and prayers. Reading David's treatment notes upon his return, Olivero became agitated. The old woman, he said, was a *bruja* very unfriendly to his village. She'd already given cancer to one member of his family, and made his niece go blind. Olivero worried that she'd taken something of his—a photograph from his desk, a business card, anything she could use for *mal puesto*, evildoing.

David assured him that they'd met in his office, while Olivero's was locked up tight. Still, Olivero would not be pacified. Did she say anything odd? Had she given David anything out of the ordinary? David said no, no, she'd paid him with a few pesos and a small cake. This wasn't unusual: poorer clients often paid in fresh eggs, tamales, fruit, whatever they had of value.

"What kind of cake?" Olivero wanted to know. "Was there anything distinctive or unusual about it?"

"No, no—just a little sweet cake, with the number twenty-one stenciled on it in green sugar."

"Where's this cake now?" Olivero asked.

"I ate it," David said. "I was running behind and hadn't eaten lunch."

"And you're sure it said 'twenty-one' on it," said Olivero.

"A lucky number," David said, "and a lucky cake, since I was so hungry."

This cake was not lucky, Olivero told him, not lucky at all. Most probably it was made with the *veintiuno* herb, which kills a man in twenty-one days.

David had never heard of *veintiuno*, and he wasn't too worried; he felt fine, and besides, many folk herbs and concoctions were placebos. But he did call his uncle and teacher, Rafael Flores, back home in Rito. Rafael didn't answer, and David remembered he'd gone to Arizona for two weeks. David then put in a call to a toxicologist at USC. Yes, the man said, there actually was a poison called *veintiuno*, and a few documented fatalities from it, but not many, and none since the fifties. Nobody knew how or why the herb was fatal: the plant itself contained no known toxins. The poisoned, it seemed, scared themselves to death.

David laughed, relieved by the absence of toxins, and promptly forgot about the *veintiuno* until a week later, when, as he was drawing his long, thick brown hair into a ponytail, a sickening clump fell out in his hands. For the next two days, hair sloughed from his head and terror mounted in his gut. When he called this time, his uncle was home. "You better come on up," Rafael said in English. "The twenty-one can be tricky."

David told Pauline he had urgent family business, loaded Sally, his old bluetick hound, into the Land Cruiser, and drove north. Around Anaheim, he heard a faint rumble in one of the wheels. By downtown Los Angeles, it was a grating noise: a wheel bearing, possibly, if not the whole rear end. Wasn't it natural law that cars always break down only an hour before the repair shops close on Saturday afternoons?

At the Toyota dealership in Glendale, mechanics clucked over the Land Cruiser's advanced age and said obtaining parts could take from two days to two weeks. David's cousins in nearby Atwater gave him a couch to sleep on. He woke up on Sunday morning in their living room, more lost hair forming a detached shadow on the pillow. What I need, he thought, is a meeting.

A woman at the AA Central Office directed him across the Hyperion Bridge to Silverlake. The meeting was called the Night-crawlers Sunday Speaker and it started at noon. Even fifteen minutes early, David had to stand in the back of the overcrowded church auditorium.

IT WAS one of those things that sounded good from four months off—to give a forty-minute talk at the largest of all the Nightcrawler meetings. How would Lewis have known back in February that Lydia would dump him, then leave for Paris on the very date he'd agreed to speak?

A loose-knit AA group Lewis had fallen in with on his return to Los Angeles, the Nightcrawlers were mostly under fifty, mostly actors, artists, and writers who rented the auditorium for daily meetings. Lewis had made a lot of friends there, including Barbara, the woman who'd asked him to speak. An actress with long, curly light-red hair, see-through skin, and the endearing, perpetually worried expression of a pretty little girl squinting into the sun, Barbara was probably his best friend. Though they'd briefly dated, she quickly decided his attentions were too inconsistent. Once they each found someone else, Barbara had offered an avid, demanding brand of friendship. He had resisted—didn't return her phone calls, wouldn't meet for coffee—but she wouldn't relent. Now they spoke daily, in person or by phone. Barbara browbeat him for the details of his life—what was he feeling, thinking, eating?—and he somehow had come to rely on this. She was like an emotional clearinghouse: "So, how do you feel about that?" she'd say, or "This one's for your shrink, I think," or "Maybe Harry could help you there" (Harry being Lewis's present sponsor).

As for this speaking commitment, Barbara refused to let him off the hook; it might even, she said, distract him from self-pity. And she was right: to command the podium, he had to pull himself together or else look like a fool. The group laughed, as they always did, at how he worked Step One thinking he was writing PR material for Round Rock Farm. They gasped hearing how his first sponsor stole his girl-friend. And when he told them Lydia had scuttled, concern flickered in their eyes and he'd had to pause, catch hold of himself, accept the Kleenex Barbara held out.

Afterward, people stood in line to shake his hand. He was numb with relief. Barbara slid up to him and whispered, "Tops," meaning she and a few others were going to the Tops coffee shop and he should meet them there.

"You going back up to Rito today?" said one Latino guy.

"No, no, I haven't been there for years."

"I thought you worked there."

"No, not for almost three years."

"I couldn't hear well way in the back," he said. "But my car broke down and I thought, if you were going up . . . It did seem too good to be true."

"Hey, sorry, man," Lewis said. "Good luck."

By the time Lewis shook every well-wisher's hand, two women had slipped him their phone numbers and three newcomer men had asked for his—all of which might have cheered him up, if he'd wanted anything besides a phone call from Lydia proclaiming her change of heart.

AT TOPS, Lewis found Barbara and a fair sampling of the core Nightcrawlers in a large corner booth.

"Our fearless leader," said an actor named Kip, who moved over to give him a seat.

Celia, a rock singer, spoke in her throaty voice. "I was thinking, Lewis, that maybe you should be a minister." She turned to the others. "Don't you think Lewis would make a good minister?"

"What, was I too preachy?"

"No, no. I didn't mean that." Celia turned to Barbara. "Jesus. I thought *I* twisted things around."

"You *would* make a good minister," Kip said. "You're funny, smart, sufficiently spiritual. You think well on your feet."

"I fornicate, I blaspheme, plus I don't believe in God, per se."

"Who cares?" said Kip. "You're a natural speaker."

"And you cried, Lewis," Celia added. "That was so sweet it killed me. I don't think I've ever seen you cry before."

"Are you kidding?" said Barbara. "He's a total sponge-face."

"When I quit smoking," said Lewis, "I was furious at everybody for about a month, and then I started getting weepy at Pepsi commercials." He sat back so the waitress could pour his coffee. "Although I never actually *cry* cry, much less sob. Just leak from the eyes."

Kip laughed. "And I always love hearing about how your first sponsor stole your girlfriend. That's really rich."

"I say that for effect, but the truth is, I'd already broken up with her."

"So you said. But the body wasn't cold."

"I don't want my friends going out with my ex-lovers," Barbara said. "People should find their own mates, not pounce on your leftovers."

"Did you really punch your sponsor?" Renee was a robust young woman with thick straw-colored hair and clear blue eyes; she looked more like a picture of the right life than a girl who used to unplug the phone, lock her bedroom door, and retire for the weekend with a couple quarts of vodka.

Lewis bowed his head. "It was awful, actually, to boil up so fast. It was like watching someone else. I still feel like shit about it."

"Sounds to me," said Kip, "like you need to make amends to yourself."

"Yeah, well . . ." Steam tumbled upward from Lewis's coffee cup in a small shaft of light.

"So you made amends, right," Renee said, "for hitting him?"

"Renee's about to make her amends—can't you tell?" Barbara, who sponsored Renee, gave her an affectionate glance.

"Good for you," said Lewis. "I didn't start feeling lighter and freer *until* I made my amends. But no, I never did with Red. I like to think that staying the hell away from his girlfriend was amends enough." He tried to laugh, but what came out was a humorless hack. "Look, can we change the subject? Or do we want to spend the rest of the day on what an asshole I am?"

"Hey, hey," said Kip. "We're all assholes here. Isn't this Assholes Anonymous? Or am I in the wrong program?"

Big sighs at this old joke, then the waitress came up to take their food orders. Lewis was too keyed up to eat. He had liked being on the podium, but it wore him out. After three cups of watery coffee, he felt scorched around the edges, and his friends were beginning to look like unflattering caricatures of themselves.

"You okay?" Barbara asked.

"It just caught up with me," said Lewis. "I need a nap." He stood and threw two dollar bills on the table.

Barbara's face darkened. She considered his naps "another place to hide," an escape only slightly less contemptible than drinking.

"I've got to," Lewis told her. "Just a quick one."

"Well, thanks for speaking. You were great, Lewis. I really appreciate it." She stood and put her arms around him and kissed his cheek.

As if suddenly fragile, he walked slowly back to his car. Each time he remembered anything he said at the meeting, it seemed stupid or corny. Had he really snuffled over a woman in front of all those people? *Quel* dope. No wonder Lydia was leaving for Paris without him.

The neighborhood Lewis walked through had Spanish-style homes with red tile roofs and tidy yards. Cars, cleansed from yesterday's rains, sat in driveways. Not a soul was in sight. Sunday: the day of deep family burrowing. Throughout his childhood, other kids couldn't play on Sundays—they had to go to church, visit relatives, sit down to the ritual Sunday supper—and not much had changed. Families and friends were still huddled indoors around hot meals, and here he was skittering through the empty streets, alone and unhinged.

He'd been so good for so long now: sober, well-intentioned, consistent in schoolwork, meditation, AA, returning phone calls and library books, paying taxes, getting his teeth cleaned. The list could go on forever, yet the women he loved still left.

DRIVING across the bridge, who did he see but that man who'd asked him for a ride to Rito. He was walking at a good clip, his jacket flapping.

Lewis pulled over and rolled down the passenger window. "Want a lift?"

"Great, thanks." The man climbed in the car. "I'm staying just a few blocks away." He extended a hand. "David Ibañez."

Lewis shook hands and introduced himself. "You live in Rito?"

"Tijuana. But I grew up in Rito." said David. "On your drunk farm, as a matter of fact. You know the farmworkers' housing on the west end?"

"Yeah! I worked in one of those bungalows. What do you think about your birthplace turning into a drunk farm?"

"I love it. One of God's great jokes. And much better than having it subdivided or paved into an industrial park. I only wish I'd gotten sober there."

"You always could, you know."

David laughed. "I'm not sure I have another recovery in me. Bleeding from the eyes kind of got to me the last time around." He wore a nubbly sport jacket and, under that, a purple knit vest with iridescent hairs and a band-collar dress shirt: beautiful clothes, undoubtedly expensive.

"You sober long?" asked Lewis.

"Seventeen years." David pointed to a Chinese restaurant. "Take a right here, please."

David's destination was a small house on a treeless block. Lewis parked and, suddenly loath to relinquish the company, turned off the engine. "What do you do in Tijuana?"

"I work in alternative medicine. I guess you'd say I'm a healer."

"You mean, like, hands-on healing?"

David lifted his hands. The fingers were long and tapered, the skin an even brown. He flipped the palms up, showing pinker skin with creases like lines depicting rivers on a map. "I use my hands some," he said.

"I always wondered how someone knows they have the power to heal. You just discover it one day?"

"It's more an affinity than a power," said David. "And I grew up in the Mexican healing tradition. My uncle's a *curandero* and he always said I had *el don*, the gift for it."

"And you can actually find jobs doing it?"

"Hospices, holistic health clinics, rehab centers, you name it. A lot of *curanderismo* is very helpful in treating alcoholics and addicts."

"Really?" Lewis had an image of cravings being pulled from the body, hand-over-fist, like thick orange yarn. "How so?"

"Oh, Western doctors constantly misdiagnose certain conditions as flu or depression when it's actually *susto,* a disease of fear that's epidemic in addicts."

Lewis promptly experienced a surge of fear himself; maybe *he'd* never been properly diagnosed. "How do you know if you have it?"

"The symptoms are similar to depression—weight gain or loss, lethargy, irritation, volatility. But *susto* also means loss of soul, and that's what makes it so much more helpful a description than depression. People with *susto* have lost any sense of true or higher self. They react to things only out of fear or guilt or shame."

Lewis tried to keep a keen interest out of his voice. "What's the treatment?"

"Herbs to relax. Conversation to examine the fears. A ritual to cleanse the person and reconnect them to both a higher power and a firmer sense of self."

"Well, I could probably use some of that myself."

"Come on in." David smiled and nodded toward the house. "I've got time. I'll give you a *barrido*—a quick, ritual sweeping. Fix you right up."

"Better yet . . ." Lewis articulated the idea as it occurred to him. "Why don't I drive you up to Rito? It's a great day. I don't have anything to do."

"Oh, I'll rent a car. I'd just thought if you were—"

"Hey, I'm happy to go."

"I wouldn't want to put you out."

"No, really, I'd like to."

"May I bring my dog?"

"Sure," said Lewis.

David went into the house to fetch his things. Alone in the car, Lewis reconsidered his impulsive offer, which obviated once and for all the possibility of intercepting Lydia at the airport, hurling himself at her feet, and begging one more time.

David emerged from the house with a blue blanket, a leather knapsack, and an ancient spotted hound. He spread the blanket over the backseat and helped the dog into the car. A female. White-muzzled, with huge droopy ears and filmy eyes, she gave Lewis a doleful look and slumped against the seat, exposing a belly of festering sores. The car filled with a moist, sour smell like rotting bacon.

Lewis opened his window, breathing in cool, fresh air as David sat down in the front beside him. "What's wrong with her, anyway?" Lewis asked.

"Her oil glands have stopped working."

"How old is she?"

"Seventeen."

"She already smells dead." When David didn't reply, Lewis said, rather more nicely, "Isn't that old for a dog?"

"Especially such a large dog." David leaned into the backseat, stroked the dog's head, then pulled his door closed.

The door shut with a muffled click, a subtle and final sound that triggered images of Lydia with acute, almost hallucinatory clarity: the curve of her long neck; her small, exquisite head. Barbara said Lydia, at twenty-five, was simply too young for him. Lewis felt Lydia's disinterest, whatever the cause, was inevitable. The miracle was that she had *ever* enfolded him, all his meagerness and angst, in those slim, tennis-sculpted arms.

"Hey," he said to David. "I don't mean to mooch free medical advice or anything, but I was wondering: do you know a treatment for someone whose idiot heart has been kicked to a bloody pulp?"

"What's that again?"

"You know, a cure—or maybe not a cure exactly, maybe just a salve—for a guy who's just lost the most brilliant and beautiful girlfriend?"

They were on the freeway now. Trucks trundled alongside them. The car was incubator warm. "Oh," said David. "What you need is a *guayanchero*. These men and women in Peru are world experts in love magic. Actually, they're wonderfully pragmatic. I met a man who went to one because his wife had stopped loving him. The *guayanchera* went into a trance, burned herbs, consulted dead birds, and then she said, 'Well, if your wife doesn't love you, maybe you'd better start looking for someone who does.' "

"I'm glad I didn't fly all the way to Peru to hear that."

"It's not what anybody wants to hear." David thought some more. "There's always the literature cure. Take a big box of books out to the desert and read until things shift. *Bleak House* can cure anything."

Lewis smacked the steering wheel. "*Bleak House* is about my favorite fucking book in the world." He couldn't wait to tell Barbara and the chair of his thesis committee he'd spent the day with a *curandero* who prescribed *Bleak House* for a broken heart. You can't make up something like that.

They settled into a relaxed, motoring hum. Lewis explained his dissertation on Flaubert, Turgenev, and Paris in the 1860s. David Ibañez described his childhood on the Sally Morrot ranch.

GROWING UP in the workers' village, said David, was like living on a feudal estate: a prescribed, simple, unquestioned hierarchical arrangement in which Sally Morrot spoke the word of God.

His earliest memories were smells. Wood smoke and dirt, a gamy mixture of chickens and compost, the orange groves' pungent dust and perfume. As a small child, he could smell water, before it rained or when the river was full. On certain February days, he'd get a whiff of spring, the moist balminess peculiar to afternoons in April, May, and June. People smelled then, too, and he could identify them by their particular tangled blend of food, sweat, and soap. He gauged moods by the onion scent of fear, the baked-goods aroma of contentment, the rankness of alcohol rising off skin.

He might've joined the twentieth century earlier, he said, had he gone to public school. Rito's elementary school had been built in the thirties, an institutional version of the popular Mission Revival style, with tiled roofs and long, arched arcades. But Sally Morrot believed in a Catholic education. By subscribing all the village children to St. Catherine's, she singlehandedly preserved in Rito a small, reactionary order of Carmelites, an odd assortment of monastics exiled to this obscure valley for too great a love of earthly things, poor relations with others, an excessive interest in lonely women or young boys. When David was in the fifth grade, the nuns informed Sally Morrot that he was exceptionally gifted, whereupon she summoned him to the mansion, fed him sugar cookies and a pale, woody drink he later identified as milky tea. She administered a series of writing and mathematical problems of her own devising and, finding his performance indeed remarkable, overrode his parents' humble objection—he was their only child—and sent him to a private Catholic boarding school in Ojai.

Sally Morrot monitored his progress and later, during summer vacations in his high-school years, expected him at her home every

Thursday night for dinner, where he joined five or six other young people in whom she took an active, often financial, interest. Some were children of her litigious, ruined relatives; others were collected from the valley's dwindling aristocracy. The young people were expected to dress for the occasion, so David wore the white shirt and gray corduroy slacks of his school uniform. His relatives answered the door, served the food, cleared the table.

Sally was incredibly old by that time, her hair vividly white. Her arms were light as cornstalks and her skin a mass of large, round freckles; she looked as if she had been covered with transparent pale-brown leaves. She presided over these dinners with her live-in companion, an elegant, elderly Chinese woman. Dora, whose father had been a diplomat from Hong Kong, spoke with an upper-crust British accent. Sally and Dora asked the children questions to sharpen their conversational abilities: Who has a story to tell? What amusing things happened this week? Who has read a good book? In their more vigorous years, Sally and Dora had traveled all over the world, so they were always saying, "When we dined with Alberto Moravia . . ." or "When we lunched with Josephine Baker. . . ." None of the teenagers knew who these people were, but the implication was that some day they, too, might eat a meal with Moravia or Baker or Irwin Shaw or General So-and-so, the second-in-command of the French Foreign Legion.

After tea in the study, they were sent home in the black Cadillac driven by Sally Morrot's driver, who was David's uncle, Rafael Flores. Crammed inside the car, the teenagers routinely referred to the two women as "old stick-birds," mimicked Dora's accent, and mimed the quavery, underwater motions of Sally Morrot's undiagnosed Parkinson's disease.

One by one, Rafael dropped off the teenagers until only David remained in the car. As the village *curandero* and spiritual leader, Rafael also took an interest in David's education. What have you learned about trees? he'd ask. What have you learned about people? You're studying *fisiología*—what have you learned about the body? And *religiones, mijo,* what have you learned about God? Although he loved his uncle, David had become ashamed of Rafael's heavily accented English and superstitious beliefs. His *curanderismo* seemed like something in the educational films on primitive cultures David watched in social studies classes. More than a decade would pass before he asked to learn his uncle's art. At sixteen or seventeen, David felt only embarrassed for and protective of Rafael, and answered his questions politely yet evasively as the older man parked the Cadillac in its garage by the warehouse. Together, they walked the quarter-mile to the village, into the range of Umberto García's woozy accordion and the battered, permanently dazed fighting cock who crowed night and day, into the smells of fertile dirt and hot lard and fried spices, and up the stoop into his mother's warm, spotless kitchen.

"It was schizzy," David said, "and obviously, my allegiances were torn. My parents were pleased I was being educated, but it broke their hearts. And Sally wanted total control over my life. She wanted me to advance so far, but no farther. She was such an old snob, yet very unusual."

Even in her eighties, he said, Sally Morrot had walked a portion of the irrigated groves every evening, sometimes with David's father, or Dora, or Albert, her amanuensis. Other nights she kept her own company, or singled out one of the local teenagers she'd taken under wing. David was sixteen the first time she asked him to "do water" with her. "You don't begin to know something profoundly until you've observed it for at least a year," she told him. "And after fifty years . . ." She'd point a trembling finger at a tree, and for the briefest instant David could see the singularity of this one tree, as if it had been created new and whole in that exact moment.

They tramped in knee-high rubber boots and carried hoes to plug up gopher holes with mud. Sally lectured him urgently on her own ideas for social reform, a peculiar system she'd developed based on her reading about Thomas Jefferson and the Shakers. She admired the Shakers' business acumen, their ambisexual God and distaste for sexual intercourse. Like the Shakers, she advocated adoption over procreation and repeatedly expounded a theory, which David never quite grasped, having to do with redistributing the world's children sensibly, granting them to whoever had the resources to properly raise them. With Jefferson she shared the belief that America was meant to be a nation of farmers augmented by whatever simple manufacturing was unavoidable. The evils of industrialization, urbanization, and corporate inhumanity arose when the country deviated from its agricultural base.

Sally confused him, David said, and bored him, and often seemed off her nut. Yet she was also devoted to him, and staunchly supported him when he resolved to go to medical school. "I won't brook law school," she told him. "My brothers and their families have been ruined in the courts. But you'll make a good doctor; you can come back here to care for your people."

David enrolled in premed at Cal-Berkeley. When he came home for Christmas his freshman year, Sally sent for him. Dora, she told him, had gone to visit her sisters in Hong Kong, suffered an aneurysm, and died. "I can't stay here alone," she said crisply. "I'm too old for this life, this big old house. If I stay on, I'll do nothing but ache for Dora." She was going to live with her nephew in Oxnard. After consulting with David's father and her accountants, and with the help of the University of California, she had set up the ranch in such a way that it could run itself more or less indefinitely. Since none of her younger relatives were agriculturally inclined, she thought this the best plan. "I'll close down the house for a while, in case I want to come back. Eventually somebody will have to live here."

She assured David his status would not change. "Even if something should betake me, you will be able to complete your education." That was the last time he saw her, although she faithfully wrote him once a month, a few large, painfully crumpled words on ecru stationery: "The best doctors, I am told, major in English as undergraduates. . . ." "Being widely read will serve you well. I am rereading James and can recommend *The Ambassadors*. . . ." "First-class essay, but do not use contractions, please."

Her generosity so resembled a set of rules, it would be decades before David identified love among the snarled strands of duty, resentment, fear, loyalty, and inferiority he felt at every mention of her name. In college lit classes, he discovered her in assorted dowagers in the work of Dickens, Wharton, and, of course, James. Later, after traveling the world and living on the East Coast, he understood that Sally and Dora were lesbians as well as members of that well-established minority, of the eccentric rich. Despite everything, though, whenever his spiritual teachers instructed him to imagine or meditate on pure white light, David would think of radiant snow, backlit clouds, and Sally Morrot's star-white hair.

AS SOON as Lewis turned off the Santa Bernita Highway toward Rito, round rocks began to appear: first a single boulder-sized speci-

men at the mouth of a private drive; then a granite honeydew atop a
concrete pillar; and finally, in profusion, gradated cannonballs bor-
dering a weedy bed of roses, a yard filled with gray basketballs.

Rito was more or less as Lewis remembered it from three years
ago—cluttered yards, cacti in lard buckets, chickens pecking in the
foxtails—and a homesickness he'd never felt welled up within him.
So many things about the town seemed comic and benign, like stray
parts of a joke: a pony tethered to a palm tree; dogs sleeping stretched
out, belly up, in the street; a butter-yellow Oldsmobile station wagon
stalled in the middle of Church Street, hood up, as six men gazed,
rapt, into the engine cavity. I was so lost when I lived here, he
thought, yet it was so funny. And safe.

David's uncle lived two miles out of town and down a gravel lane
in a dusty, weathered orchard cottage. The porch sagged with bougainvillea and morning glories. Roses, delphinium, and ranunculus
bloomed in the yard with preternatural good health.

They were greeted by a tiny, raffish wirehaired mutt and a small
flock of colorful bantam chickens. Lewis and David exchanged phone
numbers, and Lewis refused an invitation to come inside to meet
David's relatives. "I'm thinking," he said, "I might pay a surprise visit
to Round Rock."

David shook his hand. "Good luck, and keep in touch."

THE FIRST time Libby became truly angry with Red was shortly after they started spending every night together. Joe was due down for a weekend, and Red not only suggested they sleep separately for those two nights—Libby had no argument there—but also felt they shouldn't see each other at all. "You mean you don't want Joe to know we're together?"

Red blushed profoundly, hemmed and hawed. She had never seen him so bollixed. "I need time," he whispered.

This was not a line Libby liked to hear. "Time for what?"

"When Joe was here last, you were sleeping with Lewis," he said. "The switch seems, well, kind of *quick*."

She saw he was ashamed of his—their—actions, and she argued that children need to see that adults, too, can move gracelessly, and sometimes stumble into the right thing.

Red wouldn't agree. "I'd rather model appropriate behavior."

"Do what you feel is best, then," she told him as he left for the airport. "But you can save that jargon for your drunks. And I can't guarantee I'll want to see you come Sunday, or ever."

It never occurred to them that Little Bill had long since informed Joe of the romantic reversal. When Red met him at the gate, Joe's first words were, "Where's Libby?" He made Red call her from the nearest pay phone. "Don't blow this one, Dad."

The second time Libby felt that deep, potentially life-shifting anger was over two and a half years later, the night Lewis showed up out of the blue at Round Rock.

She and Red had been at the new house with the plumber, who needed a light. Libby was already in a bad mood; if they had a real plumber instead of an ex-resident moonlighting as one, he'd possess the right equipment and they wouldn't have spent all Sunday afternoon running errands for him. "I'll dash in," she said when Red pulled up at the garage.

The door was unlocked, surprisingly. She immediately spotted a caged shop light on a pegboard on the far wall and started for it.

"Hello?"

She stopped. In the far bay, a man unfolded before her. She gave a short yelp even as she recognized him. *"Lewis?"* He looked helplessly young, even vulnerable. "What are you doing here?"

"I stopped by to see Red, but he wasn't home. Then I remembered these dashboard knobs I bought for the Fairlane."

She moved forward and could see what looked like ivory acorns scattered at his feet. Radio and heater knobs. She looked back to his face; the beard was gone. His lips were so thin as to seem almost nonexistent.

"What are *you* doing here?" he said.

"Oh, God." She was shaking. "We're building a house up on the ridge and the plumber needed a light. . . ." She pointed to the pegboard behind him. He turned and automatically plucked the light down for her. The orange cord was tangled with a black cord and he began shaking them apart. "Who's 'we'?"

"Red and I. We're married, you know."

"No. I didn't know." He looked up from the cords. "How would I know that? *Married?*"

"For two years now."

"No shit?" He started coiling loops of cord around his elbow and the crook of his hand. "You married that fat old guy?"

"And what fat old guy would that be?"

Lewis flinched as if shocked by the cords he held. Red Ray stood behind Libby, framed in the door.

"You!" Lewis yelled. *"You* fat old guy!"

The air crackled with three-way glances, swaying crazily between hostility and joy. Then Red stepped forward, hand extended in welcome.

As soon as the initial trauma subsided, Libby found herself serenely indifferent to Lewis, for which she liked herself enormously. She didn't begrudge Red his obvious elation, either. Red had mourned Lewis so often in the last few years, growing suddenly pensive with thoughts, not of Lewis's misbehavior—dumping Libby, punching Red, abandoning his job—but of his own blunders. "By continuing to sponsor him after I'd started seeing you," he told Libby often, "I betrayed his confidence."

They delivered the light to the plumber; then Red took Lewis on his evening rounds while Libby napped. When they returned, Lewis came in for coffee but refused Red's dinner invitation.

"No, n-no, that's okay," he stuttered before leaving. "I'll call you soon."

Once the Fairlane vanished down the roadway, Red had turned to Libby and looked so pleased, so bright in the face, she was almost happy Lewis had come.

After dinner, she put in a load of laundry and was surprised to find Red lying in the dark on their bed, staring at the ceiling. She curled up next to him.

He stroked her hair. "Was having Lewis here upsetting to you?" he asked.

"I didn't rush off to kill the fatted calf, but I'm glad he came. You seemed so happy to see him."

"I am happy, and a little relieved, too."

"Then it's worth it," she said.

Red searched her face in the dim light. "If it's all right with you, I'm thinking I might ask him to help out at the house. Just until we replace John."

The former house manager, acting out his version of tough love, had driven a nineteen-year-old to Happy Yolanda's. "You don't like sobriety?" he asked. "Then drink. Right now. Here's a twenty." The kid had gotten out of the car and called his parents, who promptly sued Round Rock for reckless endangerment; John's dismissal was part of the settlement. Since then, Red had brought in a series of interns from the Ventura College counselor-training program, but nobody, so far, he wanted to hire on a permanent basis.

"Would Lewis even be interested?" Libby asked.

"Said he needed a summer job."

"It's kind of a shame," she said. "Here these guys go to school to be professional counselors, and you want to give the job to somebody without any training."

"Yeah, but these damn interns all go straight from recovery houses into the training program. It gets so airless and *cultish*. At least Lewis has been slugging it out in the real world."

"But, honey . . ." Libby snuggled into his neck. "You went to work in recovery right after you got sober."

"And look what I did. I hid. Took me over ten years to pull my head out of the sand—and I never would've if I hadn't met you." He nipped her ear. "I wish I'd gotten out there like Lewis has."

"What? As a student? You give him too much credit. But I don't care, go ahead and hire him if you think that's best."

Red kissed her eyebrow. "Only if you're okay with it."

She mentally tested images of Lewis to gauge her own response—his curly hair and long limbs, his porous, sandy skin—and found no residual longing or even interest, except perhaps for the way laughter could catch him by surprise. When Red had shown him the jars of deflated, tarlike rotten eggs, he shook helplessly, his eyes brimming. That was the interesting Lewis, the part outside his ego's jurisdiction.

"I won't want to see him socially," she said.

"That makes sense." Red rocked her in his arms.

"And don't be disappointed if he turns you down. You know Lewis. He does what he wants to do when *he* wants to do it."

Libby stood and started taking off her clothes. Red was on his back again, staring at the ceiling. Libby felt a wee lurch and turned on the light. "You already offered him the job, didn't you?" Rage was quickly making her head feel curiously weightless and hot.

Red, wincing, covered his eyes with his hands.

ALL THE way back to Los Angeles, in those stretches where he forgot to calculate just where in the air Lydia might be, Lewis would think about his visit to Round Rock, laugh, and hit his palm on the steering wheel. Red and Libby—*married*! He'd never considered their alliance as anything more than a bomb in his own life. Red, he always assumed, had stepped in as a form of chivalry—a way of saying "Enough!" to Lewis—and Libby had allowed it for temporary protection. That they might still be together had never occurred to Lewis; he'd never thought it through that far. And yet Libby had slid into his former job! That made Round Rock a real mom-'n'-pop operation, especially now that she was pregnant. *Pregnant.* He could see the baby: Red's shrimp-pink skin, Libby's droll, round eyes. And as if all those bungalows weren't enough, they were building a house on ranch property. A sprawling, one-story new home strung out over the top of a high ridge, each room equipped with a lordly view of the realms. *Well*.

Lewis came home to six messages, surely one of them from Lydia. He listened as he threw open the windows. The first four were from Barbara: thanking him for speaking, asking him out to dinner, saying they were leaving for the restaurant, saying they were home and where was he, anyway? The fifth message was from his sponsor, Harry, who was in Cuba making a film. "Called to hear how the speaking went. . . ."

It seemed as if five years had passed since he'd stood at that podium.

The last message said, "Hey, Lewis. This is David, David Ibañez. Just wanted to see if you got home all right, and to thank you for driving me up here today. Let's see . . . I hope you're doing okay with the girlfriend stuff. Call if you want to talk about it some more. Guess I'll be up here for a while. Thanks again for the ride, and the company. If you feel like it, give a shout."

It wasn't too late—nine-fifteen—so Lewis called back. "Things worked out pretty well," he said. "My old sponsor actually offered me a job at Round Rock."

"What kind of job?" said David.

"House manager. It's a live-in position. You keep an eye on things, make sure nobody's chipping. Not anything I'd be good at or even interested in. But it was flattering he asked. It means, like, everything's forgiven."

"But there really is a job?" said David.

"A couple jobs, in fact. Red fired the house manager, and then the cook's mom had a stroke and he's leaving too."

"And you're sure you're not interested?"

"Nah," said Lewis. "I want a summer job, but I have to finish my dissertation. All those needy newcomers? Couldn't do it. The cook job I might have considered. Cooking's fun, and there's not so much truck with the inmates."

"If you're seriously not interested in the house manager job," David said, "I might be."

"*You?*" Lewis never would've thought someone with David's exotic, arcane background would consider working at a remote drunk farm. "What about the pain clinic?"

"I need to make a change," said David. "And I could use a break from chronic pain. And sooner or later, I've got to stop working for the woman I'm sleeping with." He exhaled loudly in almost a sigh. "Mostly, I'm just dying to move back to the valley. My uncle's old, the place is changing; it'll be housing developments and strip malls in ten years. And I like working in recovery. I did it for two years in New York."

Lewis gave him Red's number. "Call him," he said. "Tell him I sent you, and I'll want a finder's fee. Just joking—but he'd be lucky to get you."

Lewis fell asleep instantly, and woke at around three a.m. Lydia, he calculated, was over the north Atlantic, her plane a speck above the turquoise sea. A tightness in his throat and chest made him think he'd been crying for hours, possibly years, without knowing it.

"GUESS who showed up Sunday?" Libby said. She and Billie were eating lox and bagels and fresh peaches in the adobe's courtyard. Billie had a table set up between beds of flowering ginger; around them, dark, waxy green plants sent out arcs of spattery red and yellow blossoms.

"I don't know. Joe? Your parents? *Red's* parents?"

"Red's parents are dead. Nope, your favorite: Lewis."

"Lewis who?" Billie grinned. "I hope you put arsenic in his cat-fish."

"He didn't stay for dinner, thank God. But he's still sober, and even quit smoking."

"Is he on the arrogance wagon too?"

"Don't get all excited now. He's still a hundred percent Lewis."

"Maybe he needs another ride in my truck."

"You may get that chance. Red offered him a job."

Billie closed her eyes.

"Don't worry. He wasn't interested. You think Lewis would move back here from La-la Land? All his friends are movie stars. But he might've found us an amazing house manager. A guy who speaks Spanish, sober about a zillion years. Oh, and he actually grew up on the ranch. He wants to come home, reconnect with his past."

"Yeah? What's his name?" Billie sounded suspicious, as if such a person couldn't exist.

"David Ibañez. Distant cousin to Victor. Seems kind of weird that he wants to move back to where he grew up—you couldn't pay me to move back to Montrose. But this *is* the most beautiful valley. And *you* never left."

"Listen," Billie said. "I know about him. He's bad news."

"Oh, everyone was bad news in this business," Libby said. "The last house manager was a heroin addict."

"This guy's a swindler, a con man, a charlatan."

"Really? He seems so intelligent."

"He makes a good first impression, all right. That's part of it."

"Even since he got sober?"

"What does sober matter? That whole family is backward: it's a level of ignorance and dealing with the world that's not erased in one generation or even two."

"You like Victor Ibañez," said Libby.

"Victor's a joke. And only a distant cousin. David's family is all black magic and thieving. They sacrifice animals. They won't see doctors. The kids die from staph infections, the women die in child-birth."

"But this guy lived all over the world. He's educated, articu—"

"He's a pathological liar, Libby. I'd be surprised if he's been east of Arizona. I know: those big brown Bambi eyes. The great *brujo*, Shaman of the Week. Try Sleaze King of the Decade. Did he tell you about his clinic in Tijuana, where desperately sick people pay thousands of dollars for coffee colonics?"

"I thought it was a chronic-pain clinic."

"Sorry to be the bearer of bad news."

"Uh-oh. Red really fell for him."

"I love Red," Billie said, "but Red's a chump. He's the only person in town who'd hire that snake."

RED SHOOK his head. "Listen, I'd take anything Billie said with a grain of salt."

"But she knows him and we don't," Libby said.

"She knows everybody in Rito, and if it's a man, she'll have some grudge against him. If I went by Billie's opinions, I wouldn't have hired our framer, our electrician, our plaster man. Every man she's done business with, she bad mouths."

"Except you," said Libby.

"She's had her problems with me, too."

Red would not be swayed. This was something Libby had come to understand: he had blind spots regarding certain people and championed them to the end, no matter how difficult, irascible, asocial they were, from Frank Jamieson and Lewis, to John the house manager and Ernie Tola.

Libby couldn't help but consider Lewis the source of this present unpleasantness. Hadn't he sent David to them? Once more, however subtly and indirectly, Lewis had raised expectations only to dash them.

"LISTEN," David said. "I just spent most of the day with Red Ray. When I told him what you said about cooking, he said he'd love for you to cook. He doesn't care if you can only do it for two months. He said, 'Why didn't Lewis tell me he wanted to cook? Of course he can cook.' "

"Red said that?"

"Yeah. So how 'bout you cook and I manage the house? We'll take over the place."

The fact that David Ibañez and Red both wanted him up there was like a flattery cocktail. "It's a thought," said Lewis.

"Think it over. I can't give Red a definite answer myself until Wednesday."

"Wednesday?"

"Just a few loose ends," David said.

RED BROUGHT David home for dinner in order, he said, to put Libby's fears to rest. Still, she found herself mistrusting David's good looks, that square jaw and long brown hair and graceful, muscled body. He did have an appealing alertness that was especially enchanting when directed her way—all part of a con man's repertoire? He didn't laugh, she noticed, or not much. And in the odd moment, during a pause in the conversation, he pulled into a dark quietness. Something was wrong with him, she thought, some weightiness or grief. When talk started up again, he shuddered slightly, shrugging off a tangible gloom.

"It looks," Red said, "like Lewis might come cook for the summer."

"Lewis wants the cook job?" she exclaimed.

"He says he likes to cook," David said.

"And he's good at it," said Red.

"This is what he's going to do with his Ph.D.?"

"It's just till September, Lib," Red said.

"He's actually taken the job?"

"He's coming up Saturday to do a little reconnaissance," said David. "He's bringing a friend."

LEWIS'S friend, Barbara, wore shiny, skintight bicycle shorts, a ribbed undershirt, and a leather vest. A peculiar outfit, Libby thought, to wear to an all-male recovery house; she had more hair than clothes on her back. Next to Barbara, Libby felt fat and bland and provincial and prudish and enormously pregnant. No wonder Lewis dumped her, when he could have this: impossible thinness, billowing apricot-colored hair, skin the color of drywall dust.

Libby also envied Barbara's expressiveness and her ease with the residents; she joked with them at lunch, belting out a deep, loud laugh at their jokes and talking easily, knowledgeably, about sobriety.

After lunch, walking toward the village, Red, Lewis, and David wandered ahead, out of earshot, leaving Libby alone with Barbara, who asked when the baby was due (October) and if the sex was known (a girl, although sonograms can be deceiving).

Libby decided to jump in with her own line of personal inquiry. "So, how long have you and Lewis been together?"

Barbara squinted at Libby and broke into a broad smile. "Oh, no, we're not together. Heaven forbid. No, I live with a guy."

"And he doesn't mind you hanging out with Lewis?"

"With Lewis?" Her smile sweetened, as if this question, while forgivable, was preposterous. "No, he doesn't mind at all."

"Sorry," said Libby. "I guess I assumed . . . You know, he's male, you're female. Very unenlightened of me."

Barbara moved closer. "I did go out with him real briefly a couple years ago."

"Me too," Libby said. "Before you."

"So I've heard. You lasted a little longer than I did."

"Yeah, but you two ended up friends."

Barbara directed her squint at Lewis's back, smiled again. "I love him."

"I can't say that."

"Oh, Lewis has an affectionate nature. I have to beat it out of him sometimes, but he can be incredibly loyal and helpful in his own way."

"Red likes him, too."

At the village, the three men and Barbara went to look at the refurbished bungalow where Lewis might bunk, and also at the boarded-up bungalow where David grew up.

Libby, claiming the excuse of pressing duties, ducked into the office, lay down on the sofa, and immediately drifted off. One of pregnancy's few boons: the instant nap. A few minutes later, footsteps on the porch woke her up.

"So tell me," Lewis said. "What do you think so far?"

"I like it here," Barbara answered. "It's so tranquil. And Red Ray is a babe. A total babe."

"You think so?"

"Yeah. And Libby too. She has such a great face."

"Libby hates me," he said.

"Yeah, well," said Barbara. "And David's adorable."

"He's already taken, Barb. He has a rich girlfriend down in T.J."

"Lewis, please. You mean *I'm* already taken."

Libby didn't have to guess that it was Lewis who kicked a porch support. A long silence followed—had they gone away?—then Lewis finally said, "You won't miss me too much if I take the job?"

Barbara's laugh was so long and loud, it would've yanked Libby from the deepest sleep. "Lewis, Lewis, Lewis. Let's get this straight. Who's gonna miss whom?"

ON A Monday morning, Red dropped his '46 Ford at the Ruiz brothers' garage, then walked up Main Street. The pickup needed its carburetor rebuilt, a job Red didn't trust to anyone presently working in the Round Rock garage. He had considered waiting on the carburetor until Lewis came back up, but there was no way of telling if he was actually going to take the job. Convincing him to come cook at the farm was like luring a skittish animal to hand-held food. Red had been careful not to push or get his own hopes up, while making it clear that Lewis was wholly welcome. Libby didn't understand—and Red wasn't so sure he did, either—why he so yearned to have him back at the farm. Some people you had business with in this life, and Lewis was one of those people in Red's. Libby felt Lewis had already fulfilled his function in bringing the two of them together. Perhaps so;

and he'd also helped Red see his own shortcomings as sponsor, friend, confidant—an unpleasant but useful lesson. Still, Lewis's return was much prayed for, a second chance to set things right and, from there, assess what business might remain.

Red walked until he came to the wood-slat bench outside his former law office, now vacant except when an accountant rented it at tax time. Red had overestimated how long it would take to hand his truck over and had fifteen minutes before Libby would pick him up on the way to her doctor's appointment in Buchanan.

The bench was in the shade of the building, but a sharp line of sunlight inched toward him. In one of the upstairs apartments over the laundromat a woman sang in a light, clear voice: "I'll see you, when your troubles are like mine, I'll see you, when you haven't got a dime, weeping like a willow, moaning like a dove. . . ." This song and the pending sunlight made Red think of Frank. Even when they were children, Frank cared for nothing so much as a prime spot in the sun and a brand-new cigarette.

Frank now lived at the Buena Vista Rest Home in Buchanan, having run away so many times, there was no option but supervised care. Red had kept him out of such institutions for years, fearing that he'd be neglected and left to disintegrate. But Frank slid into life at the Buena Vista so smoothly it was almost a reproach. He had a reliable source of not only cigarettes and sunshine but also friendship—specifically with an elderly schizophrenic man and another large mute accident victim. Red invariably found the three parked, smoking, around a small trickling fountain in the courtyard. Orderlies called them the Terrible Three—not because they caused any trouble, but because it was so difficult to get them inside for meals or bed.

When Frank left Round Rock, some central vortex at the farm had lost its pull. If Frank, the one eternal resident, could leave, why not the other diehards? In firing John, then accepting Ernie's notice, Red had feared Round Rock itself might be drawing to a close, especially since he never was any good at hiring people.

After Billie's allegations, Red had called up David's references: a Park Avenue psychologist, the director of a Manhattan recovery house, and a New Mexican M.D. with a homeopathic practice. The calls produced the usual bath of hyperbole as well as a few insights:

"such a gifted practitioner" . . . "remarkable composure in times of crisis" . . . "works intensively with others without suffering burnout." The downside? "Runs behind in his appointments" . . . "unstable female clients cathect with him." Could he be trusted around money? This question provoked a laugh from the Manhattan therapist. "Definitely, but he sure can't be motivated by it. . . ."

Last night, when David came to the AA meeting, Red took him aside during the coffee break. They walked down the driveway until the house sat on the hill behind them like a lit-up stage. Roses fogged the air with moist, lemony scent.

Red crammed his hands into his pockets and, after two years off cigarettes, longed for nicotine to ease the moment. "Your references, everything I've seen about you, makes me want to hire you," he said. "But a good friend of ours here in Rito says you're not to be trusted."

David, walking, stiffened as if alerted to danger.

"Do you have any idea what this is about?" Red asked.

"I think so."

"Want to tell me?"

"I'm not at liberty to," said David. "You'll have to go by what she says."

"She wasn't specific, either," said Red. "And I don't need to know the details. She implied you took some money."

"Twenty years ago, when she and I last had any dealings with each other, I did take some money that was offered to me."

"Oh, so this is wreckage from the distant past?"

David paused and turned to face him. "I will say, for what it's worth, I've made what amends I could. The money given to me was repaid with interest. And other amends were attempted. Although I can't say they were taken in the spirit I'd hoped for."

In David's careful syntax, Red caught the unmistakable whiff of Billie's intractability. "What, she never forgave you?" Red gave a short, knowing snort. "No? Now how did I guess?"

They stood at the foot of the lawn. Sprinklers hissed in the groves. Voices wafted down to them from the house. The bell clanged for the meeting to resume. "I need to know," said Red, "if this could interfere with your work here."

"Not with my work, no," David said. "But I'm afraid it puts you in an awkward position."

"Please. I don't hire people based on whether or not my friends like them."

Later that night, when Red started to relate this conversation to Libby, she interrupted him.

"I don't care who you hire." She grabbed hold of his waistband. "I'm sorry I stuck my two cents in. You know what you're doing. I wash my hands of the whole business. Now, can we please get this house built and furnished? I feel a serious need to drag heavy furniture around." She pulled him roughly toward her, pushed him up against the bed, and tugged off all his clothes.

It surprised Red how much Libby still wanted sex as her pregnancy advanced, how she'd scramble onto him, cling to him, pull him this way and that.

Red ran a finger along the bench's rusted iron armrest. The sun now sat in his lap, and when he looked up, Libby was parked at the curb in the beige Mercedes. Twelve years old and in tip-top condition, the car had been his one-year anniversary present to her. But this obvious ploy to make her ditch the eternally faulty Falcon had caused unforeseen embarrassment. Hadn't Yvette driven a black Mercedes? That Libby might know this, or care, had somehow eluded Red, who was therefore deeply mortified. He'd explained, awkwardly, that he respected, indeed revered, older Mercedes Benzes, to the point he'd want *any* wife of his to drive one. And maybe he did, on some level, want to re-create his former marriage; he'd enjoyed it, even thrived in it, although he no longer missed Yvette. Libby, high-colored and possibly amused, had allowed these stumbly confessions. Red offered to trade the car in on a Volvo or Saab or anything else she wanted. No, no, Libby said, she wasn't a fool, it was a beautiful gift, and at least this car wasn't black.

Red walked up to the driver's-side door. Libby was wearing sunglasses, red lipstick, her hair in a high ponytail. He tasted salt in her kiss. "Sweetheart. What's wrong?"

She spoke to the ground. "I'm having cramps and spotting."

Red drove. Libby tied the black leather strap of her handbag into fat knots. "It's that abortion I had in New Orleans," she said.

Red knew about this; Libby had been dating Stockton only a few months at the time, and they'd agreed early on to terminate the pregnancy. "I didn't know they could affect pregnancies," he said.

"It wasn't a real abortion. I mean, it was real enough. Stockton knew this script doctor who'd been disbarred, or whatever, for writing too many prescriptions for Seconal and Quaaludes and stuff."

"I know what a script doctor is," Red said dryly.

"Anyway, he was making his living doing illegal abortions. He did them in his house. Cheap. That was the draw—a bargain abortion. A bedroom outfitted with hospital equipment. He didn't have a suction thing, just scraped you out. I was conscious as hell but all drugged up. It really hurt. I just couldn't summon the energy to resist. Then, in the middle of things, he tells me I had a beautiful cervix. What can you do? So, I got an infection anyway and ended up in the hospital. Those doctors said this was bound to happen, and if I ever got pregnant again, I'd probably have trouble carrying full-term. You know, you're twenty-two, you're invincible, you think it's cool to know criminals. Nobody will ever hurt you and all the bad stuff happens to somebody else."

"That's youth all right," Red said, careful not to exhibit his distress.

"I never imagined it would hurt a real living baby. Or you."

"If anything happens," Red said, "nobody would ever blame you."

At the doctor's, Red told the receptionist that Libby might be having a miscarriage and she was called in right away. He sat in the waiting room trying desperately to stay calm. Next to him, a woman glugged from a large bottle of Evian between whimpers. Red tried to read a celebrity magazine, but the sentences didn't follow one another in any coherent fashion. After ten minutes or so, a nurse called him into the room, where Libby, now dressed, sat on the examining table while a doctor jotted notes on her chart.

A few dots of blood and cramping, the doctor said, was nothing out of the ordinary, nothing to be alarmed about. He was a pleasant, boyish man with blond hair, at least five years younger than Libby. There was no dilation, he said. Nothing wrong with her blood. No sign of miscarriage. Libby was healthy and everything was normal. Even the dark, irrational fears were normal. The doctor nodded encouragement to Libby. So far, there were no signs she might have any trouble carrying to term. And if there was any loss of womb strength from a poorly administered abortion, they'd put something called a cerclage around the cervix to hold it shut, and prescribe bed rest for the duration. But this was the worst that could happen.

On the way home, Libby's spirits were buoyant, elated. " 'Cerclage.' Such a beautiful word if you don't think about what it does —lassoes the cervix. Now, Red, did you happen to notice how enormous the doctor's head is? I pity his wife when they have kids. I'd be terrified my whole pregnancy just thinking about having a baby with a head that big. I'd sign up for a C-section right off the bat. Now you, Red, you have a beautiful head. A dream head."

DAVID stayed inside Tuesday morning. *Día veinti-uno*. Day twenty-one. He read and talked to his parents and cousins on the phone. Around noon, he moved outside with the dog under the shade of the plum tree in his uncle's backyard, amid the drunken buzzing of flies and soft conversation of chickens. He shucked sweet corn for his aunt and helped her with dinner. "I can feel people's prayers," he said. His uncle had been working with him daily, praying with him, giving him a bitter tea that made his blood race. "You must kill off a part of yourself to satisfy the poison," Rafael said. "Otherwise, it takes all of you."

They ate outside on the picnic table, staying until it grew dark and the earth exuded dampness, then moved inside, where David and Rafael did a small ritual, a sweeping, with herbs and a prayer. They smudged the house with rosemary and sage and chanted more prayers. His aunt Gloria lit candles at the kitchen altar, where the votives flickered in red and blue glass and the virgin revealed her flaming heart.

They sat around the kitchen table under the portrait of Jesus, who stood, arms apart, in brown robes the same color as his hair, his halo a fuzzy yellow light. The old dog slept under the table on David's feet. They spoke quietly in Spanish. David told about the time his father got so mad, he threw a pot of *nopales* in a boiling green wave onto the floor; and how, for years, David's mother found tiny dry squares of cactus throughout the house, even in the attic, as if they'd migrated under furniture and carpet and up the walls after the original spill. Rafael told how his brother-in-law Umberto García got drunk and accidentally butchered his prize fighting cock for Sunday dinner.

The dog's snoring became a rhythmic rasping. They drank cool water from a clay pitcher. "The thing is," David said, "I feel so wide and full and clear, I'm willing for anything to happen. Some of it's fear. But this fear is so spacious, and full of energy, and not dark at all—more dim, with a dull glow, like an empty cathedral."

At midnight, everyone laughed a little and embraced one another. David went into the bedroom where he was staying. He lit a few candles of his own, said a prayer: "I am grateful to rejoin those who don't know when they're going to die." The old dog curled up on a rug at the foot of the bed. David slept and did not dream, but woke in an hour or so to a room full of devils as a guttering candle sent shadows stretching up the walls. He blew out the flame, slept again. He awoke once more, this time convinced all the air had been sucked from the room. The night was so still, he thought for a moment he was indeed dead. He had the distinct sensation of a claw drawn across his chest. He leapt up and before he was halfway across the room, he knew what had happened.

He called Lewis the next day. "I'll be starting at Round Rock on Monday," he said quietly. "And the dog who already smelled dead? We buried her this morning."

AND SO, David and Lewis went to work.

Ernie had agreed to stay on to train Lewis. Grayer, older, still precision-coiffed, he initiated Lewis into his meat-filing system in the deep freeze, the hot and dead spots on the griddle, the recipe for his much-adored Chicken Luxurioso—chicken parts baked in a murk of dried onion soup, apricot jam, and Thousand Island dressing. Together, on Monday night, they prepared Ernie's last supper, a tribute to fifteen years of nonstop, super-fatted starch. Red Ray played host as dozens of alumni showed up to eat potato and macaroni salads, ham, biscuits, green bean casserole.

Lewis expected Red to show up the next night, too, for his first solo supper, but he didn't come once all week. Although Lewis had moved into the bungalow right across the street from Red's, he saw him only at the morning staff meetings, those rushed, fifteen-minute coffee klatches.

Lewis's new residence was furnished like a tourist cabin from the forties: clunky blond bedroom set, the sofa and chairs he used to nap on in the office, a slack-stringed Steinway upright. Homey enough, except at night, when it was so quiet Lewis could hear mice chittering in the groves. How had Red stood it all those years—the lone resident in his own private ghost town?

At the fake-wood dinette in his breakfast nook, Lewis tried to write the last chapter of his dissertation; the effort invariably sent him straight down for a nap. He tried going to Denny's again, but Phyllis, the waitress who'd afforded him squatter's rights in her section, was gone, and it was too far to drive all the way to Buchanan just to piss off somebody else. David, his erstwhile partner in a drunk-farm takeover, had no time to spare, since the drunks clamored for his company, sought him out, hung close all week; then, on his days off, David made the exhausting roundtrip to Tijuana to straighten things out with Pauline. Lewis mourned Lydia and the Nightcrawlers, especially Barbara, and ran up a deadly phone bill calling L.A.

Heading home after serving dinner one night, he saw Red in the roadway hosing out the back of his truck. The lights were on in Red's bungalow, and a round, lidded barbecue smoked in the yard. "Hey," said Lewis, "I thought you guys lived at Libby's."

"Oh, it's been back and forth since day one," Red said. "My house *is* more convenient, but there's always someone at the door. Then Libby has cats that need to be fed, and neither place has room for all our things, which is why we decided to build the castle on the hill." Red walked around the truck and turned off the water. "Your little place working out okay?"

"Yeah, great. Stop by later and I'll make you a cup of decaf."

"Maybe I will."

It was a hot night, all his windows were open, and Lewis could hear them across the way, their voice tones and bits of their sentences, Libby's delighted laugh. Then, she played the violin, the first movement of Sibelius's Violin Concerto, music so sad and haunted, Lewis had to pace. He'd never heard her play before; when he'd known her, she'd been entirely disaffected with the violin. He drank coffee, waited for Red's knock, roamed his four small, dingy rooms, which looked anonymous, like a film noir set, a good place to blow your brains out. By eleven o'clock, the occasional, indistinct syllable still floated through the windows, Red's truck was still parked across the way, but all their lights had been extinguished.

BARBARA came up with Celia and Kip; they ate dinner at the Blue House, where the company of women, as always, was highly appreciated. Then, the three spoke as a panel at the AA meeting. Although Lewis had told him about it, Red didn't attend. Afterward, Lewis and his friends drifted back to his bungalow.

"It *is* spooky here." Barbara gave him a worried look. "You doing okay?"

"I came up here thinking it'd be old home week. Instead, I feel like an employee."

"You *are* an employee," Barbara said.

He hated her for saying that.

She only laughed. "Maybe you need to tell Red you'd like to see more of him."

"Oh, right." Even imagining such a conversation made Lewis pull at his own face.

Celia opened the Steinway, played a chord. "Who needs to drink? Just play this thing," she said, and sang two new songs, which did indeed sound drunken and hilarious with such atonal accompaniment.

When everyone left, Lewis lay down on the bedroom floor, his cheekbone against the pine planking. He inhaled dust, exhaled a frustrated sob, and another, then stopped, having forgot what he was supposed to be crying about. Then remembered: I am so fucking lonely, God, I need a little backup here, please.

In the morning, a large brindled dog stood on the porch. He had goofy ears and a terrier's coarse hair, matted and filthy. He cowered but wouldn't move more than a foot when Lewis tried to run him off. He was all bones, clearly starving. Consulting the midget refrigerator, Lewis found only a hard cinnamon roll and last week's fried chicken, no doubt teeming with salmonella. He took the chicken off the bone and put it in a bowl: gone in a snap. Same with the cinnamon roll. This dog was possibly more pathetic than David's dead hound. Very funny, God, thought Lewis.

He placed an ad in the *Rito River News* and tacked up a sign at the Rito post office. As he expected, there was no response. Nobody wanted this dog. Someone, obviously, had dumped him.

When Lewis patted his head or talked to him, the dog wagged his tail, growling and pissing at the same time. He might wander in through the open door, but if Lewis spoke suddenly, he'd spurt outside, as if caught raiding the henhouse. Lewis tried coaxing him into the car, just for some company, but the dog, cringing and snarling, wouldn't come; then, as Lewis drove off, he hurled himself against the fenders, barking insanely.

Lewis named him Gustave, after Flaubert, who also seemed willfully lonely and yet craved companionship, but then misbehaved whenever anyone actually took an interest in him.

LIBBY stood in the living room measuring windows. With her arms up over her head, she looked visibly pregnant for the first time. The windows offered an almost aerial view of the valley below. The Blue House, with its peaked roofs and turret, looked like a castle in a miniature golf course. "Red's down the hall," Libby told Lewis.

"How are you doing?" he asked.

She wrote down a figure before answering. "I've got to get these measurements."

Lewis waited, thinking she'd talk to him when she finished writing, but she walked over and began measuring another window.

He found Red staining shelves in the library, a wood-paneled room with a large fireplace built of oblong riverstone. Red's T-shirt had sickening-looking brown smears on it.

"Need some help?"

"Well, hello. Sure," said Red. "My carpenter's wife broke both her legs, so he's got to take care of her. My painter can't start for two weeks. And we need to move in *before* this baby arrives." He went off to find another brush and Lewis heard him talking to Libby in a low voice.

"Should I leave?" he asked when Red returned.

"No. Please. I've hardly seen you since you got here." Red handed him the brush. They applied a first coat of urethane to finely made, floor-to-ceiling bookshelves. Lewis could see Red in here in his dotage, the color bleached from his hair, his skin papery and pink, eyes twinkly as he read to his children—or grandchildren, maybe—*Little Red Riding Hood, Snow White and Rose Red, The Red Balloon.*

"Been hearing good things about your cooking," Red said.

"Come see for yourself."

"Thought I'd give you some time to get the hang of it."

"I'm ready. Bring Libby too, if she wants. . . ."

"Will do. And you and David might think about coming to the Old Bastards. You're welcome, you know."

"Even if I only have three and a half years of sobriety?"

"It's open to all professionals," Red said. "Might make working here easier on you."

"I'll think about it," Lewis said.

They got into a rhythm, slapping the brushes this way and that. Several times, Lewis almost mentioned his disappointment in not seeing more of Red. But here they were, painting side by side, a paragon of male bonding. Why make a big deal out of it? He was dragging the drop cloth over to the fireplace mantel when Libby appeared in the doorway. "Red," she said, ignoring Lewis completely, "I'm starving. If I don't get something in my stomach right away I'm going to throw up this baby."

LEWIS found David behind the mansion working on a float for the Fourth of July parade. Men were trimming the trailer, looping red, white, and blue crepe paper around bales of hay while one guy was trying to figure out how to secure a flagpole to the trailer bed.

"Can I borrow you for a minute?" Lewis asked, and they walked a distance from the float builders. "I think I need one of your . . . you know . . . ritual things."

"Let's do it," said David.

Before he moved into his second-floor quarters in the Blue House, David had removed all the furniture, taken up the carpet, painted the walls a clean white, sanded the floors, and applied coats of polyurethane until the mottled hardwood looked like still brown water. In the first room was a low, round table with a glass globe filled to the brim with *agua preparada*, the *curandero*'s clear, basic medicinal fluid. An altar occupied one corner of the room—candles and branches, bones and flowers, arranged beneath large painted-tin *retablos* of Santo Niño and the Virgin, around which hung smaller *retablos* and, on dressmaker pins, many silver and tin *milagros* of animals, disembodied limbs, hearts, stomachs, and tiny trucks, buses, passenger cars.

David closed and locked his door.

"It's Libby," said Lewis. "She hates me."

David had adopted the basic Round Rock uniform of jeans and a white T-shirt. His long hair was twisted into a knot at the base of his head; his brown skin was smooth, his arms rivered in veins. A red string with bone beads hung around his neck. He lit the candles in front of his altar, then swept a space on the floor and asked Lewis to lie down. He gave him an egg to hold in one hand and a short, sturdy stick for the other.

"I feel," Lewis said, "like I'm being prepared for burial."

David smiled. "You are, in a manner of speaking," he said, and crossed Lewis's hands over his chest, pulled one leg a little to the left, aligned his head with his spine. David's touch was gentle, confident, matter-of-fact. Once satisfied with how Lewis was laid out, he pulled a clean, coarse white sheet over him and tucked it close. The cloth smelled vaguely of corn. Lewis was relieved to be covered, especially his face; it eliminated his considerable self-consciousness.

"I'm going to call you several times," David said, "and each time you must answer, 'I'm coming.' Now, take a deep breath. . . . Let it out. . . . Another breath. . . . Keep breathing."

Lewis lay there breathing for a long time, maybe ten minutes. The room was hot and still. He heard David moving quietly, the birds outside, and distant pops—people setting off fireworks. Then the room brightened and the air smelled sharp and crisp, as if the smoke of a medicinal campfire were blowing through.

The floor creaked. Something touched Lewis very lightly. A shadow descended. At first, he thought David was touching him with his fingers; then he understood from the whispery, scritching sound that David was pulling a small broom over the length of his body. He was speaking Spanish in a low, soft voice, a prayer or chant. Lewis recognized only *Dios* and *Cristo*.

"Come, Lewis," David said firmly. "Don't stay there."

"I'm coming." Lewis's voice sounded strange to him, sudden, as it did when he blurted something out loud to himself. The broom moved across his chest, grazing his crossed hands holding the egg and the stick. David prayed continuously in Spanish, his tone gentle and straightforward, as if prayer were the most reasonable discourse. "Don't stay there, Lewis," he said. "Come here."

"I'm coming," Lewis said, and meant it.

David, praying, swept around Lewis in a circle. The broom's work was hypnotic, soothing; the adjective that came to Lewis was "loving." Suddenly he was keenly thirsty, and drops of water instantly fell on him; it was alarming how loud they sounded landing on the cloth.

"Lewis, are you here with me?"

"I'm coming."

"Are you here?"

"Yes, I'm here," Lewis said, flooded with relief. His eyes welled up. He heard David sweeping all around him, chanting softly; it was like being a child in the room of a mother so quiet and gentle, all you could feel was her devotion. David swept in a wider and wider circle, then came close and knelt down. "You are here, now." He touched Lewis's forehead, his belly, each of his shoulders. He lifted the sheet off his face and smiled, as if in recognition, then slowly removed the sheet, folding it up length by length and setting it to one side.

David took the egg from Lewis's hand, made the sign of the cross over him, and set the egg on the sheet. Taking the stick from Lewis's other hand, he again made the sign of the cross and set the stick next to the egg. He wrapped both the stick and the egg in the sheet and stood up with the bundle. "Rest a minute," he said. "Sit up when you're ready, and I'll bring you a cup of tea."

David went into his bedroom and Lewis heard him put the water on. When the water started to hiss in the pan, Lewis sat up.

The tea David handed him was astringent, strong, head-clearing. Eucalyptus, pepper, and lemon, and God knows what else.

They sat quietly in the hot room for a few more minutes—until the men decorating the float came knocking on the door. Their work was finished, they said, and beautiful. They wanted David to see it, and Lewis could come too.

EWIS set out covered trays of bacon and sausages and assorted pastries over Sterno flames. He slung bags of bread onto the buffet table with butter, jams, honey, halved grapefruits, wedges of cantaloupes. There were urns of regular and decaf coffee, pitchers of half-and-half, whole and skimmed milk. Now he was free until lunch prep on Tuesday and would slip down to Los Angeles, catch the Nightcrawlers' Sunday meeting, see some friends. But first, he stuck a thermos of decaf and yesterday's leftover brownies in his knapsack and tossed it into the front seat of his car.

He missed the spur on the first pass and had to turn back. Up the narrow dirt road, he parked next to Libby's Mercedes. The sun was strong, the air smelled of hot sage and warm, standing water. Parallel jet trails had blown into broad horizontal stripes, like an overarching rib cage. The lake water was dark green, shiny and wrinkled. Orange barrels bobbed by the dam. A steady, persistent northerly breeze made Lewis's clothes flap and flutter against his body.

The air was calmer down in Libby's spot. She had only one line in the water, the pole propped against her folding lawn chair. Her hands rested over her rounded belly. She gazed out at the lake from under a black mesh bill hat. Afraid to startle her, Lewis rolled small rocks past her chair until she glanced around. Immediately, she turned back to the lake.

"I hope I'm not disturbing you," he said.

She pursed her lips. One eyebrow lifted as if on a string. Her hat read RITO, CALIFORNIA in red stitching.

"I'll leave if you prefer."

She whisked an iridescent green fly off her shoulder and maybe, *maybe*, gave the slightest shrug.

Lewis hunkered down beside her. A swarm of the shiny green flies buzzed over the ground. The sun was hot, and he wished he'd brought a hat. Libby slapped at another fly.

Lewis looked down at the familiar crackled mud. "You know, Libby, I was pretty messed up when I met you." He peeled a corner off one mud tile and tossed it into the water. "You were so kind and generous. I have nothing but good thoughts about our time together." He took a steadying breath, pushed on. "I never meant to run out on you, but I short-circuited. It's pretty unforgivable, I know." She was staring straight ahead. "Just the same, I wish you'd forgive me. And I think you can, because given the same circumstances, I know I wouldn't do the same thing again."

Just when he decided she'd taken a vow of silence, Libby began to speak. "In a way, Lewis, I do forgive you: I wish you well. I want you to teach, publish, stay sober—whatever you want most for yourself. But the damage is done. I don't say that to be vengeful. But something happened with us—to me, at least. On a physical level. Maybe being pregnant exaggerates it." She caught a loose strand of hair and mashed it back under her hat. "I have this reaction now: you come into a room and I want to leave it. I see you, I reflexively look the other way. It's nothing I *decide* to do. It just *is*. You did what you did, and this is the result. It's like aversion therapy that worked."

Lewis thought of saying, Well, I didn't want it to work that well, but something told him not to joke—at least not about this, not yet. "Do you have an aversion to brownies?" He held up his knapsack.

She didn't smile, though her shoulders registered another minuscule shrug.

He poured coffee into styrofoam cups and unwrapped the brownies.

She took a bite and frowned.

"That bad?" he asked.

"Raisins? In a brownie, Lewis?"

"No good, huh?"

"Not really." She kept chewing, took another bite. "I'm hungry, though."

His legs grew tired, so he sat down on the mud flat, hugging his knees. The sun baked his head. Libby, he could tell, was barely tolerating his presence. Last night, a man at the AA meeting said that to feel good about himself, he would line up all the women he ever slept with in his mind. Just seeing them and remembering their sweetness calmed him down, comforted him. This technique, thought Lewis, would never work for him. Sitting next to just one ex-lover made him want to explode.

"I'm sorry," he said. "And I've been wracking my brains about how to make amends to you." This was not true. He'd assumed a simple apology would dissolve her hostility. "I had this idea," he said, talking off the top of his head, "maybe I could help with the new house. I could work, oh, three hours every Sunday. I'll stain like I did last week, or pound nails. I don't really care. Whatever needs to be done."

"We have contractors," Libby said. "Anything we do up there is because we want to have some hand in it."

"I can do stuff contractors don't want to, like dig a garden or wash windows. You won't ever have to see me. I'll work Sunday mornings. You'll be here fishing."

Libby popped the last of her brownie into her mouth and spoke with her mouth full. "You get used to them, the raisins."

"Leave me a note saying what needs to be done. 'Stain wood-work.' 'Spade garden.' Or leave the punch list. I'll go up to the house every week until . . ." He tried to think of a reasonable length of time. "Until it's done."

Libby brushed off her hands, flicked chocolate crumbs from her sweatshirt, and hazarded a look his way. It was true: her eyes couldn't rest on him. "It's hard to say if that would change anything," she said.

"I'd like to try, anyhow," Lewis said. "A shot in the dark."

Back at his car, the right front tire was so low, it was almost flat. When he opened the trunk, he remembered he had no spare. In town, he filled the low tire, but couldn't get it fixed because Fritz's Texaco, the only gas station, was closed. He could risk the drive and make the last half of the Nightcrawler meeting, but a flat on the freeway would be expensive. He went instead to Round Rock and lay down in his bungalow until the phone rang. "You *are* home," said David Ibañez. "Come play softball. The Doodads are low on men."

"I'm not up to it," Lewis said, "and I'm a Shithead anyway." He spent the rest of the day in bed.

LETTUCE, David explained, contains a faint opiate; his mother and aunts used to make a tea from the leaves to soothe their restive babies. If Libby was having trouble sleeping, she might try some. If she needed something stronger, he told her, throw in two tablespoons of poppy seeds.

Libby obeyed this advice and had her first good night's sleep in weeks. Try as she might to see things from Billie's point of view, David did not seem, finally, a con artist. He was too soft-spoken, thoughtful.

She had conducted her own investigation. "So, you worked with cancer patients in Tijuana?" she asked when he came to the office to read client files.

"Not specifically," he said. "Only those with chronic pain. I worked with one woman who had terrible joint pain after chemotherapy, and a man who had a tumor in his neck—benign, actually —that caused obliterating headaches. So, I haven't had much experience with cancer, no."

"If you have any bright ideas to see me through this thing I've gotten myself into, please"—Libby drummed fingers on her belly— "let me know. It seems like everybody I meet has a new horror story of an eighty-hour labor."

"I'm no expert on childbirth," David said. "I've only attended one birth, in New Mexico, and the only thing I remember is that the father cooked the placenta and gave a tidbit to everyone present. It was no worse than other organ meats. A bit chewier, maybe."

Libby clapped her hand over her mouth, spoke through her fingers. "We won't be having my placenta for lunch."

"No?" He smiled. "I do know, though, that the general principles for pain management apply to labor. So much of pain is resistance to pain—you know, what they teach you at Lamaze."

"When in doubt, hyperventilate?"

Red came in as David left, and Libby made the big concession: "He's pretty nice."

"David? Yeah, he's working out really well."

How had she ever found, much less married, a man who didn't gloat?

THE NEW house was locked up tight. No note. No punch list. The roof had gone on, so Lewis walked around the site picking up scraps of roofing felt and broken cedar shingles. Also, the drywallers had evidently made great sport sailing odd pieces of sheetrock out of windows. He picked up these scraps, too, and kicked at the chalky stains in the pink dirt, a precise expression of the dejection he felt for this lonely, thankless task he'd assigned himself.

Red, arriving around nine, was surprised to find him there. No, Libby hadn't mentioned anything about Lewis working at the house. "But this is great," Red said. "I wasn't looking forward to being by myself." They stained window and door casings and applied coats of urethane. Red grew talkative and reminisced, describing Round Rock in its first years, when only six or eight guys rattled around in the mansion. "Doc Perrin or somebody from Social Model Detox was over almost every night to baby-sit, make sure we weren't having keggers." Then he told Lewis how the large Victorian came to be its unusual shade of blue: "The same day I headed out to buy a hundred gallons of white exterior latex, an itinerant band of housepainters rolled into town. I ran into them at Victor's. Their estimate, paint and labor, was substantially lower than my paint cost alone. Seemed like a miracle at the time. Of course, the color choice was limited. 'Seafoam,' I think it was called. At any rate, they primed nothing, masked nothing, just fired up a wheezing air compressor and shot paint in the general direction of the house until everything—windows, limestone, all the shrubbery—was covered." Red paused for a moment, then frowned. "Forgive me, Lewis," he said. "Maybe the prospect of being a father again has made me introspective. I've been thinking and thinking about my life, like it's some long, complicated dream."

"That's *très* Buddhist," said Lewis.

"Hey, you should come over for dinner soon. I'm a barbecuing fool these days."

"Sounds good."

"I'll see when she's up to company."

At noon, Libby herself came in, carrying a box of antique door knobs and window hardware. Her cheeks were flushed from lakeside sun and wind. "Hello, Lewis," she said with a trace increase of warmth, then disappeared into the back bedrooms. Red kept poking his head into the hall, clearly torn between keeping Lewis company and seeking her out.

Lewis stuck his brush in thinner. "I'd better be moseying along." For the rest of the day, he stayed close to home in case Red came through with a dinner invitation. He held out until eight-thirty, then drove into Buchanan for a spinach omelette at Denny's.

NAPPING one afternoon between lunch and dinner prep, Lewis was awakened by Gustave's furious barking. A gray Saab had pulled up in front of Red's office, and Gustave was at the driver's door, feinting and baying like a hyperactive hellhound. Lewis came out to his porch and called, but the dog was too crazed to notice, so Lewis had to walk over, grab hold of his collar, and pull him back.

The woman who stepped out of the car was older, maybe fifty, with short graying hair in a mannish cut. Putty-colored linen pants. Crisp white shirt. Heavy gold at neck, wrist, ears. Lewis pegged her as a state inspector, or one of many fund administrators who came out for a look before awarding Round Rock a grant.

"Sorry," he said, pulling Gustave into the house and slamming the door. When he turned back, the woman was gazing about, shading her eyes with her hand. She appeared confused.

"Looking for Red Ray?" he asked, walking toward her.

"No, but this *is* his bungalow, right?"

"The very one."

"I'm supposed to meet David Ibañez here at two." She dropped her hand from her brow and offered it to Lewis. "I'm Pauline," she said, and they shook.

It was David's birthday, she told him, and Red was lending them his bungalow for the night. Lewis was incredulous. Women swooned over David, and somehow he'd chosen this refined, older matron, as formal and self-possessed as an elk.

"Uh-oh," Pauline said, as Gustave burst through a window screen. Lewis caught him at the foot of the steps and was again dragging him toward the house when David appeared, on foot, in the roadway. "Sorry I'm late," he said as he walked up. "The Land Cruiser has a flat."

While David and Pauline embraced, Lewis got Gustave back into the bungalow. He closed all the windows and left him locked inside when he went to cook dinner. When he came home and let him out around nine, the hot and airless house stank of dog, and Gustave had chewed up a library book and a sofa cushion. The dog had another barking fit at midnight, and Lewis looked outside just as David and

Pauline climbed out of the Saab. Under the mercury-vapor light, David looked soft in the face, thick in the middle, the gray streaks in his hair conspicuous. He, too, looked unequivocally middle-aged.

Lewis caught Gustave's collar. "Good birthday dinner?" he asked.

"Quite good. Red grilled swordfish," Pauline said. "Libby baked an orange cake."

Back in his bungalow, Lewis called Barbara. "Sorry to wake you," he said, "but I'm desperate to talk to somebody. I am so far off the social registry up here, I feel like a goddamn leper."

Barbara yawned. "So what are you going to do about it?"

"Quit?"

"I don't think so," she said languidly. "Sounds to me like the perfect place to finish your dissertation."

LITTLE Bill Fitzgerald took a summer job in his uncle John's West Hollywood law firm. Billie and Old Bill drove him down, helped him get settled in John's house in Bel Air, and stayed on for a month themselves. The moment Billie came home, she phoned Libby. "Come over right now," she said.

When Libby arrived, she encountered what must have been the entire Neiman Marcus baby department. Dresses, jumper suits, T-shirts in deep, beautiful, saturated colors, all so much nicer than the river of cheap pastel-pink polyester items arriving from Libby's mother and aunts. Even the diaper covers were beautiful—deep purple, teal, royal blue, and, as Libby couldn't help noticing, twenty-six dollars a pop.

"There's so much great baby stuff these days," Billie said. "It's enough to make me think about having another kid."

"God, wouldn't that be something," said Libby.

"On second thought, you have the baby and I'll just buy the clothes."

"This baby's already better dressed than her mother ever was."

"So why don't you let Red finance a new wardrobe?"

"I don't believe in spending a fortune on maternity clothes," Libby said. "You only wear them for a few weeks."

"Good God, girl, live it up for a change! You have a rich husband now."

"Or *had* one," Libby said, "before we started building this house."

"It wouldn't hurt you to spend a little on yourself."

"Words of wisdom from the doyenne of muddy jeans."

"That may be so," said Billie, "but I don't have to keep a man attracted to me."

"What, you think Red's that superficial?"

"All men are—especially when it comes to pregnancy. It grosses men out. Women get fat and emotional, and the guys freak."

"Some men more or less revere it."

"Did you say 'revere,' Libby? That's good. *Revere*."

"You know what I mean," said Libby. "Red's pretty cool about the whole thing."

"Oh, they like to reproduce, all right," said Billie. "But they're so squeamish. Ever want to scare a man off, just say 'vaginal discharge.'"

"Not all men," Libby said. "David Ibañez *ate* some placenta."

"Placenta?" Billie looked as if she were about to throw up, or cry. "He is such a liar."

"I don't think so," said Libby. "Why would he lie about something like that?"

"So Red went ahead and hired him?"

"Yeah, and the men are crazy about him. He must've worked through whatever problems he had when you knew him. He's so open and friendly, way more than most straight men are."

"Maybe he *is* gay."

"No, no." Libby laughed. "I'm just saying I can talk to him really easily. And he's definitely not gay. He has this brilliant girlfriend. We had the two of them over the other night."

Billie's distaste, she saw, had turned into glazed boredom. Billie did that, turning off whenever a subject displeased her. Libby stood and started folding the baby clothes. "Look at this sweatshirt with all the beets," she said with forced cheer. "Oh, and this skirt has carrots and beets. It's a total vegetable look." She waved the miniature articles of clothing like white flags. But Billie was gone. After almost five years in this friendship, Libby recognized it, that instant chemical shift. Billie's eyes sank into her skull, grew large and dark, her face seeming windblown.

"You okay?" Libby asked. "You're not getting a migraine, are you?"

"No."

Stacking the clothes in a neat pile, Libby tried one more change of subject. "So how does Little Bill like working for your brother?"

"I can't talk about that right now." Billie hunched up, covering her face with her hair like a furious twelve-year-old girl.

"Oh, Billie," said Libby. "I miss him too. I miss him hanging around with us, his incredible sweetness."

Billie pulled her hair back to reveal dull, menacing eyes. "I just told you, I don't want to talk about my son."

"Sorry." Libby stuffed the teeny garments into their shopping bags. "I didn't mean to hurt your feelings."

Billie gave a broad, backhanded wave, as if to sweep Libby and all the baby clothes out of the house.

Putting the baby presents in the trunk, Libby saw that the Mercedes had a flat tire. She didn't want to go back inside, so she started trying to change it herself. She had to stand on the tire iron to get the first bolt off, which seemed exactly like something the doctor told her not to do. She was about to start walking home when Billie's foreman, Rogelio, arrived and took over.

Later that afternoon, she called and got Billie's answering machine. "Sorry if my asking about Little Bill upset you. I was so happy to see you—and all those amazing gifts, oh my God! I just wasn't thinking very clearly."

She didn't hear back, and told Red about it that evening. "She's just so changeable. A fortune in baby clothes one minute, a face full of mud the next."

"You and I both need a vacation," Red said. "Now that the house is almost done, and the farm's running smoothly"—he knocked the pine table—"let's get away. God knows when we'll have another chance once this baby pokes her head out."

YVETTE called and offered them three days in mid-August at the Ahwanee Hotel in Yosemite. She and her husband always reserved these dates, but this year they were going to Greece instead. If Libby and Red didn't mind paying $160 a night, they could have the room.

"Did Red tell you we were thinking about a vacation?" Libby asked her.

"No. I haven't spoken to him lately. We just thought you two might be interested."

Red didn't care how much it cost. Summertime reservations at the Ahwanee, he said, were impossible to get, so this was a real coup.

"Did you and Yvette go there every year?" Libby asked.

"No, I never stayed at the Ahwanee with Yvette. Must be a Bob thing."

Libby called Yvette to accept the offer. When Red took the phone to thank his ex-wife, he became monosyllabic and grunty, as he always did when he spoke to her, and signed off quickly.

"I can't imagine the two of you together," Libby said.

"She reigned and I obeyed," Red said, "except when I vanished for three days at a stretch. Our marriage was a kind of drunken opera."

"It's even harder to imagine you drunk."

"I was a merry drunk—up to a point. After that, you don't want to know."

LIBBY was pulled from sleep by a low, focused growling: a song, it seemed, of pure evil. She opened her eyes to see, inches from her face, bared teeth and a lip snagged over a curved yellow incisor. Her scream, taking root somewhere near the base of her spine, tore through her body and emerged with such force and volume that, instantaneously, the beast vanished and Lewis and Red materialized in its place.

"A huge, wild dog," Libby rasped. Her throat would be raw for a week.

"It's only Gustave. He's adopted us." Lewis was trying not to laugh. "He's not wild, just not highly socialized. But he's harmless. Sorta like everyone else I know."

"Guess what?" said Libby, "I don't find it funny."

"Gustave's okay," Red said.

"You didn't see him snarling."

"He doesn't mean any harm," Lewis said. "That's how he makes friends."

"I'll show him how *I* make friends," Libby muttered. "I'll drive him straight to the pound."

"Good luck getting him in the car." Lewis turned and walked out the door.

Libby gazed up at Red: snarling dog replaced by frowning husband.

"You really don't cut Lewis any slack," he said.

"So?"

"He's obviously lonely up here. He likes that dog."

"Nobody forced him to take the job." Libby pulled herself into a proper seated position. She remembered the dog chasing her car a few times and had assumed it belonged to the junkyard down the road. She didn't know he was the new farm mascot.

Red reached forward, brushed his fingers over the top of her ear. "Lewis is doing me a big favor," he said. "And he was over here in a second when you screamed. He's trying, Libby."

"Well, he can keep trying."

"You know, he washed all the windows at the new place yesterday."

"I know."

"You might leave him a note. If not a thank-you note, at least a suggestion of what you want done."

"I have the feeling that if I ask Lewis for anything, or appear grateful, or reveal one tiny spot of need or vulnerability, that's where he'll get me. He can do stuff at the house all he wants. But if I start expecting it, that just gives him another chance to disappoint me."

"Can you expect the worst," Red said, "and still be disappointed?"

Libby thought about this. "You're right. I do expect him to fuck up. I'd be more surprised if he followed through."

"So maybe, if you wrote him a little list of things to do on Sundays, you wouldn't be giving him an opportunity to let you down, but a chance to grow up and prove he can actually keep a promise."

"Yeah, yeah, yeah," said Libby. "But why do I owe him anything at all?"

"You don't. That's the beauty of it."

Libby thought, and not for the first time, It's hard being married to a saint. "But honey," she said, "I like being angry. I like being implacable. I like being stern and unmoving and unforgiving toward Lewis. Don't you understand? I'm having some fun."

LUCKILY, Libby noticed the new flat tire before Red went on his rounds in the morning. She couldn't believe it, and since she hadn't fixed the flat she'd had at Billie's, there was no spare. Red threw both tires into the back of his truck and together they drove to Fritz's Texaco. While Fritz put in plugs, they ate breakfast at Happy Yolanda's. And such, thought Libby, was the big difference between her two marriages. The same unpatched-tire situation would've sent Stockton into a sulk for days, possibly weeks, and there wasn't so much as a peep of reproach from Red, who in fact seemed happy for the diversion.

Billie was sitting at a table with Rogelio and her dad. Libby had left her several messages and had hoped that she was out of town again, maybe on a creep, and couldn't call back. But no: here she was, and clearly still angry. Greetings were perfunctory. Red and Libby weren't asked to join them.

"What do you think it is?" Libby asked Red as they settled into a booth in the far corner. "A temper tantrum over my pregnancy?"

"Whatever," said Red. "I wouldn't take it personally."

"I can't help it. I need my women friends right now, and she's about the only one I've got. I'm a little worried about this pregnancy, and I need somebody else to talk to."

Shortly, the doctor tried to reassure Libby. Everything was fine, although now, since the spotting hadn't stopped, he said the abortion or those weird IUD infections she had in her twenties might have weakened the cervix; the longer she was pregnant, it seemed, the more her past came back to haunt her. Nothing to worry about yet, the doctor said, so long as she avoided jumping off walls. And acrobatic, vigorous sex.

ANOTHER day, another flat. One of the tires Fritz had fixed the day before blew out as Libby was driving over to Round Rock from Howe Lane. Two fishermen stopped and changed it for her; then she drove straight back to Fritz's. "Maybe the plugs popped out," she said.

Fritz put the tire in a tank of opaque gray water, chalked where the bubbles emerged. "Nope," he said. "Whole new punctures. You have any enemies?"

"No," she said, although her black heart made its own suggestions.

She found Red picking roses in front of the Blue House. "Honey," she said. "I just had another flat, and Fritz thinks somebody is stabbing my tires."

"Then somebody is stabbing Lewis's tires too," said Red. "He also had a flat this morning—his second this week."

"You don't think Billie's crazy enough to do that, do you?"

"No," Red said. "Absolutely not."

"I wish I could be so sure."

When Red's truck and Libby's car both had flat tires the next morning, she suggested they call the sheriff. Red called Lewis and he, too, had one. "David's taking it to town right now to get it fixed." Two minutes later, he called back. David's Land Cruiser had another flat.

"Maybe I'm paranoid," Libby told Red, "but I think Billie's behind this. I think she's paying someone. I don't have any idea why, but she's really mad at me. Besides, it's the only explanation that makes any sense."

"It doesn't make sense to me," said Red. "When Billie Fitzgerald wants to make a point, she does it cleanly. Like dropping her lease here."

"Has she done that?"

"Yup," said Red. "I got the letter from her lawyer yesterday."

"Jesus," said Libby. "What are you going to do?"

"Oh, I'll just give the lease to Sunkist. It doesn't make much difference financially, but Billie took such personal interest in the trees."

"I wish I knew what's going on with her."

"I heard she's moving," Red said. "This might be her way of saying goodbye, by pulling back. But I don't think she'd stoop to flattening tires."

Red put the spares on both of their cars and threw the flats into his truck, then drove over to the farm to pick up Lewis's and David's flats.

To distract herself, Libby reclined on the sofa and wrote thank-you notes for all the baby presents that were piling up.

IN VENTURA, after picking up a large grocery and dry-goods order and buying a set of luggage and a Yosemite guidebook at the mall, Red stopped at a coffeehouse to buy a decaf latte for the ride home. He tried calling Libby from the pay phone out front to tell her that he'd solved the mystery of all the flat tires, but he kept getting the Round Rock voice mail after one ring, which meant she or somebody else was talking on the office line. He didn't leave a message; he wanted to hear her reaction, that peal of laughter.

"You have reached Round Rock Farm for Recovering Alco-holics." Hearing his own voice gave him a momentary chill. He remembered how this morning, half awake, he'd reached for Yvette—the first time that had happened. Luckily, he stopped short of speaking Yvette's name. "Nobody can come to the phone right now."

That strange lapse had startled him, accompanied as it was by a brief, involuntary shiver. As he and Libby made love—they did so now with harrowing gentleness—and later, too, while he waited for the grocery order, he'd had a quick, dark, icy taste in his mouth. "It is important," his voice said, "that you leave a message."

The girl behind the counter was close to Joe's age, and not unlike Joe in other ways as well: long and limber limbs, ash-brown hair, that lovely pearly skin. The girl seemed stuck on the boy working at the cash register. They talked back and forth about some friend who'd won a swimming award. "Decaf latte," Red said.

He could've sworn the girl dispensed the ground coffee for his latte from the same glass container she'd been using for all the other orders. Taking the cardboard cup from her hand, he said, "Are you sure this is decaf?"

"Decaf?" She twisted a silver hoop in her ear as if it were a hear-ing device. "Sure."

Outside, Red tried Libby again. Again, the voice mail picked up, so he dialed the kitchen number at the Blue House.

"Blue House, Lewis speaking."

"Just me. I'm heading home now, unless you can think of anything else you need."

"We're fine here," Lewis said.

"Hey, I figured out all those flat tires." Red had to tell someone.

"Oh, yeah?"

"It's that tire biter of yours."

"What's that?" Lewis said.

"That tire-biting dog of yours."

"*Gustave?*"

"I left the farm today, and he chased me down to the stop sign the way he always does. You know how he hurls himself against the car? On a whim, I got out to have a look, and I could actually see the punctures, plus a little dog saliva. I'm not kidding. The punctures weren't all the way through yet, but by the time I got to Rito they'd worked their way deeper and the tire was losing air. I had to stop and get Fritz to put in a plug."

"A dog can puncture a tire? Are you *sure*?"

"Those incisors are designed to bring down running animals."

"Never thought of that," said Lewis.

"Listen, don't say anything to Libby," Red said. "I want to see the look on her face when I tell her."

"Don't worry" said Lewis. "I'll leave that to you."

ALONG the coast it was cool and clear, but the temperature rose dramatically once Red had driven about five miles inland, and he broke into a drenching sweat.

Sticking his arm out the window, trying to scoop enough breeze inside to cool off, he wondered about his body—its sensitivities and weaknesses—and then about Libby's attraction to it and to him. This morning he'd held her close against him, inwardly chanting her name, and the willingness and affection of her response again made him ache with longing. How did it happen that she wasn't repelled by his cumbersome gut, his age, his indissoluble shortcomings? If anything, his character defects engaged her curiosity: "I wonder why you have such trouble firing and hiring people," she'd said with no trace of an edge in her voice. Where Yvette had seen parental failure, Libby merely said, "You're so sweet and shy around Joe, as if you can't believe he's really yours." She even appeared to love his mild but stubborn dyslexia; he often set a table backwards, or had to stop and think which was his right hand, which his left. Red had lived all his life waiting for such endless, generous interest.

Turning onto the Santa Bernita Highway, he felt the caffeine in a tidal rush of jittery energy. His hands were sweaty again. It had been so long since he'd been dosed with the stuff, he was definitely buzzed, even dizzy. Powerful drug, caffeine, though he'd hardly noticed its effects back when he poured gallons of coffee into his system. Now, eight or ten ounces generated an anxiety attack, complete with nausea.

Red caught himself patting his pockets for a cigarette. The caffeine, he thought, jump-starting that old craving as well.

Bamboo thickets flashed by. Round rocks. Smudge pots. All the many things he'd done wrong in his life. He embarrassed himself all the time. Talking a senile streak while slapping on stain up at the new house—God, he'd never talked so much to anybody. Poor Lewis. Red resolved to make amends for those sentimental benders. And to tell Libby again that he wants Lewis to come to supper. If necessary, he might have to put his foot down—especially since Libby's grudge against Lewis lately appeared more a source of amusement than a necessary distancing.

He slowed for road construction, Cal Trans workers taking down a whole screen of eucalyptus trees to widen the highway to four lanes. Red downshifted with an ominous grinding of gears, and he had to fish for second gear. Now, it seemed, the truck's transmission was going.

Several huge, shaggy old trees lay toppled, their roots tangled in snaky whorls, which, given the size of the trees, were smaller than he'd expected. A difficult sight, those toppled trees—they signified the end of this quiet, untrammeled agricultural landscape.

The first time he saw the valley, Red had flown down in secret on a February workday. Landing in Santa Barbara, he'd rented a big Buick, bought a bottle of Dewars and a sack of ice, and glided on the scotch's smooth edge into this land of old home places, purple peaks, and the citrus-soaked air of his childhood. By then freeways and housing tracts had swallowed up Pomona, Ontario, and Rancho Cucamonga. But time had moved more slowly in the Santa Bernita. A more rustic, genteel, and politically backward era had persisted for decades, although development's tendrils were now becoming visible. Walnut groves in the eastern end of the valley had given way to row crops, the first step in the developers' process—hadn't Beverly Hills arisen from lima bean fields, Orange County from celery? A city planned for the east end would put eighty thousand people where a hundred scattered souls now lived.

Coming up behind a dump truck, Red had to downshift again. Another moment of mechanical suspense before, ah, second. He could put the truck in the shop next week; they would take the Mercedes to Yosemite, anyway. He hadn't been up there since he'd gone with Frank years and years ago, even before he was married to Yvette. Late in the fall, they'd rented a tent cabin—two cots with stiff white sheets and green army blankets, a small tin woodstove, with a tidy stack of split pine and aspen alongside. They built a snapping fire, then got down to work on a quart of bourbon. A storm came up, and all night long they heard rocks bouncing down the valley walls: that weird granite clink, an interior noise, like rocks hitting underwater, or small bones breaking in the head, almost unbearable. The next morning—ragged, unshaven, feeling much more cheerful after the morning heaves subsided—they'd set out for the Tioga pass, destination Reno, but rocks the size of Oldsmobiles had slid from slag heaps and closed the road.

Up ahead, a dump truck turning off toward the landfill slowed almost to a stop. Red stayed in second. Then, accelerating, he heard a new sound in the truck's engine, the sound water makes. Maybe it was just gas sloshing around in the tank, though it seemed to be coming from up front. Hoping to isolate and identify the noise, he slowed and opened his door, trying to hear better. Hearing nothing, he slammed the door shut, and an air bag seemed to detonate between his chest and the truck's steering wheel. Had he hit the dump truck? No, there was no dump truck, only the wheel clasped by his freckly pink hands, and the white buttons on his blue chambray shirt. No air bag, no object of any kind ballooning between them. He still felt it, though: a tough sac blown up to the bursting point, pressing into him.

And now his father was in the car—or was it Frank? They were going to the water gardens. He could see the trees in the distance: the leaves, the branches, the fruit, all the crystal, silvery arcs of water.

It was not a water garden, he saw now, but a hall of people, all lined up, leaning toward him. Nobody he recognized. Their clothes were from the thirties and forties, gabardine and crepe in autumnal colors: tailored jackets in rich browns and wines on the women, the men in full-cut suits of cinnamon, chocolate, charcoal gray. An AA meeting, it seemed, or the first AA meeting, before it broke into fifty thousand splinter groups. Red searched for Bill Wilson, the founder, and his wife, Lois—he would so like to meet them. He raised his hand to shake theirs, and all the people vanished. In their place stood a row of eucalyptus trees, upright, rooted, stubborn with life. His mind clear as rain, Red thought, I lost it, damn it, and tried to swerve, but the truck hit the dirt berm and, for the next long moment, flew.

LEWIS was in the kitchen waiting for bread dough to rise. The phone had been ringing constantly—Red called a couple times from Ventura, David called from the office and asked Lewis to look in his room for a client's discharge papers. Ramón, the breakfast cook, called to say he'd like to work more meals. When the phone rang again, Lewis considered not answering it, then picked up. "Round Rock, Lewis here," he said.

"It's me, David." His voice came from a noisy, echoing place.

"Where are you?"

"Buchanan General," he said. "Look, I have some very bad news."

Lewis knew as much from his intonation. David had recently told him about taking a rare folk poison, and Lewis's first thought was that the toxin had somehow, belatedly, kicked in. He drew a breath, let it out. He was standing in the Blue House kitchen, at the desk in the back. Through the window he could see the black silhouette of an oak tree backlit by the sun. If the news was bad enough, he knew, this could become a place he'd never seen before. He sat on the desk. "Okay," he said.

David said, "We lost our good friend Red Ray today."

"Red?" Surely David meant someone else—Frank Jamieson, perhaps. *Red?*

"He had a heart attack driving back from Ventura. Drove his truck into a tree. The ambulance crew started resuscitation, but they couldn't bring him back."

"Oh my God," Lewis said, not because he truly felt any emotion or pain yet—he was numb as ice—but because the immensity of the fact was right around the corner. "And Libby? Was she with him?"

"No, he was alone. She's in there with him now—with his body."

Red's body?

Lewis heard squeaky rhythmic noises on David's end and thought, Someone must be wheeling a gurney past. Then he realized David was crying.

I'll be crying soon, too, Lewis thought.

"I'm worried about her, though." David sounded calmer than Lewis would've ever thought possible. "She's been cramping badly. I'm afraid she might lose the baby. I was there at the office when Burt came and gave her the news. It's a big shock." David took a deep breath. "She managed to call Joe and Yvette, but that's it. Can you handle the house for a while? And maybe get ahold of Perrin?"

"I'll call a house meeting," Lewis said. "And I'll call all the Old Bastards. I can do that. It hasn't hit yet. I know it will, but it hasn't yet."

"Thanks," David said. "Because I want to stay with Libby until her parents arrive."

When Lewis hung up, before he went to tell anyone the news, he walked out of the back door of the kitchen. Across the driveway was a grove of Washington navels just blushing orange, and overhead the sky was streaked with high gray clouds. The late-afternoon light was soft and slanted. Lewis cried just a little, skimming off the first thin foaming-up of grief. "Red," he said in a reasoning voice, as if calling him to reconsider this last, drastic action. The sky shimmered. "Red," he said again, as if Red were indeed close by. Oh, the dark, leathery leaves, the spherical fruit, the trajectory of a swallow! The more Lewis looked around, the more exquisite everything seemed, those wispy clouds, the fine sparkle of mist and dust. He could see the glint of pale golden sunlight on everything—dried blond weeds, granite rocks, even on the pollen and motes in the air; all of it was shining, shining, as if Red's love had burst upon the world and settled evenly, briefly, over everything.

HUNDREDS of the farm's sober alumni and every recovery professional in a fifty-mile radius showed up at the Blue House for the AA meeting that night. The ballroom was SRO. Barbara, Celia, and Kip had driven up from Los Angeles. Lewis stood against the front wall and watched people arrive, greet each other, hug. Everyone looked stunned, their faces swollen, their movements awkward.

About ten minutes after the meeting started, David slipped in beside Lewis. "Libby's still in the hospital," he whispered. "She started bleeding and the doctors are afraid she's going to miscarry."

Julie Swaggart led the meeting. She told everyone that Red had suffered a massive heart attack; it was unlikely he would have survived even if he hadn't lost control of the truck. He was probably dead before he crashed.

Julie said Red embodied experience, strength, and hope for all alcoholics. She said he'd been as dear and necessary to her as her own husband and children. "I remember when I first saw him in meetings. He was around forty and still limping from his accident and trying to sort out his life. He was so sweet and lost. Worried about his son, and couldn't decide if he should continue practicing law. . . .

"Six years later, when I came to work for him, he'd become the Red Hornet. Couldn't sit still. Coffee, cigarettes, and go-go-go. He used to say, 'Julie, everybody should be happy to hire the alcoholic. They have to do the work of three people to feel as good as one.' But he always made time for the men. Whenever I couldn't find him, I knew where he was—glad-handing the sorriest guy at the house, the one everybody else had written off as a lost cause.

"Red imprinted everybody he met," Julie concluded. "And his imprint was love."

She called on a man named Luke, a little bald guy who had been one of Round Rock's first residents. "Oh, we had a ball here that first year," Luke said. "I did the cooking when Ernie wanted a night off. Everybody pitched in, with everything. Red was just one of us. Red and Frank. Sure, Red supposedly had his own place over the other side of the ranch, but most mornings we found him sleeping in the library.

"We'd go into Buchanan for meetings, and on the way to and fro we'd stop in at the Copper Coffeepot with Frank. Always the Copper Coffeepot. And every goddamn time, even if he'd just done it two hours ago, Red gave the waitresses five bucks to sing Frank 'Happy Birthday' and bring him a slice of cake with candles. Frank would light his cigarette off the candles. . . .

"To this day, when I'm in a mess or don't know what to do, I always think, What would Red do? And it's always the same thing. Pray. Write some kind of inventory. Talk to another alcoholic. Pause, give yourself a little room to think."

Gabriel, who spoke next, had known Red in his drinking days. "If you think he was generous sober, you should've seen him drunk. He'd buy drinks for fifty people all night long. I waited five years after Red to get sober myself. He was my scout. He looked good to me, happy, and that's what gave me courage. I'd say to myself, Look at Red Ray. He loved his drink, but now he loves his life.

"I came to Round Rock just when Red started the Sunday softball games, and I never figured out where he learned to pitch like that. He'd send you these way-out, swoopy thunkers you couldn't hit off. The more sober you got, the more those pitches confounded. . . ."

Gabriel stepped down and Doc Perrin, weeping openly, came to the podium.

"I remember the day fourteen, fifteen years ago when this rank damn crippled newcomer says he wants to turn his estate into a drunk farm. A crazy fucking deal. Thing was, we needed a house. There wasn't any kind of halfway facility anywhere around here, unless you count the Good Brothers Home, where they fed you oatmeal and Jesus at every meal. We'd send people out to Camarillo and Acton back then. They'd bounce back to us in a few months, worse than ever, livers shot, yellow as baby damn ducks.

"I said, 'Red, you get a board of directors and a good lawyer and let's go to work.' Like Luke said, Red got sober with this farm. He grew up here. And everyone on the farm grew up with him. He took whoever was here through all the phases of his own sobriety. Around two and a half years sober, he went spiritual on us. Hired a farm chaplain, mostly so he could have long, theological discussions with him. Is George here?"

A man waved from the center of the crowd.

"Well, you'll remember," Perrin said. "For months, maybe years, it was Meister Eckhart all the time. 'God is neither this nor that' . . . 'God is the foundation without foundation.' Remember how he was always quoting? 'Flee and hide yourself before the storm of inner thoughts, for they create a lack of peace.' Remember?

"Then he hooked up with this Jungian therapist, and all he wanted to talk about were dreams. He had these wild theories. He'd tell you his dreams and analyze yours. He was good at it, too. I used to call him up with dreams all the time and he'd say to me, 'Is it right, Doc? 'Cause a dream isn't interpreted until the dreamer says it is.'

"Next it was transcendental meditation. He'd pay out of his own pocket if anyone wanted to learn to do it. He put out hundreds of dollars getting people to meditate. He even got me to, only he made me pay my own way. He was generous, but he wasn't a fool.

"Greatest thing that ever happened to me was Red asking me to be his sponsor. He's kept me sober all these years—you know, the drunk's overdeveloped sense of responsibility. If I slip, I thought, who'll keep an eye on that crazy SOB and all you sorry drunks at the house?

"I'm gonna tell all of you hardheaded bastards something. You think you kick alcohol, you're in the clear. But the other stuff is just sitting there, waiting to jump you. This disease moves sideways, right into cigarettes, coffee, sugar, food, gambling, women, adrenaline, you name it. So if you guys want to do something in memory to Red, throw away those damn cigarettes. Start drinking water."

Before closing the meeting, Julie took a straw poll. "Just out of curiosity," she said, "let's see the hands of the people Red sponsored in this room." About forty people, including Lewis, raised their hands, and then everybody else's hands went up, too.

BARBARA AND LEWIS drove to the hospital early, before he had to start lunch. They'd picked a large bouquet of roses, which Barbara took up to Libby's room. Lewis went to see Red's body, but an orderly at the morgue told him Red had been sent to the coroner's for an autopsy and after that would be cremated.

Lewis couldn't stop thinking about the last time he'd seen him. Before leaving for Ventura, Red had come to get the food order. He told Lewis he was taking Libby to Yosemite in a few days. He seemed harried, distracted. "Oh, live it up, Redsy," Lewis told him. "You guys deserve a break."

Then that conversation on the phone—was he the last person to talk to Red?—and the revelation about Gustave. . . . Last night, before all the people poured in for the meeting, Lewis tied the dog to a tree and left him howling and baying his terrible cry.

After being turned away at the morgue, Lewis went up to the hospital's third floor. He didn't know if Libby would want to see him, so he waited outside her door for Barbara. Pacing the hall, peering into rooms, he saw extremely old people sprawled in their beds. Why Red? he thought. Why not these people already fragile as tissue?

When Barbara came out of Libby's room, she was crying. Lewis held her, breathing through her crumpled curls. "She wants to see you," Barbara said, wiping her eyes on her sleeve. "She's *really* distraught, so just ride it out with her. It's okay if you give in to it."

Libby's face was gray, her eyes sunken. She looked drugged and gaunt, and Lewis was frightened both for her and by her. An older, deeply tan woman with a cap of white hair sat in a chair close to the bed. "Mom?" Libby said, and the woman stood up on cue and moved toward the door.

"I'm Evelyn, Libby's mother," said the woman. She regarded Lewis with evident, probably chronic disapproval. "Please don't stay long. She doesn't need so many visitors, it's getting her all worked up."

"*Mom,*" Libby said.

"The doctor told you to stay quiet," she said, then left before Lewis could introduce himself.

Libby motioned him to sit down in the now-empty chair. "I was hoping you'd come," she said.

He sat there, not knowing what to say or do.

"Here," she said, reaching out. She took his hand, smoothed it flat, turned it over. "I remember this hand. Your yellowish skin. Long fingers." She clasped it between her hands. "Red would always say to me, the two men he loved the most were you and Frank."

"He saved my life," Lewis said. "He knew I wanted to get sober even before I did. He saw that far inside me."

"He saw inside a lot of people. But he got a kick out of you. He wanted me to lighten up toward you." With hair matted against her head, Libby looked like her own ghost. "He asked me to cut you some slack, to stop being so mad." She put the back of one hand to her mouth, holding Lewis's hand fast with the other. "I was mad, but mostly I was playing around." Libby bit her hand, trying not to sob. Tears coursed from her eyes. "I . . . I . . . I . . ." She kept trying to speak until the effort became spasmodic, like hiccups. Frightened, Lewis stood up, but she held on to him. It took every ounce of self-control for Lewis not to cry, too. He thought his throat and chest would split open from the effort. Not crying felt like swallowing a dagger sideways.

He took some deep breaths and Libby followed suit. Somehow, they both calmed down.

She managed to speak, finally, in a half-whisper. "He wanted you to come over for dinner, and I wouldn't invite you. He wanted to spend more time with you. He wanted the three of us to pal around again. If I'd known *this* was going to happen, I would've had you over for dinner every night." She put her hands over her face.

Lewis found a washcloth, wet it with cool water, and squeezed it out. Sponging Libby's face, he said, "Don't worry. Besides, I couldn't have come every night. I had to cook dinner at the Blue House." Warmth rose from her body. Her skin smelled familiar. Before he could stop them, his tears fell onto Libby's chest. Then he got ahold of himself and again they calmed down.

In a normal, factual tone, Libby said she and Julie Swaggart were working on funeral arrangements. "We only want three people to speak. Otherwise, it could go on for a year. But we want you to speak, Lewis. You have to speak." Her voice tightened again. "I wanted Billie to speak, too. She's known him since he came here. But Julie called and Billie said no." Libby put her hands over her face. "I called her yesterday—she was the first person I called after I found out, even before Joe. I got her machine. Mom called her again last night, but she won't pick up the phone. She hasn't come to see me. Do you have any idea why she's doing this?"

"Libby, Libby," Lewis murmured. "Please don't worry about all that now. Billie will come through, I'm sure she will."

Libby curled up in obvious physical pain. Lewis went looking for her mother, for a nurse, for anyone who might know what to do.

THE FUNERAL that took place the following Saturday was well organized, simple, and short. Too short. The drunks were stiff and awkward and restrained in St. Catherine's sanctuary—or maybe numbness had set in. A lot of people looked as if they'd been crying for days. The room seemed to dwarf them, with its forty-foot ceiling and wide wooden beams. Statues of the saints lined the walls, interspersed with dark, clumsy oil paintings depicting the fourteen stations of the cross. Except for a gruesome, life-sized crucifix, the altar was spare.

Libby was still in the hospital. The doctors were going to let her attend the service, but when she got up to get dressed that morning, the bleeding started again. David stayed with her, and her parents arrived alone at the church. They sat in the front-right pew with Ernie Tola and Frank, who had an unlit cigarette in his mouth. Lewis sat in the left-front pew between Doc Perrin and Joe, who was dry-eyed but trembling. On Joe's other side was Yvette, a regal-looking woman with white hair.

Julie Swaggart sang "The Lord Is My Shepherd" in a rich, roomy voice. George, the former Round Rock chaplain, who had officiated at Red and Libby's wedding, led everyone in the Lord's Prayer and then read a passage from Meister Eckhart:

> Hold fast to God and he will add every good thing. Seek God and you shall find him and all good with him. To the man who cleaves to God, God cleaves and adds virtue. Thus, what you have sought before, now seeks you; what once you pursued, now pursues you; what once you fled, now flees you. Everything comes to him who truly comes to God, bringing all divinity with it, while all that is strange and alien flies away.

Doc Perrin spoke the main eulogy, and kept it clean and short for the lay audience: a list of awards and accomplishments. Luis Salazar gave a formal speech filled with hyperbole: "My great friend . . . the most God-loving man. . . ." Lewis told how he and Red used to drive all over Ventura picking up supplies, and how long it took because Red fell into conversations at every stop. From the pulpit, Lewis spotted Billie Fitzgerald in a black suit sitting in the back bracketed by the Bills.

Libby's father got up and said how happy Red had made his daughter, and conveyed Libby's thanks to all their friends for coming as well as her request that any contributions be made to Round Rock's residential financial aid fund.

All the speakers were so afraid of taking too long, they didn't speak long enough. The funeral was over in thirty-five minutes.

Afterward, a lunch was held in the town park. Lewis stayed for a few minutes; then he and Barbara drove back to the Blue House and started making lasagna for dinner. It felt good to be doing something, anything, even browning meat and stirring a big vat of spattering sauce. Lewis couldn't stop thinking or talking about Red. "I got a lift every time I saw him. He was so comfortable to be around. More comfortable than anyone, ever, in my family. He was always so even-tempered, so amused by life."

Barbara let him talk. "Grief seems to be a form of obsession," she said when he apologized for going on so. "You have to go over and over everything, if only to fully discover what you've lost."

As soon as the men were served, Lewis and Barbara drove back to the hospital. Libby was sleeping, her mother said, and sedated. So far, there was no miscarriage. They were going to stitch her shut and she would have to spend the rest of her pregnancy in bed. "She'll come home with us," said Evelyn. "That's best."

Lewis and Barbara stayed with Libby so her parents could get some dinner. Lewis liked sitting in the dim, quiet room. At one point, when Barbara went out to call her boyfriend, he cried a little. He rinsed out another washcloth and held it to his own face until Libby spoke. "Lewis? Are you all right?"

He told her his version of the funeral. "The ceremony was a little short."

She closed her eyes. Let out a long breath.

"I'm going to be okay, I think," she said. "I'm going to carry this baby full-term and all of us are somehow going to be okay."

Hearing this, Lewis's chest started to jump. He couldn't stop it. First, he made a high, soaring whine, then began to sob. He held the washcloth against his mouth as a kind of muffler—he didn't want the whole hospital staff running in to see what all the racket was about. Libby looked on, tears streaming from her bright eyes. Lewis bent over, bellowed into his lap, and she touched his hair, his forehead, the edges of his arms, whatever part of him she could reach.

LIBBY'S refusal to go home with her parents caused some bad feeling, especially between mother and daughter.

Initially, she wanted to go back to her house on her property, but David and Lewis suggested she move into Red's bungalow on the farm so they could keep an eye on her. After some consideration, she agreed. This caused further ill will: Evelyn was convinced that staying at Red's place would be gratuitously distressing, while David and Lewis argued that Libby wouldn't feel so isolated, and also she could work there, from the bed, once she felt up to it.

Lewis spent Monday afternoon at Libby's bungalow catching her two young cats, then set up a bedside desk at Red's with her computer and telephone. The next afternoon, Libby came home from the hospital. When Lewis stopped in to see her, Evelyn was in the kitchen unpacking groceries. "It almost killed her to walk in here," she told him in a harsh whisper.

Hot with shame, Lewis tapped on the bedroom door.

Libby smiled, though her eyes and nose were red and her cheeks were wet. The cats curled like round pillows on the bed, one black, one calico. "Great desk setup," she said. "And these monsters . . ." She scratched the calico's head. "You haven't seen Billie, have you?"

Lewis gave a short laugh. "Billie and I don't exactly hang out much."

"Not even in town or driving around? I'm just curious to know if she's here or gone."

"Here, I guess, unless someone else is driving her truck."

Libby pulled the sheets over her face and he could see her body quaking.

Evelyn came in behind him. "Oh, honey, you can't keep this up. . . ." She sighed and turned to Lewis. "I told her it would be too emotional for her to be here."

Every time Libby collapsed, Evelyn blamed it on her being in Red's house, and spoke in sharp, hurried tones, as if a week of grief were already excessive. After three or four days, there was a scene and Libby asked her mother to leave. Barbara came up for the next ten days and Libby still cried frequently, but was less prone to wild bouts of self-reproach.

Together, everyone at Round Rock moved slowly out of a stunned lethargy. In retrospect, the first week following Red's death—the huge nightly AA meetings, the funeral—seemed lit in rich, somber tones and executed in slow motion. Bit by bit, Lewis felt himself jerked back into the harsh glare of daily life with all its demands and the awful knowledge that Red would not be joining the staff for coffee in the mornings. He would not be telling stories while painting at the new house. He would not walk by on his morning rounds or clatter past in his old Ford truck.

The truck was at Harry Zeno's junkyard, and Libby asked Lewis to decide whether it should be repaired, sold, or junked. The sheriff had brought in the groceries and new luggage that were strewn in the ditch at the accident, but nobody had gone through the cab.

The junkyard was a small field of wrecked cars sunk in weeds, with a teardrop trailer for an office. Red's truck was right by the front gate, its toothy grille snarled as if still frozen in the anticipation of impact. The accident itself wasn't much more than a fender bender—the fan wasn't even smashed into the radiator. There was not nearly enough damage to kill anyone.

The heated-up cab smelled strongly of old oil, hot dust, and decomposing rubber, the smells Lewis remembered from that first ride he took with Red Ray from detox. His fingers went numb around the glove-compartment clasp, his vision suddenly darkened. A cardboard coffee cup lolled on the floorboards. The glove compartment contained maps, a half-full bottle of Excedrin. Lewis's lips tingled, as if charged with electrical current: the smears on the steering wheel and floor that looked like dried chocolate ice cream were Red's blood.

Lewis curled up on the front seat. It seemed unfair, cruelly ironic, and unspeakably sad that Red, who devoted so much of his life to chiseling away at human desperation and loneliness, was alone when his heart exploded, when his truck sprang for the trees.

Lewis had the Ford towed to a body shop in Rito. Once it was repaired, he and David caravaned south and sold it to a prop house in Burbank.

CLEO BARKIN, as president of Round Rock's board of directors, served as the temporary director; that is, she signed the checks. Lewis took over the supply runs and helped Libby with the secretarial tasks. David coordinated the staff and volunteers and split the intake and exit interviews with the psychologist. By each taking a few of Red's duties, they kept the place operating, but any long-range planning was put on hold. For Red, Round Rock had been an ongoing, dynamic picture in his head, and he knew instinctively and absolutely what should come into that picture and what should go out. Countless small decisions were made against his sense of the larger whole: when to call a repairman, arborist, or psychiatrist, when to just fix the problem himself. Nobody else had Red's overview, not yet, and slowly a sprung or fractured quality crept into farm life. No single thing faltered, but on some days it felt as if a good gust of wind could sweep the entire enterprise off the map.

LIBBY was confined to bed. She stretched this to mean sitting on pillows on the back stoop, sunning her legs. Barbara and Lewis moved bookshelves and a large bow-front dresser out of the bedroom to make way for a white wicker bassinet. The top of a small, low dresser became a padded changing table. Red's closet was emptied and refurnished with Formica shelves filled with cloth diapers, receiving blankets, and stacks of doll-sized clothes. Red's wardrobe was heaped in the living room in languorous bales of lightly starched dress shirts, plastic-wrapped, custom-made suits. Given his choice, Lewis took two cashmere sweaters and three silk ties.

When Barbara left, David arranged for his aunt Gloria to come in mornings and evenings, prepare meals, and sit with Libby. During the days Libby read books, tried to do office work. She called Lewis at all hours, at his bungalow or in the kitchen. "I hate to bother you," she said. "Can you talk?"

"Sure." Holding the phone to his ear with his shoulder, Lewis would chop onions, flip turkey burgers.

"I was thinking," Libby said. "Maybe Billie really was in love with Red all these years. She showed up for his funeral, after all. Have you heard anything about her moving?"

"Maybe you should write about this in your journal," said Lewis.

"I wouldn't know where to start," she said.

"Pretend it's a letter. Pretend you're talking."

Sometimes, after Gloria went home at night, Lewis came over, and they read or discussed farm business. She didn't know what to do about the new house on the hill, which was being painted, tiled, and carpeted according to schedule. "I say I want to stay in this valley, because that's where my friends are, but when I actually look at what I mean by that, I see that Red is dead and Billie won't talk to me, and you're going away to teach soon and David I'm just getting to know. . . . Do I want to ramble around the new house all alone with a baby? Should I move back to Los Angeles? I don't have any friends there, either."

"Maybe now isn't the time to make any big decisions," Lewis said. "Let's concentrate on having a healthy baby first."

"Since when do you sound like a shrink, Lewis?" Libby laughed, then began to cry. "Oh, I know Billie's not your favorite person. I wish I knew what happened. Do you have any idea?"

"She has a mean streak," he said.

A few days later, Libby handed him a letter to read.

> *Dearest Billie,*
>
> *I love you and miss you desperately, and yearn to talk to you, to hear your voice, to see your beautiful face.*
>
> *I'm afraid I hurt your feelings in a way I'm too dense to see—I feel helplessly, damningly oblivious. I'll do whatever I can to make it up to you.*
>
> *I can't live in this valley without your friendship. Please come see me or call, or at least write and tell me what I can do to clear the way for our friendship to resume. If this is not possible, at least let me know why not, and where my insensitivity lies.*
>
> *Love,*
> *Libby*

"Should I mail it?" she asked Lewis.

"I don't see why not," he said.

LIBBY sometimes played the violin when she couldn't sleep. It wasn't loud enough to keep anyone else awake; Lewis was already an insomniac. She played Bach cello suites, transposed for the violin— dry, vigorous workouts designed, it seemed, to carry the listener down some endlessly branching path deep into the soul. Or she'd take up a fiddle tune—"Sweet Georgia Brown," "The Maiden's Prayer," or "I Don't Love Nobody"—then break it down into variation after variation, complicating, tangling, slurring, sometimes deconstructing the melody into a few coughy, unrecognizable phrases sawed this way and that; and then, gathering energy, she'd slowly tool her way back home.

One night, prodded by the violin's restless meanderings as if by an insistent finger of smoke, Lewis hauled himself to the kitchen table. The last chapter of his dissertation was the one place where, after citing some two hundred secondary sources in the preceding pages, he could actually express his own opinions. Without looking at any notes, Lewis wrote the first sentence in longhand: "Fondness and abiding mutual interest characterize the friendship of Flaubert and Turgenev. . . ."

LIBBY dug out her journal: *First time I've written since you died, Red. I couldn't face the page. Lewis has been after me. He's only being nice, though. He never did like my journal. Pretend it's a letter, he says. And I thought, I could write to you, which filled me with relief. Am I refusing to let you go? Who cares? I'm as entitled to denial as to the other four stages of grief. And you do seem close by. I suspect you are seeing and hearing everything.*

It was odd to keep a journal where the big events were lacunae. Red's death was missing, and—Libby counted—the four weeks that followed. A month. Is this how life was going to be, she wondered, a dreary accumulation of time without Red?

I'm housebound in bed. How nineteenth century. The invalid— what a strange, accurate word. One does feel so marginalized, so out-

of-life's-flow, so stumped by sadness here in this bed. It makes me cry to write to you, Red. Who could cry this much?

THE THOUGHT of writing to Red woke Libby up each morning. She couldn't wait. So she went batty for a few months, nobody would blame her. There was something deliciously dotty in writing to her dead husband while wearing his pajamas. She had new empathy for her mother's friend Betty. When her husband died, Betty wore his clothes every day for over a year—pants cuffed broadly, the sleeves of his shirts rolled up around her wrists in thick doughnuts—as if to re-animate them. Such visible, guileless grief had made Libby's mother frantic, of course. But Libby now understood the quaint and harmless charm of Betty's actions; and who could've guessed Red's cotton pj's would be such perfect maternity wear?

My mother calls last night. I try to tell her about Billie, how she still hasn't phoned or answered my letter.

Oh honey, you can't let every little thing bother you, Mom says. You've just got to pull yourself up by your bootstraps.

Mom, I say, I look down and can't even see my feet. And even if I did, it's been weeks since I could tie my shoes.

Wouldn't it be easier not to be reminded of Red everywhere you look? she says. You should be in a place where time can work its cure.

But I don't want to be cured, Red. I want to have this baby in your house. I want her to have a sense of you. I want her to feel the way this bungalow feels, see the endless rows of trees, smell the groves, inhale the cool morning fog. After she hears the voices of your friends, once she gets your world in her blood, then, if need be, we can leave.

"BILLIE hasn't answered my letter," she told Lewis. "It's been over a week."

"Sounds like let-it-go time, Lib."

"If only I could. I try and I try, but she made it possible for me to live in this valley after Stockton left. I'm not sure I know how to live here without Red *and* Billie."

"You're not going anyplace tonight, or tomorrow either," Lewis said. "Come on. I'll sit with you until you fall asleep."

"You better lay in supplies, then. You might be here a lot longer than you think."

"I think I know just the sleeping aid you need." Lewis went over to his house, brought back the last chapter of his dissertation. "It's just the first draft," he said, and began reading aloud to her. Libby tried her damnedest to stay awake. She failed.

Dearest Red, You're dead, baby. I know that. I don't expect you to walk in the door. I don't expect mail from you. With Billie, there's always a chance that the phone will ring and it will be her, that the next car pulling up to the house will be that ridiculous white truck.

Hazy hot day, Red. A day to sweat.

Joe came by with a U-Haul to take some furniture for the apartment he and Little Bill have rented in Palo Alto. We had a long talk about names for the baby. He votes with you for Susanna or Elisabeth. Little Bill, he says, wants me to name her after you, more or less: Rosie. I love Little Bill, but . . .

I wish you could see the cats tease Gustave. He's tied up under the oak tree. The cats know exactly how far his rope goes. They prowl the perimeter, tails in the air. God help them if he ever gets loose.

Oh Red. I can feel you fading.

THE BOARD met in Libby's bedroom to discuss restaffing: if David became the director, as everyone hoped, the farm would need a new house manager. Since Libby didn't know how much she'd want to do once the baby came, at least a part-time secretary was necessary. And the Blue House needed a new full-time cook right away.

"Or part-time," said Lewis. "A lunch cook. That way I can help out with more secretarial and just do dinners."

"Yeah," Libby said, "but you're leaving in a week."

"Says who?"

"You have to go teach, Lewis."

"Not this semester."

Libby appealed to the men and women clustered in chairs around her bed. "He's going to go teach."

"Too late," said Lewis. "I already put them off. The old family-emergency excuse."

Libby waved her hands at him. "Lewis, please . . ."

"I can stick around until January."

"What was the point, Dr. Fletcher, of finishing your dissertation if you're not going to teach?"

"I want to see what this baby looks like."

"Please, everybody," Libby said, "tell him to take that job."

Lewis held up a hand to halt any protests. "Besides, somebody has to take Gustave to obedience school."

HE STAYED because he could. He stayed because he hadn't when Libby's trailer burned. He stayed because he was frankly worried about Round Rock and because one-year appointments in freshman English composition weren't so goddamn precious. He stayed because it seemed like something he could do to honor Red. He stayed to demonstrate to Libby—and to himself—that he actually had changed, mended his ways.

Lewis hoped, too, that he could relieve Libby's anxiety about being alone, all of which she channeled into her breach with Billie Fitzgerald. Recently, she was trying not to talk so much about Billie—knowing it was neurotic and tiresome, a weird manifestation of her sorrow. Yet she couldn't help it: "Has Billie left town? Do you ever see her at the grocería?" She tried to sound offhand, but her voice invariably rose in pitch. "I know I should let her go. I just need more information. How can I let go of something that's gnawing away at me?"

Lewis tried to think of how Red would handle the situation. He phoned Doc Perrin, who listened closely, wheezing into the receiver.

"I don't know if there's anything I can actually do," said Lewis. "I'm not even sure if it's any of my business."

"Jesus Christ, of course it's none of your damn business," Perrin said, then paused. "You prayed about it?"

"Sort of."

"What'd God say?"

"I don't know."

"Well, if you can't figure out God's will, sometimes it's good to try the one thing you swore you'd never do. The thing that scares the holy hell out of you."

THE DRIVE up to the Fitzgerald adobe was flanked by a particularly graceful type of eucalyptus, their trunks virtually bark-free, pink and naked as scalded flesh. Although he'd once fantasized that this historic rancho would be half his, via the state's community property laws, Lewis had never seen the place: the massive, stuccoed structure sat high on a riverbank and looked more like a California mission than a private home. The roof was faded red tile matted with eucalyptus debris. Creeping fig and passion fruit vines overspread the walls. In places, stucco had fallen away, quaintly revealing the thick, crudely formed clay bricks. There was even a tower complete with rusty iron bell. Recessed windows and doors were sage green, and the front door was thick, dark wood bolted together with daunting iron straps, like the gate to an old castle or prison.

"Okay, God, you gotta stick by me," Lewis muttered as he put the Fairlane into park, "because a wild fucking bitch lives here."

Billie answered the door herself. Seeing him, her pupils constricted. "Hello, Lewis," she said. In black slacks and a loose gray sweater, she appeared well groomed, wealthy, graciously middle-aged. Her spongy black hair, pinned in a twist, was white at the temples. Her lipstick was wine red. "So, you're the ambassador."

She turned and walked into the house, leaving the door open behind her. He followed her through a cool, dark entryway, where he saw himself—T-shirt, jeans, in need of a haircut—float through a mirror the size of a billboard, and out into a large interior garden.

The house that looked so massive from the outside was, in fact, mostly garden within. In the center, arched bronze dolphins held multiple tiers of a fountain in which water trickled a whispered music. The path was decomposed granite, raked clean. Round rocks bordered beds of exotic cacti and succulents and fragrant tropical flowers. A mature, wide-spreading California oak grew in one corner, and Billie walked into its shade. A movement further down the path caught Lewis's eye: a man in gray work clothes was on his knees, cutting blades off an aloe plant with a machete.

"Libby doesn't know I'm here," Lewis said. "I came because I'm so worried about her."

"Oh, I know. Terrible about Red."

"She doesn't understand why you haven't come to see her."

"No? Do you?"

"I know that when I'm in pain, I have a tendency to pull back, keep to myself, lick my wounds."

"Please." Billie snorted. Her lips curled. "Besides, Libby has more than enough friends to comfort her."

"That's not true. She needs you. You're her closest friend."

"Not really," said Billie.

Lewis looked around. Billie's garden had more round rocks than he'd seen in one place, all of them perfectly formed. Dozens cobbled the base of the oak and hundreds more lined the beds. Several huge rocks, three to four feet in diameter, slumbered among the cacti.

In the corner, the gardener worked steadily. Each juicy vegetal slice sounded like someone whacking through bunches of celery.

Billie gave a low chuckle. "Now that Red's gone, she'll probably marry Dave, don't you think?"

"Dave who?" said Lewis. "I don't know all their friends."

"She's certainly rich enough for him now—if Red left her as much as I think he did." Billie cocked an eyebrow at Lewis. "She do okay, or were there prenupts?"

"I don't know," Lewis said, confused. "I'm sure Red was generous to her."

"Or were you planning to move back in?" She winked.

"No, no . . ." He had to turn away. The fountain sang its weak tune, counterpoint to the machete's juicy whacks. How had he ever considered this woman even remotely attractive?

She moved closer. "Tell me something, Lewis. Does Libby seem smarter to you now that she's rich? Is her mind—how did you put it?—lively enough for you?"

"Ow," he said, and briefly faced her. "I did say those things, didn't I? What a jerk, eh?"

Billie shrugged lightly, as if to say, Hey, we're all jerks, so what?

Heartened by this concession, Lewis said, "If you'd just tell her why you aren't speaking to her. That's what drives her crazy: not knowing what she did."

"Oh, she knows."

"I don't think so," said Lewis.

Billie's black shoes had a spade-shaped opening at the toe, from which peeped wine-red nails.

"Okay. I'll tell you what. You tell her I'll come back around once she gets rid of David Ibañez."

"David Ibañez?" Lewis couldn't make sense of this information. The man chopping aloe stood and brushed off his knees. He had laid the aloe branches on a burlap sack, which he now dragged by one corner to the rear of the garden. "What do you care about him?"

Billie fingered her forehead, as if locating a headache. "Tell me, Lewis, do you think Red would be so happy to see Libby consorting with a Mexican gigolo?"

He laughed involuntarily. "Libby's eight months pregnant. Her husband just died. She's not 'consorting' with anybody."

"Oh, don't be naive. This started long before Red died."

The man with the aloe trimmings was going through a door in the garden wall. Lewis wanted to call out to him, to retain some link to the reasonable human world. Would you come witness this, please?

Lewis said, "I better go."

"Here's your hat, what's your hurry?" Billie, chuckling, trotted after him as he retraced his steps through the garden and house. At the front door, Lewis stopped. He had no idea how to open it. Fear and disgust sang in his limbs. Billie glided up next to him, brushing his arm, lingering. "Believe me, Libby's just fine without me," she confided.

"I know that," he said, taking in a noseful of her dense, expensive scent. "*She* doesn't."

Billie chuckled, approving his retort, then slowly slid the flat, wrought-iron hasp aside. Lewis sprang, gasping, from the house.

Yet Billie followed. Lewis opened the car door, and she was at his elbow. He turned. She crossed her arms over her chest, flattening her breasts. "I just wish you'd seen Libby when she first came here. She was married to that worthless architect. A rich kid. You know the story, right?"

Lewis shook his head.

"Mr. Daw had been disinherited in college for selling drugs. So he found Libby and married her. She worked three jobs, sent him through school. He won some big award right out of the gate. Young Architect of the Year. His work hit the magazines, his parents reclaimed him. I'm talking old, rotten Savannah money. He didn't need Libby anymore, so he stashed her up here, found himself an actress, hid all his assets. Hid 'em so well that during the divorce, it looked as if Libby would have to pay *him* alimony. She felt lucky to get the land—and that's all she got. The land and that death-trap trailer. She couldn't finance a doghouse when he was done with her."

Billie gazed up at the trees. "I found her out in the groves bawling her head off. We took her home, gave her dinner here. Took her to movies, restaurants. Dad tried to *give* her money to build herself a home, enjoy some independence. First close friend I'd had since college."

Billie nudged his arm. "No offense, Studly, but I had Red picked out for her long before you came along. She needed somebody stable, devoted. Somebody who liked her and wasn't afraid to show it."

Lewis, he told himself, just keep your ears the hell open.

"Then, when her trailer burned down, Libby moved in with us. And where were you then, oh friend of friends?"

Lewis considered this a rhetorical question.

Billie rolled on. "Red was over every night, of course. They were up there in her room doing some kind of weird no-sex routine. They must have worked it out eventually—she got pregnant, didn't she?—although there's no telling who the father really is. . . ."

She backed off a few paces. "I gave her a wedding shower. I bought her the suit she wore at her wedding. Two thousand bucks worth of Jil Sander. I was her maid of honor. And what does she do? She takes up with the person who ruined my life."

Lewis was halfway through a full-body surge of guilt when he realized Billie couldn't possibly be talking about him.

SINCE taking on more administrative tasks, David Ibañez had fashioned a small office in what was once an old sunporch on the first floor of the Blue House. Lewis found him there scheduling speakers and panels for the AA meetings.

"Hey, Lewis," he said, glancing down at the open datebook on his blotter. "Want to lead the meeting tomorrow night?"

"Maybe." Lewis paused. "Look, I went to see Billie Fitzgerald."

David looked down at his calendar, then up at Lewis. His face was still as glass.

"She won't have anything to do with Libby unless you leave."

"I was afraid it would be something like that." David closed his eyes. "What do you think? Should I go?"

"Don't be stupid."

They listened to the small air conditioner laboring in a window.

"I left this valley for twenty years," David said, "against my will. To humor her. I had that health scare recently, and realized I had to change some things. When this job came up, I really—"

"You don't need to explain anything to me," Lewis said. "But Libby has to be told."

David scratched his pen on the blotter, drawing a craggy rock formation or febrile heartbeat.

"Right away," Lewis added.

"Okay." David slowly closed his appointment book. "Will you come with me?"

LIBBY was in bed, reading a parents' magazine. Gustave was on the rug next to her, tied to the bedpost, when Lewis and David filed into the room. "Uh-oh," she said.

"Well," David said, "there is something I need to tell you."

She turned to Lewis, scanning his face. He nodded: she could handle whatever was coming.

"What is it?" she said.

"Bill Fitzgerald?" said David. "I guess you call him Little Bill?"

Libby's hands went instinctively to her belly, as if the news might be perilous to her pregnancy. "Is he okay?"

"He's fine," David said. "He's my son."

LEWIS had heard parts of this story before, from David. But what he hadn't heard riding up in the car from L.A., was that Billie Fitzgerald also attended Sally Morrot's Thursday-night dinners, and that she often showed up in the groves those evenings when David was walking the irrigation lines with Sally.

Billie was called Mina then, short for Wilhelmina. She wasn't one of Sally's charity cases, of course, and in fact seemed to have formed a voluntary attachment to the old woman, and clearly admired her style and respected her half-baked utopian discourse. Mina even dressed like Sally, same muddy boots and jaunty hoe.

One night, after they walked Sally back to the mansion, Mina drew David into the trees and kissed him with her mouth open. For the next three years, they met secretly in the groves and hills during the summer. During the school year in Ojai, where they went to different private academies, they met discreetly on trails and in the stables at Mina's school. They had to be careful. For all her free thinking, Sally Morrot never would have condoned David's incursion into her elite corner of the social fabric. And David's uncle Rafael, who knew without being told of his nephew's involvement with Mina, warned him: "Watch yourself, *mijo*. El Cuarto kills for less"— El Cuarto being Mina's father, William Fitzgerald IV.

"Old Bill," said Libby.

"Yes," David said.

Sally passed away midway through David's senior year, when he and Mina were living together in San Francisco. He was at Cal, she a junior at Stanford. Each left dorm rooms unoccupied to share a gloriously squalid studio apartment on Eddy Street in the sorriest part of the Tenderloin. They commuted to school by day, and at night studied in coffeehouses, smoked pot, drank cheap red wine, and lived on tomato sauce dumped from the can onto boiled spaghetti. Heaven. The winos, prostitutes, addicts, and assorted desperadoes who were their neighbors seemed exotic and unexpectedly kind, bringing them trinkets from Chinatown and shooing drug dealers away from their doorstep.

Mina attended Sally's funeral, where she heard that the nephew had turned the ranch over to an agribusiness corporation that pledged to halve operating costs in the first two years. Immediately rumors flew that the resident workers would be evicted, although nobody believed such a thing was legal or enforceable. In a separate maneuver, the nephew soon discontinued David's stipend and the stipends of all the other people Sally Morrot had supported. David, in no position to contest a will he'd never seen, took a job busing tables in a restaurant on Market Street.

Coming home from a double shift at midnight, he unlocked the apartment's door and found Mina sitting on the bed and staring straight ahead. She was either in a trance or very stoned. The only light in the room came from a sand candle on the nightstand. His first thought was that somebody else had died. "I'm pregnant," she said. "Four months pregnant."

David oscillated between baths of masculine pride and clear, liquid terror. She'd been so certain of her elaborate rhythm method that he couldn't understand how this had happened. He wanted to clean out one of Mina's trust funds and move to Mexico or Thailand. "We'll write our folks when we're already married, when the baby is born."

Mina surprised him with a naive conventionality. She wanted a wedding, a large and elaborate ceremony, and was confident her parents would concur. "Oh, they'll bitch and moan and try to browbeat me, but after a while they'll give in and accept you."

"No," David said. "They'll send you to South Africa and kill me. I'll be hit by a bus or I'll simply disappear."

"Dad'll yell, Mom'll cry, and that'll be that. Then you'll be one of the family."

David did not want to be one of the Fitzgerald family, with its autocratic father, soused mother, and much-belittled son who had long since fled. David had his own family, and there was no talk of Mina becoming one of them. Once, after his first year at college, Mina had half-begged, half-dared him to bring her home for dinner. His mother served the meal, then refused to sit down at the table. His father never looked up from his food.

In their tiny Tenderloin apartment, they talked and wept and held each other, while all around them junkies and pimps moaned and beat their heads against walls.

Weeks passed without any decision; then David received news that his father had been fired, the villagers evicted, and that they had moved en masse into the Rito Town Park. David and Mina returned to Rito immediately. David, finding his family and former neighbors living in cars and tents, went straight to the park's pay phone. Union leaders and lawyers arrived within hours to organize the villagers and fight a coalition of valley ranchers led by Mina's father, who wanted the villagers evicted from the town's park as well.

Mina, visibly pregnant, had gone home to the Fitzgerald adobe. Given El Cuarto's current temper and David's role in the opposing camp, she knew better than to name the baby's father. "I'll tell them some guy," she assured David. "Some guy who got me drunk and took advantage after a football game." She'd never been to a football game in her life.

She and David agreed to meet daily in a small, neglected tangelo grove way up by the lake.

THE TANGELOS were an abandoned strain, yellow and the size of large lemons or small grapefruits, with pale orange meat. Their sweetness was tempered by quinine, whose bitterness inflamed and then numbed the back of the throat. Though the fruit was popular as a novelty item in the 1920s and '30s, sweeter strains had since been developed, and so few people found the quinine tang compelling anymore, the grove went unpicked.

David acquired a Huffy bike with fat, leaky tires. The tangelo grove was five or six miles uphill, near the lake and deep in Fitzgerald property. He went the last ten minutes on foot, through the trees.

The pregnancy had made Mina enormous and emotionally fragile. She accused David of not loving her, of abandoning his own child, of preferring politics to love, and drinking in bars instead of spending time with her. She threatened to tell her parents about him. "They'll *make* you marry me," she said.

"Or have my legs broken."

"They'll learn to love you because I do."

He begged her not to tell them, not yet, fearing that El Cuarto would exact his revenge on the villagers.

Invariably, Mina broke into tears and, mortified by her emotions, fled. He was tempted to follow and soothe her, but he was also relieved to see her go.

FROM living outside in the wet spring, the dispossessed villagers came down with flu and bronchitis. Many also suffered from gastrointestinal ailments due to drinking from park spigots whose water was piped directly from the river. Even with donations from nearby churches, food supplies were insufficient. The park had flush toilets, but no showers or hot water. David, in meetings with union negotiators, lobbied for sturdier temporary housing, yet nobody had any clear ideas about what that was or how to go about constructing it. Meanwhile, the lawyers lamented that the workers had left their village, thereby relinquishing their squatters' rights—never mind that they'd been intimidated by poised bulldozers and armed guards.

During the day, when not strategizing with lawyers and activists, David gathered with the men at the El Nido, the cafe in Rito that predated Happy Yolanda's. They drank coffee, sat at tables, and were relieved to be indoors, dry, away from the damp tents and suffering women. David stayed in the El Nido longer and longer, switching from coffee to beer after lunch and sometimes forgetting to climb down off his bar stool when the time came to start the long uphill bike ride to the tangelo grove. He began keeping the company of a few older men who were known for their drinking capacities.

He was half drunk in the El Nido when news came in that Mina Fitzgerald had taken a bad fall down stairs in her father's adobe. She'd broken an arm, and someone said she'd gone into premature labor. That was too bad, the village men agreed, but bad luck ran in that family. First, the *doña* drinking herself ill, then a daughter pregnant without a husband, now this. The men laughed a little. No matter how rich you are, they said, trouble sniffs you out, finds your door.

David sat at the bar until nobody would associate his leaving with the news about the rich, knocked-up *gringa*. He hitchhiked to the Sisters of Mercy Hospital in Buchanan, where he found Mina sitting up in bed. One arm in a cast, she gazed at him with such deadness that he already felt forgotten.

"You okay?" he whispered. "Is the baby okay?"

With her good hand, she waved him away. "It's over," she said. "My father will talk to you."

El Cuarto materialized behind him.

Even at such close range, William Fitzgerald IV wasn't a large man. He was actually rather delicate: white-haired, soft-spoken, executive in manner, his clothes the color of sand. "I believe we can settle this little matter quietly, in a civilized fashion," he said, or something like it; David would never have a precise memory of this scene, which sat in his mind as a blur of undifferentiated pain. The two men moved out of the room, down the hall, where El Cuarto produced a cashier's check made out for fifteen thousand dollars. "To help you finish medical school. No strings attached."

David would remember arguments, but could never be sure if he spoke them aloud. At some point, a private cop materialized in regulation blue.

El Cuarto, calm and condescending, went on as if speaking to a child who didn't know the language. "Your name will not appear on any birth certificate. You will not have to pay for anything, ever. Nothing more will be expected of you. Nothing more desired from you. So far as we are concerned, Mina was the victim of an unfortunate encounter in college."

David demanded to speak to Mina again. There was a scuffle, the security man's creak, the abrasive brush of ink-dark gabardine. Once David was pinioned, another paper was held up for his scrutiny: a restraining order, he was told, signed in Mina's half-cursive printing.

David didn't know, of course, that a summons and a hearing were required before a true restraining order could go into effect. For him, the document produced a silent, raging clarity. The room with its chairs, the cop, El Cuarto's quiet, raspy voice, seemed to be crystallizing. "Just let me talk to her," he said.

"That, my boy, you will never do again."

The check reappeared.

"I'll only tear it up," David said, which made the father laugh out loud in his muted, genteel, sand-colored voice. "I wish you would. Oh, how I wish you would."

David did not tear up the check. He cashed it and gave ten thousand dollars to Rafael to be used for the villagers. The rest he used to travel in Thailand, Malaysia, India.

DAVID was in Goa, drowsing on the beach, thinking he was extremely depressed, not yet aware he was in the first stages of hepatitis B, when he noticed a tall, striking woman walking out of the ocean. Her wet hair was dark, her body full-bellied, deeply tanned, soft. Not fat so much as large, big-boned, well-fleshed-out—a largeness exaggerated by the tiniest bikini. Her face was intelligent, if not beautiful. The closer she came, the older she appeared, perhaps decades older than he. One breast bore a thin, arching scar.

Divorced, wealthy, recovering from breast cancer, Gayle Sterling was thirty-eight. Her two children were only a few years younger than David. She was in Goa studying meditation and tantric healing with an iconoclastic Buddhist teacher. She guessed David was a Sephardic Jew and laughed when he said no, a California Mexican.

At Gayle's invitation, David went to her house that evening to use the telephone. She'd rented a bungalow on stilts, all polished wood; blue paisley curtains roiled out of windows in the ocean breeze. He called Rafael, who explained that the villagers had won large financial settlements in lieu of the right to return to their homes and jobs. "Mina had a son," Rafael said finally. "He is El Quinto. And she is Bill now, too. Billie." David hung up the phone and found he couldn't get up from Gayle's sofa. This would become their joke: "David came to use the phone and never left."

The doctor said David would die unless he made it to a U.S. hospital, so Gayle booked a flight. She told no one he was sick, or he never would have been allowed to board the plane. David would say he died en route, in the air over Burma. "I saw the bright light, and felt this enormous, sweet calmness, like falling into the most magnificent mattress." At this point of the story, if Gayle was present, she'd burst out laughing. "He may have felt calm, but he terrorized everybody on the plane—moaning, raving, screeching like a demon. They kicked us off in Singapore and I had to bribe an entire airport bureaucracy to get us out of there."

David spent a month in the hospital, then convalesced in Gayle's Upper West Side apartment. Looking out the window into the quavery springtime air over Central Park, David understood what Sally

Morrot had given him along with all the conversation, the coaxing, the education: an uncanny, life-saving ability to connect with wealthy women.

Once his liver recovered, he started drinking again and couldn't seem to stop. When the hepatitis came back, Gayle threatened to kick him out unless he went into treatment. His first sixty days of sobriety were spent in a private recovery center in the East Nineties. Upon his release, Gayle presented him with a puppy, a bluetick bitch he named Sally.

David lived and traveled with Gayle for twelve years; together, they compiled material for an international encyclopedia of alternative medicine. Then, after a remission so lengthy that doctors had called it a cure, Gayle's breast cancer returned to kill her.

Over these years, David had news of his son from the "Mexican telegraph," his relatives in Rito. His second cousin Carlota was Little Bill's nanny; she smuggled snapshots and announced when the boy walked, talked, learned to swim.

When he was three years sober, David wrote to Billie, enclosing a cashier's check for five thousand dollars to begin repaying what he'd come to regard as his debt, and begged to meet his son. The money was refused. He went to Rito hoping to talk to her and was met with a court summons alleging harassment. David didn't fight the restraining order: too many of his relatives worked for Billie Fitzgerald, and he didn't want to endanger their livelihoods. He put the five thousand dollars into an account that would pass to Little Bill at the age of eighteen, and kept paying into it until the sum amounted to over thirty thousand dollars.

"I told myself I was making amends to Billie by staying out of her way, by letting her dictate the terms," David told Lewis and Libby. "But maybe I was just taking the easier, softer way."

Libby kicked at her bedclothes. "Yes, because Little Bill's the sweetest human being. It's too terrible that you don't know him."

"Oh," David said softly, "but I do."

THE SUMMER after Gayle died of breast cancer, David went to stay with his aunt and uncle in Rito. "I needed to come home, whatever that meant." He obeyed the restraining order, kept off all

Fitzgerald property, laid low, and finally began learning *curan-derismo* from his uncle. He helped treat patients, met with other *cu-randeros*, gathered medicinal herbs, slowly pulling through his grief. In the afternoons, he took long hikes in the hills. On the Chapman Peak trail, up above the lake, maybe four miles from any road, he rounded a bend and saw his son picking leaves off a manzanita bush.

The boy was blocking the trail and David had to stop. He'd spied on his son for years, though always at a great distance, and to see him this close and alone was a confusing, complicated shock. Bill was twelve then, strongly built, his warm brown skin smooth as water, his hair thick like David's, curly like his mother's.

"I was terrified," David told them. "I'd trained myself to think of this moment only as a liability: it meant I was breaking the law, cross-ing Billie, possibly endangering all my relatives employed by the Fitzgeralds. I'd never once imagined how the love would swallow up every other concern."

The boy talked to him as he would've to any other adult. He was collecting leaves for biology and needed three of each type. "Are these obovate?" He held up a manzanita sprig.

David didn't recall much leaf typology, but told the boy that if you smashed manzanita leaves and berries together, then made a tea from the mash, you could soothe a sore throat.

The boy listened, placed the manzanita leaves carefully into a nylon knapsack, and proceeded up the trail to a sage bush. "These are lanceolate," he said.

"Steep a couple handfuls of those leaves in a pan of hot water," David said, "and you could ease your aching feet."

They proceeded from sage to monkey flower, lemonade plant to sugarbush, their first conversation a cataloging of the chaparral. Bill classified the leaf and David recited its medicinal properties until, without warning, the boy said, "Okay, that's it. Thanks a lot," and trotted off down the trail.

David sat on a rock waiting to get his breathing back to normal. The boy was so lovely, so much his very flesh.

Taking the same trail the next day, he found his son at the same manzanita bush. David tried to be cavalier. "Picking more leaves?"

His son faced him with an expression of contempt only adoles-cents can muster. "Look," he said. "I already know you're my dad."

On a dare from friends, a classmate in catechism at St. Catherine's had run up to Little Bill and said, "Your father's that crazy *brujo*, David Ibañez."

"Is that what you think I am?" David asked. "A crazy *brujo*?"

"No," said the boy. "You look more like a rock star."

They saw each other every day after that, up in the hills, in many of the same spots where David and Billie had once met.

"I showed up every day, rain or shine," he told Libby and Lewis. "I showed up until he knew I was there for him. When I was offered a job in New Mexico, Bill helped me decide to take it. We've been in close contact ever since."

"And Billie never knew?" Libby was incredulous.

"It's the only secret this town ever kept," David said. "Berthe Kipness once saw us in a restaurant in Los Angeles, and Rogelio spotted us at that campground on the Dennison Grade. Either Billie didn't believe them, or they never told her."

The three of them sat quietly in Red Ray's former bedroom. The late-afternoon breeze, bearing a cool tone of ocean, flapped the cover of a magazine, shifted hairs on their heads. Lewis had taken a chair by the bassinet, in which the calico cat lay curled and sleeping.

"Billie had told him his father was some kid," David told them, "who'd died in a car wreck before he was born. When Bill was ten, he asked about his other grandparents and aunts and uncles on his father's side. Why didn't they want to meet him? That night Billie took fifty Valium, and he never asked about his dad again."

"She really wants things her own way, doesn't she?" Libby said.

"Don't we all?" said David. "This spring, I was given an herb that kills you in twenty-one days unless you make enormous changes in your life. Warriors and sorcerers used to take it as part of their initiations; in more recent times, it's been classified as a poison. As my uncle says, it makes you grow up or die. I finally had to forgive myself for my childhood crimes. I had to stop capitulating to Billie, and stop running. I really had to come home."

"I know," Libby said. "This damn valley. You yearn for it even when you're here."

"I knew this job might be problematic," David said. "Red and I talked about it."

"You told Red?" said Libby.

"Only in the most general way."

Libby's eyes filmed with tears. "Okay," she said. "Thank you." She handed a water glass to Lewis. "You guys go back to work. I need some time to think."

SHE PHONED Lewis at the office the next morning and invited him to stop by for a bowl of Gloria's *albóndiga* soup. "That's meatballs to you, Lewis," she said.

He walked across the roadway to Libby's house. Gloria, a tiny woman with a thick gray braid, had the darkest eyes he'd ever seen. She was on her way out the door, but put down her purse and ladled out a bowl of soup for him. *"Contenta hoy."* Gloria nodded to the bedroom.

Libby sat propped up in bed, eating her soup. She looked happy. The back door was open. The calico cat sat on the stoop, having a stare-down with Gustave, who was tied to the oak tree. Every now and then, Gustave let rip an excruciating, bloodcurdling whine.

"Don't you love soup on a hot day?" Libby pursed her lips to suck in the skinny vermicelli. The air in the room seemed light as helium.

"I gotta get this recipe," Lewis said.

"Lard—that's the secret," said Libby. "When Gloria was browning the meatballs, I asked what smelled so good in there. '*Manteca*,' she said. Pig fat. Nectar of the gods."

"I read that lard's actually better for you than butter. Less cholesterol, more amino acids, something like that."

"Hey, you're preaching to the converted."

They slurped up their noodles.

"So, I called Billie," said Libby.

"You *talked* to her?"

"No way. She didn't pick up. I left a message." Libby regarded the meatball balanced on her spoon. "I said, 'I just have one question. What gives you the right to deprive your son of his father? That's the most selfish thing I've ever heard. Every child has that right!' Oh, I was really on my high horse." She raised the meatball to her lips. "And I also said, 'Come to think of it, you haven't been very nice to me, either. Until you deal with some of this stuff and start treating people with some compassion and honesty, I don't think I can be your friend." Libby popped the meatball into her mouth.

"You said that?"

"I know, I know," Libby said with her mouth full. "Can you believe it?"

Lewis started to laugh. "*You* dumped *her*?"

Libby paused to swallow. "I know David's far from blameless, but at least he tried to correct his mistakes. I believe in him. He and Little Bill do seem to have a good, open—"

"Wait a sec, Lib. You told Billie you wouldn't be her friend anymore?"

"This is what gets me," Libby said. "Billie always says people don't change. It's her war cry. But she's the only one who never changed. I mean, look at all of us. Who knew we'd end up here, together, slogging through all *this*?"

BEDIENCE TRAINING for Adult Dogs was taught Saturday mornings in Buchanan's Plaza Park. Before he could enroll Gustave, Lewis had to take him in for shots. The vet said he was about fifteen months old, healthy as a horse, and probably half large terrier—Airedale or schnauzer—and half Great Dane.

When Gustave met the other dogs, he spooked, barked like a hellion, did his usual cower-and-piss routine, and otherwise identified himself as the class problem. The teacher, a middle-aged corgi breeder named Beverly, was reassuring. "Obedience training exists to help dogs like Gus."

The Santa Bernita is a small valley, so Lewis wasn't surprised to know two of the other dog owners. One was Carl, his first roommate at Round Rock, who had stayed sober and was still teaching high-school biology; Lewis had seen him briefly at Red's funeral. Carl had a shiny chocolate Labrador named Valrhona, Val for short. They walked to the drinking fountain during the break, dogs lunging on their leashes. "I'm still in shock over Red," Carl said.

"I really miss him," said Lewis.

They stood kicking at the grass until the dogs whined and pulled them back to the present.

Lewis's other acquaintance was Phyllis, formerly his favorite waitress at Denny's. He didn't recognize her at first because she'd stopped bleaching her hair. She was now a short-haired, nondescript brunette, boyish, still skinny, though not quite so severe-looking as before. Phyllis's dog, Tessie, was a peculiar little terrier mix that looked more like a badger.

"Denny's was a cesspool," she told Lewis after class. "My boss stalked me, called me up drunk at all hours. I had to quit." She had moved in with her mom and gone to massage school. "I found out I liked learning physiology and anatomy." Now she was working toward a nursing degree, making straight A's, and giving massages at a physical therapy clinic in Buchanan.

"Wanna meet Ralph?" she asked.

Ralph, her son, had parked himself away from the class because Tessie couldn't concentrate at all if he was in sight. A skinny teenager lying on a blanket in the sun and reading a book, Ralph had stringy brown hair, a sunken chest, and an undernourished pallor. He shook Lewis's hand, said it was nice to meet him, and looked him in the eye. Lewis liked him right away. Phyllis gave Ralph a ten-dollar bill to buy burritos and Cokes. "You want something?" she asked Lewis.

"That's okay," he said.

She turned to Ralph. "Don't let them put that fire juice on mine or I'll kill you." Ralph started smirking. "Don't think I won't," she growled. "I'll wring your neck." Her son danced off, waving her money.

"He's a good kid," she said.

They sat down on Ralph's blanket and Lewis saw he was studying algebra and Spanish.

Phyllis touched Lewis's arm. "Where you been?"

Her eyes were gray-green, her skin freckled. She was a good listener; she nodded at appropriate moments, made sympathetic noises. When Lewis told her about Red's sudden death, and his own decision to stay on at Round Rock, she said, "It sounds like you're a good friend to those people there. I hope they appreciate you."

"Oh, they do."

"So what's anybody doing for you?"

"They're all *nice*, you know."

"Nice?" Phyllis said. "All right. Lie down." She patted the blanket. "On your stomach." Lewis did as ordered, resting his chin on the edge of the blanket. Grass blades speared his nose. Tessie and Gustave chased each other in large circles around them. Quickly, Phyllis straddled his rump and placed her hands on his upper back. She pushed her fingers into his shoulders and neck. It had been so many months since Lewis had been touched that he was flooded with gratitude and something cool and shadowy, like sorrow.

"Take off your T-shirt," Phyllis said. She moved instinctively to little pockets of stored pain and crunched them with her thumbs until he squirmed and groaned. She lifted his arms and jiggled them.

"Relax," she said. "Give me all your weight. Let go. Give it up, Lewis, for crying out loud."

The sun bore down. Phyllis's hands ranged up and down his spine, quarrying pain with alarming precision. The dogs barked and ran around them faster and faster, their paws thudding, sometimes so close that grass and dirt sprayed the side of Lewis's face and he felt the near-rasp of a toenail.

Phyllis slowed down, then rested her hands on his back. His body rang. She climbed off, and he pulled himself up to look at her. His arms were wobbly. They gave each other a long look, the kind that usually ends in a kiss. And Lewis meant to reach up, grasp the back of her neck, pull her to him. But he made no move. With Phyllis, he saw, it could go either way, kiss or no kiss. She wore a sly smile. The air itself seemed taut. He liked looking at her sharp, pretty face, those deadpan eyes, the slightly upturned lips. Kissing *would* break the tension. He held off for a moment, and a moment after that, amazed that anyone could actually stop to consider such things, and then amazed again at how keen and sweet the holding off itself was, as if the anticipation alone had bloomed into some bright, open space.

Abruptly, the dogs threw themselves down, panting, on the grass nearby. Their tongues were pink and very long. Phyllis burst out laughing; then, gazing past Lewis, she pointed. "Look, here's Ralph, bearing burritos across the park."

A BAND of contractors had slid into Rito in late summer and built fifteen townhouse condominium units across from the packing plant. The construction crews worked so fast with truckloads of prefabricated products, that a model unit was ready for viewing by early September.

The condos, Libby asserted, proved that Billie Fitzgerald was moving away, because otherwise she would have fought the zoning variance with routine ferocity.

Most of Rito's inhabitants had never lived in a brand-new place, and some of the women were taken with the air conditioning, wall-to-wall carpets, and dishwashers. When word came that a number of the condos would be leased, and that the management would accept social-service housing vouchers, a contingent from the Mills Hotel walked down to check out the units. They walked home decrying paper-thin walls, windows flimsy as cellophane, tiny toilets. The wall-to-wall, they said, smelled like fish. A few young couples made down payments and moved in, but most of the units remained empty.

At Round Rock, David Ibañez became the new director. He talked Pauline into leaving her pain clinic for consulting work; she would move up in two months. They didn't yet know where on the farm they'd live, because Libby hadn't decided which place she'd inhabit after the baby came: the new house on the ridge, her old house on Howe Lane, or Red's bungalow in the village.

Lewis's friend Kip became the new house manager. He couldn't make a living with his acting, he said, and helping drunks recover might beat waiting tables, at least for a while.

The farm's unwritten no-women rule was broken when David and Libby hired a young woman from the Culinary Institute. Lewis, then, went back to working full-time in the office. After much fine-tuning and fretting, Lewis finally turned in his dissertation the last week of September. Promptly accepting it, his committee wanted to see him for the defense in two weeks' time.

Libby grew enormous. "Maybe I'm having a pony," she said. "That would be fine, so long as she's healthy." Libby's face puffed up, her ankles swelled. Turning over, she claimed, was a major endeavor. Barbara came up two weekends in a row, and the two of them watched marathons of videos and planned the birth, which began to seem more like an open house than a hospital procedure. A Lamaze home tutor came; Barbara and David Ibañez both took the instruction so that one, the other, or both could coach her through labor. Pauline was also invited to attend the birth, and Gloria, of course, and even Lewis.

"Me?" Lewis said to Libby. "You want *me* there?"

"Yes, I do."

Dearest Red, It's over eight months now. The cerclage was removed yesterday and any time, the doctor says, we can have a healthy baby. I have a monitor now—it's for a baby, but it's also wired to Lewis's house, so I can be alone here for the night without worrying that I'll be too whacked out to remember anyone's number.

I can't tell you how glorious it is to walk outside. I've been so bored in this bed all these large, long days. I think I have missed you with every cell in my body, one by one. I have cried my weight in tears—certainly in tears and also, probably, in phlegm. (Why is it nobody ever talks about that part of weeping?)

WHEN Lewis returned from the successful defense of his dissertation, he and David spent the rest of the afternoon teaching Gustave not to run at cars. Libby watched from her back stoop. David had Gustave on a heavy-duty retractable leash. Lewis would peel out with all the provocation his Fairlane could muster and when Gustave leapt, David yelled *"No!,"* threw on the lock, and pulled as if he were setting the hook in an eighty-pound yellowfin. "Sit!" he thundered.

Gustave sat, and David rewarded him with a hunk of hamburger. Gustave remained sitting, shivering madly. Lewis backed up, over and over. Again and again he hit the gas. Gustave was a fast learner: after four leaps, he sat through every kind of fishtail or popped gear. Enough hamburger, thought Libby, and that dog could learn English.

Next, Lewis switched to the Mercedes, and then to David's Land Cruiser. Poor Gustave, unleashed, quaking in all his subdued instincts, allowed the vehicles to pass without incident.

Lewis gave the dog's head a jubilant, thorough scratching. "He really should've won Best Dog at obedience school, and not just Most Improved."

Libby clapped, and Gustave ran free for the first time since the day Red died.

Okay Red, now this. Lewis says, since he's finished his dissertation, he has to have a big project, one that will keep him going. He's going to write a novel. A novel for our entertainment. Starring him, he says (big surprise). But we can all have supporting roles (such largesse). I promised I'd read through my journals for the juicy bits. He already wrote the prologue and read it to David and me last night. We laughed at every sentence; it's all about the Santa Bernita Valley, and the oddballs who live here. He makes some stuff up about people—he made Yolanda into a nun! And you, it includes you, baby. You're there, you and this crazy drunk farm.

JOURNAL in hand, Libby knocked on Lewis's door. "You can't believe how good it is to walk again. Even though I've metamorphosed into an elephant."

Lewis wasn't expecting company. Clothes were clumped everywhere, stacks of papers listed, dust bunnies drifted over the floor. "Sorry it's such a mess," he said.

"Looks like a bachelor pad, Lewis. Do you want me to send my housekeeper over?"

"No. Thanks anyway. The inability to take care of myself is one of the few things I have left to attract a woman."

"Attracting women has never been your problem, Lewis," Libby said flatly, and pulled out a chair at the dinette. The pile of papers on the chair slid onto the floor. Libby looked on helplessly as Lewis gathered them up. "So," she said, "is there, uh, one particular woman for whom you're setting this irresistible bait?"

"No, not really," he said, straightening the papers. "Sometimes I think about Phyllis."

"Not the masseuse? Now, she's a kick in the head," said Libby. "So funny. But tough."

"Yeah," said Lewis. "She fed her ex-husband ant poison."

"My God! Did he get sick?"

"That's exactly what I asked. Shit, yeah, he got sick. He ate ant poison, for God's sake."

"Well, it sounds like she'd keep you in line. And think of all those free massages." Libby lowered herself carefully onto the now-empty chair and held up the journal. "I brought this. I wanted to read to you about our wedding."

"It won't upset you?"

"I'll probably cry, if that's what you mean. But I *do* want to read it to you." She opened the journal, smoothed the pages. Her face had taken on a healthy pinkness. "It doesn't make you uncomfortable, hearing about Red and me?"

"Oh, maybe a little," said Lewis. "But I *do* want to hear it."

She smiled. "Okay, then. I should say that originally, we were going to be married in Bakersfield by George, who used to be the chaplain here. Then we'd go on up to the cabin in the Sierras we'd rented for our honeymoon. It was supposed to be no big deal. But Billie wanted to be at the wedding, so Red arranged for George to meet us at the park in Fort Tejon. All to pacify Billie. Although I liked the idea of being married outside in the middle of winter. Okay. That's the intro."

Libby lifted the journal and began to read.

"*The fourteenth, Valentine's Day, was a beautiful, clear winter day. Glassy white sun. In the seventies in the Santa Bernita, although freezing in the shade. Billie and the Bills pick me up five minutes early. She has a garment bag for our jackets.*

"*The Bills, that unusual trinity, carry me to my future in the great white truck.*" Libby paused. "Also Billie's idea. That we'd meet Red there, so the bridegroom wouldn't see the bride."

"Right, that traditional thing."

"*Billie has selected Handel and Debussy to accompany us. The cottonwoods along the river, bare but for their high tufts of flame-yellow leaves, light our way. Old Bill dozes. Little Bill snaps pictures. We find the park—it's right off the highway. Red and George are waiting in the parking lot. Red is in gray slacks, elegant salmon-colored shirt, no tie, jacket slung over his back. (Why are men never cold?) The expression on his face could only be described as comic dread.*

"*I assume that he's stewing in hideous second thoughts. What's up? I ask.*

"*He says, Oh, nothing really, although I don't know what it portends for married life: It seems we've stumbled into the Civil War.*

"*And it's true, as we walk up into the park, there are hundreds of people in Civil War dress milling around. Bluecoats and graycoats, and women in long cotton skirts and shawls, lots of cleavage. The softball diamonds are a battlefield. Regiments assemble in straggly phalanxes. Men carry muskets. The smell of cordite hangs in the air. Sporadic, heart-seizing Rebel yells erupt. Concession stands and vendors sell black powder, medals, bedrolls.*

"*Red says, I've always sort of admired Stonewall Jackson.*

"*Billie says, I told you we should've had this wedding in my courtyard.*

"*We find a semi-quiet space on the far side of a large, covered pergola. George says, This won't take long.*

"*Billie and I go to the bathroom, a stone building with hosed-down concrete floors, rust-stained sinks. It's full of war wives.*

Women dressed like ancestors. I feel self-conscious pulling on the crisp ivory jacket to my suit. Billie pins a corsage to my lapel and tells all the women, She's tying the knot. The women cluster. I hear Oklahoma twangs.

"Gettin' married in pants? That takes nerve! says one woman—admiringly, I think.

"Billie looks terrific in a gray Armani suit and pearls.

"I take a deep breath.

"Billie tells me to join the men while she hauls our discarded sweaters to the car. I walk over, heels poking into the grass, and stand awkwardly, squeezing—no, wringing—Red's hand. I'm afraid to sit on the picnic benches in these glowing, tusk-colored clothes.

"Red has wet and combed his hair, his face has a naked look. Big eyes. Little Bill's snapping a lot of pictures. Billie takes her time. I spot her talking to two women who scuttle off like plump partridges. Oh god, I mutter. She's up to something.

"We move into the small grassy space enclosed by a fence covered in dark green honeysuckle; it's quieter. George positions himself in the corner. Red and I stand together, facing him. Old Bill is next to Red, Billie next to me. Little Bill is our diligent chronicler. Some of the women from the bathroom watch from a respectful distance. I shiver, though the sun is strong. Guns pop. Trucks lumber and downshift on the highway. George starts talking. It is a reasonable ceremony—I can't recall a word of it. We manage the vows although one prolonged Rebel yell during Red's recitation makes me giggle and briefly I'm afraid I'll never stop.

"It's done, we kiss.

"And shots explode, ring out, so close and loud, I'm sure we're already dead. Red and I leap apart. Behind us, a dozen laughing men, blue and gray, raise their smoking muskets."

Libby closed the book, wiped at her cheeks.

Lewis handed her a paper towel. She blew her nose loudly. "Thanks for listening, Lewis," she said. "I really wanted you to hear this."

LITTLE BILL came bearing gifts. He brought his own copy of *Goodnight, Moon*, a clever wooden rattle, and a tiny Stanford T-shirt sent from Joe.

"So you know about my dad and all," Little Bill said.

"Yes," said Libby. "And I'm sorry. Having parents shouldn't be so difficult."

Little Bill shrugged. They smiled awkwardly at each other. "Mom just closed on a house in Bel Air."

In a recent conversation, Joe had told her that Billie was house-hunting, but this information caused in Libby a general physical loosening, as if all her muscles had gone flat. So. Now she knew.

"I hope she finds what she wants," Libby said. "And what will become of the house here, and the ranch?"

Little Bill shrugged. "Rogelio will run the groves. Some producer wants to lease the house. If that doesn't work out, she might sell."

"How do you feel about that?"

"I don't know. I don't want to live here. Maybe later, but not now."

Libby could hear David's timing in Little Bill's careful way with words, and see the same inimitable sweetness in the boy's eyes and face.

"And Old Bill—what's he going to do?"

"Grandpa's moving into Uncle John's," Little Bill said. "He lives only two blocks from Mom's new place."

"Well, that makes sense," said Libby, "the family close together like that. It's still hard to imagine your mother living anywhere but here."

Little Bill smiled his kind smile. "I keep telling her she'll be miserable not walking her irrigation lines every night. She says no, *that* was misery, and she'd much rather walk the aisles at Barneys. Who knows, maybe she'll marry a movie star."

"Think you'll ever tell her that you see your dad?"

"I want to. I told my uncle John when I went to work for him. He was pretty cool about it. He thinks we should tell her, but only after she moves, so he can keep an eye on her. Actually . . ." Little Bill frowned. "Uncle John says we should check her into a hospital and then tell her, in case she flips. But I think, *Right*, and how do we get her into the hospital?"

"You might feel relieved when everything's out in the open."

"Maybe," he said. "Maybe not."

Billie must have done many things right with this boy, Libby thought, for him to end up so measured and quiet and wise.

"I'll miss you," she said.

"Oh, I'll be up all the time to see my dad. At least that will be easier. Next week, and Joe's coming along. He says . . ." Little Bill paused, suddenly embarrassed.

"He says . . . ?" Libby prompted.

"He says maybe his new sister will be here by then."

"Tell him I'm working on it."

25 October 1:22 a.m. Dearest Red. Labor woke me up. I haven't called anybody. Nothing severe so far, only the sensation of large hands tightening around my back, almost an embrace—I like to think that it's you. I'm not scared yet. I'm going to take a bath.

2:39. My skin's all pruney, but somehow, warm water felt exactly right. Also, the shower jet on my back was great. Big movement afoot. I'm not uncomfortable yet. Except that I miss you so much. I'm writing this by candlelight. Cat on the chair next to me.

Twelve minutes apart. It's exciting and strange, and there's a little pain creeping in. It comes almost after the contraction, almost an accompaniment to the thought, oh, that one's over. A twinge, a little kiss of things to come, each one a little tighter than the last.

In a way it almost seems polite, this pain. I'll give you a little glimpse of me, it seems to say. Let you get used to me bit by bit.

There's a great urge to call somebody, and I'm going to yield to it in a minute. Oh, I wish it was you, Red. I won't say it again. But I want to state it clearly, before I start this work. I wish you were here. I hate that you're not. I want to register this complaint, just

*once, just here. I have your friends, your trusted servants, but they're
not you.*

I do see you moving through them.

Baby, if I don't write to you for a long time, you'll know why.

LEWIS was deep in a dream of an old section of Los Angeles,
where he was driven over a bridge lit with acorn-shaped street lamps
and into a realm where nomads' fires burned across a plain. Something called his name, the syllables squawky, swaddled in static.

"Huh . . . what?" Speaking, he woke himself up.

"It's started." Libby's voice came from the monitor.

Lewis took in her words with a breath. Then they hit. "Jesus
Christ!" he cried, and was out of bed, feet in pants, in one fluid move-
ment. Then, his fingers were so uncooperative that he had to dial
David's number twice. "Libby's in labor."

"I'll be right there."

The three of them took the Mercedes, Lewis driving.

"It doesn't really hurt yet," Libby would say, then make the most
scrunched-up face.

"Long, smooth breaths, Lib," David said. "Don't forget."

The moon had set and trees, houses, hills, even the skies were silvery. Gloria, wrapped in a blue shawl, was waiting for them in front
of her house. Rafael, small, spry, and white-haired, waved from the
porch. A rooster crowed.

They arrived at Buchanan General at four-fifteen a.m. Since the
hospital wasn't officially open, they had to use the emergency entrance. Lewis carried Libby's overnight bag and stood to one side
with Gloria while David and Libby negotiated at the desk. She was
preregistered, but they still wanted to check her in and put her in a
wheelchair. The wheelchair took forever to arrive, so Libby and
David practiced breathing. "I'll have this girl in the lobby if they
don't hurry up," Libby said. When the wheelchair finally came, they
loaded her bag and coat into it and Libby herself pushed it down the
hall, into the elevator, and out into obstetrics on the fourth floor.

The birthing room was painted a rose-tinted peach, with not-too-
ugly watercolors of flowers and a baby's building blocks. There was
a rocking chair, a bed, a little cabinet to stash things in.

Libby didn't want to sit or lie down. She wanted to hike, climb stairs. "I need to move," she said. "If I keep going, it's like I can stay one step ahead of the pain. Or maybe I'll be like that lady in Louisiana who gave birth standing in a bank line. They had to cut open her slacks because the baby was stuck in a pant leg." Libby laughed and then gasped. David held up a finger to represent a candle, and Libby blew out air as if to extinguish it. "I don't think this cervix is so fucking incompetent," she said when the pain receded. "It's feeling pretty damn competent to me."

She did have one terrible moment, when she just stood in the hall and wept, head in hands, tears streaming down her arms. She didn't say anything, but you didn't need a Ph.D. to guess what she was crying about.

She roamed up and down the halls in Red's enormous white terrycloth robe. Barbara showed up around six with big hugs all around. She and David and Gloria and Lewis took turns walking Libby up to the sixth floor, down to the lobby and back. Whenever Libby had a contraction, Lewis felt embarrassed by his inadequacy. "Breathe," he'd say helplessly.

A mistrust and dislike of the hospital staff gave Libby a reckless buoyancy. "Somebody tell that nurse to get a better peroxide job," she said. She referred to her doctor as Big Head, with variations. "Where is Big Head, anyway? Tell him to finish his Cheerios already and get his ass down here. I can't wait all day." Passing by the nursing station, she said, "Tell Cabeza Grande to load up that epidural."

"*Oooohh,*" said the nurse with the bad hair. "Somebody's in transition." She herded everyone into the birthing room and a different doctor came in and measured Libby. Big Head was allegedly on his way.

Once Libby's legs were up in the stirrups, Lewis got that fizzy feeling in hands and lips. He strayed to the periphery of the action, gave a good long look at the painting of those building blocks. After some time, the doctor said, "Okay, go ahead, push. *Push.* . . . Yes, yes. Beautiful. . . . That's great—you're doing great." Lewis lasted for about two pushes. Seeing Libby's entire body constricted in pain, hearing her whimpers and rough groaning, was more than he could take. Frankly, the whole thing was a tad too gynecological for him. Looking at those peachy walls, he had a wild urge to find someone, anyone, who could just stop the whole process. Then the gray linoleum floor slid upwards in a slick, waxy wave.

"One's going down," someone said, and two attendants grabbed Lewis's arms before he hit the floor.

"Let's find you a chair," one attendant said. "You're pale as a ghost." He led Lewis out of the room. "We don't need people passing out in there."

Lewis was too busy not throwing up to argue. In the waiting room across the hall, the walls were mercifully yellow. The attendant brought him a paper cup of water and instructed him to lower his head below his heart until he felt better. Lewis hung his head between his knees. By then, it was close to noon.

"Hello? Are you okay?" A tall woman with brown hair and brown eyes was looking down at him. White blouse. Cotton flowered skirt. Hose and sensible shoes. Hospital ID card on her shirt pocket. She looked to be in her mid-thirties and was pretty in an appealing, midwestern way: big-breasted and buttoned-up.

"Just catching my breath," Lewis said. "Got a little intense in there." He waved toward the birthing room.

"You with María Mendoza?"

"No, no—Libby Ray."

"Oh, so this is your first?"

"The first birth I've seen, yeah," he said.

"I saw my first one yesterday," she said. "Of course, I gave birth sixteen years ago, so there were no real surprises. Still, it's unbelievably moving. And, of course, I also knew it would be over soon. It will be over for you too—before you know it."

Lewis looked at her more closely. "Are you a doctor?"

"No, a chaplain. A student chaplain. I'm in seminary, and I have to do this clinical-pastoral internship before I can be ordained. This is my second day. I have no idea what I'm doing. They tell you to be a presence, to just sit there and listen." She caught herself, then laughed. "And here I am blabbing away."

"That's okay. I don't have anything to say. I almost passed out. I'm still a little shaky." The woman's badge did, in fact, say "Clergy." Lewis held up a vibrating hand. "I mean, it's educational, but God— so much pain. I'm never going to complain about my mother again. Makes me queasy just to think about it." Lewis put his head back down between his knees, speaking up at her sideways. "It's funny. Some of my friends say I should be a minister. The only problem is, I don't have a religion. I mean, I have spiritual leanings, and I meditate, but I don't believe in God. Major hitch."

"Oh, I don't know if I believe in *God* God," she said. "I'm pretty much a Hindu myself."

"Don't you have to believe in God to be a minister?"

"I don't know. I don't think so." She laughed gaily. "At least nobody's made me sign any loyalty oath."

Her name was Linda. She was a Unitarian, she said, and practiced Hindu chanting meditation for serenity, Buddhist breathing meditation for insight.

Lewis heard thudding and sprang to his feet. He made it into the hall and saw a blond-haired doctor sprint past and push through the clot of people standing in Libby's doorway. "Oh!" Lewis said. "Something's going on." His head buzzed. He didn't know what to do.

"Want me to go see?" asked Linda.

"Please."

Alone, Lewis took a deep breath. *God,* he thought, *or whatever, don't let anything happen to Libby and that baby now.* He limped over to the waiting room's window, steadied himself against the sill. Outside, a roof was the color of cigarette ashes, with pink vents and large aluminum air-conditioner cowlings. Farther off, the tinder-dry hills were the color of lions. The sky was milky, the glare intense. Libby's pain was going to be over soon, Lewis told himself, no matter what.

Linda reappeared almost immediately, hair flying, eyes ablaze, skirt swishing with her sudden turn at the door. "Hey!" She grabbed Lewis by the hand. "Hurry up! Come meet your beautiful baby girl!"

CALIFORNIA'S OVER
by Louis B. Jones

In this funny novel of the 1970s, a seventeen-year-old self-described novelist who calls himself Baelthon turns up at the decaying house of James Farmican, a renowned poet who killed himself three years before. Farmican's heirs hire Baelthon to haul off Farmican's chattels as they prepare to sell the family house, but he finds himself entangled in the Farmican family scams and secrets while falling in love with the poet's sullen teenage daughter.

Fiction/0-679-74600-5

HORACE AFOOT
by Frederick Reuss

Quintus Horatius Flaccus (or Horace) has taken the name of a Roman poet, forsworn automobiles, and entertains himself by telephoning strangers to ask them what love is or what they think of St. Bernards. His neighbors think he's wacko and this suits Horace just fine, since all he wants in life is the serenity of not caring. But people in the Midwestern town of Oblivion are conspiring to make Horace care about them, as he finds himself involved with an irascible dying librarian and a mysterious assault victim.

Fiction/0-375-70378-0

THROUGH THE SAFETY NET
by Charles Baxter

In these eleven stories, Charles Baxter plunges into the undertow of middle-class American life as he explores the unruly desires, inexplicable dread, unforseen tragedy, and sudden moments of grace that mark those lives. A drunken graduate student hurtles cheerfully through a snowstorm to rescue a fiancee who no longer wants him. A hospital maintenance worker makes a perverse bid for his place in the sunlight of celebrity. A man and a woman who have lost their only child cling fiercely to the one thing they have left of her—their grief.

Fiction/Literature/0-679-77649-4